Stop [illegible]

ALSO BY LEIGH RUSSELL
FROM CLIPPER LARGE PRINT

Cut Short
Road Closed
Dead End
Death Bed

Stop Dead

Leigh Russell

W F HOWES LTD

This large print edition published in 2014 by
W F Howes Ltd
Unit 4, Rearsby Business Park, Gaddesby Lane,
Rearsby, Leicester LE7 4YH

1 3 5 7 9 10 8 6 4 2

First published in the United Kingdom in 2013
by No Exit Press

A CIP catalogue record for this book is available
from the British Library

ISBN 978 1 47126 108 4

Typeset by Palimpsest Book Production Limited,
Falkirk, Stirlingshire
Printed and bound by
www.printondemand-worldwide.com of Peterborough, England

This book is made entirely of chain-of-custody materials

Dedicated to
Michael, Jo and Phill

GLOSSARY OF ACRONYMS

DCI	–	Detective Chief Inspector (senior officer on case)
DI	–	Detective Inspector
DS	–	Detective Sergeant
SOCO	–	Scene of Crime Officer (collects forensic evidence at scene)
PM	–	Post-Mortem or Autopsy (examination of dead body to establish cause of death)
CCTV	–	Closed Circuit Television (security cameras)

PROLOGUE

She dashed across the cold kitchen floor. The sound of his feet pounded in her ears as he raced down the stairs. It wouldn't be long before he caught up with her. Her thoughts spun wildly. She had to get away. Hide somewhere. Anywhere. As the back door swung shut behind her, the evening air felt cool on her tears. She stared around in terror at the darkness, searching for somewhere to hide. The garden was overgrown with scratchy brambles. Frantically she ran across the weedy lawn, the dry grass prickly beneath her bare feet, forcing her muscles to keep going, faster and faster. Any second now he would emerge through the door behind her.

She darted into the shed. Bent almost double, she struggled to catch her breath. Her chest was burning. Her lungs felt as though they would burst. She was drowning. As her breathing slowed, she became aware that her legs ached painfully from running. They were shaking so violently she could barely stand.

* * *

He burst in, slamming the door against the shed wall. With a roar he launched himself at her, dragging her onto the ground. She hit her head as she fell, but she didn't care. All that mattered was that he was there. She grappled feebly with him, but was no match for his vigorous assault. It was happening again and she was powerless to stop him.

Over his shoulder, through her tears she saw a figure hovering in the doorway, one hand raised in a futile gesture. But there was no point calling out for help. Scrabbling on the ground, her fingers closed on the handle of something very heavy. In that instant, she knew what she had to do. With a surge of adrenaline she raised the hammer as high as she could and swung it down.

There was a loud crack, like a window breaking, and he slumped forwards. Whimpering, she struggled out from beneath him. It wasn't easy. His inert body weighed down on her, but she managed to crawl free. Groaning, he rolled away from her, onto his back, exposing his genitals. Yelling in fear and ecstasy she raised the hammer again.

CHAPTER 1

Amy glanced fearfully at her watch.

'I've got to get going. He'll be expecting me.'

She sat up and swung her slim legs out of the bed.

'Stay a bit longer. You only just got here. Stay.'

'You know I can't.'

'Of course you can.'

Guy propped himself up on one elbow and leaned across to pat her pillow with his free hand.

'Come back to bed. Can't you forget about him for once? What's he going to do? You're not his bloody prisoner.'

Amy twisted round and caressed his smooth chest delicately with the tips of her dark red nails. Blonde curls swung around her face as she shook her head.

'You don't know him like I do. You don't know what he's capable of when he's in a temper.'

Guy lunged forwards, grabbed her by the wrist, pulled her back down onto the bed beside him and kissed her, savouring her perfume and the smell and feel of her body still warm from lying in bed.

* * *

Guy had never met anyone like Amy before: on the surface so intimidating with her sophisticated, knowing manner, yet beneath that show of confidence more vulnerable than anyone he had ever known. At twenty-three his previous relationships had been short-lived affairs with shallow ignorant girls, mannequins with screechy voices. Amy was a mature woman, wealthy and classy, informed about life and the wider world. It seemed to him almost miraculous that she would treat him as an equal.

'So who's this mystery woman of yours?' his mates clamoured to know.

'I can't say.'

'She married then?'

When Guy shrugged the lads had chuckled and slapped him on the back. Only one had warned him to take care.

'What about her husband?'

'Don't be a prick,' another one chipped in. 'He's getting his leg over, isn't he? She must be a looker at any rate, and that's all there is to it. Guy's not going to be banging her forever, are you? Get out before the problems kick off, and you're alright, mate.'

'It's not like that,' Guy had begun then stopped, embarrassed to admit that he was in love.

His mates had roared with laughter.

'He's got it bad.'

A few months earlier, Guy would have shared their amusement if any of his friends had turned soft but since meeting Amy his perspective had changed completely. He couldn't stop thinking about her. Not having her to himself was driving him crazy.

Amy shook her head, pushing him away.

'Stop it, Guy. I've got to go. I'm late.'

Extricating herself from his embrace she slipped out of bed and he lay back, watching her blonde hair skim the top of her round white shoulder. Her profile didn't do her looks justice, emphasising her straight nose which was a shade too big and her pointed chin, while her long hair concealed the piercing grey eyes which were her most striking feature.

'Maybe we should just forget the whole thing,' he grumbled, watching the curve of her vertebrae as she crouched down to gather up her clothes.

'What do you mean?' she asked without turning round.

'You're never going to leave him, are you? It's the same thing every week. I mean, what the hell are you doing, staying with him? What are you waiting for?'

She turned and looked down at him, her grey eyes troubled.

'I'm working on it. I do want to be with you,

you know I do. But you've got to let me deal with this in my own way. You just have to be patient. It's the only way.'

'Amy, I want you to come and live with me all the time, now. Why does it have to be so complicated? Just leave him. What are you waiting for? Pack a bag and come here. Tonight. In fact, don't even bother going back for your things. We can get you new stuff tomorrow. I'll take the day off and we'll go shopping, I'll buy you anything you want—'

She sat down again, cupping his shoulder in her hand. He seized her wrist and kissed her fingers, one after another.

'Oh Guy, he'd take everything, the house, the car, everything's in his name. He'd even take the dog from me. You don't know what he's like when he doesn't get his own way. He's vindictive. I'm scared of him, Guy.'

'Why don't you let me deal with him then? There's nothing for you to worry about, trust me. I'll take care of everything. We don't need his money. I can take care of you.'

'You don't know him.'

She paused, watching his face closely, then looked away.

'Sometimes he can be violent when he's been drinking. He yells at me – threatens me – it's happened more than once—'

Guy sat upright, gripping her hand so tightly she winced.

'What do you mean he threatens you? Jesus, if he so much as touches a hair on your head – Just leave, Amy. Do it tonight.'

His eyes shone with passion and she smiled.

'Oh Guy, don't be so naïve. I'm not worried for myself. He won't hurt me, not really. But he'll kill you if he finds out about us.'

Guy laughed uneasily.

'Not if I kill him first,' he blustered, flinging himself back on his pillow. 'If he so much as touches you, I'll do it. I swear I will.'

Amy perched on the edge of the bed without looking at him, her shoulders tense. Although she spoke softly, he heard every word.

'You know what to do.'

She pulled on her shoes, stood up, smoothed her pencil skirt over her thighs and, with a flick of her blonde hair, was gone.

Guy lay on the bed gazing up at the ceiling, biting his lip. He wished she had the guts to leave her bastard of a husband. It was hard to ignore the nagging suspicion that she was never going to give up her affluent lifestyle to move in with him. What did he have to offer a woman like Amy? Turning his head from side to side on the pillow he considered her suggestion. She made it sound so simple.

'The restaurant's called Mireille,' she had told him, warning him not to write it down.

She made him repeat the address until he knew it.

'He leaves after it closes around one in the morning, earlier on a Sunday. All you have to do is follow him and – Well, just make sure he doesn't get home, that's all.'

At first he hadn't been sure he understood. Finally she had grown impatient.

'Oh do I really have to spell it out to you? Once he's out of the way, everything will be ours. It all comes to me. We'll be free of him, and you'll never have to work again.'

'A kept man,' he had laughed, not believing she was serious.

But she had leaned forward until her hair fell across his face as she whispered, 'You could do it for me. For us.'

He had kept silent, not knowing what to say. Thinking about it, he still wasn't sure if she was seriously asking him to kill her husband.

CHAPTER 2

It was only three o'clock but Geraldine felt like going to bed, she was so tired. She wondered if she was going down with a virus, but decided it was more likely a reaction to all the stress she had gone through in recent weeks. It wasn't much more than a month since she had moved to North London. Her salary as a detective inspector on a Homicide and Serious Crime Command wouldn't have stretched to buying her new flat, but her mother's death a year before had left Geraldine enough money for the move to Islington. The flat was perfect, with two small bedrooms, one of which she would use as an office. It could double up as a spare room when her niece came to stay. After all her enthusiastic plans when she had first moved in, after six weeks she had barely finished unpacking. Arriving in London she had been thrown into a murder investigation, which had only finished a week ago. She had just completed writing up her final report. With nothing pressing to do, she succumbed to a numbing exhaustion.

* * *

When her phone rang, she answered it reluctantly. Although she loved her job, and always felt slightly depressed by the hiatus between cases, right now she was ready for a break. But her spirits rose when she recognised the voice of her former sergeant in Kent. They had worked together on several cases, becoming friends in the process.

'Ian, it's great to hear from you.'

Just for a second she felt like crying, she was so pleased to hear his voice. Her new sergeant, Sam, was great, but Geraldine missed Ian.

'I was wondering if you were planning to come over this way some time to visit your sister, and fancied meeting for a drink?' he said.

On the spur of the moment she told him she would be in Kent that evening. Saying the words made it true.

Geraldine hung up, taken aback by the desperation of her impulse. She hadn't realised how lonely she was in London. But there was no time to question the sense in driving for two hours to meet an old friend for a drink. It wasn't as though she had anything else to do. Tidying her flat could wait. With a tremor of anticipation, she showered and pulled on jeans and a new jumper. Quickly she ran a brush through her short black hair, and flicked mascara lightly above her dark eyes to highlight her long lashes. The sky was overcast as she set off, threatening rain. Nearly October, the air had an autumnal chill and the evenings were drawing in. By the time she reached Kent it would be dark.

Two hours later she was seated in a pub near her old police station, not far from the estate where Ian lived in a maisonette with his fiancée, Beverley. They were reminiscing about a case they had worked on together.

'And do you remember his wife?' Ian asked with a mischievous grin and Geraldine laughed.

She gazed at his familiar features, blue eyes bright beneath neatly combed hair that would spring out of place as soon as he ran his hand through it. If she hadn't known the care he habitually took over his appearance, she might have suspected him of making a special effort to look smart for her this evening, with his well-pressed shirt and coordinating tie. Yet despite his efforts, he still managed to look awkward, seated at a low table that exaggerated his bulk. With his broad shoulders and huge hands, Geraldine had found his presence reassuring when he had accompanied her as her sergeant.

'You look well,' she told him, although she actually thought he seemed downcast, and somehow older than she remembered him. Even in the poorly lit pub she spotted that he was greying around his temples. His shoulders drooped forward and he appeared to have lost his characteristic exuberance. She hoped he was tired, rather than bored with the evening. It had been his idea to meet, after all. He raised his glass.

'Another one?'

'I'd better not,' Geraldine replied. 'I'll have a soft drink though.'

'Cheap round,' he grinned, standing up.

'It's good to see you again, Ian,' she said as he returned from the bar and he smiled easily at her.

'How're the wedding plans coming along then?'

His smile faded.

'My God, Geraldine, you have no idea. It's more complicated than any investigation . . . I wish we'd just gone off and done it quietly, but it's too late now. Bev's got the bit between her teeth and you'd think it was a bloody royal wedding the way she's carrying on. The sad thing is, I don't think she's enjoying it, she's so stressed, but when I suggested we drop the whole idea – of the big wedding, that is, not getting married – she went ballistic. Said we were too far committed to back out now, which I suppose is true.' He sighed. 'It's crazy. But she had her heart set on this grand occasion. Cast of thousands. She wants me to wear a bloody penguin suit.'

Relieved to discover the source of Ian's dejection had nothing to do with her, Geraldine gave what she hoped was a sympathetic smile.

'I'm hardly in a position to offer advice. I've never been even close to getting married.'

That wasn't strictly true. In her twenties, Geraldine

had lived with a boyfriend, Mark, for six years. She had taken it for granted they would end up together until, without any warning, he had left her for someone else. With hindsight she should have noticed the signs. He was always complaining she put her work first, but she had been too wrapped up in her career to realise anything was amiss with their relationship.

She turned her attention back to Ian who was bringing her up to date with gossip about her former colleagues on the Kent constabulary. He expressed surprise when she asked about the detective chief inspector who had recently retired. He shook his head.

'I'm not sure what happened to her. There was a rumour she'd gone off, travelling round the world, but then someone said they saw her in Margate. I can't remember who it was.'

'I really should get in touch with her.'

Ian gave her a quizzical look.

'I never realised the two of you were close. I thought you didn't exactly see eye to eye?'

Geraldine shrugged.

'I wouldn't say we were close, exactly, but—'

The conversation drifted back to Ian's wedding plans.

'Oh well, I'd better be off,' he said at last, glancing ruefully at his watch. 'Can't afford to upset the future missus.'

'It's good to see you, Ian. Give my best to Bev, won't you?'

He nodded and stood up.

'Will do.'

Seeing his sheepish grin, Geraldine suspected he wasn't going to tell his fiancée about their meeting. Bev had resented the close relationship that had developed between him and Geraldine when they were working together. Sometimes people outside the force struggled to understand the camaraderie that grew up between officers. Like members of other emergency services, they had quickly developed an absolute trust in one another. Without it their jobs, and at times their lives, would be in danger.

'See you at the wedding, then,' she said with forced cheerfulness, and Ian groaned.

CHAPTER 3

'The roads won't be busy at this time of night,' he assured her.

She leaned back in the passenger seat. It was a smart car, with polished wooden dashboard and leather upholstery. As they glided along dark streets she stared out of the window while he talked incessantly. She was so preoccupied, she barely noticed when they turned into a narrow alley. Tyres squealed as he slammed on his brakes beside a row of dingy lock-up garages.

'Sod it! I've missed the bloody turning. I thought this didn't look right. Too busy talking. I don't suppose you've got any idea where we are?'

She shook her head and pressed herself against the back of her seat, arms folded across her chest, heart pounding in sudden alarm.

'No. Sorry.'

'Well, don't look so worried. It's not a problem. I'll get the sat nav out.'

His teeth gleamed in the shadows as he grinned at her. She turned her head and saw peeling paintwork on a garage door before he flicked the headlights off. Darkness closed in on her.

Leaning across to unlatch the glove compartment, he let his hand drop onto her knee. At the same time, he slapped his other hand over her mouth while his fingers crawled beneath the fabric of her skirt, clawing at her thigh.

'Don't make a sound,' he hissed, his breath hot on her cheek.

The man's cheek felt rough against hers as his wet lips nuzzled her neck. She tried to reach for the door handle but terror sapped her energy, and she lay immobile. For so many years she had believed herself safe. Now he had returned and the nightmare was closing in on her once more. This time he was going to kill her. She closed her eyes and tried to block out the sour taste in her mouth, and the smell of his sweat. The hard ridges of the car seat rubbed painfully against her back.

It was soon over.

In the driver's seat once more, he made a wisecrack about getting lost on his way to finding the sat nav. He threw his head back and laughed at his pathetic joke.

'Right then, time to get the sat nav out. Come on,' he added impatiently when she didn't react, 'I want to get home tonight.'

Slowly she sat up, blinking in the darkness, trying

not to think about what had happened. A small light came on inside the glove compartment when she opened it, and she leaned forward to reach inside. The sat nav felt impossibly light, but then her fingers closed on a stout metal torch.

She was still whimpering softly when she scrambled from the car. Her ankle twisted awkwardly as she fell out onto the tarmac, scraping her knees. Without stopping to examine her injuries, she snatched her bags from the car and hobbled away, shaking with sobs. Her only thought was to get home as quickly as possible. Once out of sight of the car, she stopped and rummaged in her bag for her mirror; she looked no worse than many other women staggering about on the streets of London at night. With a quick glance along the empty street, she pulled off her coat. Rolling it into a tight wad, she rammed it into her bag so no one else could see the stains. It made her feel sick to look at it.

Every time a car zoomed past she cringed in case he was coming after her and turned her head away, trying to keep out of sight. Then she marched on doggedly, muttering to herself. 'Keep going, you'll be fine once you get home.' At last she found her way back. The pavement was empty apart from a couple of youths hanging around outside the station, smoking. They threw her a bored glance as she scurried past. The small parade of shops beside the station were all shut, and there were only a few cars on the main road as she turned into the side street where she lived. It was an effort of will to walk the last few yards, but at last the door closed behind her. Shaking, she crossed the dark hallway and sank to her knees at the bottom of the stairs.

It seemed to take her hours to climb the stairs and stagger along the landing. As if in a dream she looked around her bedroom, irrationally surprised to see that nothing had changed. Without stopping to remove her jacket or shoes, she grabbed a black bin liner and hurried to the bathroom. Ripping off her clothes, she stuffed them in the bag, together with her coat and shoes. Everything was contaminated. She tied the top of the bag tightly so his smell couldn't escape, before stepping into the shower. Her skin turned mottled purple under the flow of water which began to run lukewarm, then hot. Steam swirled around her as she scrubbed every inch of her flesh until she felt hot and raw.

In the misty mirror she was surprised to see her face hadn't changed. She tied her wet hair back in a ponytail, pushing her fringe off her face and scowling at a dripping strand that slipped out, falling to her shoulders. The flesh above her top lip felt tender when she touched it but she couldn't see any bruises where his teeth had pressed against her. Her ordeal was over, but she would never report the outrage. She couldn't bear to think about what had happened, let alone talk about it.

'You survived,' she told herself with desperate satisfaction. She was home. She was safe. He couldn't touch her again. It was over. No one else knew what had happened. Once she had disposed of the black bin liner there would be nothing left to link her to the events of that evening. No one else would ever know. The incident existed only in her head. If she could erase all thoughts of it, she knew the memory would disappear like a horrible dream. Slowly her shock gave way to a growing feeling of exhilaration as she studied herself in the mirror. Having survived this ordeal, she could survive anything.

CHAPTER 4

Taunted by the perfume that lingered on his sheets, Guy fretted for a while, unable to sleep. Finally he punched the pillow where she had been lying and sprang out of bed. Pulling on pants and a sweatshirt he went into the kitchen to put the kettle on. With a sudden expletive he took a beer from the fridge and wandered into his cramped living room where he flopped down on a chair and swigged from the bottle, irritated by the clutter that surrounded him. Everything reminded him of Amy. It was easy for her to criticise his mess. She had no idea how difficult it was to keep the place tidy with so little space. He threw his head back and gulped the last of the cold beer. One thing was for sure, he couldn't carry on like this. He had been seeing Amy for over three months but despite her repeated assurances that things were going to be different, nothing changed. He was sick of being pushed around. Enough was enough. If Amy was too scared to confront her husband, he would do it himself. He wasn't going to be intimidated by anyone, least of all some geezer old enough to be his grandfather.

* * *

He finished another beer and chucked the bottle at the overflowing bin. He watched it roll slowly across the floor and come to rest against the wall. It troubled him that Amy claimed to feel so intimidated by her husband. She didn't strike him as a woman who could easily be dominated. He wondered if it was an excuse to cover up misgivings about abandoning her marriage. It was a lot to give up. He had seen where she lived; lavish wasn't the word. Compared to his crummy little room, her house was a palace. He glanced peevishly around and scowled. He wouldn't blame her for being reluctant to leave her stunning mansion for his pokey little flat. Then again, she might bring a pile of dosh with her. He pictured moving into a neat little house, just the two of them, together every night. Her lifestyle wouldn't be luxurious like it was now, but he would make her happy, which was more than could be said for her lousy husband. With her money, they could live very comfortably on what Guy earned. If she wanted more, he would willingly put in as much overtime as it took to keep her happy.

That was how they had met, when he was working on her conservatory. He had noticed her on the first day. After that he had watched and waited, hoping for an opportunity to talk to her alone. It was just a fantasy, something to think about while he was working, but he soon discovered she was looking for an opportunity to approach him. That was where it had all begun. He'd met her husband too. A tall miserable looking git who strutted about like he was something special, just because he owned a big house near Hampstead Heath. The thought of that arrogant bastard putting his hands on Amy made Guy feel physically sick. He closed his eyes and pictured his rival's pale angular face. He bit his lip and thumped the arm of his frayed armchair, grinning at the thought of giving Amy's husband a bloody nose, and a black eye into the bargain. But what was the point of punching a chair? It didn't make him feel any better.

And what if Amy was right – what if her husband would kill him if he found out about the affair? For now Guy had the advantage. He knew Patrick Henshaw's identity, knew where he lived and worked. Amy thought Guy hadn't taken any notice of her suggestion to get rid of her husband. She didn't know that he'd waited on the pavement opposite the swanky restaurant Patrick Henshaw owned in Soho, watching and thinking. Perhaps she was right and the time had come to act, while they were ahead. The thought made him shiver with fear and excitement. He gulped down the dregs of his beer. With her husband out of the way, nothing would stand between him and Amy. She would be a seriously wealthy widow. There would be no need for her to move out of her big house. Guy could simply move in with her, after a decent interval so as to avoid arousing suspicion. She'd be able to keep her dog. Whatever she wanted. They might even get married. He glanced around his untidy room and smiled.

He fetched another beer and sat down, speculating. He knew he was slightly drunk, fabricating an unattainable fantasy, but he couldn't stop himself. It did no harm to dream. The point was to get rid of Amy's husband. But how could he possibly do that? He had to come up with a plan. Amy was a clever woman. She had told him where to find her husband.

'He's usually had a few to drink by the time he leaves the restaurant.'

'But what if someone sees?'

His question had been rewarded with a tender kiss.

'There's an alleyway runs along the side of the restaurant that isn't lit. You just have to be ready when he leaves. I'd do it myself, if I didn't think he'd overpower me too easily. But if I had the strength, it would be almost too easy . . .'

He knocked back his beer and went to the kitchen for another one, cold and refreshing. Sitting down again he imagined how it would feel to save Amy from her tyrannical husband. It was his duty as a decent man, to protect her. When his head hurt from all the thinking, he staggered back to bed. Alone – but not for much longer, because he made up his mind he was going to do it. Soon. He would move into the big house and Amy would be his whenever he wanted her. He would devote the rest of his life to making her happy.

It was late but he was too edgy to feel tired. With a burst of energy, he jumped out of bed, pulled on his trainers and went outside. In contrast to the warmth of the day, the night air felt chilly, perfect for an invigorating run. With no particular route in mind he ran in a wide circuit of quiet streets, his feet pounding a rhythm on the pavement. He ran along minor streets parallel to Holloway Road, avoiding the main thoroughfare where police cars tended to cruise, likely to stop and harass a young man running along the street at such a late hour. An occasional car sped past but he kept to side streets which were mostly deserted at that time of night. The run didn't tire him out. On the contrary, by the time he arrived home he felt more wired than before. It was nearly one o'clock and he had to be up early in the morning. His head ached with a tightness in his temples above his ears. He lay down in bed, still worrying about what to do about Amy's husband, wishing she was there with him.

CHAPTER 5

There was a fair amount of traffic when Geraldine returned home on Sunday evening. At least it was moving. The major routes into London were always busy, whatever the time. Even though it was past midnight, the queue of cars crawled past a section of the motorway that was closed for resurfacing. In no hurry to get home, she didn't mind sitting in the car with no decisions to make, no evidence to consider, no need even to think as she travelled along in limbo, helpless to do anything about her situation. By the time she arrived home it was past midnight. Turning off Upper Street she drove past elegant white and brick terraced houses and turned left into Waterloo Gardens, where high wrought iron gates closed soundlessly behind her. In the quiet of her street, it was hard to believe she was living in the centre of London. Much as she had enjoyed her excursion to Kent, she was pleased to be home.

Tired from her journey, she kicked off her shoes and padded into the bedroom. The flat had been painted in pastel colours, easy to live with, although bland and impersonal. She had been considering redecorating, starting with the pale green bedroom which reminded her of a hotel room. In pyjamas and dressing gown, she went to the kitchen where a half-drunk bottle of Chianti stood on the table, waiting to be finished. It was a nice wine, but she hesitated only for a second before putting the kettle on and making a mug of tea.

It had been good to catch up with Ian. He had helped her out of several dangerous situations in the past, saving her life more than once. Seeing him again made her realise how much she missed working with him, but London was not just a positive career move, it was an exciting place to live.

After she finished her tea, she didn't feel tired. Perched on the side of her bed, she took a small photograph from her bedside drawer. It was framed under protective glass to prevent it from fading with exposure to daylight. She gazed wistfully at what could have been a photograph of herself as a teenager – if the picture hadn't been taken before she was born. Her own black eyes and dark hair stared up at her. Only a crooked nose ruined the otherwise perfect features of the mother who had given Geraldine up for adoption at birth. She had been adopted by a prosperous family, fulfilling Milly Blake's wish to help her daughter by giving her up. Not only had Geraldine enjoyed a comfortable upbringing, she had grown up in happy ignorance of the circumstances of her birth, until her adoptive mother died. The agency that had arranged her adoption was unable to put her in touch with Milly Blake, who had flatly refused any contact with the daughter she had given away. Geraldine couldn't suppress her desire to meet her birth mother in the hope that she would change her mind about refusing contact if they met, face to face. With a sigh, she replaced the photograph in the drawer. Although she was determined to find her mother, she wasn't ready to deal with the pain of further rejection.

She overslept and arrived at work late on Monday morning. Mentally prepared to deal with a stack of paperwork to clear up from her previous case, she was surprised to find all the lights were on in her office. The bin had been moved from beside her chair. A man sitting at the other desk in the room looked up as she came in and rose to his feet, smiling. He was broad shouldered, with muscular arms. Light brown hair cut short along his temples grew longer on top of his head where it was brushed straight back from his wide round forehead so that it stuck up in a slightly comical way. Above a large blob of a nose his left eye was more widely open than the right one, as though he was caught in the act of winking, which gave him a good natured appearance.

* * *

'You must be Geraldine. I've been looking forward to meeting you. Nick Williams.'

Shrugging off a slight irritation that she was now sharing the office which had been her personal territory for her first London case, Geraldine returned her colleague's smile.

'Hello, Nick. Nice to meet you. How long have you been here?'

'Three years. You new to the Met?'

'Haven't you heard? I'm a county mounty.'

'I transferred here from the West Country three years ago, when I was promoted to inspector, but it's not so bad. London's not the friendliest of cities, but you get used to it. It's a huge force, of course, but from what I hear, you're already making a bit of a name for yourself.'

He smiled kindly, and Geraldine felt herself blush.

'I do my best,' she muttered.

'Working on anything right now?'

'No, just clearing up a few odds and ends of paperwork.'

Nick gave a sympathetic groan.

'Oh those bloody odds and ends of paperwork. I'll let you get on then. I've just been assigned a new case. I'll tell you about it when we've got time, but right now—'

He picked up the file on his desk with a resigned shrug.

When Geraldine was ready for a break she invited Nick to accompany her but he shook his head, smiling.

'Thanks, but I've got something I really need to finish.'

She was sipping coffee in the canteen when Detective Sergeant Samantha Haley entered the canteen and strode purposefully up to the servery. Geraldine had worked with Sam on her previous case and her colleague's cheerful grin broadened when she turned round and saw her. She approached, clutching a mug of coffee and a plate.

'You joining me?'

For answer, the young sergeant sat down and took a huge bite of her pastry.

'Mmm,' she grinned, her lips dusted with fine sugar. 'You really should try these, Geraldine. They don't do much that's nice here,' she added, glancing towards the servery to make sure no one could hear her, 'but these pastries are fantastic. I mean, I know they don't make them here, but even so—'

She had a tendency to speak very fast, as though she was permanently in a hurry. Geraldine watched Sam tucking into the pastry, envying the young sergeant's ability to eat so heartily without putting on weight; slim rather than thin, with well-toned arms that verged on muscular.

'So?' Sam asked as she finished a mouthful.

She licked her sticky fingers and wiped them carefully on a serviette.

'How's things?'

'Can't complain. How about you?'

Sam nodded complacently and they smiled at one another.

'I see Nick Williams is back.'

'Yes. I met him just now.' Geraldine leaned forward and lowered her voice. 'What's he like, Sam?'

'He's nice enough,' Sam answered promptly. 'If you have to share an office, you could do worse, I suppose.'

Geraldine frowned at the sergeant's evasive response as Sam turned her attention back to her pastry. Geraldine waited, sipping at her coffee, noting the tension in her colleague's voice.

'What else, Sam?' she asked at length.

'Why the sudden interest in Nick Williams?'

'It's just that I'm sharing an office with him, that's all.'

'Watch out, Geraldine, he's married,' Sam teased her, laughing. 'And he's an arsehole,' she blurted out.

Geraldine was taken aback by the sergeant's unexpected flash of anger.

'What do you mean?'

'It's nothing. I didn't mean that. He's alright. But be careful, that's all.'

Geraldine was puzzled.

'He struck me as a nice guy, that's all. Or am I missing something?'

Sam just shrugged.

* * *

'So, how's things with you?' Geraldine asked, when it was obvious Sam wasn't going to say anything else about Nick. 'Still happily single?'

Sam gave a sheepish grin.

'Actually, I might be seeing someone, but it's early days. You know how it is. There's nothing to tell yet.'

'Anyone I've met?'

'No.'

Sam didn't seem inclined to talk about her new girlfriend, so Geraldine didn't pursue the subject.

When Geraldine returned to her office Nick was on the phone. She waited for him to finish his conversation before approaching his desk.

'Nick, there's something I'd like to ask you—'

'Fire away.'

She wasn't convinced it was wise to quiz him about Sam, and resolved to be circumspect. But her curiosity was aroused. She couldn't just ignore the vindictive tone that had crept into Sam's voice when they had been discussing him. Sam could be outspoken, but she wasn't malicious.

'It's about DS Haley.'

'Sam?'

He gave a wry smile and turned away from her, leaning his elbows on his desk.

'Did you have a falling out over something?'

Nick sighed.

'You could say that. She's a bit of a firecracker, isn't she?'

'So – what happened between you?'

He turned to face her with sudden decisiveness.

'Have you ever made a thoughtless comment that appeared to trivialise an issue that someone else felt serious about?'

Geraldine nodded, suspecting Nick had made some sexist remark that had not gone down well with Sam. She waited and after a few seconds he continued.

'We were investigating a rape case, not getting anywhere, following random leads that led nowhere. Anyway, you know how it is, we were all getting irritable and I made some stupid comment about how it probably wasn't rape at all, the girl probably asked for it, that sort of thing. It was just a careless comment, I didn't mean anything by it. Anyway, Sam reacted as though I'd accused the girl of fabricating the whole thing. She was bang out of order, speaking like that to an inspector. I probably should have reported her after the way she spoke to me, but she's a good officer so I decided to overlook it. I put it down to a moment's aberration on her part, a momentary unpleasantness. There was no point in blowing it up out of all proportion. She's young.'

Geraldine knew Sam could overreact, but couldn't help thinking the incident raised a serious query over Nick's judgement.

CHAPTER 6

Patrick wasn't in bed beside her when Amy woke up next morning. Working such late hours he rarely woke up before ten. He would get up late for a leisurely breakfast before setting off back to the restaurant in time for lunch. Relieved to find herself alone, she lay spreadeagled in the cool sheets and thought about Guy's firm toned torso and muscular limbs, his youthful impatience that made her feel like a teenager again, in the flush of a first love affair. But the young man's appeal was more than mere physical attraction; his youth and passion were infatuating. In contrast to her husband's indifference Guy's love making was addictive, what he lacked in technique more than made up for by his eager gratitude. In twenty years of cold marriage she had forgotten how stimulating the company of a man could be.

After a while she got up slowly and washed, in no hurry to go downstairs. Her elegantly furnished bedroom, the en suite tiled in natural travertine with a sunken Jacuzzi bath, formed a stark contrast to Guy's shabby room and cramped shower cubicle, but she felt wretched in the lonely luxury of her home, aching for him to be with her. She went down one side of the wide curved staircase. The house was silent. The ornate dining room with its carved walnut furniture and plush velvet curtains was empty, as was the wide sunlit conservatory, and there was no sign her husband had been in the kitchen, no familiar smell of coffee and toast in there. She let out a sigh of relief.

While the kettle boiled she went in the garden and followed an elegant path that wound through landscaped terraces past a miniature lake where a large carp revolved with a lazy flick of its tail. It was a mild morning and she walked past high banks of rhododendron bushes, acers and hibiscus, admiring the fuchsias and late flowering roses. There was no denying Patrick kept the garden looking lovely. Even in late September it was packed with glorious and startling colours, every bush in place and barely a weed in sight.

Patrick expressed regret that Amy didn't share his passion for gardening but she had no intention of becoming involved. Far better to keep away from any activity controlled by her bullying husband. Nevertheless she admired his approach to gardening, the way he kept the trees neatly shaped and level, the edges of the lawns trimmed with mathematical precision and the flowers organised in patches of colour, pink with pink, white with white, and so on, with no mingling of colours in the different beds. He was obsessed with cutting and pruning, dead heading the rose blooms as soon as they started to wilt.

'Cut them off when they're dead and you get more flowers,' he'd explained, snipping at the bushes. 'Otherwise all the plant's energy goes into the hips, and we don't want seeds, we want a display.'

It seemed rather sad to Amy, the survival instinct of all those rose bushes thwarted by a man's desire to adorn his property.

She tried to put her husband out of her mind as she brewed some coffee and thought about what to do with her day. On the dot of eight thirty the housekeeper, Christina, arrived. Amy checked her diary. She had a busy afternoon with a hair appointment booked at two, followed by a manicure and a facial. Later on she would see Guy. But today wasn't a usual day. She couldn't face the inane chatter of her hairdresser and manicurist so she phoned and cancelled her appointments, saying she had a migraine. Since meeting Guy she had become an accomplished liar, she thought with a rueful smile.

After checking automatically that Christina was carrying out her tasks satisfactorily, Amy took a stroll around the garden and decided she should call Patrick's mobile. He didn't answer. She watched a bit of television, picked up a magazine, but couldn't settle to anything. The later it got the more agitated she became, wondering what to do. Finally she pulled her phone out of her bag and punched in Guy's number.

'Come on, come on, pick up, please pick up.'

She was close to tears by the time she heard Guy's voice.

'Hallo? Is that you, Amy? Amy?'

'Oh Guy, Guy—'

'Amy? What's wrong? Amy? Are you all right?'

'I'm fine. It's nothing like that. I haven't seen him today. He hasn't been home. I don't think he came home at all last night.'

'Thank Christ for that.'

'No, no, you don't understand.'

She was almost hysterical.

'I'm scared something might have happened to him. I'm really scared, Guy.'

'What do you mean? Amy? What are you talking about? There's nothing to worry about.'

'But what if . . . what if he followed me? What if he knows where you live? What if—'

Guy interrupted her, forcing a loud laugh.

'Don't be daft, Amy. What could possibly have happened to him?'

'I don't know, but—'

'He's bound to be fine. Tell you what, let's make the most of it. I'll say I'm feeling rough and go home and you can come round. What do you say?'

'What?'

'Come over now. Or we could meet somewhere if you like. Go out together.'

They had only ever been to Guy's rooms since their affair began. Amy was too nervous to meet Guy in public in case anyone saw them.

'You know we can't, Guy. It's too risky,' she protested.

'Maybe it's time we started taking a few risks,' he replied testily. 'I'm sick of all this having to hide away all the time. Look I didn't mean meeting anywhere public.'

'What then?'

'I'm not suggesting we parade up and down outside your house arm in arm.'

She giggled.

'But why don't we go to a posh hotel in London? Meet in a nice bedroom for a change. What do you say?'

She was tempted, excited by his eagerness.

'Where were you thinking of?'

There was a pause and Amy realised he probably didn't know any decent hotels.

'I'll book a room, shall I, and text you the details?' she suggested.

'Great. I'd do it but I'm still at work. It's awkward.'

Hearing the relief in his voice it occurred to her

that he had never booked a room in a hotel, an uncomfortable reminder that she was seventeen years older than him, old enough to be his mother.

'Leave it to me,' she said.

Amy booked the hotel and texted Guy to meet her there after lunch. Then there was nothing to do but wait for the cleaner to finish. She sat in the conservatory leaning against the high curved back of a bamboo chair. Gazing at the arched windows and brilliant white frames, she remembered when the construction had been installed. She had noticed one of the builders straight away, his muscles tensed beneath a damp white T-shirt stretched taut across his back. When he'd turned unexpectedly their eyes had met in a flicker of mutual interest. Amy had been nearly forty then, but she took good care of herself and there was no doubt the young man had looked at her with significant intensity. Amy had looked away first but not before his eyes had registered a hot blush that spread over her cheeks. After that first silent exchange she had kept an eye out for the young labourer, seizing on the first opportunity to offer him a cold beer. Dazed and terrified, she wasn't sure whether to hope he would realise that a beer wasn't all she wanted to offer him. The danger somehow added to her excitement, and when he made his first tentative advance she had found him irresistible.

* * *

She went up to her dressing room to decide what she was going to wear for her rendezvous with Guy. She had wasted enough of her life fretting about Patrick. It was time for her to start enjoying life, while she was still young enough.

CHAPTER 7

Keith had barely started his breakfast when the doorbell rang three times in quick succession. It didn't sound like the postman. 'Someone's impatient,' he thought, surprised to have a caller so early in the morning. The bell rang again. Faintly uneasy, he wondered if Jenny had come home unexpectedly, without her key. But his next door neighbour was on the doorstep.

'What the hell are you playing at?' Dave demanded, his large square face flushed with fury.

'What do you mean?'

'Your bloody car's blocking my garage and I'm going to be late. Move it, will you? Right now.'

Keith shook his head in bewilderment.

'She's not back till tomorrow.'

'What?'

'Jenny's gone to see her sister in Luton and she won't be back till—'

Dave's face turned a shade darker. He inched forward. Keith took an involuntary step back so that his infuriated neighbour stood poised with one foot on the threshold.

'I'm not interested in your wife. What's she got to do with it? I'm talking about your car, parked right across my garage door and—'

Keith shook his head again.

'But Jenny's taken the car and she isn't back till tomorrow.'

'I'm talking about the Mercedes.'

'What Mercedes?' Keith frowned. 'I haven't got a Mercedes, it's a Vauxhall.'

He gave a rueful smile.

'I wish it *was* a Mercedes.'

Dave took a pace back to stand squarely on the step outside.

'Well, some selfish bugger's gone and left a dark green Mercedes right outside your lock up and it's blocking my garage. I need to get my car out, I'm due in Bedford at nine and if I don't get off soon, I'm going to be late.'

'Well, it's not mine and I don't know whose it could be.'

'I'll have to call and tell them I can't make it for nine,' Dave grumbled. 'But you'd better do something about getting that Merc moved. It can't stay there.'

'Not sure what I can do.'

'Call the police. Report it. Or get onto a garage, I don't care. Just get it moved.'

Disgruntled by the encounter, Keith returned to his breakfast. What the hell did Dave expect him to do about some wretched Mercedes? It wasn't his responsibility. But as he munched cold toast and sipped lukewarm coffee, he had to agree that his neighbour had a point. If Jenny couldn't get the car in the garage they'd have a problem parking. They paid a fortune to use that garage. By the time he finished his breakfast, he was as outraged as Dave. He went storming round the back to see what was going on. He hoped the Mercedes would have gone, but rounding the corner into the narrow access lane he saw it, gleaming dark green, positioned right across the front of his garage, its boot jutting out past Dave's garage door.

'Bugger!'

He felt his heart begin to race.

'Selfish bloody bastard.'

No one with a scrap of decency or common sense would park like that, blocking access to someone else's garage. Such stupidity suggested the car had been stolen and abandoned there, in a quiet corner off the main road. Joyriders. Kids, most likely. All the same, Keith hesitated about calling the police straight away. They might want to talk to him and it was already quarter to eight. If he hung around much longer he would be late for work. It was a smart car and there was a chance the owner had been too drunk to drive home and had left it there for the night intending to return for it during the day, in which case the problem would simply go away. He decided to give it a day, and get onto the police if the Mercedes was still there that evening when he returned from work.

After a difficult day at work, Keith was in no mood for any more aggravation, but the dark green Mercedes was still parked right outside his garage when he arrived home, gleaming in the moonlight. Although he couldn't have said why, he had an uneasy sensation something was wrong. Frowning, he approached the vehicle for a closer look. He couldn't see anything through the tinted side windows. Moving to the front he peered through the windscreen. It looked as though a man was sitting slumped in the driver's seat. Keith ran round and tapped sharply with his knuckles on the driver's window.

'Oi! Wake up!'

Stepping back, he noticed a trickle of dark oil had oozed into the road from the bottom of the driver's door. It appeared to be leaking from behind the door, nowhere near the engine. In the meantime, there was no response from inside the car. Keith must have been mistaken. Frustrated, he went home to have something to eat and think about what to do. As if his day hadn't been bad enough, he saw a dark smear appear on their new beige hall carpet. He must have trodden in the oil leaking from the Mercedes. Slipping off his shoes he went into the kitchen. Before he did anything else, he opened a beer.

He almost knocked the bottle over when his mobile rang, startling him. It was Jenny.

'How are you doing?'

'Fine,' he fibbed.

It was almost true. He would soon have the oil patch cleaned up, and the owner of the Mercedes was bound to come back for it and drive off before long.

'How about you?'

Jenny chattered for a few moments about her trip.

'I can't wait to see you,' she finished.

'Me too.'

He gulped down the last of his beer, promising himself another one after he had sorted out the hall carpet. Clutching a wet rag and a bottle of washing up liquid he dropped to his knees and scrubbed wretchedly at the stain, hoping he could clean it up before Jenny saw it. After a moment's furious exertion, he sat back on his heels and a worried frown spread across his face. The patch had altered as he rubbed at it, turning from black to blood red.

With a burst of energy he sprang to his feet and ran into the kitchen. He rummaged frantically in the drawers where he knew Jenny kept a torch. At last he found it. Torch in hand he pulled on his trainers, grabbed his keys and ran outside to circle the green car, careful to avoid treading in the dark slime again. To begin with, all he could see was the reflection of the torch beam, and the shadow of his staring face behind it. He left it until last to go round to the front of the car and shone the torch through the windscreen. There was definitely someone in the driver's seat, his head hanging forward so his face was hidden. Keith gazed at the stranger's grey hair and shivered.

'Hey! You in there!'

His voice trembled and the torch shook in his hand. The sleeper didn't stir. Keith tapped on the windscreen, then went around to the side of the car and rapped more forcefully on the window nearest the man's head. He returned to the front of the car, trying to ignore the obvious. An inert figure, blood red liquid.

'Wake up! Wake up! You in there!'

Behind him a window was flung open and someone called out.

'Oi! What's all the racket? Put a sock in it, mate.'

Keith switched off the torch and ran back home.

On the point of calling the police Keith paused, phone in hand, wondering if he was overreacting. But there was no getting away from the suspicion that there was a dead body in a car outside his garage. Feeling lightheaded, he opened another beer. He had to call the police.

'Police please. And – can you hurry up. This is serious.'

In a trembling voice he gave his name and phone number.

'There's a body, at least I think there is, someone dead, in a car outside my garage. He's been there all day. He isn't moving and there's blood on the ground. It's dripping out of the car.'

'Blood dripping out of the car.'

His words repeated by the calm voice at the other end of the line made them sound far-fetched.

'Yes. I trod in it. I thought it was oil—'

He shook with relief when the operator took his address and told him a patrol car was on its way. As he waited for the police to arrive, he wondered if they would want to know why he hadn't called them in the morning, when he had first become aware of the Mercedes parked outside his garage. He was asking himself that same question, wondering if the body in the car had still been alive then. If he had acted promptly, he might have saved a man from bleeding to death.

CHAPTER 8

Geraldine was at her desk when Nick Williams arrived on Tuesday morning.

'Right,' he said briskly, 'I don't know about you but I've been thrown straight back in. Hopefully—'

He broke off as her phone rang. After taking the call Geraldine replaced the receiver with a rueful grin.

'Oh well, that was the duty sergeant. I'm off.'

She stood up.

'Catch you later,' he said with a smile.

The bulky figure of Detective Chief Inspector Reg Milton was standing in the Major Incident Room, waiting for silence. Stuck behind a desk most of the time his athletic frame was beginning to run to fat, but he held himself with the confidence of a physically powerful man. Despite the grey streaks in his hair, he looked like a man in his prime.

'You all know me,' he began.

When Geraldine had first met him his clipped upper class accent had come as a surprise.

‘A man’s body has been found in a car somewhere just off the Caledonian Road.’

He read the address aloud and paused briefly, glancing round the room to check that he had everyone’s attention.

‘The body was discovered in a vehicle parked outside a row of lock up garages at the back of the houses. It was found by one of the householders, Keith Apsley. We’ll need to question him, and talk to the neighbours, find out if anyone noticed anything unusual. The Assessment Team have confirmed that we’re looking at murder. Scene of crime officers are at work checking the car and we’re conducting a thorough search of the area for a weapon. Credit cards in the wallet in the victim’s pocket give us the name Patrick Henshaw, although he hasn’t yet been formally identified. The car was registered in the same name. Any questions?’

No one spoke.

‘Right then, let’s see what we can find out.’

Geraldine was pleased that Detective Sergeant Sam Haley was working with her again. After a rocky start, their professional relationship was developing into a firm friendship. Sam was usually optimistic, but this morning her features were twisted into a scowl.

‘Well, this is going to be a complete waste of time,’ she grumbled as she drove Geraldine across London towards Caledonian Road. ‘The body’s gone to the morgue so what exactly are we expecting to see, apart from an empty car parked outside a locked garage in a street packed with nosey bystanders hoping to see a murder victim?'

Geraldine didn't answer. They drove in silence to a quiet side road not far from their destination, where a sign on a lamp post displayed a list of complicated parking restrictions.

'How the hell is anyone supposed to make head or tail of that?' Geraldine asked.

'Perk of the job,' Sam replied, pulling up right beside one of the notices.

The day was overcast and it was threatening rain as they stared along the street of well-maintained terraced brick houses. There were no front gardens but many of the houses displayed brightly painted window boxes and plants in large pots in the narrow paved strips that served as front yards. The scene had a comfortable air of normality – apart from the forensic tent and a team of uniformed police officers making their way painstakingly along the street. Geraldine and Sam donned protective gear and entered the forensic tent, where a dark green Mercedes was being closely examined by scene of crime officers. It looked like a gigantic green slug with white larvae crawling over it. Geraldine walked slowly around the car. The side windows were heavily tinted, obscuring the interior of the vehicle. Through the windscreen a scene of crime officer could be seen inside the car, carefully collecting evidence samples. Reaching the driver's door she peered at the seat, which was soaked in blood. The inside of the door was also drenched in blood, which must have sprayed there as the victim lay dying. Behind the front tyre a thin stream of blood had trickled under the door and onto the road.

'There's a hell of a lot of blood,' she muttered.

'Yes, it looks as though the victim bled to death,' a scene of crime officer agreed cheerfully, pausing in his work and twisting his head round to talk to her.

'Is there any sign of a murder weapon?'

'Not yet. We've been conducting a search of the area but nothing's been found so far. We might still come across something but my guess is the killer took the weapon away with him.'

'We know the car was registered in the victim's name. So if Patrick Henshaw was attacked in his own car, how did his assailant get to him? The window wasn't broken. He must have opened the door.'

She frowned, trying to work out what had happened.

'Perhaps he was abducted,' Sam broke in with sudden enthusiasm. 'It's an expensive car. He must've been a seriously wealthy bloke. It could've been a kidnap attempt gone wrong. Henshaw opened the car door, a couple of men jumped him, one of them drove while the other was restraining him in the back, only things got out of hand—'

'Like your imagination,' Geraldine interrupted her quickly. She was pleased to see that the sergeant's usual good humour had returned, as she smiled at Geraldine's gentle reprimand. Sam was never bad-tempered for long.

'For a start, the victim was in the driver's seat. Apart from which we've seen nothing to indicate any attempted kidnap. Keep it real, Sam. Anything's possible at this stage,' Geraldine continued. 'So let's not muddy the water by allowing our imaginations to run away with us. We're here on a fact finding exercise so let's focus on the job and gather as much information as we can while we're here.'

'But you told me yourself facts alone aren't enough. We have to envisage the bigger picture. I'm not imagining, I'm *envisaging*.'

Geraldine felt faintly uneasy that her young sergeant seemed to remember everything she said. Of the two of them she was the senior officer, but there were times when the responsibility of knowing that Sam took her words so much to heart made her uncomfortable.

'That's true, Sam, but without facts we don't have anything to base our theories on. We can't just come up with ideas from nowhere.'

'Righty ho.'

* * *

'How long is this going to take?' Sam enquired after a pause.

'Do you have somewhere you need to be?' Geraldine asked sharply.

She had never had reason to doubt her sergeant's commitment before.

'I want to look around a little longer and then see if the witness who found the body is home. Is there a problem with that?' she added, seeing Sam grimace.

'No, but – it's just that I haven't eaten anything since breakfast. I wouldn't mind, only it's hard to focus when you're starving. It's distracting.'

Geraldine couldn't help laughing.

'I should have known you were thinking about your stomach. Come on then, I think we've seen what we need to see here for now. Let's go and grab something to eat – but I want to be back here soon to question the witness who discovered Henshaw, if he's in. The sooner we speak to him, the better, while it's still fresh in his mind.'

Sam looked shamefaced.

'We should really see him now, shouldn't we? I can wait, of course I can. Work comes first.'

'You're sure of that?' Geraldine asked, her sarcasm lost on Sam who nodded seriously.

'Come on then, it's number thirty-six. Let's get this job done.'

* * *

They left the tent and removed their suits, gloves and shoes before returning to the street where a small crowd of onlookers, mainly women, had gathered just beyond the police tape that cordoned off the narrow lane leading to the lock ups. Muttering to one another, shuffling and waiting for information about the dead man who had unexpectedly shattered the monotony of their street, they fell silent, watching, as Geraldine emerged from the narrow side turning and looked up and down the street of houses.

'Hey, miss,' one of them called out.

'What's going on?'

'We've got a right to know.'

Geraldine approached a uniformed constable and spoke quietly so members of the public wouldn't overhear her.

'There's no chance any of it was caught on CCTV I suppose?'

'No ma'am. There's no cameras this far from the main road, and even if the car was filmed driving past the station, or somewhere else in the area, we're not going to see a dicky bird through those windows.'

'No, I suppose not.'

As she turned back to the onlookers, a few more voices called out to her.

'Who is it in there?'

'What's happening here?'

'Has someone been murdered on the street?'

* * *

Ignoring the demands from the crowd, the two detectives walked past them to number thirty-six. Geraldine pushed open the gate and Sam followed her across the narrow front yard. It began to drizzle as they waited on the doorstep.

'At least the rain will send the spectators packing,' Geraldine said, nodding in the direction of the neighbours who showed no sign of dispersing.

CHAPTER 9

'The witness who found the body is called Keith Apsley,' Geraldine reminded Sam as she rang the bell.

A moment later a man opened the door. Tall and pale, he stared anxiously down at them.

'Keith Apsley?'

'Yes. Is it about—'

Geraldine held out her warrant card and introduced herself and her sergeant.

'We'd like to ask you a few questions.'

'Yes. That's OK. I've been expecting you,' he mumbled.

Geraldine detected a whiff of alcohol on his breath as he spoke.

'I've been trying not to think about it, but I just can't get it out of my head. How can I, knowing what's out there? To be honest, I didn't sleep at all last night, what with the shock and being on my own and all. They have taken it away, haven't they – should I say him?'

'The body's been taken to the morgue, Mr Apsley, but the forensic tent will stay there and the area of the lock ups will be cordoned off while it's examined by forensic officers.'

'How long will all that take? Only my wife's coming home this evening and she'll need to put the car in the garage.'

'As long as it takes for the forensic team to complete their search. I'm afraid I can't say how long that will be.'

Keith stood aside to let the two women in. Entering a neat narrow hallway Geraldine's eyes were caught by a smear of blood on the light carpet. Noticing the direction of her gaze he started forward.

'It's not how it looks,' he stammered.

'How does it look?'

'You think it's blood, don't you? Well, I think so too. That's why I suspected something was wrong in the first place, but he never came here. I didn't know him. It was my shoe, the blood was on my shoe—'

Keith was babbling nervously.

'Perhaps you'd like to sit down and start at the beginning, Mr Apsley.'

'Yes, of course. Come on in. Let's go in the living room.'

'We'll get that checked forensically,' Sam said, pausing and looking down at the stain.

'There's no need. I know where it came from. It's from that car. I trod in it, you see. Look.'

He darted forward, picked up a trainer and held it upside down.

'See?'

He waved the shoe at them before turning to lead them into a small square sitting room, furnished in pine and light blue. Plonking himself down on a chair, he launched into a rambling account of his discovery of the body.

'My wife's sister just had a baby, so Jenny's gone over there. I'm here on my own. Yesterday morning one of my neighbours knocks on the door making a fuss about a car parked outside my garage, blocking his garage. That was the first I knew about it.'

'What time was it when your neighbour called on you?'

'Early, about seven maybe. I'd just started breakfast.'

He gave them his neighbour's details and returned to his narrative, describing how he had gone to the lock ups to take a look at the car.

'You didn't report this until after seven yesterday evening, nearly twelve hours later,' Geraldine pointed out.

'I know, but I had no idea there was anyone inside. I didn't take a close look at it at first, I just clocked it was there and went to work. I hoped it would be gone by the time I got home but it was still there in the evening so I went up for a closer look and saw there was someone in the driver's seat. That's when I trod in the blood. At first I thought it was some kind of oil although it wasn't leaking from the engine—'

He broke off with a puzzled frown.

'I couldn't see much. I thought he was asleep, only he didn't move, even when I shouted at him. I called out and banged on the window but he still didn't move. So then I thought he must be drunk. I didn't realise I'd trodden in anything until I came in and saw the mess on the carpet.'

'You tried to clean it up.'

Sam's comment sounded like an accusation.

'Yes, I know. I didn't want Jenny to see it. She's always on at me to take my shoes off in the house. We've got this cream carpet in the hall. I told her it wasn't the best idea, but she insisted it would be all right. And it was, until this. We've had it for two years.'

'So you tried to remove the blood stain from your carpet,' Sam interrupted Keith's panicked babbling.

'Yes.'

'Didn't you wonder where it came from?'

'I thought it was oil.'

'Oil?'

'I just assumed because it looked black to begin with, but when I started rubbing it with water it turned red and that's when I knew.'

He raised stricken eyes to Geraldine.

'Thank you. We might ask you to come to the

police station to answer a few more questions but that's all for now, Mr Apsley.'

He accompanied them to the door.

'Inspector, can you tell me the best way to get rid of blood stains? I need to clean the carpet before Jenny—'

'Please don't touch the blood stain on your carpet for the time being, Mr Apsley.'

'But I can't just leave it. Jenny'll go ballistic if she sees it.'

'We'll need to send a scene of crime officer in to examine it first.'

'Why do you need to examine it? I told you where it comes from. You know what it is.'

'And we'll need your shoe—'

Keith stared at her, belligerent with sudden fear.

'What for?'

His voice rose in agitation.

'And when are you going to move that car? I told you, Jenny will be home this evening and she'll need to put the car in the garage. There's no parking round here without a resident's permit. We haven't even got one because we don't need it. We've got a garage—'

He paused and took a step back.

'I'm sorry. It's just – I'm not feeling quite myself. This whole thing's been horrible.'

'Mr Apsley, we'll send a scene of crime officer in as soon as possible,' Geraldine assured him. 'Once they've finished I'm sure they'll be able to advise you the best way to remove the blood stain from your carpet.'

'Thank you.'

'Did you think there was something a bit dodgy about him?' Sam asked as they walked back to the car.

Geraldine shrugged.

'My guess is he's been drinking this morning. Not a good idea when you've missed a night's sleep after a shock.'

'But it's a bit of a coincidence, isn't it?' Sam persisted.

'What is?'

'His wife goes away and suddenly a dead body turns up on his doorstep.'

'There's nothing to suggest he had anything to do with it. Someone just happened to deposit a body by the lock ups. It's a quiet enough spot.'

Sam wasn't satisfied.

'What about the blood stain on his carpet?'

Geraldine looked thoughtful.

'He gave a reasonable account of how that got there. If he was implicated in the murder, why would he report it to us? And would he be so quick to show us the blood in his hall and on his shoe if he was guilty?'

'We could hardly miss seeing the blood on the carpet. He didn't exactly show it to us,' Sam argued.

* * *

Geraldine shook her head.

'No. It doesn't add up, Sam. He could easily have covered up the blood stain with a rug, or spilled red wine over it to mask it, or something, and we'd have been none the wiser. Why would he draw our attention to it? And why show us his shoe and admit he'd stepped in the blood right by the car when he could have disposed of the shoe without our seeing it and we might never have known he'd been anywhere near the door of the Mercedes. He could simply have reported what he'd seen through the windscreen, or just reported the car and not mentioned he knew there was someone inside it at all.'

Sam scowled.

'Well, it all seems a bit odd to me.'

'We'll certainly check him out, and his missing wife, but I don't think someone who's just committed a murder would be in such a hurry to summon us, and go out of his way to draw suspicion on himself. Why would he?'

'To put us off the scent,' Sam argued. 'He didn't exactly rush to call us. The car had been there all day, maybe longer for all we know. He said himself he saw it when he went out yesterday morning. He must've realised someone would report it eventually and it's parked right outside his garage. He probably thought it would look odd if he didn't report it himself.'

'Well, maybe, but I don't think so.'

'Why not?'
'For a start, he seemed far more worried about his wife's reaction to the stain on the carpet than about the body outside his garage.'
'Transference?'

'Maybe. Now come on, we've got an important job to do.'
Sam's face fell.
'Oh Jesus, what now?'
Geraldine turned to her with a laugh.
'Lunch of course. Or aren't you hungry any more?'
Sam grinned.
'Ravenous,' she replied. 'I know this great Chinese chippy not far from here.'

CHAPTER 10

'This place must have cost a few bob,' Sam said with a low whistle as they cruised along an elegant tree-lined avenue in Hampstead and drew up outside a large detached house. She stared around in admiration before following Geraldine through an iron gate into a small front garden.

'I reckon some of the windows at the back must have a view over the heath.'

'Put your eyes back in,' Geraldine smiled.

The door was opened by a slim blonde woman in her late thirties, well groomed rather than beautiful. She was wearing a figure hugging dark green pencil skirt and matching shoes, with a pale green silk blouse which set off blonde hair as glossy as that of a model in a shampoo advertisement. Grey eyes peered at them through a long fringe. There was something guarded in her solemn expression. Whatever other emotions she might be feeling, the widow was clearly frightened.

* * *

'Amy Henshaw?'

'Yes.'

Geraldine held out her warrant card.

'I'm Detective Inspector Geraldine Steel and this is Detective Sergeant Samantha Haley. May we come in?'

'This is about my husband, isn't it? Has something happened to him? He hasn't been home since Sunday and I've been so worried—'

She raised a manicured hand to her mouth.

'Let's go inside, shall we?'

Amy led them across a spacious hall into a living room comfortably furnished with armchairs, a small settee, and several occasional tables neatly positioned within easy reach of every chair.

'I suggest you sit down, Mrs Henshaw.'

'What is it? What's happened? Tell me he's all right.'

She was chattering nervously, seeming far too jittery considering she had no idea yet what had happened.

'I'm afraid your husband's dead, Mrs Henshaw.'

'Dead? He can't be!'

Her surprise seemed genuine.

'It's not—'

For an instant Geraldine thought she caught a glimpse of real terror in Amy's expression before she threw herself forward, hiding her face in her hands, her shoulders shaking with noisy sobs.

* * *

Geraldine gave Sam a quick nod and the sergeant set off to find the kitchen.

'Detective Sergeant Haley's gone to make you a cup of tea,' Geraldine said quietly. 'When you're ready, I'd like to ask you a few questions.'

'Questions?'

Her shoulders were motionless now, her face still hidden.

'What sort of questions?'

'We're investigating your husband's death.'

'Investigating? What do you mean?'

'Mrs Henshaw, your husband didn't die from natural causes. He was murdered.'

Amy Henshaw shuddered. Dropping her hands, she peered up at Geraldine through her fringe and spoke rapidly, almost hysterically.

'I don't understand. You haven't told me how he died. What makes you think he was murdered? That's insane.'

Her grey eyes glared at Geraldine.

'It's a horrible thing to say. No one would have wanted to harm Patrick. No one. What happened? Was it a drunken brawl? He liked to drink sometimes . . .'

Her voice petered out.

Geraldine leaned forward, watching Amy's expression closely.

'Was your husband often involved in fights?'

'No. He wasn't. He was never involved in any

fighting. What makes you think he was ever in a fight?'

'You said he drank and you thought he might have been in a brawl. It was your word.'

The widow's eyes flickered round the room, avoiding Geraldine's gaze.

'Was he a violent man?'

'No, he wasn't violent. He was . . . . He was a good man.'

'Were the police ever called when he was in a fight?'

'No, no, there was nothing like that. No one was ever hurt. He just used to drink a bit. It was nothing serious.'

Amy dropped her eyes and stared at her hands, while her fingers fidgeted with her wedding ring.

'Two months ago you reported your husband for domestic violence.'

'I retracted it,' Amy whispered.

She looked pale.

'It wasn't true, it was just . . . a mistake.'

'A mistake?'

'Yes, that's right,' she went on, her voice stronger. 'It was a mistake. It was my own fault. I thought Patrick was seeing someone else, but he wasn't. He was just working long hours. I made a mistake.'

Amy stood up abruptly and walked over to the door.

'I'd like you to leave now.'

Geraldine didn't move. Amy spoke angrily.

'I don't want to discuss this any more. Please, just go. I've just lost my husband.'

Geraldine made no move to leave.

'My sergeant will be here with a cup of tea for you soon, and then I'll need to ask you a few more questions.'

'No, no, I can't, not now. Not yet. I can't talk about this. It's all too – too confusing.'

Amy sat down again and flung her head in her hands. Geraldine could see nothing of the widow's face behind its trembling screen of hair.

'Don't you want to help us find out who killed your husband?'

Amy Henshaw sat up suddenly as though she had been stung, tossed back her hair and glared at Geraldine.

'Of course I do.'

Sam came in holding a delicate china cup and saucer decorated with blue flowers.

'Here you go,' she said, handing the tea to Amy. 'I'm sorry, this tea set was all I could find.'

Amy took a sip of tea and pulled a face. She put the cup down on the nearest table.

'I don't take sugar.'

'You've had a shock, Mrs Henshaw. Sweet tea is the best thing for you right now. Drink it.'

'And then we would like to ask you a few questions,' Geraldine repeated gently.

'Can't you leave me alone?'

'We'd like to run through a few routine questions first.'

Reluctantly, Amy sipped the tea and nodded, her eyes downcast.

'Go on then. Let's get this over with.'

'Mrs Henshaw,' Geraldine leaned forward. 'Were you aware of any bad feeling towards your husband? Anyone he might have had a falling out with?'

Amy shook her head.

'Can you think of anyone who might have wanted to harm him? Anyone who had a grudge against him? An aggrieved employee, perhaps?'

Amy put her cup and saucer down on the table beside her.

'Patrick didn't discuss his work with me. I don't know anything about it. He never said anything.'

'Did he ever mention any names? Any arguments he might have had?'

'No. I told you, he never brought his work home.'

Her voice was clipped, curt, and she didn't look up, every inch the bereaved wife in shock.

Despite feeling that Amy Henshaw was playing a role, Geraldine spoke more gently.

'Had you been married for long?'

'Twenty years.'

'Was it a happy marriage?'

'What do you mean?'

'Your marriage. Was it a happy one?'

'Yes. Of course it was. Patrick is – he was – a wonderful husband. Whatever I wanted—'

She broke down in tears, hiding her face in her hands.

'We'll leave it there for now, Mrs Henshaw.'

Geraldine stood up.

'Here's my card. Please call me if you want anything, or if you think of anything else you'd like to tell me. Now, would you like us to call anyone? You might not want to be alone—'

'No, I'm fine. Just leave me alone.'

'So what did you make of the grief stricken widow?' Sam asked as the front door closed behind them.

'I'm not sure,' Geraldine admitted. 'It was a bit much of her to claim he was never violent, just two months after she accused him of beating her up, or at least hitting her. Did she think we wouldn't know about that?'

'Well, there was something distinctly odd about her, if you ask me,' Sam said.

'Odd in what way?'

'I don't know, really. There's nothing I can put my finger on, but I didn't believe a single word she said.'

Geraldine nodded.

'I thought that too. She's covering something up, but what? It might have nothing whatever to do with her husband's death, but she was definitely frightened.'

'Yes, that's the impression I had, which suggests—' Sam left the sentence unfinished.

CHAPTER 11

The pathologist's report made unpleasant reading. The vicious injuries inflicted on Henshaw seemed to suggest the killer had known his victim. If that was true, with luck it could make the case relatively easy to wrap up; sooner or later painstaking investigation into everyone who knew Henshaw would lead to the murderer. In the meantime, Reg Milton was waiting impatiently to find out what information had been gathered so far. After spending most of the day studying reports, there had been little time to deal with a pile of paperwork that was growing on his desk, trivial but pressing.

The detective chief inspector had summoned his team for a late afternoon briefing and waited while they all gathered in the incident room. Geraldine and Sam entered together, both clutching cups of coffee, smiling at something they had just been discussing. Watching them, Reg felt a pang of regret at the camaraderie he had relinquished in moving up the hierarchy. He greeted them all cheerfully before turning to Geraldine.

'You questioned Keith Apsley, didn't you?'

'Yes.'

'And what did you make of him?'

'I think he was on the level, sir.'

'My name's Reg,' he reminded her with a smile.

'Sorry. Old habits die hard. I'm used to working in the Home Counties.'

When Geraldine returned his smile, Reg thought that perhaps he had been right to go for promotion after all. Forming an effective team out of a disparate group of strangers was just a different kind of challenge to those faced by officers working out in the community. Even behind a desk he could make a difference. He turned his attention to what Geraldine was saying.

'Apsley was irritated that the Mercedes had been left right outside his garage, so he checked it out. At first he thought the man in the driver's seat was asleep, probably drunk, but after a while he realised something was wrong – he noticed blood outside the vehicle and wasn't able to rouse the man, so he called it in. That seems to be the extent of his involvement.'

'Why did it take him so long to call us?' someone wanted to know.

Geraldine shrugged.

'That part of his statement's not altogether clear. He claims he didn't realise straight away that there

was anything wrong. He didn't notice the body in the morning.'

'Didn't notice it?'

'Yes sir – Reg. The thing is, it's possible, because the car's got tinted windows. I believe him. He was in a hurry to get off to work and thought he could leave it till later to deal with. He was hoping someone would come and remove the car by the time he got home yesterday evening.'

Samantha Haley shook her head impatiently and looked as though she was about to speak, but Reg turned to a detective constable who had been doing some research into the witness. He wanted to share some facts before listening to any more speculation about whether or not he was telling the truth.

'Has he got form?'

'No. There's nothing on him or his wife. Both working, nothing on either of them.'

Reg turned to another constable who had been looking into the victim's background. It was similarly uneventful.

'Not so much as a parking ticket, and that's quite a feat considering they live in Hampstead. He wasn't born to money. Grew up on a council estate in South London.'

'So the money came from his wife?'

The constable shook his head.

'Patrick Henshaw was a self-made man. In his

twenties he made some very lucrative investments – shrewd or lucky, maybe both. Anyway, he made himself a tidy packet. By the time he reached forty, he was worth millions. When he married Amy he was forty-five and she was just twenty. He retired from business when they married then five years ago he bought a swanky restaurant in Soho. God knows why, he didn't need the money.'

'Perhaps he was bored,' Reg suggested. 'So his wife's twenty-five years younger than him which would make her forty. He was more than double her age when he married her.'

'Yes, she's forty. She must be a very wealthy woman now.'

Sam broke in briskly.

'Which makes it more likely it's a crime of passion, something to do with his wife. Why else would the killer have been so violent? And if she's inherited a fortune—'

Reg turned to her with a nod to indicate he was listening.

'I don't think we should be writing Keith Apsley off just yet. I think he might somehow be involved in it.'

Eagerly she outlined the reason for her suspicion, the body having arrived outside Keith Apsley's house just when his wife was away.

'It just seems a bit of a coincidence. It's possible Keith Apsley was having an affair with Amy Henshaw. What if he killed her husband so they could get his money?' she concluded triumphantly.

'We're not ruling anything out for now,' Reg replied. 'Not until we know more about what happened, but I agree it sounds as though Apsley might be implicated.'

'You haven't even spoken to him,' Geraldine pointed out.

'As I said, I'm not ruling anything out just yet,' he repeated, a trifle sharply.

He considered Sam's suggestion. On the face of it, the idea seemed reasonable. It was certainly an odd coincidence, a man's body appearing outside the Apsleys' garage just when Keith's wife was away. But Geraldine's explanation was equally plausible. He had only worked with her on one case, but her gut feeling then had proved spot on. He wondered if that had just been luck, or if she was one of those rare officers who possessed an uncanny instinct for the truth. There was no doubt she had an impressive track record.

'Well,' he concluded. 'We'll keep our minds open and carry on. See what we can find out.'

CHAPTER 12

Geraldine was annoyed that Reg had taken Sam's theory seriously. Reg hadn't even met Apsley, and they had found nothing to suggest he was having an affair with Amy Henshaw. She hoped the investigation wouldn't be led astray by fanciful speculation. As her mentor, Geraldine had already warned the sergeant against unsubstantiated speculation. She had another go at impressing on Sam the importance of resisting committing to a theory without any evidence.

'So you think I've got it all wrong, is that what you're trying to tell me?'

'I'm just saying we need to keep an open mind. Cases can throw up all sorts of surprises.'

'I have got an open mind,' Sam replied crossly and they drove the rest of the way to the morgue in silence.

Geraldine arrived at the morgue irritated with Sam, and even more annoyed with herself for handling the situation so clumsily. The pathologist met them with a smile. He had clear hazel eyes and light brown hair tinged with red. Although he must have been older, he looked about twenty.

'I've been waiting for you,' he said with a hint of impatience in his voice.

He introduced himself as Miles Fellows. While Geraldine responded to the friendly greeting, Sam stepped forward for a sight of the body. She flinched and Geraldine threw the sergeant a sympathetic glance, aware that Sam felt queasy around corpses.

'I'm afraid he was a bit of a mess when he was brought in,' the pathologist began, sounding apologetic, as though he was somehow responsible for the victim's injuries. Horrified, Geraldine and Sam studied the cadaver. The dead man's face was bloodless, the effect emphasised by his dark staring eyes and gaping mouth. From one side his face was white and intact. With curiously angular features, he looked like an android. As Geraldine approached she saw a deep weal on his left temple surrounded by a bruise that extended from the edge of his straight eyebrow to disappear beneath his hair. But that wasn't what held her attention.

'Oh my God, what happened to him?' Sam asked.

'This was a vicious attack,' Miles replied quietly. 'The attack began with an injury to the side of the head.'

He pointed to the gash on the victim's temple.

'It may appear superficial, but the internal

damage is considerable, a single blow inflicted with considerable force at close range. It would probably have been enough to stun the victim, if not knock him unconscious. And after that – as you can see – the victim was severely battered.'

No one spoke for a few seconds as they stared at the dead man's pulverised genitals, a mess of bloody flesh.

'That's disgusting,' Sam muttered at last.

Her voice sounded thick and slurred, as though it was an effort for her to move her lips.

'There was a hell of a lot of blood in the car where he was found,' Geraldine said. 'Would it all have been the victim's or—'

It seemed too much to hope the killer might have left his DNA at the scene.

'The blow to his head might well have knocked him out, or at least it would have dazed him for a few seconds, but he was still alive when the other injuries were inflicted. I can't imagine he would have remained conscious for long and the shock and blood loss would have finished him off pretty quickly even if he'd weathered the blow to his temple. But between the two injuries that could well account for very extensive bleeding,' Miles told them.

There was another pause.

'I daresay you already know a great deal about the victim. He was well nourished, worked out or exercised regularly, and looked after himself. My first impression was that we were looking at a man in his mid-fifties, but closer examination suggests he was past sixty.'

Geraldine said Henshaw was sixty-five when he died.

'Can you give us an estimated time of death?'

'Sunday night between ten thirty and eleven thirty.'

Sam had been staring in horror at the victim's injuries.

'Why on earth would anyone do that? The killer must've really hated the victim, so he must've known him.'

'Some hatred,' Geraldine muttered.

'At any rate, the killer must have known him,' Sam insisted. 'If you ask me it was a jealous rival who did this. Either Henshaw was sleeping with the killer's wife, or the killer was sleeping with Henshaw's wife. Nothing else explains this.'

She pointed at the victim's mutilated genitals.

'It's an act of revenge. And if it's Henshaw's wife they were fighting over, there's money at stake as well.'

'That's two possibilities certainly,' Geraldine agreed cautiously, 'but it's just guesswork.'

A sulky expression crossed Sam's face as Geraldine continued.

'All we can say with any certainty so far is that his name was Patrick Henshaw, he was sixty-five, married, with no children that we know of.'

'He was a heavy drinker,' the pathologist told them. 'He'd been drinking shortly before he was killed. I've not got the toxicology report yet but I could smell it on his breath and his stomach contents. He'd eaten a couple of hours before he died – steak and salad – and he'd been drinking too. I'm pretty sure I smelt beer and I'd hazard a guess at whisky too.'

'OK, we'll check his credit card payments, see if we can find out if he was on his own that evening.'

'What was the actual cause of death?'

'That was a nasty wound on his head. Resultant internal bleeding would probably have caused permanent damage, if it hadn't in itself proved fatal, but as for the actual cause of death, that was blood loss, compounded by shock.'

He nodded his head in the direction of the injuries to the victim's body.

'What if he'd been found earlier? Could he have been bleeding to death for a while?' Geraldine asked.

'Placing the time of the attack earlier than the time of death, you mean? No, there's no way he was going to survive those injuries for very long. He would have bled profusely over a short period of time, ten or maybe twenty minutes at the most.'

'It had to be a jealous rival,' Sam insisted. 'Why else would anyone do something like that? Nothing else makes sense.'

* * *

'It's a vulnerable area,' Geraldine said. 'Is it possible the murderer wanted to be certain the victim was dead? I mean, I'd have thought that was a pretty good way of making sure.'

She addressed her question to the pathologist who shook his head.

'It was certainly a frenzied attack,' he agreed. 'But as for the motive, that's for you to discuss. Now, is there anything else I can tell you?'

'We're looking at a vicious murder all right,' Geraldine said as the two detectives arrived back at her office.

'Horrible,' Sam agreed.

'Murder most foul, is it?' Nick asked with a smile.

Geraldine was surprised to hear him quote Shakespeare and picked him up on it.

'You a Shakespeare boffin then?'

'Huh?'

'You quoted *Hamlet* just now.'

'And you recognised it. Does that mean we're both boffins?' he replied and they both laughed.

Sam turned away and it occurred to Geraldine that Sam might resent her rapport with Nick. Geraldine turned to her.

'Let's go and get a coffee and mull over what we know.'

Sam's face immediately brightened. Geraldine would need to handle her efficient young sergeant sensitively.

* * *

Sam was still convinced they were dealing with a crime of passion.

'It makes sense, Geraldine. Henshaw is playing around with another woman, her husband finds out and – there you are. It explains the injury. Revenge by a jealous husband. I'll bet he was having it off with Keith Apsley's wife!'

'Unless Henshaw's wife was the one playing around,' Geraldine said. 'And had a jealous lover who wanted her husband out of the way.'

'And Henshaw's death leaves her a wealthy woman,' Sam added, her eyes alight with enthusiasm. 'Maybe she put him up to it.'

'They could have been in it together.'

Despite herself, Geraldine was catching the sergeant's fervour.

Geraldine made a quick phone call and discovered Amy Henshaw had already been to the morgue to identify her husband's body.

'Damn,' she said as she rang off. 'I thought I might catch her there. Sometimes people let their guard down when they've seen the victim. She might've been more likely to talk. We'll speak to her again soon. In the meantime, let's see what else we can find out about the Henshaws, and if you discover one of them was having an affair, so much the better.'

CHAPTER 13

Petrie and Waterman's door was sandwiched between a kitchen showroom and a beauty salon in Temple Fortune. Geraldine rang the bell and was buzzed in. A carpeted staircase led to the solicitors' premises. She introduced herself to a receptionist who ushered her into a small, neatly furnished office where a distinguished-looking older man was seated behind a wooden desk.

'A police inspector is here to see you.'

'Oh?'

The solicitor raised his eyebrows and half rose to his feet.

'Please take a seat. I'm Jonathon Waterman. How can I help you?'

He glanced at her warrant card as Geraldine sat down on a hard leather chair and introduced herself.

'I'm enquiring about Patrick Henshaw's will.'

The solicitor looked suitably solemn.

'Patrick Henshaw? He was my client. So you're investigating his death?'

Geraldine glanced around the office without responding. The room was at the back of the building, and strangely hushed after the London traffic to which she had grown accustomed. Horizontal white shutters at the window were open a crack to let in the daylight between the slats, but it wasn't possible to see out.

'I take it the circumstances of his death were suspicious?'

'What makes you say that?'

'Why else would you be here?'

Geraldine smiled in acknowledgement before asking to hear the terms of the dead man's will.

'It was fairly straightforward as I recall,' Jonathon Waterman said, 'but I'm afraid I can't divulge any details. We're not reading the will until tomorrow so the beneficiaries don't know the details yet.'

Geraldine sighed and leaned forward in her chair.

'Mr Waterman, I'm conducting a murder investigation. If you have any information that can assist us in our enquiries, it will of course be treated in confidence. Did he leave much?'

She paused.

'Mr Waterman, the sooner I can access this information, the more helpful it might prove.'

A frown crossed Jonathon Waterman's face.

'I appreciate the position, and there are certain details I can let you know in advance of the reading of the will tomorrow. George Corless is already aware that he became sole owner of the jointly owned restaurant on Patrick Henshaw's death under a contractual agreement between them, but the other details of the will are as yet confidential. However—' he hesitated. 'Under the circumstances, given this is a murder enquiry—'

Geraldine watched him cross the room, select a file from a metal cabinet and extract a document. Still standing, he scanned down the page before returning to his seat and reading aloud. Geraldine noted down the relevant details.

'To summarise,' he concluded, forthcoming now that he had begun, 'Patrick named three people in his will. His share in the restaurant went to his business partner, George Corless, Miss Stella Hallett of Ladbroke Grove inherits his liquid assets, and he left his property to his wife, Amy.'

'What can you tell me about the restaurant?'

'Patrick part-owned Mireille – you may have heard of it. It's a very prestigious restaurant in Soho. Very profitable.'

Geraldine said she thought the name sounded familiar.

'There was a television documentary about it recently. It focused mainly on the clientele. Mireille is patronised by celebrities and stars of the media, people of that sort, and the chef is himself well-known, of course, Henri Gilbert. I gather he's something of a television personality in his own right.'

He proceeded to name a string of pop stars, several of them well-known for their on-off relationships with high profile footballers.

'My understanding was that the previous owner was struggling for some years and the place was rapidly going downhill when Patrick and his partner bought it. They turned it around and it became fashionable with the in crowd. It's a real success story. Patrick had a talent for making money.'

'So he didn't leave his share in the restaurant to his widow?'

'No, his share in Mireille went to his partner, George Corless, who now owns the place outright. That's quite a goldmine he's got his hands on.'

He rubbed his manicured hands together and Geraldine wondered if Waterman acted for George Corless as well.

'A real success for him as well then,' Geraldine said.

The solicitor looked thoughtful.

'There's something else, isn't there?' Geraldine asked, seeing the look on his face. 'Something you're not telling me?'

'The two men have been in business together for years. But George introduced other issues—'

'Other issues?'

'Patrick wasn't a gambler until he went into business with George. Of course he was always a gambler in some sense, all successful businessmen take risks, but George spent a fortune making the bookies rich.'

'And Patrick Henshaw followed his example? Is that what you mean?'

'I'm afraid so. I believe he invested in Mireille as a business venture because he was bored in his retirement. But there's no doubt George was interested in Mireille to fund his habit, addiction you might call it, and Patrick was drawn into it.'

'Did his behaviour change at all as a result?'

'His behaviour? No.'

Noting a slight hesitation, Geraldine pressed him and the solicitor shrugged.

'His behaviour as such didn't change, but he was clearly stressed. He looked terrible.'

'Did you have much to do with Henshaw?'

'No, not really. I drew up his will for him, dealt with contracts, that sort of thing. And I saw him socially from time to time.'

'Socially?'

He smiled at her evident surprise.

'Amy and my wife were friends for a time, then we drifted apart, after he bought Mireille. Socialising became difficult after that with him keeping such unsocial hours, at the restaurant every evening. There was no falling out; we just moved on.'

Geraldine nodded.

'This,' he tapped the will on the desk in front of him, 'makes George Corless a seriously wealthy man.'

'And what can you tell me about the other beneficiary, Stella Hallett?'

She waited but the solicitor didn't respond.

'What can you tell me about Stella Hallet, Mr Waterman?'

He shook his head.

'I'm afraid I can't tell you anything about Stella Hallett. I've no idea who she is. I encountered her name for the first time in Patrick's will. Other than that she's just inherited almost a million pounds, I'm afraid I don't know anything about her. I'll be meeting her for the first time tomorrow, if she turns up to hear the will read.'

Jonathon Waterman inclined his head before rising to his feet and crossing the room to replace the will in its drawer.

'So the restaurant was left to George Corless, almost a million to Stella Hallett, whoever she is, and the wife inherits the rest of the estate which must be worth how many million?' Geraldine asked.

The solicitor shrugged. He sat down again and rested his elbows on the desk, his chin on his clasped hands.

'The will is being read tomorrow so I don't suppose it can do any harm if I tell you that things aren't quite how they might appear. But you must keep this under wraps for now.'

Geraldine nodded vigorously.

'Of course. But what did you mean, things aren't how they appear?'

'Patrick was experiencing some difficulties.'

'What sort of difficulties?'

'Having amassed several millions, he retired in his mid-fifties but complained he grew bored with his newfound leisure and – well, there's no reason I shouldn't tell you now – he took to gambling in a serious way.'

'I see. How much did he lose?'

'Almost everything, apart from what he'd put into the restaurant.'

'So his wife gets the large house in Hampstead, and that's all he left her?' Geraldine asked.

The solicitor nodded uncertainly.

'I see. Did she know about his financial position?'

'I'm not privy to what her husband told her, but he was anxious to keep his gambling debts concealed from her, so she might be under the impression that her husband was a very wealthy man, and my guess is that she'll be anticipating hearing that she's extremely well off after his death. A wealthy widow.'

'And is she?'

'Inspector, I'm afraid I've already told you far more than I should have.'

'Is there much equity on the house?'

'Very little, I'm afraid. It's going to come as quite a shock to Amy if she really had no idea about Patrick's financial position.'

CHAPTER 14

It was quiet in the restaurant. The tables were laid with white table cloths and linen napkins, silver cutlery and crystal glasses. Gleaming ice buckets stood on tripods and there was an air of subdued bustle as waiters in crisp white shirts and black waistcoats glided smoothly between tables. Doubtless the prices reflected the upmarket ambience. A bald waiter approached Geraldine discreetly, his words conveyed rather than spoken.

'Table for two, madam?'

When Geraldine held up her warrant card and asked for the manager, he turned and vanished through swing doors.

'Just look at that!' Sam muttered.

She stared enviously as several plates of food were delivered to a nearby table. A team of waiters materialised to serve the accompanying vegetables and wine.

'God, I'm starving,' Sam went on, wistfully. 'It'll be chips for us on the way back, I suppose.'

Geraldine smiled.

'I don't think expenses would run to dining here.'

The head waiter returned as soundlessly as he had departed, and ushered them out of the dining area.

Polished double doors swung closed behind them. At once the atmosphere changed. Pans clashed, cutlery clattered, white clad figures scurried past, while a frenzied voice shouted out orders in a thick French accent. They followed their guide through a brown baize door to a dimly lit office where a middle-aged man was sitting behind a large wooden desk. He rose to his feet extending a sweaty hand and introduced himself as George Corless.

'Please, take a seat,' he added, wheezing as he sat down again. 'Thank you, Bernard.'

He nodded at the waiter who left, closing the door softly behind him.

'Now, Inspector.'

He leaned back comfortably in his large leather armchair.

'I hope this won't take long, only I've got a stack of work waiting. What's the problem?'

Geraldine studied George Corless, a fat, balding, round-shouldered man in his sixties. Black eyes returned her gaze without blinking from beneath bushy ginger eyebrows, his sharp gaze giving the lie to his offhand words.

He gestured towards a couple of chairs and they sat down.

'We're here to speak to you about your partner.'

'Desiree? What's happened to her?'

The ruddy glow faded on his broad face and he shifted in his chair.

'I'm talking about your business partner, Patrick Henshaw.'

'Patrick? What about him?'

Geraldine couldn't decide if his shock was genuine when she told him Henshaw was dead.

'Dead?'

'You must have noticed he was missing.'

'No. That is, I wondered why I hadn't seen him. He's usually here, but I thought something must have turned up and he'd be along later.'

'What about yesterday? Didn't you wonder where he was?'

'We don't open on Mondays.'

Corless sat fidgeting with a box of cigars that lay open on the desk top. He gazed around the room uncertainly until his eyes lit on a decanter. He rose heavily to his feet, crossing the room to pour himself a tumbler of whisky. Throwing his head back, he downed the liquor in one gulp and refilled the glass. Geraldine watched his back, shirt stretched across wide shoulders, trousers taut on his buttocks and barrel shaped thighs.

After a moment he turned and waddled slowly back to his desk, clutching his drink in a hand that shook slightly.

'Are you telling me Patrick's actually dead?'

'That's exactly what I'm telling you, Mr Corless.'

'But – what the hell are you doing here, if you don't mind my asking – unless—'

He paused, his forehead creased in a puzzled frown.

'Patrick Henshaw was murdered,' Geraldine said.

The fat man sat down abruptly, oblivious of whisky sloshing in his glass. It splashed the papers on the desk in front of him, its scented aroma permeating the air between them.

'Mr Corless, I'd like to ask you a few questions.'

He stared at the glass in his hand as though dazed by what he had heard. Beads of sweat appeared on his forehead.

Geraldine leaned forward. She kept her eyes fixed on his face as she spoke.

'From what we've heard, you and Patrick Henshaw didn't exactly see eye to eye.'

'What the hell is that supposed to mean?'

'With Patrick out of the way, the restaurant belongs to you. You're free to do what you want with the place.'

She wondered if it was obvious she was fishing.

'Let me get this straight. Patrick's been murdered and you think *I'm* responsible?'

He set his whisky down and flung his hands in the air, stung into animation.

'That's complete bollocks. I'm the last person on earth who would want anything to happen to him. Apart from the fact that we were friends, we've got a great business here. Only an idiot would want that to change.'

Geraldine spoke quietly.

'You argued about your business plans, didn't you?'

He looked puzzled.

'I'm not sure what you're implying. Sure, we had different ideas. Business partners do. What's wrong with that? We weren't bloody identical twins.'

He stood up abruptly.

'Please tell me you're not going to try and pin his murder on me, because you'll only end up making yourself look like an idiot. I've got to say, it's the stupidest idea I've heard in a long time. Patrick was my partner. We've known each other for years. Why would I want him dead? If he really was murdered. What possible motive could I have for killing him?'

'Money is a powerful motive.'

'That's ridiculous.'

Corless looked uncomfortable. He drained his glass and resumed fidgeting with his box of cigars, but when he next spoke his voice was firm.

'Look, Inspector, you're barking up the wrong tree. Mireille's a great business, but our success is down to Patrick, so it makes no sense for me to want to get rid of him. Why would I?'

He sighed and rubbed his chin with the fingers of one hand.

'Mr Corless, you must be aware that Mireille now belongs to you, making you an extremely wealthy man. Patrick Henshaw was very generous towards you in his will.'

'It was a reciprocal agreement. We go back a long way, me and Pat. God knows how I'm going to manage this place without him. Believe me, no one is going to regret his passing more than me. Jesus, I depended on Pat to make this place work. Without him, I'm really in the shit.'

He sounded genuine, but Geraldine wasn't sure whether to believe him. With so much money at stake, anything was possible.

CHAPTER 15

Amy had wanted to speak to Guy as soon as the inspector left her house, but she had been nervous about contacting him. The police might be listening to her calls. By Wednesday morning she was desperate to speak to him. She dialled his number from a payphone in a pub, but he didn't answer. He must be at work. She would have to wait until the evening. Catching sight of herself in the mirror when she went to the bathroom, she was shocked by her face, white with red and swollen eyes. She took a deep breath. Whatever else happened, she couldn't let Guy see her looking so haggard. Usually she could get away with admitting to ten years younger than her forty years, but right now she looked closer to fifty. Imagining herself standing beside Guy gave her a tremor of panic.

Removing all traces of make-up she took a long shower, before lying down with cooling eye patches to reduce the swelling around her eyes. It was impossible to relax. Finally she got up, dressed, and reapplied her make-up carefully until she looked reasonably presentable. Then she went out to try the payphone again.

'I need to see you,' she blurted out as soon as he answered. 'Something's happened to Patrick.'

Her voice shook as she told him she thought she might be in trouble with the police. They had cunning techniques for putting pressure on vulnerable people. She was careful not to say too much in case anyone was listening.

Having lost her husband, Amy might be about to lose her freedom as well. Then everything would be over: the sex, the money, the whole future they had planned together, all snatched away. The phone trembled in her grasp. She tried to think, but her mind seized up. Patrick had always taken care of everything. He had taken care of her. Now she would have to look out for herself. Guy was too young and inexperienced to take charge of the situation.

'When can you come round?'

He sounded curiously keyed up. Amy barely paused before agreeing to go there right away. Far better confront him face to face with what she needed him to do.

'Amy, what have you done?' he asked as soon as his door closed behind her.

He moved aside to avoid her embrace and gazed at her in consternation.

'Done? What do you mean?'

She moved forward to kiss him, but he pushed

her away and repeated his question. He wanted to know exactly what had happened. Keeping her at arm's length, he studied her face carefully.

'Amy, you look terrible. What's wrong? Tell me what happened. What did he do to you, Amy? Why are you looking at me like that? Don't worry, whatever happened, whatever you've done, it's not your fault.'

Amy was watching his face closely as he spoke. When she answered her voice was terse.

'I haven't done anything, Guy.'

She was shocked. If Guy blamed her, what hope did she have of convincing the police she was innocent? She turned away.

'He's dead.'

Amy turned back to him in time to see Guy's eyes narrow, calculating.

'Patrick's dead,' she repeated solemnly, and was surprised to see him grinning.

'But that's great! I can't believe it! He's gone, really gone, out of our lives. I don't care what happened, all that matters now is that he's gone and we can be together all the time!'

Amy looked up at him, tears spilling from her eyes. Gently he reached forward to wipe a tear from her cheek with one finger.

'What is it, Amy?'

'Patrick was murdered. Guy, this is horrible.'

* * *

He put his arms around her, pulling her close.

'So what? What difference does that make to us? He's dead, isn't he, and that's all that matters. It's not like he didn't deserve it. Come on, Amy, don't cry. He's dead, and we can be together all the time. There's nothing to stop us now. That's what's important. And it's hardly a surprise that someone finished him off, is it? He was a vicious bastard. He got what was coming to him and that's the end of it.'

His smile faded as Amy pulled away in alarm.

'I mean, I'm sorry he's dead, of course,' he added quickly. 'And to die like that. I wouldn't wish it on anyone, but—' he lowered his voice, speaking very clearly, 'I don't blame his killer, and nor do you. Your husband got what was coming to him and good riddance.'

Amy took a step backwards, her eyes fixed on Guy's face.

'I haven't told you what happened yet,' she whispered. 'How do you know how he died?'

'You said he'd been murdered. That's all I need to know.'

'What if they find out?'

'What do you mean?'

Guy shrugged his shoulders.

'Don't even think about it. Think about me, about us!'

'It's not that easy. It's . . .'

Amy broke off, incoherent with sobs.

* * *

Guy put his arms around her again and led her gently into the kitchen where he put the kettle on and poured out two mugs of tea.

'Do you want sugar in it?' he asked, solicitously. 'It's good for shock.'

Amy grimaced and he grinned.

'I'll take that as a no, then.'

He put the tea on the table in front of her.

'Now, do you want to talk about it? Tell me what happened at the police station.'

He watched her lips pucker as she blew on her tea.

'If you'd rather not talk about it – or about his death – that's alright. Whatever you want. We can talk about what we're going to do, if you like. Because it will all be yours now, won't it? The house, the car – the dog!'

Finally he was rewarded with a tentative smile and he sat down, cupping his own hot mug in his hands.

'He can't take anything away from you now, and he won't ever hurt you again. You're free, Amy, a free woman.'

She smiled weakly.

'And a rich one,' he added in a quiet murmur, almost inaudible behind his tea.

He put his mug down and leaned forward.

'But I don't give a stuff about the money, Amy. All I care about is being with you. And whatever happened to him had nothing to do with either of us. It's just our good luck to be finally rid of him for good.'

'I know. It couldn't have been either of us,' she replied.

All at once her voice became firm.

'It couldn't have been us, because we were together when Patrick was killed. We were both here *all* Sunday night.'

'Until you left at—' he broke off, understanding.

Amy reached across the table and stroked his bottom lip with her finger.

'Enough talking. Whenever it was done, you were with me. All night.'

She stood up, walked round the table and bent down to kiss him. Guy surrendered to her embrace.

CHAPTER 16

As Geraldine was about to go out for lunch the next day she received a call from the forensic team. Several long brown hairs had been found on the passenger seat of Henshaw's car, along with smears of make-up. Geraldine frowned. Amy was blonde. The forensic evidence indicated that someone else had been sitting beside the driver on his last journey.

'So at some point a dark-haired woman was sitting in the passenger seat,' Geraldine said.

'Sitting or possibly lying back.'

'What makes you say that?' she asked, suddenly interested.

'The hairs were found on the seat, hairs and flecks of dandruff, but there were also specimens on the back of the head rest, as though the woman had been lying with her head pushed back. It's just a possibility. Make-up was found on the back of the seat as well, suggesting she was lying with her face turned sideways, pressing against the seat.'

'Why would anyone sit like that?'

'Search me. I'm just reporting on what we found in the vehicle.'

Geraldine thanked the forensic scientist and asked to be informed as soon as they had an identity from the DNA provided by the hairs.

Stella Hallett was a dumpy little woman in her thirties. With mousy hair that fell to her shoulders and a plump figure, she was an unlikely choice of mistress for the husband of glamorous Amy Henshaw – which had been Geraldine's first suspicion on hearing the terms of the will. Looking at her, Geraldine thought Stella was more likely to be a relative; Henshaw's younger sister or a daughter, perhaps. Yet a woman with brown hair had been lying on the passenger seat of Henshaw's car not long before he died, and Stella's hair was brown.

Stella was the first person to express any grief on hearing about Henshaw's death. Visibly shocked, her face lost its colour and she clutched at the door frame as though in need of support.

'Patrick's dead?' she repeated several times.

Geraldine waited for her to absorb the news that Henshaw had been murdered.

'I'm afraid so. I'm here to ask you a few questions, Stella. Shall we go inside and sit down?'

'Yes, please come in. But how did you find me?'

Geraldine didn't answer. She didn't yet know if Stella had known about Henshaw's will. If she had, that might provide a motive for wanting him dead.

When they were settled in Stella's tidy but threadbare living room, she dissolved in tears again, hiccupping and snuffling into a large tissue.

'I'm so sorry,' she stuttered, 'it's just such a shock. I had no idea anything had happened to him. I haven't seen him for five years.'

Geraldine sat back in her chair and waited for the other woman to regain her composure. She couldn't help thinking Stella's grief was a disproportionate reaction from someone who hadn't seen the dead man for so long. And Stella had dark hair.

In a calf length brown skirt, cream shirt and beige jumper, Stella looked dull, although her clothes were clean and neat. Her skirt wasn't creased and her shirt must have been starched, the points of the collar were so perfectly symmetrical. Her flat was equally spick and span, with shelves gleaming as though they had just been polished. Gazing around, Geraldine recognised a younger Patrick Henshaw in a framed photograph on a shelf. Turning her head, she saw another similar framed photograph hanging on the wall. It took her a few seconds to realise the slim woman smiling at his side in both pictures was Stella. It seemed strange that she would have photographs of Patrick displayed in her living room, if she and Patrick were no longer seeing one another.

'Yes, that's me,' Stella admitted with a shy grin, following the direction of Geraldine's gaze. 'I've let myself go a bit since that was taken!'

Her eyes watered again.

'Tell me about your relationship with Patrick,' Geraldine said gently.

'Like I said, I haven't seen him for five years. We were together for two years and of course I knew all along he was married. I knew he'd never leave her for me, really, although I still hoped. You do, don't you? When you love someone. I never stopped hoping until – until now—'

She broke off, her voice wavering, her face creased in an effort to control her sobbing.

'There's never been anyone else—'

Stella was convincing, but Geraldine had to question whether there was something strange about her extreme attachment to Henshaw. If they had been apart for so long, it seemed unlikely he would still be the man in her life, the one whose photographs she wanted to see every day in her living room. On the other hand, why would she lie about it, unless she wanted to distance herself from his death? That would suggest she had been involved in his murder.

'How did you meet?' Geraldine asked.

'We met about eight years ago. I was his personal

assistant then. That's how we met, at work. He was married so I never wanted anything to happen between us, but somehow—'

She shrugged.

'But I'm not sorry,' she added, her voice rising with a flash of spirit. 'I knew he was married when I met him, but once we started seeing each other I didn't care about that any more. And I wanted him to leave her, I actually prayed their marriage would fall apart. Was that so terrible? He wasn't happy with her and I knew I could make him happy. I wanted to be the other woman, the marriage wrecker – only it never happened. She was so glamorous and I'm so ordinary. But like I said, you always hope, don't you? And then—'

She fell silent, lost in her memories. Geraldine wondered if sexual jealousy had prompted the particularly nasty attack on Henshaw.

'What happened?' Geraldine prompted her.

Stella heaved a shuddering sigh, dropped her head in her hands and began to rock in her chair, wailing.

'Stella, perhaps you'd like me to come back later—'

The weeping woman shook her head and raised her glistening face, wiping her cheeks with the back of her hand. Then she smiled apologetically and assured Geraldine she was fine.

'I'm so sorry,' she hiccupped. 'I think perhaps – that is, can I offer you a cup of tea? Or something?'

Geraldine shook her head.

'But please go ahead if you'd like one.'

'Yes, I think it might help. It's been a bit of a shock.'

Her eyes began to water again. Muttering that she would only be a moment she hurried off leaving Geraldine alone in the living room.

Geraldine gazed around the room registering the worn carpet, faded curtains frayed at the hem and broken springs in the chair beneath her, and wondered if Stella had known the terms of Patrick Henshaw's will. It looked as though she could do with the money.

'Here, I thought you might like to look at this,' Stella said. She handed a photograph album to Geraldine who flicked through it with a show of interest: Stella and Patrick by the sea, the pair of them sitting by the river, Stella on a park bench, Patrick on the same bench. Geraldine closed the album and turned to Stella.

'Tell me what happened,' she repeated.

Stella stared straight ahead while tears rolled unheeded down her round cheeks. She spoke in a flat voice, barely louder than a whisper.

'I think he was only with me because he wanted a child. He didn't want me, not for myself. We'd been seeing each other for just over a year when I fell pregnant. He seemed so happy about it. He said he'd leave her and marry me. And I believed him. I think he really meant it. He made me give up work, said I had to look after myself, he'd take care of everything. But then I lost the baby and that was the end of everything. Nothing was the same after that. He became distant, cold, then one day he didn't come round. He didn't say anything but I knew he wouldn't get in touch again. He stopped paying my bills and I had to move out of the flat I was renting and I've been here ever since. I never saw him again. And now I never will.'

Stella's bottom lip wobbled and Geraldine spoke briskly before she broke down again.

'We need to eliminate you from our enquiries, Stella.'

'Eliminate me?'

'Where were you last Sunday evening?'

'I don't know. Sunday evening? Was that when it – when he – when it happened?'

Geraldine inclined her head without speaking.

'I didn't go anywhere on Sunday. I was here. I don't go out much.'

Stella had no witnesses who could vouch for her whereabouts on the evening Henshaw had been killed.

Stella appeared surprised when Geraldine asked her to go to the police station so a sample of her DNA could be taken.

'What do you want that for?'

'So we can eliminate you from the enquiry.'

'But—'

'It will be better for you if you come willingly.'

'Yes, alright.'

'You do know you're mentioned in his will?' Geraldine asked cautiously.

Stella raised bloodshot eyes to stare at her.

'Am I? So that means he did remember me – still thought about me. Do you think he still cared about me, deep down?'

Geraldine could only speculate about whether Henshaw had been motivated by affection or guilt when he chose to leave his money to Stella. She glanced around the spotless room, wondering if Stella was lying when she had claimed to know nothing about the will. It was possible her tears were phony; and even if her emotion was genuine, there was still no way of knowing if her tears were prompted by grief or remorse.

CHAPTER 17

After reading through all the reports, Geraldine tried to put the investigation out of her mind when she went to bed. There was nothing more she could do now. In the morning she would ask around and see what else she could find out. But she slept uneasily, her dreams haunted by images of Patrick Henshaw's mutilated corpse. After a hurried breakfast on Thursday morning, she drove straight to Hampstead hoping to catch Amy early. Arriving at eight thirty she opened the gate in time to see a small dark-haired woman approach the front door. Geraldine watched from the gate as the woman rang the bell and waited, oblivious of Geraldine standing a few yards behind her. No one came to the door. The woman fidgeted impatiently, looked at her watch and rang the bell again, several times. At last she turned away and as she walked back down the path caught sight of Geraldine hovering on the pavement.

Geraldine stepped forward, blocking the woman's exit.

'I'm looking for Mrs Amy Henshaw.'

'Mrs Henshaw lives here, but she's not in. She knew I was coming. I'm here every Monday and Thursday to clean for her. She always lets me know when she's not going to be here. Do you think she's forgotten?'

The little woman's face twisted in irritation.

'Well, she'll have to pay me. It's only fair. I've come all this way for nothing. So how do you know her?' she added, suddenly suspicious.

Geraldine introduced herself without explaining the reason for her visit. She learned the woman's name was Christina.

'You know the household. I'd like to ask you a few questions about Mrs Henshaw.'

Christina's black eyes narrowed in alarm.

'Where's Mrs Henshaw? What's happened to her?'

'Calm down, please. Nothing's happened to Mrs Henshaw, but I'd like to ask you a few questions.'

At first the cleaner was reluctant to divulge any information. She insisted she had to get home, but wavered when Geraldine offered to reimburse her bus fare.

'Mrs Henshaw gives me breakfast,' she said promptly.

A veiled threat, added to the offer of breakfast and her bus fare, clinched it; a small price to pay for what might prove key information about the Henshaws.

* * *

Seated in a dingy café Geraldine sipped lukewarm milky coffee, while Christina tucked into greasy egg, bacon and toast. A plate of food and a mug of tea on the table in front of her loosened her tongue, as Geraldine had hoped; Christina became positively garrulous. Chomping on her breakfast, she explained she had been visiting the house twice a week for about six years. Only when Geraldine enquired whether the Henshaws were happy together did Christina clam up.

'That's not my place to say.'

'Christina, we're investigating the circumstances of Mr Henshaw's death. I'm afraid you have no choice but to answer my questions, unless you want to find yourself facing prosecution for obstruction.'

Christina's mouth fell open in surprise and the knife and fork she was clutching dropped onto her plate with a loud clatter. Geraldine turned away from the disagreeable sight of half masticated egg and bacon and took a gulp of coffee before resuming.

'Now, I'll ask you again. In your opinion, was the marriage a happy one?'

Carefully Christina wiped a piece of toast round her plate mopping up egg yolk, her eyes fixed on her breakfast. At last she raised her head, apparently making up her mind.

'I don't want to speak ill of the dead, but he was

a foul-tempered man. If you ask me, poor Mrs Henshaw couldn't possibly have been happy with a man like that. No one could. He was a lot older than her and I don't think he paid her much attention. Money maybe, but that's about all he gave her. If you ask me,' she leaned forward in her chair, 'that's why she married him in the first place. For his money.'

'Was he seeing other women?'

'Mr Henshaw?'

Christina sat back in surprise.

'Now how would I know a thing like that?'

A slight belligerence in the way Christina spoke drew Geraldine's attention.

'What about Mrs Henshaw – was she seeing anyone else?'

Geraldine was surprised to see Christina blush.

'Oh well, I suppose you're going to find out anyway so there's no harm in spilling the beans. Yes, she was. She had another man, and I can't say I blame her.'

Geraldine sat, pen poised, but Christina merely sipped her tea without saying any more.

'Who was he?' Geraldine prompted her at last.

'Who? Her fancy man? I don't know. I don't know anything about him. I never saw him but he was on the phone to her all the time.'

'Are you sure it wasn't her husband she was talking to?'

'Oh yes. I used to overhear her sometimes though I'd blush to repeat some of what she said. And it wasn't her husband she was talking to, I can tell you that for a fact.'

'How can you be so sure?' Geraldine pressed her.

'Well, for a start, I heard her promise to leave her husband, only she said it was difficult, and she asked for more time. Then she said how much she loved him and wanted to be with him, and how she hated having to keep the affair a secret, and I can't remember what else besides, but more on the same lines. I don't know who she was talking to, but it wasn't her husband.'

Geraldine looked up from her note pad.

'Are you sure you can't tell me anything about him? Did you ever hear his voice?'

'Yes. I answered the phone to him several times. *Just tell her it's me,* he said. It wasn't Mr Henshaw's voice.'

'Are you sure?'

'Sure as I'm sitting here.'

'What did he sound like?'

Christina shrugged.

'Like a man, you know. He had a man's voice. He sounded young and—'

She paused, thinking.

'Eager. Like he was impatient to speak to her, like he was always in a hurry.'

* * *

'So have you found out anything from Amy Henshaw?' Sam asked Geraldine when she returned to the station.

'I think so. Not about Henshaw himself, but – well, you met his wife.'

'Yes, and—?'

'It seems she was having an affair with a young man.'

'I said it was a crime of passion!'

Geraldine couldn't help laughing at the triumph in Sam's voice.

'What did she say exactly?'

Geraldine shook her head.

'I didn't see Amy Henshaw, but I spoke to her cleaner who's been going to the house twice a week for the last six years. She was very forthcoming, and I can't see any reason to doubt what she told me. So we need to find Amy and find out who this other man is. You met Amy. What do you think? Could she have killed him herself?'

Sam considered, her expression serious.

'It was certainly a vicious attack, with marked sexual aggression, which means the killer was probably a man.'

'Probably,' Geraldine sounded a note of caution. 'Let's not jump to conclusions. Remember—'

'I know, I know. I'm only saying. Alright, so we think the killer was probably a man. They usually are. I did think when we saw the body that the injuries might have been inflicted by a jealous husband, if Henshaw had been messing around. But maybe it was Amy's lover who was jealous. This young man she was having an affair with, whoever he is.'

Geraldine nodded.

'Yes, this opens up new possibilities.'

'What you mean is, you have to concede I was right all along,' Sam grinned.

'Right? About what, exactly?'

'That this was a crime of passion, carried out by a man in a fit of jealousy.'

'It's one possibility. But you're forgetting the DNA found on Henshaw's body. It was female.'

'Does that mean Amy was there when he was killed? The young lover came in and found them at it and in a jealous rage pounced on his hated rival! Or perhaps,' Sam went on in a more serious tone, 'Amy and her lover were in it together.'

Despite her confusion, Geraldine couldn't help laughing at the gusto with which Sam outlined her theories. There was something infectious about the sergeant's enthusiasm which made her company invigorating.

CHAPTER 18

In a dark suit and clean shirt, George fumbled with the knot in his tie.

'Here, let me,' Desiree said as she climbed out of bed.

He grinned sheepishly as she fiddled at his throat, not wanting to be distracted by her naked body, as though focusing on the approaching meeting could make a difference to the will. There was no reason for him to feel nervous. He and Patrick had drawn up an agreement that if one of them died, Mireille would become the sole property of the remaining partner. There was no way the agreement could be altered without their joint signatures. It was a good arrangement for whichever partner outlived the other. He and Patrick used to joke about doing away with each other, agreeing that poison would be the most appropriate method, with a restaurant at stake.

Now Patrick was dead, George could do anything he wanted with the restaurant. He was free to sell it if someone offered the right price. He couldn't help grinning. Mireille was a substantial windfall and it had come in the nick of time, because George's lucky streak had stopped abruptly about a year ago, and since then his debts had been spiralling out of control. Pipped at the post with every decent sized bet he placed on the horses, winning and losing in equal measure at the casinos, he had been unable to take care of his financial difficulties. Whichever way he turned, the debts mounted. It was as though he'd been cursed. All he had needed was one lucky break as he kept losing and losing until he dreaded opening the post, and daily expected bailiffs to come knocking at his door. In one stroke all that had changed with his business partner's death.

'You take care now,' Desiree fussed. 'Call me as soon as it's over. I'll be waiting.'

George wasn't sure if she appreciated the enormity of this meeting which was going to solve all his problems. Even though he knew what Patrick's will contained, he wouldn't be able to relax until he heard it from the lawyer with his own ears. Patrick was a tricky bastard. George wouldn't have put it past him to have pulled some devious stunt at the last minute, swindling his business partner of his share.

It was impossible to park at the offices of Petrie and Waterman and, in any case, he could afford to take a taxi now. He knew to a penny how much the restaurant was turning over and his share of the profits had doubled overnight. Plus there was always the chance his partner had left him an additional nest egg. He had no idea how much money he had accumulated. Patrick had always been secretive about his personal finances. Lately he had become quite touchy whenever the subject came up.

'We're business partners with the restaurant and that's as far as it goes. My personal finances are none of your fucking business,' he had told George, leading him to surmise that Patrick had a stash of winnings that he was keeping quiet about.

The taxi dropped him outside Petrie and Waterman with five minutes to spare. Nevertheless, he was the last to arrive. There was only one chair left unoccupied in the solicitor's office. He nodded a greeting at the grey-haired man sitting behind the desk who half rose to his feet, motioning him to a chair.

'George,' Jonathon greeted him in a familiar drawling voice. 'It's good to see you again, but I'm sorry to be meeting under such circumstances. My condolences.'

George glanced at the two people who were already seated, facing Jonathon's desk. Amy looked a class act in a black skirt that skimmed the top of her knees, and a tailored jacket. The outfit was appropriate for a grieving widow while showing off her neat figure, slim legs and flat stomach. She looked about twenty, although she had been married for nearly that long. No woman her age had the right to look that good. He smiled at her and her lips twitched in response. He glanced down at his own sagging gut, resting on his broad thighs, then back at Amy who was gazing demurely at the solicitor.

His eyes slid past her to a woman in a green coat. She didn't look round when he entered the room but sat without moving, staring straight ahead, giving no sign that she was aware of his furtive scrutiny. If she had chosen her clothes carefully, taken the trouble to have her hair styled, and worn make up, she wouldn't have been unattractive. At first glance George had thought the woman was about fifty but a closer look revealed her to be closer to thirty. It was a shame to see a woman looking so unkempt when she could have made so much more of herself with very little effort. George almost felt sorry for her, but his overriding feeling was aggravation that she might be a contender for a share of Patrick's fortune.

Amy took a small cotton handkerchief from her bag and dabbed gently at her eyes, taking care not to smudge her make up.

'I want to know when I can bury my husband,' she said softly, and dropped her gaze mournfully, the picture of a grieving widow.

'I'm afraid that's out of our hands,' the lawyer told her. 'You just have to be patient.'

At his side George heard her shift in her chair as Jonathon picked up a document.

'We're here to read Patrick Henshaw's will.'

He looked at each of them solemnly in turn, then putting on glasses with narrow lenses, began reading in a dull monotone, his diction clear and impersonal. George tried not to switch off at the familiar opening formula. His ears pricked up at the mention of an amount in excess of nine hundred thousand quid. The name Stella Hallett seemed to ring a bell but George couldn't remember who she was. He didn't have the faintest idea why Patrick would be leaving her such a lot of money.

'Who's Stella Hallett?'

Amy's angry demand interrupted the flow of Jonathon's voice and he looked up at her over his glasses. Before he could answer the woman in the green coat spoke.

'I am.'

Amy and George turned to her in surprise.

'You? You're Stella Hallett?'

'Yes, I'm Stella Hallett.'

Unexpectedly, she began to cry.

'I don't understand.'

Amy turned to George, her bottom lip pushed out in a pout that was somehow ridiculous in a woman her age.

'Who is this woman? I mean, why did Patrick leave her nine hundred thousand pounds? Who is she?'

Jonathon turned to Stella for an answer but she was crying so hard she couldn't speak. He turned back to Amy.

'Stella Hallett is named in Patrick's will. That's all that concerns us here,' he informed her in his dry, clinical voice.

CHAPTER 19

George thanked Jonathon Waterman in his gruff voice and left, followed by Stella Hallett, snuffling into a tissue. She turned in the doorway as if she wanted to thank the solicitor, but catching Amy's eyes on her, she waved her damp tissue and shuffled quickly out. Amy watched them leave. They made a right pair, both overweight and unattractive, with George's balding head and beer gut, and the woman's thinning hair and plain face. As soon as the door closed behind Stella Hallett's hunched figure Amy sat back down and looked anxiously at the solicitor who gazed solemnly at her over the top of his glasses. She cleared her throat, eager to question him further about her own inheritance.

She had always known about the agreement regarding Mireille when either of its owners died. Patrick had gone first and his toad-like business partner had got the lot. That was bad luck. If George had died first the whole lot would have belonged to Patrick, and she would have inherited it when Patrick died. According to Patrick, it had been a gamble with more than decent odds.

'He's overweight, and he smokes like a chimney.'

Other than the restaurant, she had expected Patrick to leave everything to her. The odd woman in her hideous green coat had taken her completely by surprise, but at least everything else was hers, including the house. She just wanted to know how much it was all worth. How much she was worth.

'I'm ready, so do your worst,' she concluded, suppressing a smile.

That Patrick had left almost a million to another woman was an outrage she would deal with later. For now she just wanted to be assured of her share of the fortune. She might even pay the smarmy solicitor to go after Stella. Clearly the other woman must have exerted some influence on Patrick. She had no such hold over Amy.

'The house is yours.'

Jonathon hesitated, glancing down at the documents on the desk.

'How much is it worth? Three million?'

Jonathon didn't answer.

'Don't worry, I'll get onto the estate agents tomorrow, have it valued. I might even sell—'

Registering his expression she broke off and dabbed delicately at her eyes again.

* * *

'I'm afraid you're not as well off as it might at first appear,' he said gravely. 'I'm not sure if you're aware that Patrick remortgaged the house?'

'Remortgaged the house? What do you mean?'

She stared at him in bewilderment.

'The truth of the matter is that the house is currently worthless to you.'

'Worthless? What do you mean?'

'The debts owing on the property are quite possibly greater than its value.'

For a moment she stared at him, too shocked to speak.

'I don't understand,' she said at last. 'This is a mistake, it has to be a mistake. The house is mine.'

The solicitor shrugged and raised his eyebrows.

'I'm afraid it's worth nothing to you, Amy.'

'But – but how can the house be worthless?' she stuttered. 'The house over the road sold for nearly three million last year.'

'It's worse than worthless, I'm afraid.'

He spoke very slowly.

'Patrick remortgaged the house which means he's left you with a large mortgage and very little besides. There's the house contents of course, but they won't go anywhere towards paying off what you owe on the property.'

He paused.

'The debt is now yours, as the house is in your name.'

* * *

'The debt?' she echoed, barely audible.

'The mortgage.'

'How – how much?'

Amy started when he gave her the figure. For a moment she felt stunned. She struggled to grasp where everything had gone so horribly wrong. When she had married Patrick, he had been a wealthy man, a self-made millionaire many times over, someone she could respect and admire. She had thought she loved him. She had always understood she was no more than a trophy wife, a beautiful young companion for him to hang on his arm and display, with an obligation to keep herself looking good. She had spent a fortune on make-up and hair products, workouts and yoga. It beat going out to work, and when she wasn't at the salon or the health club, her time was her own, which was just as well once she met Guy.

And now, after enduring twenty years of loveless marriage, contrary to all her expectations she found herself worse than penniless: she was heavily in debt. She couldn't understand why Patrick had done this to her. She hadn't been such a terrible wife. She had known about the restaurant, and it was certainly unfortunate the way things had turned out; it was a gamble that hadn't paid off. But she had no idea why Patrick had left so much money to an ugly stranger called Stella.

* * *

'I'm going to contest this,' she protested. 'I'm not going to let that woman take my money.'

'I'm afraid there's nothing you can do about it. I appreciate you may not be happy with the terms of your husband's will, but it's a legal document and there are no grounds for challenging it. I'm sorry.'

'But it's not fair! There must be something you can do.'

Amy didn't want to sound petulant, but she had every right to feel outraged, having been cheated of money that belonged to her. Cheated by a complete stranger.

'It must be a mistake. Who is this woman anyway? I've never seen her before. I'm his wife. She's nobody, nothing to us. I don't even know who she is.'

The lawyer sat drumming his long fingers on the desk.

Amy had promised to phone Guy as soon as she left the lawyer's office. There was no reason why he shouldn't come round to her house now. In preparation for a private celebration, she had left a bottle of champagne in the fridge before leaving home that morning. She knew Guy preferred lager, but she'd had plans to improve his tastes. Now she couldn't even afford to keep him in beer. After hearing Patrick's will, she barely managed to reach home before she surrendered to a paroxysm of weeping.

* * *

Startled by the phone she sat up, wiping her eyes and pulling her fingers through her hair. Guy's cheerful voice grated on her nerves. His tone altered when he heard she couldn't see him.

'What's up?' he demanded. 'You sound terrible.'

There was a pause.

'Amy, have you been crying?

She stifled a sob.

'That's it,'he said, 'I'm coming round.'

Amy hung up and ran to the bathroom to press a cold flannel on her swollen eyes and repair her face as best she could with a film of make up. Not only was she destitute, she looked awful.

As she worked on her face she fretted about how Guy would react to the news that she was broke. It was going to take them years to pay off her debts. But as soon as she opened the door and he swept her up in his strong arms she knew that she couldn't tell him the truth just yet. He had to go on thinking she was wealthy; she couldn't bear the thought of his leaving her.

'You poor thing,' he greeted her, stroking her cheek. 'You've had a bad time of it, haven't you? But it's over now. Thanks to you he's never going to bother us again. First thing we'll do,' he went on before she had a chance to respond, 'we'll take a holiday. How do you fancy going on a Mediterranean cruise? Do you fancy that? Or what do you think about the Seychelles? It's supposed to be fantastic. A mate of mine went there for his honeymoon. It cost him an arm and a leg but what the heck? We've got money to burn!'

He threw his head back, laughing. Amy watched his Adam's apple move up and down in his sturdy neck and knew she couldn't risk losing him. Having longed to be free of her husband, it was ironic that the fulfilment of her wish had thrown her into poverty that might drive Guy away. She felt a surge of rage against Patrick. Even after his death he was ruining her life.

'Let's not rush into anything,' she whispered. 'I've just lost my husband.'

She raised her head and smiled to hide her desperation.

CHAPTER 20

In the light of the DNA detected on Henshaw's body, there was now some urgency about questioning his widow further so Geraldine returned to the large house in Hampstead later that afternoon. This time Amy was at home. The polished white door opened at once, as though she had been expecting a caller, an impression reinforced by her evident disappointment on seeing Geraldine.

'Good afternoon, Mrs Henshaw. I'd like to ask you a few more questions and then we'd like to take a routine DNA sample.'

When Amy expressed surprise, Geraldine explained that traces of a woman's DNA had been found on her husband's body.

'A woman's DNA?'

She sounded puzzled.

'Yes. I appreciate this must be very difficult for you, but we do need to ascertain whether the DNA belonged to you or another woman was involved.'

'Another woman?' Amy echoed. Her expression hardened. 'It was Stella Hallett, wasn't it? I hope you lock the bloody cow up and throw away the key.'

'What makes you think she's responsible?'

'Isn't it obvious? With nearly a million pounds to gain, anyone would—' She broke off, realising what she was saying. 'Come on then, let's get this over with. Do whatever you have to do.'

She turned and led the way to the back of the house.

Geraldine glanced admiringly around a spacious kitchen, elegantly appointed. A huge square picture window overlooked a series of narrow terraced gardens which led down to a row of trees.

'What a lovely view.'

'Patrick did the garden,' Amy said curtly as she perched on a padded kitchen chair holding herself stiffly upright.

'Where were you on Sunday night?'

'Here.'

A dark red flush rose from Amy's throat to her cheeks.

'Were you here all evening?'

'Yes . . . er . . .'

Amy fell silent.

'Mrs Henshaw?'

'Well, I might've gone out briefly – to post a letter—'

Amy gazed helplessly around the immaculate kitchen. Once again, Geraldine was sure the widow was lying. She gave her an encouraging smile.

'That's fine. The post mark will confirm what you've told me. Which letter box did you use, and who was the letter addressed to?'

'No – I mean, I could be wrong. I'm so confused right now. It might not have been Sunday. I can't remember. I really can't remember.'

Geraldine read aloud from the notes she had taken down, careful not to betray any hint of the scepticism she was feeling.

'So you were here at home on Sunday evening. You might have gone out to post a letter, but if you did you returned home straight away and didn't go out again, is that right?'

Amy nodded.

'Is there anyone who can confirm you were here all night?'

'No. I told you, Patrick didn't come home. I was here on my own.'

Her worried expression cleared.

'I tell you what, my cleaning lady came round first thing Monday morning. She'll tell you I was here. Ask Christina.'

Geraldine didn't reveal that she had already spoken to the cleaning lady.

'Tell me about your affair,' Geraldine hazarded, impatient to move things on.

'Affair?'

Amy arched her eyebrows with an expression of surprise that was also wary.

'What affair?'

'We know you're having an affair with a young man,' Geraldine said softly. 'It's no use pretending otherwise. And it's not clever to lie about it, not when we're investigating a murder. It's better not to keep secrets at a time like this.'

Amy rose to her feet, agitated. Her shoulders slumped forward but her eyes were defiant.

'I've no idea what you're talking about. I don't know what you're implying, but it seems you've been listening to some silly gossip. Who have you been speaking to? Where did you get hold of this ridiculous idea?' She paused, gulping to catch her breath. 'I loved my husband. Patrick was everything to me.'

There was no mistaking the genuine emotion in Amy's voice. At the same time, there was no way of knowing whether it was driven by grief for her husband or fear of discovery that she had been implicated in his death.

In the face of Amy's consternation, Geraldine wondered whether Christina had been telling the truth. It was feasible her account had been mistaken, or malicious.

'Mrs Henshaw, please sit down. Good. Now, you were having an affair, that much we know.'

She hoped it wasn't a false accusation.

'It would be far better for you if you simply tell me what I need to know. Adultery isn't a crime.

I really don't understand why you'd want to conceal the truth, now there's no longer any risk of your husband finding out. If you persist in lying, I'll have to conclude that you have something else to hide.'

Amy closed her eyes while tears gathered and spilled down her cheeks. Geraldine waited.

At last Amy gave a deep shuddering sigh and opened her eyes.

'Yes.'

Her voice was hardly above a whisper.

'I was seeing someone. But it's over. I haven't seen him for – six months.'

Hesitation gave her away, indicating the affair was still going on.

'Who is he?'

Amy shook her head.

'It's over,' she insisted. 'I don't think it's relevant who he is.'

'I'll decide what may or may not be relevant, Mrs Henshaw. Why did you lie about it?'

Amy began to cry.

'It's over,' she insisted. 'It's over.'

Geraldine leaned forward.

'We know that's not true,' she fibbed.

She couldn't be sure the affair hadn't finished – but when Amy's eyes widened, Geraldine knew her accusation was accurate. Abruptly, Amy dropped her head in her hands and broke down in tears. After that, it didn't take Geraldine long to learn the identity of Amy's lover.

'He's got nothing to do with all this,' Amy insisted tearfully. 'Please – please—'

She broke off, weeping noisily.

Now that she had discovered what she needed to know, Geraldine stood up. She felt sorry for the woman's distress, but her sympathy was tempered by the suspicion that Amy might be responsible for the cold blooded murder of her husband. It was a horrible thought, but there was no time to dwell on it. She informed Amy that someone would be round shortly to take a DNA sample in order to eliminate her from the enquiry, and left.

It was hard to focus on anything else while they waited for the results of the DNA test, especially with Sam so hopeful that Amy was at least implicated in the murder.

'I'm guessing it was the two of them in it together, her and the boyfriend,' she told Geraldine. 'I can't wait for the results of the DNA test. Amy's already tried to pull the wool over our eyes about her affair. Why would she lie about it now her husband's dead, unless she's got something else to hide? If she's prepared to lie about that, for sure she'd lie about killing her husband.'

Thinking it all over when she got home, Geraldine thought she could understand why a forty-year-old woman might want to conceal her relationship with a twenty-three-year-old man, even if her husband hadn't just been brutally murdered in what appeared to be a very personal attack. There were all sorts of reasons why she might want to keep her two lives separate. For a start, the young man might not know how old his mistress was. Lost in speculation, Geraldine was startled by her phone and nearly dropped it as she lunged for it on the side table. She was neither surprised nor particularly pleased to hear her sister's voice.

'Geraldine, how are you?' Celia asked earnestly, as though Geraldine was suffering from some sort of terminal cancer. 'We haven't heard from you for ages.'

Geraldine assured her she was fine and asked after Celia's husband and daughter. That was a mistake. Celia could talk about her daughter for hours. She listened politely for as long as she could contain her impatience before she interrupted, insisting she had to go. Promising to call back when she had more time, she rang off.

CHAPTER 21

Guy was traced to a company that installed double glazing and bespoke conservatories. The next morning, Geraldine and Sam went to question Amy's young lover.

'Guy Barrett?' the woman on reception repeated. She checked a ledger and nodded uncertainly.

'Yes, he's out on a job right now, but I'm not sure I can give you the customer's address – I mean, I don't think Mr Reynolds would like it if you interrupted the work, but I should have Guy's address here somewhere. I'll have to fish around for it. The system's down, I'm afraid.'

With a sigh she began flicking through a file.

At five o'clock they arrived outside Guy's flat just off the main Holloway Road. He didn't answer the door, so they returned to the car to wait for him to come home. The mild September was changing with a hint of cold weather to come and a light steady drizzle began to fall as Geraldine settled further down in her seat. Just before half past six a young man entered the building. They waited a few moments before hurrying across the glistening road.

Tall and sturdily built, in his early twenties, Guy had a broad high forehead, dark curly hair and boyish features. He folded his bulging arms and leaned against the door frame, staring from Geraldine to Sam and back again, chewing gum and glaring like a sullen adolescent. When Geraldine introduced herself he straightened up, arms dangling, eyes downcast.

'May we come in, Mr Barrett?'

He gave an awkward shrug without meeting her eyes.

'Or we can talk at the police station.'

With a grunt the young man led them through an untidy kitchenette. Several empty beer bottles stood on a narrow work surface, a crusty saucepan rested on the hob beside a greasy frying pan, and a pile of plates was stacked, unwashed, beside a sink full of cutlery. One soiled tea towel was scrunched up beside the sink, another lay discarded on the floor. They passed into a cramped living room furnished with a dark red carpet, chairs too large for the space, and curtains an inch too short for the window. An unsightly crack stretched diagonally across one wall from floor to ceiling.

Guy remained standing, stammering awkwardly as he answered Geraldine's questions. To begin with, he denied knowing the widow, but his lies were clumsy and he soon abandoned the pretence.

'Oh Mrs Henshaw,' he mumbled, frowning as though he had just recognised the name, and blushing. 'Yes, I know her. That is, we've met. I was on a job at her house in Hampstead last year. That's where I met Mrs Henshaw. And Mr Henshaw. I met them both.'

He glanced furtively at Geraldine under long thick lashes, before his eyes flicked away again.

'Was that when your affair began? Last year?'

'Affair?'

He turned his head and spat his gum into an open bin where it stuck, glistening, on top of an empty cigarette packet.

'What affair's that then?'

Geraldine almost felt sorry for the gauche young man. He didn't strike her as particularly intelligent.

'We know about your relationship with Mrs Henshaw so it's pointless lying about it,' Sam said firmly. 'You're not protecting her. It was Mrs Henshaw who gave us your name and told us about the affair.'

Barrett drew his broad shoulders back and raised his head, his face creased in a belligerent frown. He stared at Sam. He wasn't much younger than her but he sounded like a stroppy teenager talking to his mother.

'So? What of it? It's not a crime to be seeing a

woman, is it? And I don't see that it's any of your business either.'

'No. But it is a crime to kill someone.'

'Kill someone? What are you talking about? I thought you were talking about me and Amy. Who said anything about killing anyone?'

He shifted his weight awkwardly from one leg to the other and leaned back against the door frame again in a crude attempt to appear nonchalant. Geraldine studied his face closely as she told him that Mr Henshaw had been murdered. He scowled but didn't say anything straight away. At last he raised his eyebrows in a studied expression of astonishment. Amy had presumably already told him about her husband's death but Geraldine wondered if he had known before that. If he had been the first person to know.

'Poor Amy. This is terrible.'

He gave an exaggerated sigh.

He was such a poor liar that Geraldine challenged the young man outright about his relationship with Patrick Henshaw and he glared at her suspiciously.

'What relationship? What are you talking about? I only met him once, when we were doing his conservatory.'

'When did you last see Patrick Henshaw?'

'I told you, last year, when we had a job on there.'

Geraldine nodded.

'Fine. Now we'd like you to come along to the police station to make a statement—'

'What for? What sort of statement?'

He narrowed his eyes and took a step backwards.

'You think I did it, don't you? I'm sleeping with his wife so it had to be me that killed him. Is that it? That's the stupidest thing I ever heard so you can get lost with your stupid stereotypes. You haven't got a shred of evidence.'

He took a step backwards.

'Are you refusing to come to the station?'

'What if I am?'

'I suggest you come voluntarily, so we can eliminate you from our enquiries.'

'Do I have any choice?'

'Not if you're going to be sensible. Now come along.'

Somehow Geraldine found herself treating Guy as though he was a child. Despite his defiance, he seemed very biddable. Now that Geraldine had met him, she had to admit that Sam's theory seemed quite plausible. Amy might well have seduced her young lover into disposing of her husband.

Back at the station Sam was exuberant.

'He was screwing Henshaw's wife, for goodness

sake. And she's going to inherit a packet, I expect. That house alone must be worth millions.'

Geraldine nodded. Despite Guy's relationship with Amy, they had a lot of work to do if they were going to achieve a conviction. And she wasn't convinced that Guy had murdered Patrick.

'I'm sure he would've wanted Henshaw dead. He had powerful motives. And I can believe he was physically capable of overpowering a man in his sixties. But—'

'But?' Sam prompted her.

'We don't know he's guilty.'

'What makes you think he isn't?'

Geraldine shrugged.

'For a start, he's a hopeless liar.'

'He had a motive.'

Geraldine pointed out that Henshaw's business partner also had a pressing reason for wanting him out of the way, and asked Sam to take a careful look into George Corless's finances.

'Do you really think Henshaw's killer was motivated by money?'

'It's possible. We know George had money troubles and whatever his situation, that restaurant is a gold mine. This could've been, as you put it, a crime of passion, but greed could also be a motive with so much money at stake.'

'Yes, anything's possible. But is it likely? What

about the nature of his injuries? What's that all about if he was killed for his money?'

'Then the quicker we can eliminate George Corless from our enquiries the better. Now, enough speculation for one day. Let's get to work.'

CHAPTER 22

Wound up by uncertainty over the case, Geraldine wanted to take some time to cool off and refocus. She found Sam in the canteen where they sat in companionable silence for a while.

'Come on then, let's get back to work,' Geraldine said when she had finished her coffee.

'Time for another piece of cake?'

'No, come on, we need to crack on.'

Geraldine stood up.

'I still don't know how anyone can eat like you do without putting on weight.'

Sam patted her stomach and grinned.

'I'm not exactly size zero,' she replied.

Before her break, Sam had been looking into George's financial circumstances. Back in the office, she told Geraldine what she had discovered.

'So one way and another, he blew a heck of a lot of money,' she concluded.

'A heck of a lot,' Geraldine echoed.

'Imagine having that much money in the first place.'

'And then throwing it all away like that.'

'Why would anyone spend so much? For no reason.'

'He spent hundreds of thousands on his girl friend, Desiree. He bought her a club at one time. That lasted all of six months, and nearly wiped him out.'

'What a waste!'

They sat in silence for a moment, musing about the obscene amount of money one man had squandered. It could have bailed out a hospital ward, or paid for a raft of police officers for a year, enough to clear up many cases. With a sigh, Geraldine stood up. It was time to pay George Corless another visit.

On finding the restaurant closed, they drove to his flat in West Hampstead. It was unassuming for the owner of a fashionable upmarket restaurant, and very different to the Henshaws' imposing property. A young woman with voluptuous curves came to the door, a pink silk dressing gown draped around her hourglass figure. Her peroxide blonde hair darkened at the roots, and her nails and eyelashes were obviously false, but her smile conveyed a warmth that was entirely natural.

'What's the stupid bastard gone and done now?' were her first words on seeing Geraldine's warrant card.

A door slammed somewhere in the house behind her.

'We'd like to speak to George Corless.'

The young woman clutched her dressing gown more tightly around her waist as Sam stepped briskly forward and gave the door a vigorous push.

'Tell them to fuck off,' a man's voice called out suddenly. 'Any more of this bloody harassment and I'm calling the police—'

The blonde woman half turned and yelled over her shoulder.

'It *is* the police.'

She turned back to Geraldine with an apologetic shrug.

'He thought you were the bailiffs.'

George led them into an untidy kitchen. It stank of stale cigarette smoke. A few magazines lay strewn around the chairs. He swept them up and chucked them on the floor before waving a hand, inviting Geraldine and Sam to sit down at the table.

'Patrick Henshaw's death came at a very convenient time for you,' Geraldine commented.

'What do you mean by that?'

'You were facing financial difficulties.'

'That was nothing new. It's not a crime to owe money, is it?'

'What did Patrick Henshaw say about your gambling debts?'

'Nothing. It was none of his business any more than it's any of yours.'

He pulled a cigarette out of a packet and tapped

the end of it on the table before lighting it. Leaning back, he exhaled slowly, avoiding Geraldine's eye.

'And now you're a very rich man,' Geraldine continued. 'You inherited your business partner's share of the restaurant just when you needed it. That's going to sort out the bailiffs for you.'

George rose to his feet in a sudden swift movement, his face flushing darkly.

'What the hell are you saying?'

'I'm just stating the facts, Mr Corless. You were in trouble. Couldn't pay your bills. Now you're home and dry – until you gamble it all away again, that is. It's very convenient for you, Henshaw dying just now, isn't it?'

She sat back and watched him smoking and scowling.

'Is that all?' he responded at last. 'Only I've got a business to run. How long is this going to take?'

Geraldine ignored his question.

'Did you get on well with Patrick?'

'What do you think?

'Answer the question.'

'We were partners.'

'Yes. And did you get on well?

'I'd say so, yes. We were mates. We go back a long way.'

'Tell me about how you met.'

'Oh for Christ's sake! It was years ago. We were

working for the same construction company. The company went down the pan but we kept in touch. A few years later he invited me to join him in a small business venture – I was flush at the time so we put up the money together and one thing led to another. Then Mireille came up. It was a good deal, and we knew we could work together, so we went ahead. That's all there is to it.'

Geraldine quizzed him about the finances for the restaurant.

'We both put money in. It was a joint venture. Equal partners.'

'Tell me about your disagreements.'

'What disagreements? We never had any disagreements. If you're going to put words in my mouth, I want my lawyer present.'

He glanced nervously at Sam, notebook open in her lap, pen poised.

'You told me you had different ideas,' Geraldine insisted.

But however much she pressed him, he revealed nothing that might implicate him in Henshaw's murder.

'I already told you, he was the business brains behind the restaurant. I'm in the shit without him. Why would I want to kill him? Now, can we hurry this along if you've got any more questions, and let's get this over with. I need to get off to the restaurant soon.'

He glanced at his watch, his face twisted in anger. His hands shook as he lit another cigarette.

Geraldine tried a different tack.

'Mr Corless, where were you on Sunday evening?'

'Sunday evening?'

He took a deep drag of his cigarette, thinking. She wondered if he was really trying to remember, or if he was taking his time, concocting a convincing alibi.

'What time are we talking about?'

'Some time around midnight, say between ten and one in the morning.'

'I'd have been here. We close early on a Sunday, and it wasn't too busy so I left around ten. Patrick said he'd lock up.'

'Can anyone vouch for that?'

'Ask Desiree. She'll vouch for me.'

Geraldine wondered if Desiree's word was as false as her nails.

CHAPTER 23

She hated having to stand on a crowded train, even for a short journey. The heat from other people's closeness made her cringe; their smells suffocated her: body odours, the stench of stale cigarettes mingled with cloying perfumes and hair gels; strangers coughing and sneezing beside her, breathing on her. She made a point of walking right to the far end of the platform, where she was more likely to get a seat. At least sitting down she had some space of her own.

Her attention was arrested by a face staring blankly at her. There was no mistaking the glaring angular features; his face haunted her dreams. Squinting, she tried to make out the words below the photograph but it was impossible to read the text across the carriage as the page trembled with the bumping of the train. All she could distinguish was the headline: 'Police Hunt Killer.' Passengers shuffled along the packed carriage obstructing her view of the newspaper. She shifted sideways in her seat but by the time the paper reappeared in her line of vision the commuter had turned the page.

Gripped by a sense of urgency she scanned the carriage but there weren't any other papers in sight so she stayed where she was, fretting with impatience. Reaching her station she hurried out onto the street, bought a paper at the nearest newsagent and stood on the street reading, oblivious of the light rain that began to fall, spattering the newspaper in her hands while she skimmed through the report. A smile spread slowly across her thin lips as she read how he had been found, dead, in his car. Justice had been done. She hoped he had suffered.

She reread the article, wondering how much the police knew. They weren't to be trusted. They were asking if anyone had seen the victim on the night he was killed, but they knew a lot more than they let on. Reading the report once more, she tried to work out what it meant. The police were making out they didn't know who the killer was. That might be true, but they could be lying. Either way, she had no intention of admitting anything. She had more than seen him, she had felt his sweaty hands on her face and the weight of his body on hers, smelt his foul breath. For a second she was back in his car, struggling helplessly. And now he was dead. It served him right. Death was too good for him.

* * *

Someone bumped into her, startling her from her reverie. A middle-aged woman was peering at her and she realised she was standing in the middle of the pavement in the rain. Without answering she turned on her heel and walked off. Passing a litter bin she tossed the paper away, barely pausing in her stride. She wouldn't help the police hunt down whoever had killed that monster. It was raining more heavily now and she pulled up her collar, cursing herself for coming out without an umbrella.

Hurrying home, she had a hot shower before switching on the television. His face was there on the news, while a round-faced policeman appealed for witnesses to come forward. Like the newspaper reporter, he said a woman had been with the victim on the evening he died. The police were asking her to come forward to help them with their enquiries. She smiled. If the police had any idea who they were looking for, they would have been dragging her down to the cells, not issuing vague appeals for information. They didn't have a clue.

He had got what he deserved, that night in the car. One thing was for sure, the woman who had been with Patrick Henshaw on the night he died was never going to share what she knew with the police. If they wanted to expose his killer, they would have to do it without her help. She was free of him now, and she intended to stay that way.

CHAPTER 24

Reg Milton was up to speed with all the reports entered on the system and he was now ready to pump Geraldine and her sergeant who had been out asking questions of anyone involved in the case. The public, interested only in results, had no idea of the hours of work that underpinned a murder enquiry, or that the occasional unsuccessful investigation represented months and sometimes years of painstaking and dedicated police work. Even though they usually got a result in the end, everyone on the team lived in fear of being responsible for allowing a killer to walk free, possibly endangering more lives. None more so than Reg who was in charge of the investigation.

It was time to share ideas and impressions. They were all aware that they could throw ideas around endlessly, but in the absence of proof it was ultimately pointless. He sighed as he opened the door to the Incident Room. At least they had several lines of enquiry going. So often in a murder case they struggled to point the finger at anyone, but in this instance there was more than one suspect and Reg listened intently to the members of his team as they endeavoured to fit all the pieces together.

Geraldine had been questioning Henshaw's business partner. It was understood that George Corless had a lot to gain from Henshaw's death.

'He certainly needed the money,' Geraldine said. 'His finances were in a hell of a mess, gambling debts up to his ears and a high-maintenance girlfriend. He had a pressing motive, and could easily have found the opportunity. They saw each other every day. It might explain what Henshaw was doing on the Caledonian Road, which was off his route home from the restaurant. George might have arranged to meet him there where no one would see them, and they wouldn't be recognised even if they were seen.'

It sounded plausible. They were all familiar with George's bank statements, enough to give anyone nightmares.

'But he's got an alibi, hasn't he?' Sam pointed out.

'Or we'd have brought him in by now, put some pressure on him,' Reg agreed.

'He's got an alibi of sorts.'

Briefly Geraldine described George's companion: young, blonde and empty-headed. His motive was compelling, he had the opportunity, and his alibi was dubious; yet Geraldine was convinced George Corless had nothing to do with his business partner's death.

'What makes you so sure he had nothing to do with it?'

'He said the success of the restaurant depended on Henshaw's involvement and – I just don't think he did it. I can't explain why. It's just a feeling.'

Sam gave her a quizzical look.

Reg looked at the next name on the list.

'So you think it was Amy Henshaw? Or is it Guy Barrett we should be pursuing?'

'Or the two of them together,' Sam added.

They discussed the possibility that Amy was implicated in her husband's murder.

'His solicitor was under the impression she didn't know the terms of the will before it was read, so presumably she was expecting to inherit her husband's estate,' Geraldine said. 'He told me she seemed to know nothing about her husband's gambling debts and was shocked to discover the house had been re-mortgaged. So it appears she was expecting to be very wealthy on his death. His money could have been a motive for her.'

'She could have been motivated by passion,' Sam interrupted, her eyes bright with enthusiasm. 'She might have been prepared to get rid of her husband and make herself wealthy at the same time, so she could keep her young lover.'

Reg frowned. Avarice or passion might well have driven Amy Henshaw to kill her husband.

'It's possible,' he murmured to himself.

'And what about the young lover, Guy Barrett?' he asked.

Geraldine and Sam exchanged a glance.

'He's certainly good-looking,' Sam admitted.

'Just what you'd expect from a toy boy,' Geraldine agreed.

'He's not that much younger than her, is he?' Reg asked.

'Seventeen years. She's forty.'

'Getting on then,' he mused aloud. 'In terms of having a twenty-three year old boyfriend, I mean,' he added quickly, noticing Geraldine's scowl.

'The two of them might have been in it together,' Sam said.

Reg nodded. The business partner, strapped for cash and maintaining an expensive lifestyle; the wife, eager to dispatch her husband and seize his fortune so she could keep her young lover; Guy Barrett himself, keen to save his mistress from an unhappy marriage, and gain himself a luxurious lifestyle to boot – each of them had motive and opportunity, all were suspects with flimsy alibis.

'And what about Henshaw's mistress, Stella Hallett?' Geraldine asked. 'She had a lot to gain. She was living in a shabby rented apartment. Believe me, she didn't have two pennies to rub together – and suddenly she's a millionaire. She claims she had no idea she was mentioned in the will, but surely it's possible she had kept in touch with Henshaw. They might even have taken up with each other again, for all we know.'

She paused, and Reg wondered if she was thinking about the female DNA sample found on Henshaw's corpse. The pathologist had confirmed that the deceased had intercourse shortly before his death, making his ex-mistress a likely suspect. He stared out of the window at the branches of a tree, shuddering in a gust of wind.

'We only have her word for it that they were no longer seeing one another.'

Geraldine flicked through her notebook as she spoke.

'Here it is. According to Stella, she hadn't seen the deceased for five years. But she still had his photo on display in her flat, so I'm not sure that rings true.'

Reg turned to look at Geraldine, considering the possibility that Stella had killed Henshaw for his money.

'Is it likely he would have left so much money to her, after such a long time apart?' he asked.

The question hung in the air for a moment. They all understood the significance of the DNA found in the back of Henshaw's car, and on his body. The woman he had been with on the day he died would be able to give key information about his movements on the day he was killed. If she wasn't culpable herself, she might have been a witness to his murder.

'It has to be Amy or Stella,' Sam broke the silence.

'Let's hope so,' Geraldine replied, wishing she shared Sam's assurance. It was almost impossible to infer anything else, but she had been working on murder investigations for too long to be confident about anything until they had irrefutable evidence.

'It's possible the killer isn't any of these people,' she said softly. 'It could be someone we know absolutely nothing about.'

As Sam protested, Reg threw Geraldine a sharp glance and turned away without a word. Like Geraldine, he had been around for too long to be swept away with excitement before they had any proof.

CHAPTER 25

Every time she closed her eyes she heard the words going round and round in her head: 'Nine hundred and seventeen thousand pounds to Stella Hallett, nine hundred and seventeen thousand pounds to Stella Hallett.' Patrick must have left his wife well off, but near enough a million pounds was still a lot of money to lose. He had chosen to share his fortune with Stella, and there was nothing anyone could do to change that. No wonder Amy had been furious. Stella could do whatever she wanted with all that money. After all the time she had wasted feeling abandoned, it was staggering to know that Patrick had never stopped caring about her. With her stylish outfits and expensive face, Amy had never succeeded in winning back his affection. Blonde, glamorous and smug, she looked like a rich man's wife. But he had mentioned Stella in his will. She was the other woman, even after he was dead. She smiled at the thought.

'Nine hundred and seventeen thousand pounds to Stella Hallett,' she muttered to herself, *'nine hundred and*

seventeen thousand pounds to Stella Hallett.' The practical implications of her unexpected fortune hadn't sunk in yet. The money would be welcome, when it came, but she didn't care about wealth for its own sake. What pleased her was knowing that Patrick had thought about her. She knew it was evil, but she couldn't help feeling exultant, as though she had somehow won him back from Amy – a hollow victory, because Patrick was dead. She would have traded every penny of her unexpected fortune to have him back, even if he had come to her penniless. Tears overwhelmed her at the enormity of her loss. She had never wanted things to turn out this way.

Before she met Patrick, Stella's days had passed comfortably enough, without any emotional disturbance. Her life was transformed when she was appointed Patrick's personal assistant. For the first time in her life, Stella had fallen in love. Responding to her hints, Patrick had taken her to a hotel for the night. Shortly after that, he had moved her into a flat so they could continue their affair. Patiently she had waited for Patrick to leave his wife, and for a long time he had been full of promises. But instead of walking away from his marriage, he had abandoned Stella after her miscarriage. Stella's initial shock had turned to despair which, in turn, had given way to a terrible rage. She was still angry when she remembered how badly he had treated her.

* * *

Eventually she had calmed down and found another job. Outwardly her life returned to the same dull routine she had followed before she met Patrick. But everything had changed. Claiming she suffered from migraines, she took an occasional day off work to sit in a café opposite Mireille and watch for Patrick to arrive, noticing how his hair was greying, his waistline expanding. She knew she was being ridiculous, spying on him like that, but she derived comfort from this tenuous connection to him. She looked forward to seeing him, although he had no idea she was there, watching and waiting, like a guardian angel. It became a habit, almost an addiction, to sit there once a month, daydreaming that he would walk into the café and see her. She imagined him throwing himself at her feet to implore her forgiveness, and beg her to marry him. But he had never gone into the café to tell her he loved her, and now he never would.

She gazed miserably around her living room, dull and unremarkable, just like her. She watched her forearm rise, fat and white, as her fingers reached for the framed picture of Patrick standing on the shelf. He hadn't forgotten about her. He had left her nearly a million pounds in his will. She sat down on her one comfortable armchair and looked from the small picture in her hand to his large face beaming down at her from the wall. Several times she had taken his picture down in a burst of anger. Once she had chucked it in the bin so viciously, the glass had shattered. Her fit of weeping over, she had rescued the photograph. A week later he was back on the wall, smiling down at her from a new frame.

She had never had any money to spare. Now he had made her rich. She smiled at the picture in her lap, lifted it to her lips and kissed it. Tracing the familiar contours of his face gently with one finger, she smiled again. It was the best of all worlds, she told herself fiercely, as tears threatened to overwhelm her again. Kissing the photograph one more time, she replaced it carefully on the shelf, exactly where it had stood before. Tomorrow she would have to go to the police station for a DNA test, but in the meantime she was going to enjoy her evening.

Getting a piece of paper and a pen, she sat down to make her plans. In neat columns she wrote down how she might spend all that money. She could buy a flat of her own, travel the world, or invest the money so it gained interest. Patrick would approve of that. In her head she began to discuss the possibilities with him, imagining what he would say in response to each of her proposals.

To begin with, Patrick would suggest that she go to all the local banks and find out what interest rates they could offer if she was to invest her money with them. It was a sensible idea, and would help ensure the money didn't all disappear. She had never been one for spending, but the temptation might easily prove too great. It would be better to invest Patrick's gift wisely, so that she would be taken care of for the rest of her life. *'Nine hundred and seventeen thousand pounds to Stella Hallett,'* she repeated to herself. It was a serious amount of money, hers to spend as she chose. She couldn't help smiling.

CHAPTER 26

If it hadn't been for planned engineering work on the underground, Gideon wouldn't have been stuck in a train outside Rayner's Lane station. He stared at his fellow passengers: a bespectacled middle-aged man engrossed in a document, a large woman with a clutch of carrier bags at her feet, a young woman in a distractingly short skirt who wriggled uncomfortably on her seat as she tugged at her hem and a teenage boy, the beat from his headphones audible on the opposite side of the carriage.

Gideon had been tempted to give the visit a miss. After a late night on Friday the prospect of dragging himself out of bed to travel all the way back into London from Ickenham on Saturday was off-putting, but he knew he would never hear the end of it if he didn't turn up for the birthday party his mother was throwing for his step-dad. He had felt a brief flicker of hope on discovering that the Metropolitan line was closed west of Baker Street that weekend, but his mother had pointed out that he could take the Piccadilly line to Kings Cross and change there for the Northern line just the same.

'It'll take forever,' he protested.

'It'll take longer, so make sure you leave in plenty of time,' was the last thing she had said before she hung up.

'Yes alright, but is it—'

There had been no point protesting. No one was listening.

The train juddered feebly, engine whirring, but it didn't budge. None of his fellow passengers appeared concerned that the train wasn't moving. Gideon fretted, isolated in a carriage of strangers.

After a week of showers the weather had turned sunny. Walking to the station he had enjoyed the unexpected heat but the train was airless, stifling, even though they were no longer underground. The windows on the carriage could only be opened a crack. It was better than nothing, but only just. As he looked over his shoulder to see if the window above him was ajar he glimpsed a bundle in the rough weedy strip of waste ground that ran alongside the track. Distracted by sweat dripping from his brow, he turned back and wiped it on his sleeve. The train gave another jolt and as it did so he swivelled round in his seat, and for the first time registered what he was seeing. He glanced away, blinked, and looked round again in disbelief.

⋆ ⋆ ⋆

Barely a couple of feet away from him a man's face was glaring straight at him, from beneath a busy cloud of black flies. The body was all but concealed in tangled undergrowth on an incline in the shrubbery, visible only to someone who happened to glance out of a passing train from just the right position. It could have been there for days. Gideon twisted right round in his seat to study the figure more carefully. There was no mistaking what he was seeing: a man, grey-haired, lying on his side, his ashen face partly obscured by tall grasses, nettles and other weeds. Gideon told himself the man was sleeping, some old tramp with nowhere else to go, but flies were crawling all over the inert face, and by craning his neck he was able to make out a patch of congealed blood on the man's temple. He was dead alright. Gideon turned back to the train, shocked and nauseous. There were so many flies buzzing around the body.

Just then the train shuddered into motion and Gideon slid away from the hideous sight, still hesitating about what to do. The middle-aged man packed his reading material neatly away in a brief-case, the stout lady gathered up her carrier bags and clambered to her feet, the young woman stood up and shuffled towards the door, and the teenager sprang to his feet his head still nodding in time to the rhythm of his music. Gideon decided to put the hideous spectacle out of his mind and continue with his day as though nothing had happened.

After all, nothing *had* happened. Nothing that concerned him, at any rate. The dead man would be discovered sooner or later by some railway employee, and no one would ever know that Gideon had caught a glimpse of it from a passing train; if he hadn't turned his head when the train was at a standstill he would never have seen it.

But he *had* turned his head and seen a dead body covered in flies.

He barely managed to leap from the train before he threw up on the platform, narrowly missing his shoes, faintly aware of other passengers skirting around him and rushing away. Hearing a wheezing he glanced up to catch a glimpse of disgust on the overweight woman's face as she hurried past. He wiped his mouth on his sleeve, conscious of the smell of his vomit, and walked slowly over to a bench. He needed to think, although he knew there was only one course of action open to him. He had no idea who the poor fellow was, lying out there smothered in flies, but he couldn't just walk away and leave him there.

Clearing his throat nervously he accosted a station guard at the barrier.

'I want to report an incident,' he said and paused, trying to think of the right words.

'Oh yes? Is it a complaint form you want?'

The guard gazed apathetically at Gideon.

'No. It's nothing like that.'

He hesitated.

'Is it a suspicious package?' the guard prompted him indifferently.

'No. There's a dead body.'

He had the guard's interest now.

'A dead person on the train?'

'No.'

Gideon could hear himself gabbling as he explained.

'Slow down, mate,' the guard interrupted him. 'You're sure about this?'

'I'm sure.'

Glancing up he noticed the station clock and realised he was going to be late for his stepfather's lunch.

'Look, I've got to go—' he began.

The guard shook his head at Gideon.

'You'll have to wait here, mate. The police are going to want to talk to you.'

CHAPTER 27

'Where the hell are we going now? It's not our patch. Why doesn't anyone ever tell us what's going on?'

They were sitting on the tube, travelling west to Rayner's Lane station. Normally Sam was keen to visit crime scenes and busy herself with all the activity associated with a murder investigation, anything that took her away from sitting at a desk entering reports on the system, but today she was cantankerous.

'I hope this isn't going to take too long.'

'It'll take as long as it takes,' Geraldine replied evenly, 'but it could be a long day. We'll just have to see how it goes. We can get off as soon as we've done what needs to be done.'

Sam groaned.

'You know what the job involves. This is nothing new. So what are you complaining about? What's the problem?' Geraldine asked her.

The sergeant shrugged.

'No problem – it's just that it's Saturday and I'm supposed to be going out this evening. I wouldn't mind as a rule, but it's Sally's sister's hen night and I promised I'd be there.'

Geraldine didn't bother to answer. There was nothing more to say. They both knew what the job demanded of them.

'I still don't get why it has to be us,' Sam broke her sullen silence. 'It's not our area, is it?'

'That's what makes it so interesting.'

They fell silent again, considering the implications of the summons they had received. Their presence had been requested by the Homicide Assessment team who had been first on the scene. When Sam spoke again, Geraldine was pleased that she was no longer thinking about her plans for the evening.

'Either the victim is connected to Henshaw, or it's an identical murder.'

The station was cordoned off. A couple of uniformed constables were turning travellers away at the barrier as Geraldine and Sam crossed to the platform.

'But how long is it going to be closed?' a woman was asking as they passed.

'I'm sorry, I can't say, madam.'

'What's going on? Is it a bomb?' the shrill voice persisted.

'Some selfish bastard gone and thrown themselves under a train, more like,' an irate man said.

'I'm afraid I can't give you any information.'

* * *

From the top of a stone staircase, Geraldine spotted the luminous yellow high-vis tactical vest of a British Transport Police officer on the platform and nodded at him, holding up her warrant card. He hurried up the stairs to meet them. Flushed with exertion he led them back down the stairs, past several benches and a waiting room, to the far end of the platform where a small metal gate displayed a notice: Passengers must not pass beyond this point. They descended a ramp with rusty railings running down the side of the slope furthest from the track. At the bottom the officer turned sharp right, away from the train track, to where a forensic tent stood on long grass in front of a barbed wire fence bearing a sign: No rubbish to be deposited. Geraldine was glad she wasn't wearing a skirt as they clambered over rough ground, through nettles and stout brambles that would have torn her tights to shreds and scratched her legs. As it was, thorns nicked her trousers, catching at the fabric.

'The line's suspended eastbound,' the officer explained. 'The trains are going straight through so you won't be disturbed.'

'Not by trains anyway,' Sam muttered.

On the far side of the tent, the police officer pointed to a break in the wire fence.

'That's where the body must have been dragged through – the grass was flattened and the brambles broken, but there's nothing to indicate who brought it here.'

Beyond a grass verge on the other side of the fence they could make out a narrow track.

'There's a car park further along,' their guide added, following the direction of Geraldine's gaze. 'SOCOs are still examining it.'

Inside the tent, Geraldine gazed down in surprise at a body lying in the glare of bright lights, its face horribly contorted and stained on one side with dark blood from a head wound. The victim was lying on his back with one arm flung upwards as though caught in a vain attempt to ward off his attacker. His head was turned to one side towards the train line, eyes wide open, mouth gaping in a silent cry of protest. Geraldine could only see his face, chest and legs. His torso was concealed behind the kneeling figure of a pathologist who was examining the body, but she could see that his clothes had been cut open.

She turned to a scene of crime officer who was hovering behind her.

'What's the story here?'

The officer stepped forward, his eyes peering anxiously at her above his mask.

'The body's related to your current case, ma'am. We should have an identity soon—'

Geraldine interrupted him.

'That's George Corless.'

'Who?'
'George Corless. He's the business partner of the victim in the case I'm investigating.'
'Are you sure?'
'I'm positive. I questioned him only yesterday.'
'Well, that saves us a bit of time,' the SOCO replied, suddenly cheering up.

Geraldine felt an unaccustomed sense of revulsion in the presence of death. She had seen bodies of people she had met before they died, family members she had known for years, including her own adopted mother, but this was the first victim of a violent death she had spoken to before they were killed. George had been an ordinary man, the kind of person she might pass in the street every day. He had been offhand with her, guarded in his response to her questions. And now he was about to undergo a post-mortem. Up until now the cadavers she had seen had been no more than dead victims in a case to be investigated, but for the first time she gazed at a corpse recalling his mannerisms, the sound of his voice, the way he had frowned at her. It was unsettling and totally unexpected.

The scene of crime officer's voice recalled her to the situation.
'Yes, it's a good job, you recognising him like that. Saves us a bit of hassle.'
She shook her head, frowning.

'Am I missing something here? Only I don't get it. How did you make the connection to the Henshaw case if you didn't know who you've got here?'

It was the scene of crime officer's turn to look surprised.

'I thought you knew,' he said. 'It's the pattern of injuries that suggested there might be a link.'

He shifted to one side to allow Geraldine an unobstructed view of the body.

She stepped forward so she could see past the pathologist who hadn't yet looked up from his work. Corless had a nasty wound on the side of his head, and with a horrible sense of déjà vu she saw that he had also been beaten in the genitals.

'Oh my God,' Sam blurted out.

She looked very pale.

'Now my Saturday night is definitely ruined.'

'It hasn't done much for his either,' Geraldine replied tersely. 'Oh well, that's Corless ruled out as a suspect.'

'Which means the spotlight's back on young Romeo and his ageing Juliet.'

'Hey, less of the ageing,' Geraldine said sharply, but she was smiling.

Sam nodded sheepishly. She had forgotten that Geraldine was getting on for forty herself, hard though that was to believe.

* * *

A light rain began to fall, drumming out a soft rhythm on the roof of the tent.

'Shit,' the scene of crime officer grumbled. 'It's going to be a mud bath out there. And I left my umbrella in the car. Typical.'

They hung around for a while, talking about the crime. They would be able to establish if Corless had arrived by train, in which case they might even be able to see if he had been accompanied there. The high fence between the platform and the waste ground made it more likely that he had arrived by car and made his way down the incline from a footpath that ran behind the waste ground. If that proved to be the case there would be no CCTV film of his arrival and might be few clues about whether he had been carried there post mortem, or had been killed where he had been found. And there might be nothing to indicate who had arrived there with him.

Scene of crime officers were outside examining the area around the deposition site. While Geraldine and Sam were in the tent studying the victim and speculating about what had happened, an officer entered to report that tracks had been discovered which suggested that Corless had walked across the wasteland from the direction of the footpath. It confirmed what they had already suspected.

'Was he alone?'

'We're trying to establish if he was accompanied, but it's almost impossible to ascertain in all the undergrowth, and now it's beginning to rain into the bargain. But it's unlikely there was more than one other person with him. There's not enough disturbance on the ground to suggest more than two people.'

'First Henshaw, now Corless,' Geraldine said. 'It looks like we need to pay another visit to Mireille. What do you think, Sam? What's behind it? Is it about money? Or did someone have a grudge against them?'

'That's a heck of a grudge,' the sergeant replied, glancing at the victims' injuries and shuddering. 'Who would do that?'

They stood in silence for a moment, shoulder to shoulder, observing the body. Then Geraldine turned to the sergeant.

'We'll go to the restaurant this evening, after we've spoken to the witness who found Corless. We might as well speak to him now, while we're here and it's still fresh in his mind.'

Sam nodded.

'Like you said, it's going to be a long day.'

CHAPTER 28

Sam glanced at her watch and cast a pleading look at Geraldine who gazed pointedly at her own watch.

'Is that the time?' Geraldine asked, raising her eyebrows with a show of surprise. 'I thought it was much later than that.'

'But it's already seven!' Sam wailed. 'I wanted to be away by six.'

'Did you say you're going out this evening?'

'Well—' Sam hesitated. 'It's just that it's Saturday night, and technically I'm not on duty this evening, and I'm supposed to be going out and I've still got to get home and change and I really need to wash my hair and if I don't get going soon I'm going to be late and it's a hen night and I promised her I'd be there and if I let her down again she's going to go mental . . .'

Geraldine gave the sergeant a sympathetic smile.

'Let's crack on then, shall we, and see if we can get done in time? You speak to the guard who called us and I'll question Gideon Grey.'

* * *

The witness who had reported the body was sitting in the dingy station office, sipping tea from a stained mug. He was around thirty, casual yet smart in dark jeans, a shirt and jacket. He looked up when Geraldine entered, and launched into an agitated complaint before she had even introduced herself.

'I've been kept here, virtually a prisoner, for over an hour.'

'I'm sorry sir, but we've come from Hendon. I'm Detective Inspector—'

'I don't care who the hell you are or if you've come from bloody Timbuktu, I'm supposed to be at a family party and all this has been—'

He broke off, his voice suddenly unsteady, eyeing the warrant card she was holding up.

'I'm sorry sir, but you are aware this is a murder enquiry, and we really would like to take a statement from you. Your name is Gideon Grey?'

Gideon shrugged, no longer concealing his shock behind a smokescreen of anger.

'Look, I'm sorry, really, but I'm afraid I can't help you. I've no idea who the old stiff is. I've never seen him before in my life and – I wish I never had seen him, I can tell you that for nothing.'

He heaved a sigh that shook his shoulders.

'I'm sorry he's dead and all that, but this has got nothing to do with me, it just happened to be me that saw him. When the train stopped I was sitting right opposite him or I'd never even have noticed him. He wasn't exactly conspicuous out there. He could have been there for days for all I know. Shit, I shouldn't even have been on that train. It's only because the Met line isn't working that I used the Piccadilly line at all today. I knew I should've stayed at home.'

He paused to take a sip of his tea and screwed up his face.

'This is disgusting.'

'Mr Grey, can you tell me exactly what happened?'

He shrugged, tapping the toe of a scuffed shoe on the dusty floor.

'There's not much to tell.'

His expression sombre, he described how he had been startled on catching sight of the dead man's face staring at him through the train window.

'It scared the shit out of me, I can tell you. I mean, I didn't really take it in, not at first. It's not the sort of thing you expect to see when you're just sitting on a train, minding your own business. Some stiff, right outside your window, in broad daylight. But the train wasn't moving, and there he was, right enough, dead as a doornail.'

Geraldine glanced up from her notebook.

'You knew straight away that he was dead then?'

'Yes.'

'How?'

'How what?'

'How could you be sure he was dead?'

'It was kind of obvious, really. You didn't need a medical degree to know that.'

He paused, remembering.

'It was the flies,' he explained, and shivered. 'It was gross. There were all these flies buzzing around him – those big fat bluebottles, you know? – and his eyes were open. He was just lying there, staring, without blinking. I tried to see exactly what had happened to him and I thought I made out blood on the side of his head, but it wasn't that easy to see what was what, in all the weeds and stuff. But I knew he was dead alright. No one lies that still, with their eyes open, and all those flies.'

He shivered again, raising his eyes to Geraldine in mute appeal not to talk about it any more.

She took down Gideon's details before thanking him for his help.

'We may ask you to attend your local police station to sign a statement,' she concluded. 'But that's all for now. Thank you again for your co-operation, Mr Grey, you're free to go on your way whenever you're ready.'

'Will you let me know?' he asked as he stood up, no longer quite so eager to leave now that he was free to go. 'I mean, who the guy was and what happened to him?'

'We already know the victim's identity, and you can rest assured we'll find out soon enough who was responsible for his death.'

Gideon nodded, clearly impressed.

'So who is he then – I suppose I should say who *was* he?'

Geraldine politely refused to tell him anything else.

'I suppose I'll see it on the news, or in the papers.'

'Yes, Mr Grey,' she agreed, hiding her disquiet, 'I suppose you will.'

Having delivered his statement, the witness was already recovering from his initial shock and was bound to relate his experience to everyone with whom he came into contact. Word would soon spread. Apart from Gideon Grey who had stumbled on the body, the station guards all knew about it, which meant that the network of staff across the whole underground were probably aware of it by now. It didn't take huge powers of deduction to link the murders of two men who had been business partners, and once the press sniffed out a connection between Henshaw and Corless there would be a frenzy of media interest and a torrent of reports, many of them embellished. She could imagine the headlines: *Serial Killer Targets Restaurant Owners*. Geraldine hoped they would come up with a result before the press went to town on it.

CHAPTER 29

Geraldine treated herself to a leisurely breakfast on Sunday mornings whenever she could. This Sunday she struggled to eat anything, her thoughts dominated by the prospect of telling George Corless's family what had happened to him. She had to ring the bell several times at his flat before Desiree came to the door. It was just gone eight and she had clearly just woken up. Her skin was surprisingly perfect, and without thick make up and false lashes her eyes were softly beautiful.

'Where the hell have you – oh,' she broke off and raised her eyebrows, pulling her silk dressing gown more tightly around her substantial frame. 'What do you want? George isn't here. And before you ask, I don't know where he is. He had nothing to do with that murder you're investigating so why don't you leave him alone? He was with me, all the time—'

'Desiree, I'm afraid I have to tell you there's been another murder.'

'Another murder? Well, it's got nothing to do with George so you can just—'

Desiree stopped abruptly, her eyes anxiously searching Geraldine's face.

'Why are you here? Where's George?'

Desiree's emotional outburst degenerated so rapidly into hysteria that Geraldine feared for the girl's mental stability as she howled without restraint, bending over forwards to clutch her stomach. She allowed Geraldine to close the front door and steer her back into the apartment.

'Let's sit down,' Geraldine urged, manoeuvring the weeping girl into the living room.

When Desiree finally calmed down enough to listen, Geraldine explained something of the circumstances of George's death but she was circumspect, wary of setting the girl off again. Desiree was clearly shaken to hear that he had been murdered.

'What? Like Patrick, you mean?' she asked, her voice punctuated by hiccups.

'Did you know Patrick Henshaw?'

'No. That is, I'd met him a few times, when I was with – with George, but I never really spoke to Patrick much myself. I just sat there while they talked, you know.'

'What did they talk about?'

Desiree shook her head.

'I don't know. They were always talking about the restaurant. I wasn't even listening most of the time. Menus, complaining about the chef, and the staff, problems with the plumbing, that sort of thing. And they talked a lot about money, but I didn't understand any of it.'

Geraldine thought about the balding paunchy man she had met and wondered what had inspired such devotion from the attractive young woman in front of her.

'Tell me about George,' she said gently.

Desiree sniffed.

'We never meant it to happen, him and me, but sometimes you can't help these things, can you? He said it was love at first sight for him.'

'And for you?'

Desiree shrugged.

'I was in a bad place, I'd just come out of a bad relationship.'

She sighed.

'You know how it is. I'd been a complete idiot. Oh, he was drop-dead gorgeous and I fell for him, didn't I, only turns out he was a rat, stringing me along, me and I don't know how many others. Even when I knew he was messing me around I didn't finish it straight away because you keep hoping, don't you? I didn't want anything more to do with men after that, only then George turned up and he was different, a real gentleman, treated me nice and – he was kind to me.'

* * *

'How did you meet?'

'He just bought me a drink when I'd finished my act, and we started talking—'

'Finished your act? Are you a dancer then?'

'Like a pole dancer, you mean? God no, nothing like that. Look at me! I haven't got the figure for it. No, I'm a singer. Desiree. I used to do gigs all over the place, where I could, and that's how I met George, when I was singing at the restaurant one night. It was pouring and I'd forgotten to take a coat so he offered to give me a lift home. He was kind like that—'

Without warning Desiree burst into tears again. Geraldine felt sorry for the girl who was barely more than a child, but needed to press on with her questions.

'Is there a friend, or a family member, who can come here to be with you tonight?'

Desiree shook her head and blew her nose noisily.

'No, I'll be alright. I'll phone my sister.'

Geraldine waited while Desiree made a tearful call.

'She's coming straight over. You don't need to wait, I'll be OK. She'll be here soon.'

Amanda Corless lived in Bexley, on the outskirts of South East London near the Kent border. The journey was likely to take an hour, even on a Sunday, so Geraldine set off as soon as she could. Although George and his wife hadn't been living together for three years, they were still married; nominally George, his wife and their two children had remained a family. His son and daughter had both left home and were no longer financially dependent on him. Nevertheless, he had continued to treat them generously, perhaps because he had left their mother when they were both in their late teens.

It was easy to see that George had a 'type' as soon as Geraldine set eyes on Amanda Corless. The woman who opened the door had voluptuous curves now run to fat, and shoulder length, unnaturally blonde hair. It was almost like looking at an older version of Desiree, but where the young woman's blue eyes were trusting, Amanda's were shrewd and wary.

'What do you want?'

She glared at Geraldine who introduced herself.

'May I come in, Mrs Corless?'

Amanda made no move to admit her.

'Why? What's this about?'

'It's about your husband.'

'George? Listen, I've no idea what he's done and I don't want to know either. Whatever it is, it's nothing to do with me. He doesn't live here any more. You'll have to speak to him. Leave me out of it. I can give you his address if you want.'

'Thank you, Mrs Corless. We have his details.' Geraldine took a deep breath.

'Mrs Corless, I'm here to tell you that your husband is dead.'

'Dead?'

Geraldine nodded.

'Now may I come in?'

'No, I don't want to hear about it. He's caused me enough grief.'

She frowned and took a step back, raising a hand to close the door.

'We're not together any more, so what makes you think I'd give a toss? Go and tell his whore. See if she cares. I don't. Why should I? He walked out on me for some tart and now—'

She broke off, her lips trembling.

'Leave me alone.'

Geraldine insisted she needed to ask a few questions. Amanda seemed shocked to hear that her husband had been murdered, but she insisted she was unable to help the enquiry into his death.

'You can't think of anyone who might have wanted to harm your husband?'

'What? George? No. I mean, I was mad at him, of course, when he walked out on me for some young floozy.'

She laughed, her expression bitter.

'I could have killed him then, alright, and the kids were mad at him too for what he did. But that's all over and done with. I don't have anything to do with him any more but he still sees the children. At the end of the day he is their father.'

Geraldine waited and Amanda drew a sharp breath.

'He was a selfish bastard and he walked out on me. So what? Am I supposed to fall apart now he's dead?'

She shrugged.

'I finished crying over that bastard years ago.'

She made to close the door, her eyes glittering with repressed fury, or tears, it was impossible to discern which.

'All of this has nothing to do with me and, if you must know, he had it coming. Whatever happened was no worse than he deserved.'

'Mrs Corless—'

'Like I said, I stopped crying over him a long time ago. I've got nothing more to say to you.'

She slammed the door.

CHAPTER 30

Geraldine had arranged to visit an old school friend, Hannah, that Sunday evening, as she was already half way to Kent. In her twenties Geraldine had allowed herself to become obsessed with work to the exclusion of everything else. With growing maturity – or perhaps just declining energy – she was trying to pace herself by making time in the week for some distraction from her job. She was conscious that her former detective chief inspector had suffered a coronary brought on by the stress of the job. So far the alteration in Geraldine's work-life balance hadn't proved detrimental to her work. On the contrary, what would once have felt like a dereliction of duty now seemed increasingly essential to her performance. Viewing another body had dampened her mood that morning, but her spirits rose as she left London and the pressures of the investigation behind her. It was a sunny afternoon and she sang along to an old Madonna CD as she drove, the window wound down so she could feel the breeze on her face. She felt invigorated, and excited about returning to Kent.

* * *

After the usual greetings: 'I love what you're doing to your hair these days,' and 'You're looking tired, not overdoing it in the big city, are you?' they sat round the table for dinner. To begin with Hannah's husband was quiet but he became quite expansive after an excellent dinner, talking at length about cricket, a passion he shared with his cherubic round-faced ten-year-old son. As soon as she set eyes on the girl, Geraldine understood why Hannah had been so concerned about her thirteen-year-old daughter lately. It was nearly a year since Geraldine had last seen her, and Eleanor had grown up almost beyond recognition. Her features had sharpened and her blue eyes had a shrewd look that was slightly disturbing in a thirteen-year-old. The girl moved her body with precocious consciousness of her own sexuality. Tight clothes exaggerated her well-developed figure, displaying a cleavage that was bound to attract attention from teenage boys, if not older men. She could easily have been mistaken for eighteen, her knowing expression accentuated by dark eye shadow and thick mascara framing the sullen eyes of a disaffected teenager.

'Look at you,' Geraldine greeted her, 'you look really grown up.'

Eleanor glared and Geraldine felt embarrassed at having addressed her in such patronising terms. Clearly it was no longer appropriate to address Eleanor like a child. She decided against asking about school, choosing instead to converse in more general terms.

'So how's things, Eleanor?'

The girl muttered incoherently.

'You're not supposed to call her that any more,' her brother interjected. 'She doesn't want to be called Eleanor.'

'What's wrong with that? God, the fuss. I've changed my name. I'm entitled to change my name if I want to. I don't know why you have to be so immature about it. Just because you're a stupid—'

'Now, now,' their father interrupted. 'We've got a visitor. Let's have some manners.'

'Well he doesn't have to diss me. I'm allowed to change my name. There's no law against it.'

Geraldine learned that Hannah's daughter wanted to be addressed by her middle name, Jessica. Eleanor explained that she hated her first name, had always hated it, hated her parents for saddling her with such a pathetic name, and hated her brother for refusing to call her by her preferred name. Throughout lunch the adults all addressed her as Jessica. Her brother persisted in calling her Eleanor at every possible opportunity, and she deliberately ignored everything he said to her.

'Pass the salt, Eleanor.'

'Hurry up, Eleanor.'

'Aren't you going to eat that, Eleanor?'

Neither of their parents paid any attention to

the sibling squabble which Geraldine found both irritating and amusing.

It was a relief when the two youngsters scurried off to their rooms after dinner. Jeremy offered to clear up.

'Which means he'll dump the dirty dishes in the kitchen sink and leave them for me to sort out later,' Hannah laughed.

'This isn't London,' Jeremy replied, smiling at Geraldine. 'None of your metrosexual men here out in the sticks. Not yet, at any rate.'

'Don't worry,' Hannah laughed. 'He's joking.'

'I suppose I'll have to stack the dishwasher now, won't I?' he grinned.

Hannah and Geraldine settled down for a chat over another glass of wine while Jeremy clattered about in the kitchen.

'I don't want to hear any details of your latest gruesome case,' Hannah said and they both smiled.

'So tell me how it's all going here,' Geraldine replied. 'Because I haven't really got anything to talk about except work and to be honest I'm more than happy to get away from all that for an evening.'

Hannah complained about her exasperating daughter and Geraldine sipped her wine and made sympathetic noises. Hannah's family life felt reassuringly normal, the kind of existence Geraldine had once envisaged for herself.

'She'll grow out of it,' she assured her friend.

She felt herself unwinding.

'But listen to me jabbering on,' Hannah said at last. 'What about you? How are you finding life in London?'

Geraldine considered. Ian had asked the same question. Both her friends spoke of London as though the capital was a foreign country, although it was less than two hours' drive away. When the roads were quiet she could make the journey in just over an hour.

'Well,' she hesitated. 'It's not that different really, but it feels different. It's hectic. Everyone seems busy, all the time, and everywhere feels crowded. People rush around all the time, with no time for anything, so it's not what you'd call friendly – although I'm making friends on the force,' she added quickly, noticing concern in Hannah's face. 'There's a more obvious ethnic mix, and it takes longer to feel you belong because everyone's so busy.'

'I can't say you've sold it to me yet.'

'No, but I like it. It's very exciting. There's always something going on.'

Hannah poured another glass of wine, and Geraldine made up her mind to take the plunge.

'There's something I've been meaning to tell you,' she said.

'Well? Is it a man?' Hannah grinned.

'No, no, it's more complicated than that. It's hard to explain.'

'You're not ill are you?' Hannah asked, putting her glass down and leaning forward, suddenly anxious.

'No, no, nothing like that.'

'You haven't done anything – anything . . .' Hannah paused at a loss what to say.

'It's about my mother.'

'Your *mother*?'

Hannah looked baffled. Geraldine's mother had died nearly a year earlier.

Geraldine paused.

'The thing is, the woman who brought me up, the mother you knew – she wasn't my mother. Not really. Not at all, in fact.'

'What do you mean?'

'I was adopted.'

'Oh, I see.'

Hannah looked relieved, then frowned.

'But why didn't you tell me before? And why are you telling me this now?'

Geraldine explained she had only discovered the truth about her birth after her adoptive mother's funeral.

'I didn't know anything about it until last year when the mother you knew died. It explains a lot. My sister being blonde while I'm so dark. She always looked like Mum; you could see the resemblance. I never looked like either of my parents, not really.'

'You mean Celia wasn't—?'

'Celia was our mother's biological daughter but after Celia was born there were complications and Mum couldn't have any more children so they adopted a baby.'

'You.'

'Me.'

Hannah stared at her for a moment.

'And they never told you?' she asked at last.

Geraldine shook her head and tried to keep the bitterness out of her voice.

'Celia knew. She says she thought Mum had told me and, to be fair, I suppose it wasn't Celia's place to tell – but my mother never breathed a word.'

Geraldine broke off, afraid she might become emotional.

'Oh my God, you poor thing. So how did you find out?'

Briefly Geraldine told her how Celia had passed on the paperwork pertaining to her birth and adoption after their mother's death.

'So Celia really thought you knew.'

Hannah looked stricken for an instant then shrugged.

'It doesn't make any difference to anything though, does it? I mean, she was still your mother.'

'But—'

'And she was a wonderful woman.'

Reminded that Hannah had always liked her adoptive mother, Geraldine decided not to say anything about her unsuccessful attempts to persuade her case worker to reunite her with the birth mother who had refused all contact with the daughter she had abandoned at birth.

The conversation moved on and soon they were giggling over anecdotes from school.

'Remember that geography teacher? What was her name?'

'Miss Crackpot.'

They both laughed at the nickname.

'She put me in detention for leaving the dining room eating a chicken nugget!'

'And do you remember that chemistry test when we all just made up answers?'

'Except Swotty Morgan.'

'Oh my God, Swotty Morgan. I wonder what she's doing now.'

'Probably running the civil service.'

'Or MI5.'

'I heard she went off the rails at uni and now she's a pole dancer.'

'You're kidding!'

Hannah laughed.

'Well, she had the figure for it.'

They collapsed in giggles, like the school girls they had once been.

CHAPTER 31

That night Geraldine slept fitfully, and went into work early on Monday. Nick wasn't in that morning so she had the office to herself but even that consolation palled after a couple of hours. She found herself struggling to concentrate, and wished she had lingered in bed longer, realising she could have done with another hour's sleep. She wandered along to the canteen but didn't recognise any of the other officers in there. Nostalgia for her old station hit her. In Kent she had known just about every officer on the force but London was very different.

A subdued Guy Barrett was escorted to the station. The constable who brought him in reported that he hadn't appeared surprised when he opened the door and saw a uniformed policeman on the door-step, and he had accompanied the constable to the waiting car without argument.

'I think he was waiting for us.'

'Come on then,' Geraldine nodded at Sam. 'Let's see if he's got anything to tell us.'

Secretly she was hoping it would be relatively

easy to draw the truth out of a self-conscious twenty-three year old, but she didn't say so out loud. She didn't want to jinx the interview. In any case, Sam wasn't very much older than twenty-three.

Guy watched in silence, apparently calm, as Geraldine set the interview in motion. He sat very still, his head held upright, as he waited. Quite remarkably good looking with a disarmingly ingenuous gaze and a square jaw line, he looked younger even than twenty-three. With the preliminaries out of the way, Geraldine began her questions.

'You know Amy Henshaw?'

'You know I do.'

'Tell me about your relationship with her.'

'I'm shagging her. Is that what you want me to say?'

Suddenly he flung his brawny forearms on the table, palms facing upwards in a gesture of submission.

'Look, I know what this is all about. Someone knocked off Amy's old man and you think it was me. Well, you can save us all a lot of hassle because I can tell you right now I never went anywhere near the guy, not since we did a job at his house a couple of years back. I had nothing to do with him.'

He scowled and leaned forward to rest his chin on his hands.

'But I'm not going to give you a load of bullshit about how sorry I am he's dead, because what happened to him was no worse than he deserved. Do you have any idea what he was like, how he treated Amy? I don't suppose she told you he used to beat her up? Fucking bastard. If you want to know, I'm glad he's dead. He didn't deserve any better and that's a fact.'

He leaned back in his seat with an air of finality.

Geraldine didn't reply. Instead she put a photograph of Henshaw's mutilated corpse in front of Guy and watched his reaction closely. He gaped, looking so startled that Geraldine was convinced he hadn't known the details of the assault beforehand. She watched his eyes remain fixed to the image on the table.

'Jesus!' he muttered under his breath. 'That's sick.'

Geraldine sat forward.

'You just told me you thought he deserved this.'

'What the hell happened to him?'

Guy had turned very pale. He shook his head in disbelief and she saw his fingers trembling as he passed his hand over his lips. It seemed an extreme reaction from someone who hadn't known the victim. It crossed Geraldine's mind that he might be shocked not so much by the injuries Henshaw had suffered, as by the discovery of the extent of the killer's brutality.

* * *

Guy raised his eyes and shook his head, defiant once more.

'Of course he didn't deserve to be beaten like that, no one does, but he was a bastard and I still say she's better off without him.'

'I wouldn't say she's better off exactly,' Geraldine said carefully, with a sideways glance at Sam who was sitting beside her.

'No,' the sergeant agreed at once. 'You can hardly call her better off now.'

'What the hell are you talking about? Amy's not on her own if that's what you're getting at. Far from it. Because I'm going to take care of her properly from now on.'

'You'll have your work cut out then.'

Sam smiled as though she was amused by his claim.

'She strikes me as an expensive woman to maintain,' Geraldine agreed. 'With all those designer outfits and fabulous hair treatments – you didn't think it was natural, did you? And I expect she's used to having a personal trainer and a tennis coach and goodness knows what else besides. So how are you intending to take care of all that, exactly?'

A dark flush spread across Guy's face and he looked down at his hands.

'We're going to share everything,' he muttered. 'We've talked about it. She says I won't need to work any more but I'm not going to stop, if that's what you think. I'm not that sort of a man. I pay my way. I won't be living off her money.'

'Living off *her* money?' Geraldine raised her eyebrows. 'I thought we were talking about Amy Henshaw?'

'Of course I'm talking about Amy. Who else?'

'But Amy Henshaw doesn't have any money, does she?'

Geraldine turned to Sam.

'Shall I tell him or will you? Only it strikes me that Amy Henshaw has been leading this poor boy on, making out she's a wealthy woman in her own right.'

'We share everything,' he repeated, raising his voice fretfully. 'You don't understand, we don't have any secrets. You're just trying to wind me up.'

'How's this for a secret?' Geraldine retorted sharply. 'Not only does Amy Henshaw have no money, she also has a crippling mortgage on a very expensive property that's now registered in her name. In fact, she's mortgaged up to the hilt with no funds to pay up. Financially her husband's death has left her in serious trouble. What's the matter, Guy? Did she forget to discuss her financial difficulties with you?'

Guy sat without moving, staring at his lap. When he finally looked up, his brows were drawn low over eyes no longer candid.

'I don't believe a word of it.'

His lips twisted in a snarl as he spoke, and he seemed to be short of breath.

'She would have told me. We don't have any secrets. You're lying.'

The news that Amy Henshaw hadn't inherited a fortune was clearly a surprise to her young lover.

Seizing on the opportunity to take advantage of Guy's momentary dismay, Geraldine sat forward. Her light-hearted tone had disappeared. Her eyes glued to his face, she spoke slowly and clearly.

'Where were you last Sunday evening between eleven and one o'clock?'

There was a pause.

'Think carefully before you answer, Mr Barrett.'

Guy nodded as though he had been expecting this question and understood its importance.

'I was with Amy all night,' he replied, pursing his lips primly, 'and she'll tell you the same, so don't go thinking you can pin this murder on either of us.'

Although his voice was steady his eyes flicked round the room and he shifted awkwardly on his chair, his shoulders tensed.

Sensing his discomfort, Geraldine pressed him with a series of questions.

'How can you be sure what she's going to say? Did you discuss this together? Get your story straight?'

'I know she'll tell you we were there because it's the truth.'

'Where were you?'

'She came round. We always met at my place because – well, I couldn't go to hers in case her husband turned up unexpectedly. So we were at my flat from—'

He broke off, momentarily nonplussed.

'Well, I can't remember exactly when she turned up,' he resumed lamely, 'but it was early when she came over and she stayed all night.'

He paused, staring at the photograph of Henshaw which Geraldine had left on the table, as though he was unable to drag his eyes from it.

'Look, I get it. Because I'm having an affair with Amy you think it must be me that killed her husband. That'll be good for your targets, won't it, a nice quick arrest and you're done. Very clever. Only, I didn't kill Patrick Henshaw. I never saw him again after we did his conservatory, and I never did – that – to him. So can I go now? None of this has got anything to do with me. You can't just keep me here and I've got nothing more to say to you.'

Sitting back in his chair, arms folded across his chest, he pressed his lips firmly together as though to illustrate his decision to remain silent.

CHAPTER 32

Although she wasn't convinced Guy had murdered Henshaw, Geraldine still shared Sam's disappointment that he hadn't caved in and confessed his guilt. She returned to her desk to tidy up. A wave of exhaustion swept through her as she sat down and slumped back in her chair, too tired to continue. She must have dozed off because she came to with a start, her head lolling uncomfortably to one side, her mind spinning with all the possibilities. She wondered if they had been right to dismiss Corless so readily. He might have killed Henshaw and then been bumped off in his turn, as an act of revenge. That depended on the second killer having known exactly how the first murder had been carried out, and copied it, which was unlikely. In any case, she had believed Corless' claim that he couldn't make a success of the restaurant without Henshaw. That gave him a vested interest in Henshaw remaining alive and healthy.

She stood up and stretched, stiff from sleeping in such an uncomfortable position. They were eight days into the investigation and not only were they no closer to finding out who had killed Henshaw, they now had a second victim on their hands. She knew she should be rereading early statements in the light of this new development, going over and over the same ground, but she felt an uncharacteristic sense of lethargy. Finally she went out to grab some lunch in a local cafe.

Stuffed with pasta, Geraldine drained her one small glass of wine and decided against drinking any more. Instead, she ordered coffee and took a few deep breaths, determined to clear her mind of the investigation so she could return to work with a fresh eye. Life wasn't so bad. She was happy with her neat little flat, her own private territory where she was free to do whatever she wanted, and she was fortunate to be pursuing a challenging career. Despite its frustrations she enjoyed her work, and didn't understand why she was feeling so dejected. She wondered if it was the investigation that was dampening her spirits, but she was accustomed to the problems of working on a murder investigation, and anyway it wasn't going too badly. They had several leads and if forensics could come up with a match for the DNA found on Henshaw's body, it was even possible they might get a confession for both murders and wrap up the case within a day.

Gazing around as she waited for her bill, she couldn't help noticing that she was by no means the only person eating alone. On a nearby table a young woman was intent on a kindle while she waited for her food to arrive; a little further off a middle-aged man sat contentedly tucking in to a large plate of noodles. It struck her that life in London was very different to Kent, where she would probably have been the only person sitting by herself. Even so, everyone she knew seemed to be settled in a relationship. Reg Milton and Nick Williams were both happily married, Sam had been rushing off on Saturday to see her new girl-friend while Geraldine had spent the evening sitting at home on her own watching rubbish on the television to take her mind off the case.

The morning had been a waste of time and she was feeling increasingly despondent. She was sitting at her desk when her phone rang. It was the pathologist.

'OK,' he said, 'there's good news and bad news. First of all we've got the results back from the lab concerning the female DNA we found on Henshaw's body.'

Geraldine's breath caught in her throat and she was suddenly aware of her heart pumping rapidly. There was a pause. She waited, picturing the pathologist's boyish features twisted in thought as he searched for the words he wanted.

'Yes?' she prompted him impatiently.

'The tests confirm DNA found on Patrick

Henshaw's body came from a woman, but the bad news is that it doesn't appear to be a match with either Amy Henshaw or Stella Hallett. In other words, he had intercourse with another woman some time shortly before he was killed, but the sample of DNA found at the scene isn't a match with either of your suspects.'

'Damn. Are you sure?'

'There's little room for error these days, but—'

Geraldine's spirits lifted for an instant.

'But in my opinion, this couldn't possibly be a match. It's too improbable. And you certainly couldn't use this to make a case against either of your suspects. You'd be laughed out of court.'

'There's more. This might help. The hair on the back seat of the car is a match with the DNA on the body—'

'So the woman he was with on the day he died had dark brown hair,' Geraldine finished the sentence.

'Exactly.'

'So who was she?'

Geraldine couldn't contain her impatience any longer. This was it. All they had to do was find the woman who had been in the car with Henshaw on the day he died, and they would be able to start tracking his last movements. They would discover what he had been doing near the Caledonian Road, what his movements had been before he arrived there. She might even turn out to have witnessed his murder, if she hadn't actually carried it out herself.

'I'm afraid I've told you all I can.'

'Whose was the DNA?' she insisted, but it was a desperate question to which she already knew the answer.

'We don't have a match.'

Although she knew what he was going to say, disappointment hit her like a slap in the face.

'That's it, I'm afraid. We don't have a DNA match. All I can tell you is that she has dark hair, probably shoulder length, and split ends, but that's about all we can say with any certainty because – well, there's nothing else as yet, nothing that can help your enquiries.'

His voice petered out as though he too was overwhelmed with disappointment. Listening to him, Geraldine felt a wave of lethargy flow through her. After the rush of excitement that his call had provoked, they were no closer to finding the truth about Henshaw's death.

'Thank you for letting me know,' she said automatically before she hung up. Letting me know nothing, she added under her breath. They were no closer to tracing the woman Henshaw had spent time with on the day he died, for all their forensic expertise. The thought of spending hours trawling through CCTV to find images of dark-haired women entering or leaving the street where

Henshaw's body had been found made her groan out loud.

'Why the hell couldn't the woman at least have had ginger hair?' she asked.

Nick gave her a sympathetic smile.

'We've found the haystack,' she explained. 'Now all we have to do is find the needle – a woman with shoulder-length dark hair who was near the Caledonian Road on Sunday evening. That narrows it down a bit, doesn't it? And to cap it all, our chief suspect is blonde. It just gets better and better.'

CHAPTER 33

The identity of the dark-haired woman who had travelled in Henshaw's car and had sex with him shortly before he died remained obscure. In the meantime Reg was keen to put pressure on Amy and Guy. Expecting to gain most from Henshaw's death, they remained the obvious suspects. As it turned out they became worse off after he was killed, but neither of them had been aware of the financial disaster his death would bring them. Ironically, they had both anticipated the exact opposite.

Amy was escorted in from a different interview room where she had been kept for a brief period with a uniformed female constable standing at the door. She had been left there for long enough to unsettle her, but Geraldine's hopes that the widow might be cowed by her incarceration were dashed as soon as Amy entered the room. Her hair was immaculate and her make-up apparently so freshly applied that it looked as though she had touched it up while waiting. She sashayed into the room heralded by a scent of expensive perfume, a fake smile fixed on her painted lips, looking like a hostess at a corporate lunch.

She sat down gingerly on the hard chair, and smiled at Geraldine and Sam in turn before addressing herself to the former.

'Good afternoon, Inspector. I take it this is about my poor husband? I hope you've found out who's responsible.'

'I'm afraid we can't divulge any details to you just yet—'

'Not even to me? His widow? I find that preposterous. I have a right to know who did this to my husband.'

'I understand you may be feeling impatient, Mrs Henshaw, but rest assured we are doing our job very thoroughly and whoever killed your husband will be brought to justice. Make no mistake about that. The person or persons responsible are not going to get away with it.'

'Are you telling me you have no idea who did this terrible thing?'

'That's not what I said. Now, Mrs Henshaw, if you don't mind, we'll get through this a lot faster if you let us ask the questions.'

Amy Henshaw sat very upright in her chair, a bored expression on her face. But her eyes revealed her anxiety.

'Did you have a close relationship with your husband?'

Pencilled eyebrows rose. She was clearly startled at the direction the interview was taking.

'Close? Yes, of course we were close. We'd been married for twenty years.'

Her eyes flicked to Geraldine's left hand.

'Are you married, Inspector?'

Ignoring the question, Geraldine continued.

'It seems a reasonable question under the circumstances. Your husband left you nothing in his will after your twenty years of marriage, during which you were conducting a long-standing affair. So I'll ask you again, was your relationship close?'

'My relationships in and outside of my marriage are none of your business.'

Amy was unnerved, her composure beginning to slip. With luck it wouldn't be long before she lost control of herself. Geraldine leaned back in her chair and scrutinised the widow's face, focusing solely on her left eye, until Amy began to fidget.

'Not only did he leave you destitute, he didn't even warn you about the position he was leaving you in, did he? And it's not as if he was a very young man, not like Guy. He was an experienced business man who understood very well what he was doing with his money. I'd say that leaving you saddled with a mortgage you couldn't possibly repay was pretty harsh, after twenty years. It's not as if you walked out on him. You were still his wife.'

* * *

Amy didn't answer but she looked tense.

'Why would he do that?' Geraldine pressed her, 'leave you so badly off without preparing you for what might happen?'

'Because he's a bastard, that's why.'

Geraldine nodded sympathetically. Leaning forward, she spoke gently.

'Tell me about Patrick.'

To Geraldine's relief, Amy began to talk. Geraldine already knew she had met her husband when she was only nineteen, but she kept quiet and let her talk.

'I was a child,' Amy said. 'I didn't know anything and he was forty-five when we met. He was so much older than me, he swept me off my feet.'

Geraldine thought about Amy's twenty-three year old boyfriend but said nothing. Bowled over by the attentions of an older man Amy had readily succumbed to his courtship, flattered and excited by the glamour of the wealthy lifestyle he was offering her. But the reality of their marriage had been a miserable failure. The more Amy talked, the angrier she became, while Geraldine sat listening in silence, waiting for her to slip up.

'You think if you marry an old bloke like that with so much money you'll be sorted for life, but it didn't work out that way. And now, after putting up with his foul temper and disgusting habits all this time, the bastard's gone and left me without a penny to my name and a bloody great mortgage hanging over me.'

With increasing vehemence she described the breakdown in her marriage which, in her opinion, was entirely the fault of her self-centred husband who often came home drunk and, on more than one occasion, behaved violently towards her.

'He hit me, properly. He really hurt me. And he had no respect for women. You know what I mean. Only of course I didn't find that out until it was too late.'

Under other circumstances Geraldine would have felt sorry for the abused and emotionally neglected woman, but she was concentrating on unpicking the truth from Amy's narrative, and couldn't afford to sympathise with a woman who was a suspect in a murder investigation.

'That's what he was like,' Amy concluded, 'a selfish vicious brute. He was a real pig.'

'You must have been relieved when you heard he was dead,' Geraldine said quietly. 'Before you knew about the will, that is.'

Amy nodded.

'I was pleased alright. It was the best news I'd ever had. And I'll tell you something else. I'm still pleased he's gone, even with all the money trouble he's left me in. That's just typical, that is. I mean, what husband does that to his wife? You're absolutely right in thinking I'm pleased.'

'I said relieved,' Geraldine pointed out.

'Relieved, pleased, you name it. What's the difference? Can you imagine what it was like, living with him, never knowing from one day to the next if he was going to come home off his face, ready to fly off the handle. Talk about walking on eggshells – I slept on eggshells for twenty years. You have no idea what it was like.'

Geraldine kept her voice steady.

'And yet you never lost your temper with him, never answered back or packed your bags to leave? You just stayed there and put up with this appalling treatment, day in day out, without once complaining?'

'That's about the measure of it.'

Amy looked away, refusing to be drawn any further, although Geraldine did her best to needle her into confessing that she had finally been provoked into retaliating.

'All I want to do now is get shot of that wretched house – God, when I think of the hours I put into it – and settle down somewhere else. Of course we won't be able to afford to live in London—'

'*We*?' Geraldine asked. 'That's you and—?'

'Me and Guy. There's nothing to stop us moving in together now—'

Geraldine pulled a face and shook her head.

'What?' Amy demanded, her eyes stretched wide in annoyance. 'What are you looking at me like that for?'

With a show of reluctance Geraldine explained

that Guy had appeared very shocked to learn of Amy's financial straits. Amy was immediately incensed.

'What the hell did you go and tell him that for? You had no right to share my private affairs—'

'Guy told us you had no secrets from each other, so naturally we assumed he knew all about the will. It's hardly something you're likely to forget to mention, is it?'

Amy was pensive for a few seconds.

'How did he take it? The news of my mortgage. Was he OK with it?'

'OK?' Geraldine hesitated. 'No, I wouldn't say that exactly, would you?'

She turned to Sam for confirmation.

'Well, he didn't seem too pleased when he heard that, instead of securing a luxurious lifestyle with a wealthy older woman, he'd got himself involved with a woman who was not only old enough to be his mother, but penniless as well.'

Sam made a show of searching through her notebook.

'No,' she said at last. 'I can't find it. But he said something about having to start all over again.'

Geraldine frowned, afraid that Sam had been too obvious, but Amy started forward, a horrified expression on her face.

'He said that? You mean, he's going to look for someone else?'

'Words to that effect,' Sam mumbled.
She glanced nervously at Geraldine. They both knew it was a lie.
'So he was only interested in my money all the time,' Amy fumed, unconscious of the irony. 'A gold-digger. Well, he can just whistle for it now, because he won't get a penny from me.'
'Oh I think he knows that,' Geraldine said cheerfully.

'He won't get away with treating me like this. So he's planning to dump me now, is he? That's rich, coming from him of all people. If it wasn't for him Patrick wouldn't be dead and I wouldn't be in this mess in the first place.'
Her face was working with the effort of keeping her tears in check.
'What do you mean, "if it wasn't for him Patrick wouldn't be dead"?' Geraldine prompted her.
She leaned forward, barely able to control the tremor in her voice. Her eyes flicked sideways, checking that the tape was still running.

'It's obvious, isn't it?' Amy's voice was shrill now; she was beside herself with rage and disappointment.
'He did it because he thought he could get hold of my money by marrying me. Oh my God, do you think he was planning to do away with me too? Well, go on then, arrest him. What are you waiting for?'
She began to cry, her shoulders heaving with sobs.

‘And poor Patrick. It’s all my fault. Guy did that to him, didn’t he? And it’s all because of me.’

‘Amy, look at me. Are you accusing Guy Barrett of murdering your husband?’

Amy’s eyes were still streaming but she spoke loudly and clearly through her hiccups.

‘That’s exactly what I’m saying.’

CHAPTER 34

Geraldine and Sam were in agreement that Amy's sudden accusation was unreliable. Furious on hearing of Guy's desertion, she had retaliated in the heat of the moment. While it was perfectly reasonable to suppose Guy had killed Henshaw, it seemed unlikely he would have gone on to kill Corless. Unlikely, but not impossible.

'We can't rule anything out at this stage,' Geraldine said.

'It might have been Amy herself who killed them,' Sam pointed out. 'Now she's dropping Guy in it out of revenge as a way of saving her own skin.'

Geraldine didn't need to be told that George's injuries were virtually identical to Patrick's, but she listened attentively nonetheless as the pathologist ran through the details of the second killing. George's head injury had prompted a fatal stroke, which was followed by an attack on his genitals; a nauseating repetition that seemed to confirm that the two men had been killed by the same hand.

'So he died of a stroke,' Sam asked, 'after being hit on the head and before any other injury was inflicted?'

She pointed to the damaged area of the body. The pathologist inclined his head.

'The impact of the blow to his head was sufficient to trigger an internal bleed which would have caused him to lose consciousness almost at once. He wasn't technically dead when the second injury was inflicted so there would have been blood loss, potentially fatal in itself if left unattended. But the blow to his skull and consequent internal bleed in the brain came first and that was what killed him.'

Visiting the morgue was never a cheerful experience but a sense of gloom enveloped Geraldine and Sam as they left. Neither of them uttered a word on the way back to the car. Two identical deaths in a week would have been enough to depress anyone, even if they weren't responsible for tracing the killer.

'Bloody heck,' Sam said as she got in the car, 'this is a mess.'

'What are you thinking?' Geraldine asked.

'Well, they were business partners, so this isn't chance, is it? I mean, both of them in a week.'

'No, it's certainly not a coincidence. Apart from the obvious connection between the two victims, it looks like the same killer in both cases.'

* * *

Sam nodded, her expression brightening.

'At least that gives us something to go on,' she said, brightening up. 'It's got to be someone who knew them both and that narrows it down a bit.'

'We need to pay the restaurant another visit,' Geraldine agreed, and Sam beamed.

'We could go there for dinner.'

In spite of her dismay at the latest development in the investigation, Geraldine couldn't help laughing at the sergeant's sudden enthusiasm.

'You know perfectly well that's not what I meant. As if we've got time to sit around having dinner.'

'But we could find out a lot about the place by going there—'

'Yes, and we'll find out what we can by going there and doing our job.'

'But—'

'If you're hungry, there's bound to be a chippy on the way.'

She didn't add that she was sure Sam knew exactly where they could find one.

In a fashionable parade of shops in Soho, Mireille was situated between a smart hair salon and an art shop that sold expensive prints and offered a bespoke framing service. The restaurant itself had an elegant frontage with a stylish dark blue awning, pristine blue paintwork and large windows slightly tinted to give an aura of privacy to the interior. The door was locked but a man in a dark suit opened it when Geraldine knocked on the glass. After checking her warrant card in silence he stepped back to admit them.

The restaurant would routinely have been closed on a Monday even if business hadn't been suspended due to the unexpected deaths of its proprietors. On this particular Monday Geraldine had arranged for all the staff to meet there at the end of the day. To begin with she thanked them for coming to the restaurant to give statements instead of reporting to their local police stations.

'This is going to save us a lot of time,' she concluded. 'I've no doubt you're as keen as we are to know who murdered Patrick Henshaw and George Corless.'

Gazing at a group of tense faces clustered together, she wondered what would happen to the restaurant staff now. No doubt they were wondering the same thing themselves.

The chef would doubtless find another position. Tall and imposing, with a substantial frame to support his huge belly, he looked every inch a chef. Even Geraldine, who knew nothing of gastronomy, thought she recognised his face. She suspected she had seen him on the television. Henri Gilbert was flanked on either side by two assistants, similarly attired in white, who were both young and good-looking, although one was badly affected by acne. In addition to several youngsters in casual dress who were presumably waiting staff, there was a man in a formal suit and tie and a middle-aged woman in a blue overall.

The man in the suit stepped forward and introduced himself as Jed Parker, the restaurant manager. Around forty, quietly-spoken and immaculately dressed, he seemed perfectly composed. His expression was appropriately solemn.

'This is Henri Gilbert, our master chef, and his two sous-chefs, Will and Ollie.'

The two young men nodded and mumbled, while Henri stared past Geraldine, barely deigning to acknowledge her. Jed introduced five waiters and waitresses, all in their twenties and reasonably attractive, and finally the middle-aged woman who stepped forward and stared blankly at Geraldine.

'And last but not least,' Jed concluded the introductions, 'this is Ginny who comes in and cleans for us every morning before we open.'

'Who's going to be paying us for our time today?' the cleaning lady demanded.

Jed gave no sign that he had heard Ginny, so Geraldine looked around at all the assembled staff and thanked them again for coming to the restaurant to give their statements.

'I realise it's not terribly convenient for some of

you, but this is going to save us time. And I'm sure you're all keen to help further our investigation into the murders of Patrick Henshaw and George Corless.'

CHAPTER 35

Geraldine wanted to speak to the chef first; it might be best to let him leave as early as possible. The cleaner was second on her list, as potentially the most obstreperous witness. She decided to see the manager last. Sam was talking to the waiting staff and Geraldine would question some of them herself if she finished her list first.

The lofty chef strode into the office where Geraldine was conducting her interviews and glared down at her.

'Mr Gilbert, please take a seat.'

'I remain here standing.'

'As you wish. Thank you for agreeing to co-operate with our enquiry—'

'You say there is a choice for me?'

Geraldine shrugged and launched into her questions. The chef gave brief factual responses in laboured English, and seemed offended by her suggestion that he might prefer to answer through the medium of a translator.

'I speak seven language!' he announced pompously.

'My English, it is good as the next man. You will hear.'

It was heavy going. For all her perseverance Geraldine learned only that Henshaw was a charming man, while Corless lacked any taste or manners.

'This man has no sophistication. He is a primitive.'

Probing, Geraldine discovered that there had been a falling-out over the menu.

'My sauce,' the chef pursed his lips. 'My sauce are supreme. And this animal, he ask for ketchup on the table. Ketchup, in my restaurant? Never!'

He shuddered.

'For this insult truly he deserve to die. But it is not me. I do not dirty my hand so. I am not the hooligan. If I choose the kill, it will be with poison, and no one will suspect my food. Ha!'

'And Patrick Henshaw?'

'Ah, Mr Henshaw is always the gentleman. He understand the value of the chef. It is I, Henri Gilbert, make this restaurant famous in the world! You ask yourself, what it is, my sauce? But I do not give up the secret.'

Much as Geraldine was enjoying his performance the chef wasn't helping the investigation, and she forced the conversation away from Henri Gilbert's cuisine, back to the murder of the two restaurant proprietors.

'Mr Henshaw and Mr Corless have both been murdered. Can you think of anyone who might have wanted them both dead?'

'Ah, that is the question I ask myself.'

'And?'

He shook his massive head then tapped the side of his nose with one finger.

'Who is it takes the cuisine of Henri Gilbert now? Find the answer and you have it! The reviewer say to kill for the recipe of Henri Gilbert!'

Geraldine suppressed a smile at the man's egocentricity.

'Do you think someone killed them so they could take over the restaurant?'

It was the chef's turn to shrug.

'And the other reason can be what?'

The cleaner entered the room in a huff, her blue overall sleeves pushed up to the elbow as though she was spoiling for a fight, while her small dark eyes gleamed with annoyance.

'I asked Jed, Mr Parker I should say, and he says we just have to take it on the chin, but it cost me my bus fare to come in today, not to mention my time, and if I'd known they wasn't going to pay me I'd never have come in. And now it looks like we're all going to be out of a job into the bargain. Typical. They never think of us. You know, I could have spent this time finding another place, couldn't I? What if there was something and I've missed out through being stuck here waiting, and for what?'

Geraldine invited her to sit down and Ginny subsided into a chair, still grumbling.

'You don't care, do you? I'm just the cleaner.'

Geraldine studied the wiry little woman, her short curly hair awry, her face a study in resentment.

'Ginny, this is a murder enquiry and we would have had to speak to you sooner or later.'

'I can't see what any of this has got to do with me.'

Ginny folded her arms and glowered across the desk as Geraldine began questioning her gently, aware that sometimes the people in the humblest positions knew more about what was happening within a company than anyone else. Having established that the cleaner had been employed at the restaurant for over two years, going in daily for two hours to clean the place up in the morning, she led the conversation on to the staff.

Resigned to having to waste her time at work unpaid, Ginny settled into her chair and began to talk. And once she started she was forthcoming in expressing her opinions about the restaurant. She was equally forthright in her views on the two victims. She dismissed Henshaw as a 'snooty stuck-up piece of shit – if you'll pardon my language. I'm sorry to speak ill of the dead and all that, but you did ask for the truth. I'm nowhere near important enough – or pretty enough – for him.'

'Not pretty enough?' Geraldine queried politely.

'Oh, he had an eye for the girls. You ask them what he was like. Always fawning over them, he was. He was the one wanted those girl singers, and he'd have had them do more than sing, I daresay—'

She broke off with a knowing shake of her head.

'What singers?'

'Oh, don't ask me. I never saw any of them. It was nothing to do with me. They were only here of an evening at the weekend. Apparently he thought it added a bit of class to the place. Huh. I don't think Henri thought much of that, or anyone else for that matter.'

Geraldine asked if Henshaw favoured any of the waitresses over the others but Ginny said he wasn't particular.

'Now George, he was a different kettle of fish altogether. He had no pretensions, not like Mr Henshaw. George was friendly, but not over-familiar, if you get my drift. I was sorry to hear about him. Of course I'm sorry to hear about what happened to them both,' she added quickly.

The sharply-dressed manager was glib and irritatingly self-assured. His black hair was smooth and sleek, his features perfectly proportioned, his gestures camp in spite of his sober clothes.

'I suppose they'll be closing the place down now,' he said as soon as he sat down. 'I'm already working on my CV. Shame, I've only been here for a year and just when I thought I was settled, this goes and happens. Isn't that just typical?'

Geraldine didn't answer straight away but let him talk through his dissatisfaction with his situation, hoping to glean his views on the two murdered men. He answered her questions clearly and at length, but gave little away, carefully restricting himself to bland comments on his bosses.

Geraldine asked if anyone else had been working at the restaurant on the evenings when the two owners were killed.

'Ginny said something about a singer?' she prompted him.

'Oh yes, of course. We usually have performers in at the weekends, and often on a Friday as well. It adds to the customer's experience.'

'Was anyone performing here the night of the murders?' she asked again.

The manager frowned, thinking.

'There was a girl last Friday, yes.'

'What about the previous Sunday, the night Henshaw was killed?'

'To be honest, with all that's been going on, I couldn't tell you. Patrick used to book the performers and I'm not sure if he kept any written records. If he did, they weren't here. It was all quite informal, you know.'

Geraldine didn't return his guarded smile.

* * *

'What can you tell me about the singer who was here last Friday?'

'Not a lot, I'm afraid. I didn't get involved. She was one of our regulars. She was alright, nothing special. We only have room for solo artists, a singer with a guitar, or sometimes they use a backing track. We have a few regulars who are good value, and the customers appreciate it. Live music is very popular these days, and we like to – here at Mireille—'

He broke off with a sigh.

'We'll need the singer's contact details.'

The manager went and rummaged around behind the bar, before returning to Geraldine with a shrug. He cleared his throat.

'I've got her name here somewhere, but – we paid her in cash.'

He fished through the till. They both knew he was going through the motions.

'I tell you what,' he said finally, his expression lightening with relief at having remembered something. 'She told me she sings on Tuesdays in Westfield in Shepherds Bush.'

He named a café.

'I wish I could remember her name – Inga?'

'Inga the singer,' Geraldine said, smiling.

'No, that wasn't it. I'm sorry, I just can't remember her name, but she told me she sings there regularly on Tuesdays.'

'Can you describe her?'

'Short, slight, dark hair, quite pretty.'

It wasn't much to go on.

The questioning took most of the day. As they left the restaurant, Geraldine was troubled by a feeling that they were going nowhere with the investigation. She and Sam compared notes, adding to what they already knew about Henshaw as an urbane womaniser with an acute business brain. Geraldine had the advantage that she had spoken to Corless before he was killed. He seemed less sophisticated than his partner, blunt in his views but not unkind towards his employees and his young girlfriend. It was a testament to his cordiality that, despite falling out with his wife, he had remained on good terms with his children. But while everyone at the restaurant seemed genuinely concerned about the double murder, nothing that was said shed any light on the identity of the killer.

CHAPTER 36

With George out of the running, his ownership of the restaurant went to his children, both of whom had alibis for the evenings when the murders took place. Meanwhile, Amy and Guy were still suspects. It was curious that the nature of the injuries in the two murders was almost identical, although the damage the victims had sustained suggested the murders had been prompted by personal enmity. The fatal blow against Corless appeared to have been quite powerful, making Guy the most likely out of all the suspects. In addition, Amy had accused him of killing her husband, a claim Geraldine suspected was no more than the ranting of a disappointed woman. Even so, she had to follow it up so she decided to start her day by talking to Guy again.

Her expectation that the young man would resent being recalled for further questioning was confirmed as soon as she entered the interview room. He leapt to his feet, dark eyes blazing with anger.

'What the hell's going on? I answered all your

questions yesterday, I even signed a statement, what more do you want? You've got no right to bring me back here again.'

Paying no attention to his outburst, Geraldine sat down and greeted him politely, thanking him for helping them with their enquiries. As she did so, the duty solicitor mumbled something to the suspect who sat down, grumbling quietly.

'I only met Patrick Henshaw once, for Christ's sake. Go on then, ask all your questions again if you must, but you won't find out anything new.'

He glanced sideways at the solicitor, who made no further attempt to communicate with him.

Leaning back from the table in a deliberately casual pose, Geraldine kept her eyes fixed on the suspect as she asked if he had ever met George Corless. Guy shook his head without answering.

'Mr Barrett, please answer the question.'

'Who did you say?'

'George Corless.'

Geraldine showed him a head shot of the dead man taken a year or two before his death.

'Do you know this man?'

'No. Why? Should I?'

'Look carefully, Mr Barrett.'

He glanced at the photograph without registering any interest.

'I don't know him.'

As previously, Geraldine believed he was telling the truth, but she persevered.

'This is George Corless,' she said. 'He was Patrick Henshaw's business partner.'

'I know. He's the one who gets the restaurant now. Where's the justice in that? Amy was married to him for nearly twenty years.'

'Almost as long as you've been alive,' Geraldine pointed out.

Scowling, Guy mumbled something about that being none of her business. Geraldine sat forward, suddenly brisk.

'What *is* my business is that Patrick Henshaw's business partner is now dead.'

Guy didn't enquire what had happened to him. He was interested only in the disposal of the restaurant.

'I mean, it's worth a few bob, isn't it?'

'I believe so.'

'And with Mr Henshaw's business partner out of the way, I suppose it'll be Amy's now? The restaurant, that's what I'm talking about. It's all hers now, right?'

He was alert now, his eyes alight with excitement.

'The restaurant is left to George Corless's two children, in equal measures,' Geraldine told him.

'You mean she gets nothing? After all that time. Bloody hell. Well, I'm glad she's shot of him at any rate.'

He failed to suppress a satisfied grin and rubbed

his hands together then suddenly looked abashed, as though he had just remembered where he was.

'I'm sorry he's dead, this George bloke, but I didn't know him. I never met him. I just want to get the hell out of here and get back to Amy.'

'You might find she's not so keen to see you.'

Guy frowned at her.

'What's that supposed to mean? We're together, me and Amy. In everything.'

Geraldine shook her head and heaved an exaggerated sigh.

'I'm not sure Amy sees things in quite the same way,' she said gently, doing her best to sound sympathetic. She felt a twinge of guilt for deliberately provoking the young man, but pressed ahead, reminding herself he could be a vicious psychopath.

Guy half rose to his feet, his face dark with anger, fists clenched. At his side the solicitor muttered urgently and he sat down again.

'You don't know what she's thinking,' he said, glaring at Geraldine. 'I was with her before she had all that money to her name, and I'm with her now. She's not going to dump me now. She's going to need me more than ever. She always wanted—'

'I'm afraid she may already have done it,' Geraldine interrupted him.

'What are you talking about?'

'Amy Henshaw made a statement yesterday accusing you of murdering her husband.'

Geraldine nodded at Sam who flicked through her notebook and read aloud.

'He did it because he thought he could get hold of my money by marrying me . . . Do you think he was planning to do away with me too? . . . Go on then, arrest him. What are you waiting for? . . . Poor Patrick. Guy did that to him.'

Guy stared. The flush slowly disappeared from his face as his anger faded into bewilderment.

'I – I don't believe a word of it,' he stammered at last.

He turned to the solicitor.

'They're lying. All of them. Playing games, trying to mess with my head. Amy never said that. She couldn't have done. She'd never betray me like that.'

He turned back to Sam.

'It's vile, what you're doing, trying to trip me up with your filthy lies, but it won't work, I'm telling you, it won't work!'

He was shouting now, out of control, with spittle beading at the corners of his lips, tears gathering in the corners of his eyes.

'Do you often lose your temper?' Geraldine asked softly.

Guy shut his mouth and folded his arms across his chest, glowering. Geraldine waited.

'Is it true?' he asked at last. 'What she read out?' He jerked his head in Sam's direction.

'Is that really what Amy said?'

'We could play you the tape.'

Guy thumped his fist so suddenly on the table that Geraldine jumped, startled. Even the solicitor looked taken aback. Only Sam's composure didn't falter.

'It was her,' he said, speaking very slowly as though working out a puzzle as he went along. 'Don't you get it? She did it, she killed him, to get her hands on the money. She had me set up all along. Why else would she lead me on and then drop me in it like that? She can't—' his broad shoulders shook as he heaved an enormous sigh, 'she can't have given a toss about me all along, or she'd never have done it, accuse me of killing her husband like that. And if she didn't love me, she must have been leading me on so I'd carry the can for her when she got rid of him.'

'And George Corless?'

'If she killed her husband for his money, I suppose she killed him for the same reason.'

Guy's theory made as much sense as Amy's. Some love affair, Geraldine thought, as she mused over how quickly they had switched from giving one another an alibi to accusing each other of committing an evil double murder.

CHAPTER 37

Sam wasn't surprised when Geraldine admitted to feeling under the weather. She looked exhausted. For once she readily accepted Sam's offer to go to Westfield shopping centre to track down the girl who had been singing at Mireille the night Corless was killed.

'Are you sure you can trust me to go by myself?' Sam asked, with a grin.

She had warned Geraldine in the past of her reputation for refusing to delegate tasks. They both knew the singer was unlikely to add to their knowledge of what had happened the night of the murder. Nevertheless, Sam was gratified that Geraldine trusted her enough to allow her to work alone. Any witness might provide vital information, however far removed from the action they were.

The centre was buzzing with people chattering, loaded with carrier bags, as Sam made her way past a row of shop fronts and up an escalator to the café. Stepping inside the beige interior, she saw a grand piano on a raised platform along one wall. Behind it a cream curtain hung from ceiling to floor, forming an elegant backdrop to the performance space where a girl was perched on a stool, playing the piano and crooning softly into a microphone. Her dark hair accentuated the pallor of her skin. She was slim, with thin lips and glittery make-up on her eyes whose colour was impossible to determine from several yards away. Sam stood by the door for a few moments, listening to the singing float across the room in sporadic bursts. Low notes were indistinguishable from the general chatter above which high notes hovered with a haunting quality. A few young women were sitting at a table nearby, drinking cocktails. Their easy laughter drowned out the sad music. Sam caught a few words of the lament: 'sad . . . lonely . . . lost.' They seemed to suit the girl's mournful expression. For some reason, the melancholy lyrics reminded Sam of Geraldine.

Conscious of her responsibility, Sam crossed the room to sit on a high stool at the bar where she ordered a soft drink, so she could engage the barman in conversation.

'I see you've got a singer in,' she said as the young man set her glass down on the gleaming beige top.

One of the benefits of her cropped spiky white blonde hair was that people rarely spotted she was a police officer. She didn't mind the public stereotyping her profession. It worked in her favour.

'Yes, that's Ingrid. She's here most weeks,' the

barman replied readily, leaning his elbows on the gleaming bar to chat. 'We get some great bands in at the weekends, if you're interested. There should be a few flyers on the tables, or you can always check the website to see what's going on. We're the only café that has live music every night of the week at Westfield.'

Ingrid came to the end of a song and slipped off her stool. Most of the customers paid no attention. Only one elderly man seated beside the stage applauded feebly, nodding his head with a toothless grin. Taped music began to play loudly. Sam stepped across to intercept the singer as she stepped off the podium.

'Nice,' Sam said vaguely. 'Do you write your own songs?'

'Some of them,' the singer paused, before adding, 'I'm glad you liked it.'

Now she had the singer's attention, Sam introduced herself. The girl's expression didn't alter on hearing she was talking to a police officer.

'What do you want with me?'

Sam suggested they step outside for a moment.

'Well – I'm on a break but I need to get back soon.'

'This won't take long. And I'd prefer not to have to shout.'

They found a bench in the shopping centre and sat down.

'How well did you know Patrick Henshaw?'

'Who?'

'Patrick Henshaw. He owned the restaurant Mireille. You sang there recently.'

The singer's face remained impassive. She looked bored.

'I never met him.'

Her gaze drifted past Sam to stare vacantly past her shoulder, as though she was watching for someone. Close up Sam saw that her eyes were green, and her dark hair had a reddish sheen that was probably dye.

'You sang at Mireille recently.'

'Yes. But I don't know the owner. I dealt with the manager. His name's Jed. You can ask him. I was there. It was a crap gig. You wouldn't think it, would you?'

'Why?'

'It's such a posh place.'

She turned to Sam with a sudden awakening of interest.

'Why do you want to know?'

'What can you tell me about Patrick Henshaw?'

'Nothing. I told you, I never met him. Jed paid me.'

'Did you speak to anyone else there?'

'I can't remember. There was a fat chef who shouted a lot, and that's all I know.'

'Who did he shout at? Was there an argument?'

The girl stared blankly at her.

'I don't know.'

'Can you remember anything he said?'

'It was just a load of yelling in the kitchen – zis is no good, zat is no good, that kind of thing. I didn't hear much. I think he fancied himself as a sort of Gordon Ramsay. But the food was crap.'

She pulled a face, screwing up her long nose.

'I've no idea why anyone would pay so much to eat there. Anyway, I've got to do another set.'

She turned away.

'If you think of anything that might help us, here's my card. You can give me a ring.'

'Help you with what?'

Sam hesitated. There was no reason why Ingrid should have heard about Patrick Henshaw's death, especially as she had never met him. Briefly, she explained the reason for her questions.

'Murdered?' the singer repeated. 'Bloody hell. And you're trying to find out who did it, right?'

'Yes.'

'Bloody hell, murdered,' Ingrid repeated. 'That's awful. Look, I'd like to help you, but I never met the guy and I wouldn't have a clue who his enemies were. Isn't it usually the wife?'

With a casual shrug she turned away.

Sam felt a flicker of envy. She wished she could turn away from the image of Patrick Henshaw on the slab at the morgue so easily. Much as she loved her job, and could never imagine doing anything else, it was hard. Every time she heard the phrase, 'I'd like to help you—' she experienced the same stabbing disappointment. Finding murderers mattered, yet other people shrugged off her questioning without a second thought. Ingrid probably wouldn't even keep her card. Wretchedly Sam watched the singer disappear back into the café. Before she went down into the station she dashed off a quick email to Geraldine.

'Wasted journey. Singer Ingrid never met Henshaw.'

As the train jolted and rattled underground, Ingrid's final throwaway remark lingered in her thoughts.

'Isn't it usually the wife?'

CHAPTER 38

It was time-consuming, co-ordinating the follow up investigation of all the staff who worked at Mireille. A team of constables had been occupied all day questioning every member of staff again, tracing travel cards, scrutinising CCTV film footage, and checking alibis. Only the chef, the manager and two waiters had been working on both evenings when the murders had been committed. All the other members of staff had alibis for one or other of the evenings. That reduced the police workload considerably. While it was feasible that the chef, the manager or one of the waiters who had been working both evenings could be guilty, it was difficult to see what possible motive any of them could have had. None of them stood to gain from the double murder. They appeared to have no contact with their former bosses outside work and, far from benefiting, would probably all lose their jobs as a consequence of the deaths of the restaurant owners.

Sitting over a coffee that evening, Geraldine thought about Amy and Guy. It was fairly obvious what had brought them together in a relationship that was unlikely to last. Without the excitement of clandestine meetings they would soon tire of each other. Not clever enough to realise that Amy had levelled her accusation in retaliation, in the belief that he had deserted her, Guy would eventually work out what had happened. The two lovers might even discuss it, and clear the air together. But in the meantime Geraldine couldn't help feeling a twinge of pity for the young man. He was scarcely more than a boy, and had seemed genuinely distraught. She wondered if there might have been any substance in either of their accusations; having retracted the alibi she had given Guy, Amy had made herself a suspect as well.

Back at her desk she was flicking through her expenses when her phone rang. She felt the breath catch at the back of her throat when she heard Miles Fellows' voice announce that he was calling from the forensic lab. This could be it, she thought, the detail that would identify who had committed the double murder. She struggled to keep her voice even as she replied, crossing her fingers beneath the desk.

'Which do you want first, the good news or the bad news?' the young pathologist asked, as breezily as if he was enquiring whether she preferred red or white wine.

'Just tell me what you've found.'

* * *

'Well, it's not straightforward,' he began and Geraldine sighed.

Nothing ever was.

'The good news – if it can be called that – is that we appear to have a match . . .'

In the brief pause that followed, Geraldine hardly dared ask the question. Her voice sounded hoarse and strangely flat.

'What do you mean, you appear to have a match?'

DNA evidence should be conclusive, clinical. The pathologist's hesitation troubled her.

'Well, this is where it all gets a bit complicated because as I said we *do* have a match,' he replied.

There was another pause. This time Geraldine waited, unable to speak.

'The problem is, the borough intelligence unit have come up with a match to a woman who's in prison.'

'In prison? Are you sure?'

'Quite sure. She's been locked up in Whithurst for the past twenty years.'

Geraldine found her voice.

'But you said the DNA was a match and DNA is evidence. It's conclusive. There has to be an explanation. We could have solved this case. It must be a mistake. You must have entered the wrong details or – check again. Someone's made a mistake.'

Geraldine heard the desperation in her own

voice, babbling on. To have come so close to an identification only to have it snatched away was almost unbearable. She struggled to control tears of frustration blurring her vision.

'Well, yes, clearly something's not right here,' the pathologist agreed cheerfully, 'but the DNA profile on file was entered twenty years ago when DNA testing was in its infancy. It wouldn't happen any more. Our science and our systems are much more advanced today. We're much more reliable with DNA records now than was the case in the past. Tests are becoming more sophisticated all the time. So when we're looking at samples taken twenty years ago or more, there's a large margin for error that today has been virtually eliminated.'

He spoke pompously as though he was giving a lecture. Geraldine cut in before he warmed to his subject. All she wanted to know was the identity of Patrick's killer.

'Yes, thank you,' she interrupted impatiently.

She wanted a positive result that would help solve the case, not a lecture on the scientific progress that had been made in DNA testing over the last two decades.

'So who is she?'

'Sorry?'

'The woman whose DNA matches that found on Henshaw's body? Who is she?'

'We can only say it appears to be a match,' the

pathologist corrected her. 'It can't actually have been her, of course. As I said, profiling twenty years ago wasn't what it is today.'

'Yes, alright, who is the woman whose DNA appears to match that found at the scene, if you must be pedantic,' Geraldine said, her frustration making her testy.

'As a scientist—' he began but Geraldine cut in.

She wasn't interested in his views, only in the information he was able to give her.

'Just tell me who she is.'

The DNA found on Henshaw's body matched the DNA profile of a woman named Linda Harrison, who had been convicted of killing her husband twenty years earlier. The significant factor was a slightly unusual genetic coding that featured in both DNA samples. Geraldine tried to quell an initial rush of hope that the forensic scientist's information was inaccurate, and that Linda was no longer locked up. If the prisoner had recently been released, only to kill two more men in quick succession, it would be a terrible indictment of any rehabilitation programme she had attended, and of her psychological assessment prior to her release; but it would also lead to a conviction and an end to her killing. Whatever the truth, at least they had new information that might help them find the killer.

It didn't take long to establish that Linda was still locked up in prison. Geraldine contacted the governor herself to double-check. Only when there was no longer any possible doubt that Linda was securely behind bars did Geraldine's spirits sink.

'Surely twenty years is a long time?' she had asked the governor.

'Her psychological state is such that it is felt better for her to remain in custody. She's going to be with us for the foreseeable future.'

'What can you tell me about her psychological state?'

'Linda has never shown any sign of remorse. She remains adamant that her crime was not only necessary but morally correct.'

'Necessary?'

The prison governor heaved an audible sigh.

'Look, I'm sorry, but we're going over old ground here. I can assure you we've done our best for Linda, but some people resist any attempt at rehabilitation and I honestly doubt if she'd survive on the outside now. The best thing for her is to remain where she is. Now, I am rather busy. I hate to cut this short, but was there anything else?'

Geraldine called the forensic lab to confirm that it was feasible the DNA that appeared to match Linda Harrison's had in fact come from a close family member, before she set about researching Linda's relatives. Her first set of enquiries led nowhere. Linda had never had children so there was no possibility a daughter might have followed her psychopathic example. A momentary excitement at discovering that Linda had a sister was dismissed by further investigation which revealed that the sister had died nearly thirty years ago. Reluctantly, Geraldine concluded that the DNA sample had been a false lead. Somewhere in the lab, there must have been cross contamination of samples leading to the impossible conclusion that a woman had killed Patrick and George while she was locked up in a Category A closed prison.

Geraldine went home, feeling thoroughly dejected. In an attempt to cheer herself up she stopped on the way home for a takeaway, opened a bottle of wine and put on the DVD of one of her favourite films. An hour into the film, and halfway through the bottle, she felt as miserable as ever. It was typical of her sister to choose that moment to call, as though she could sense when Geraldine didn't feel like talking. Geraldine felt slightly guilty. She had intended to phone her sister. In her preoccupation with the case, she had forgotten.

'Celia, I was going to ring you.'

'Really?'

She couldn't blame her sister for sounding sceptical.

'Did you get an invitation from dad?' Celia asked.

'No. What invitation?'

Geraldine remembered that she had never sent her new address to her father.

* * *

Over twenty-five years had passed since their father had walked out, leaving their mother with two young children. Living in Ireland with his new wife, he had sent money regularly, always remembering Christmas and birthdays. Geraldine had been quite young when he left home. It was different for Celia. She was three years older than Geraldine, and the man who abandoned them had been her real father. By the time Geraldine discovered the truth about her own birth, the man she had always believed was her father seemed like a distant relative anyway.

'What invitation?' she repeated.

'I expect yours is in the post,' Celia replied, 'or he got your new address wrong. You did write to him when you moved, didn't you?'

Geraldine gave a non-committal grunt.

'He's decided to throw a party for his birthday and he's invited us all to Ireland. Can you believe it? He's asked Jeremy and Chloe as well, all of us. I can't believe he's going to be sixty-five!'

'Are you going?'

'You are joking.'

Geraldine wasn't surprised at her sister's reaction. Celia had refused to have any contact with her father after he left. Geraldine felt sorry for him because she knew he was desperate to meet his only grand-daughter, but Celia remained adamant in her rejection of her father.

'And I hope you're not thinking of going,' Celia added.

'I can't say. I haven't had an invitation yet.'

Although she didn't admit as much to her sister, Geraldine was tempted to accept the invitation. She hadn't yet confronted her father about her adoption, face to face. He might well have information that could help her find her birth mother for whom she had been looking, so far without success.

'I don't know,' she said to Celia, thinking aloud. 'I just don't know what I'm going to do.'

CHAPTER 39

Maurice watched a group of youngsters gathered at the bar and pondered how times had changed. He remembered dropping in on a Saturday night when the pub was run by Mary and Bob, a pair of friendly faces who had registered his presence. Those were the days when another human being actually noticed when he wasn't around, even if it was just the landlord of his local.

'You alright then, Maurice?' Bob would call out to him as he stepped through the door. 'Been off on your holidays?' and they would both laugh because Bob knew he never went anywhere. Making his way to the bus stop was as much as he could manage. That was before the pub had been taken over and everything had become plastic and ersatz. Maurice never saw or heard of Bob and Mary again. He hoped they were happy in their retirement, but he couldn't help feeling let down by their departure. For years they had given stability to his lonely existence.

* * *

But all that was years ago. He had grown older and crabbier since Bob and Mary had left, his hands curled more tightly with arthritis, his eyes peering through ever thicker lenses. If it weren't for the free glasses, he would be blind as a bat by now. That would be terrible, cutting him off completely from all human contact, because he was a people watcher. Maurice liked to spin fantasies about strangers he saw in the street, or reading newspapers in the library, in the pub on his weekly outing for a drink, or on the bus home. It was the only way people touched his life these days, unless he had an appointment at the doctor's, and even then he saw a different doctor every time and recognised none of them. Nothing stayed the same any more. No one knew him, apart from Toby who just stared mournfully at him, thumping his stubby tail on the floor.

Even the beer was different, he thought sourly. For a while he had stopped coming to the pub in a fatuous act of protest, not that anyone would miss a frail round-shouldered little man with a fuzz of grey on his head and a raincoat fraying at the sleeves.

'Just the usual,' he would say, and then he would have to explain what he wanted to another stranger behind the bar.

Maurice never stayed out late. It wasn't that home was far away or a difficult journey, just a couple of stops on the bus, but he felt uneasy travelling after dark, wary of the gangs of youths who strutted around the streets at night, off their heads on alcohol or drugs. He would watch them as they staggered along the pavement, two or three abreast, shouting and jeering as though they owned the streets. Observing them from the safety of the bus as it rattled past he felt he should pity them, blasting their brains with a toxic cocktail of chemicals, their lives empty of purpose; but he envied them. They were a bunch of mindless followers, capable of committing acts of unspeakable violence, but at least they had a herd to travel with. He had gone through life doing no harm to anyone, yet he was alone in a hostile world.

A friend might have scolded him for self-pity, but it was hard to reproach himself when life was so unfair. As he stared through the bus window at a group of youths one of them happened to look up and catch sight of him watching. With a flicker of fear Maurice turned his head away and became aware of a woman sitting beside him. He wasn't bothered about women. When he was much younger he had gone with prostitutes in an attempt to fend off his loneliness, but now he contented himself watching passers-by. Engrossed in gazing out of the window, he hadn't noticed anyone sit down beside him, but sensing a body next to him, he half turned to see her looking sideways at him. She didn't drop her eyes when he saw her but continued to watch him out of the corner of her eye. She looked nervous. Emboldened, he stared right back at her.

The woman had shoulder length blonde hair framing a face that was heavily painted with bright red lips and artificially thick eyelashes. He wondered if she was a prostitute or just out on the pull. It was difficult to tell with so much make-up on her face, but he guessed she wasn't much over thirty. He considered speaking to her but bottled it and turned away. It wasn't worth the bother. A woman like that would never be interested in him. Looking down he observed her raincoat had fallen open to reveal a tight short black skirt. Turning to look at him, she crossed her legs. With a slight shock he saw right up her thigh, before she pulled her coat closed. He licked his lips, wondering if she had deliberately displayed herself to him.

She leaned back against the seat as though resting. With a shiver of excitement he saw that her eyes remained fixed on his. Her expression didn't alter, but he knew that she was conscious he was watching her. He looked away. As he did so he shifted sideways until his leg was touching hers. She moved away and he wriggled further across his seat so their legs remained in contact. It was a long time since he had enjoyed any physical contact with another person. As she stepped off the bus, she glanced back and saw that he was following her. She turned away, and he hobbled after her.

CHAPTER 40

Geraldine passed a restless night. She had gone to bed early, resolving to make a fresh start on Amy and her young lover's files in the morning, but whenever she closed her eyes she saw George, a heavy figure seated in a dimly lit office, dark eyes staring at her from beneath unruly eyebrows. It irritated her that his image haunted her in this way. After all, she spent her life dealing with murder cases. There was no reason why this particular victim should trouble her so deeply. In his sixties, George was bordering on clinically obese, a heavy drinker and smoker who no doubt suffered from stress with his wife, his mistress, his business dealings and his mounting gambling debts. But the spectre of his living figure dogged her thoughts as she tried to sleep.

She tried to focus her thoughts on the case as a whole, but everything took her back to George. It seemed unlikely that Amy or her young lover would have inflicted such horrific injuries on him. It wasn't the nature of the attack that Geraldine found disturbing. She had worked on cases with far more distressing victims: kids not yet out of their teens, frail elderly women, helpless infants. Nevertheless, every time she tried to sleep, George appeared in her mind, knocking back a tumbler of whisky while his other plump hand rested comfortably on his well-rounded stomach as he puffed on a cigarette, gesturing and smiling towards his young girlfriend, relishing the sensual pleasures in life. She hadn't experienced this disturbance before, never having questioned other victims before they were killed. Such a clear image of him while he was alive seemed to turn his brutal death into something worse than murder. It was the end of a world.

She couldn't sleep so she pulled on her dressing gown and went to the kitchen to brew a pot of tea, deciding that she might as well do some work as she was unable to sleep. But once her laptop was switched on she couldn't focus on either Guy or Amy, both obviously in the frame for the first murder. If they did turn out to be responsible for George's death as well, it would presumably be for financial motives, in which case it was hard to believe either of them capable of inflicting such vicious injuries. It was possible this had been a calculated attempt to show that both murders had been carried out by the same person. But that made no sense.

It was clear both murders had been committed by the same person, whether alone or with an accomplice. To begin with, the details of the attack on Henshaw hadn't been shared with anyone outside the investigation. For that reason alone it was hard to see how Corless could have been the victim of a copycat killer. But that suggested the killer was one person who had known both the victims, and hated both of them enough to carry out such a gruesome assault. Geraldine went back to bed and tried to relax but felt restless and got up once again. Feeling peckish, she wandered back to the kitchen and opened a packet of biscuits she had bought for her niece's next visit. Crunching miserably through the packet, she ate until she began to feel queasy. Finally she dragged herself back to bed where she lay, exhausted but irritatingly alert. There was something amiss with the whole investigation but she just couldn't put her finger on what was wrong.

She woke up late the next morning with a pounding headache that felt like a hangover, only she hadn't been out the previous evening drinking and partying, she had been at home on her own stuffing herself with biscuits she didn't even particularly like. Her excess made her feel sluggish and slow. Thoroughly wretched, she pulled on a shirt and an old pair of trousers and didn't bother to apply any make-up before hurrying off to the office, not even stopping to brew coffee. Once she got stuck into work, she would feel better.

* * *

Her first line of enquiry was to search for anything suggesting Amy might have had a personal grudge against George. Clearly she stood to gain financially from his death. If Amy had harboured a grievance against her husband's business partner strong enough to account for her mutilating him as he lay dying, then the whole case would start to make sense. They had obviously been in contact through Patrick, and there were any number of ways in which they could have fallen out. But this was all speculation.

Geraldine grabbed a coffee from the canteen before she made her way to her office, planning her day as she strode along the corridor. All she wanted to do was sit quietly and mull over what she knew, but as she opened the door to the office, she saw Nick apparently having a clear out. His desk was covered with papers that had spread out across the floor. Files were stacked beside Geraldine's desk. There was even a small pile on her chair. He turned and beamed at her, the hair sticking up on top of his head no longer striking her as comical, but intensely irritating.

'Good morning.'

The cheerful greeting grated on her foul mood.

'Most people would have asked before putting stuff on my chair,' she snapped.

Nick looked surprised. He half opened his mouth as though about to reply, then turned away.

'You weren't here,' he said, his tone frosty.

Geraldine looked pointedly at her watch.

'It's not even nine. I'm hardly late. It would have been courteous to wait until I arrived before spreading your papers around.'

'This is because of DS Haley, gossiping behind my back, isn't it?' he demanded unexpectedly.

His face had tautened with repressed fury, but his voice was steady.

'Sam Haley. She's been spreading stories about me, hasn't she? What has she been saying?' He scowled. 'I never should have let it go, that first time, when she gave me a roasting for a careless remark. Ever since then she's been nothing but trouble.'

Geraldine was suddenly sick of the whole place. As if the stress and pressure of a murder investigation wasn't bad enough, she now had to share an office with an irate colleague who was making an increasingly poor job of concealing his hostility towards her sergeant. It didn't help to know that Nick's grumbling was a knee-jerk response to her own bad temper. Much as she valued her job, she sometimes felt there must be more to life than the pursuit of those who ended it for others. But she knew she could never do anything else.

CHAPTER 41

Geraldine had been in the job far too long to be surprised by anything that came up, so she didn't question being called to the scene when a body was pulled out of the canal near Highbury. It wasn't immediately apparent how this victim was related to her current murder investigation. As she drove to the canal she couldn't help worrying that the body was that of a dark-haired woman whose DNA matched that found on Patrick. Her concern was irrational; there was no reason why the body in the river should be the witness they were seeking.

They needed to find the unknown witness urgently. Without an opportunity to question her, they might never work out Patrick's movements on the day he was killed. If that was the case, the identity of his killer might forever remain a mystery. They had all been quietly hopeful that questioning the woman who had been with Patrick on the day he died would help them to work out what had happened. But although the DNA sample gave them a profile, it remained worthless without a viable match.

It was barely light when Geraldine reached the canal, and early enough to be cold. She thrust her hands into the pockets of her thin grey jacket, pulling it more tightly around her as she walked along the deserted canal path. A fine mist lay on the waste ground alongside the water, lending the scene an eerie atmosphere which was intensified by the forensic tent looming ahead, a vast apparition dimly visible through the haze. As she approached, the silence was disturbed by a muted murmur of voices punctuated by an occasional shout.

'Over here!'

'Get a move on with that tape!'

'Watch out!'

In keeping with the surreal quality of the scene, a tall dark figure materialised as abruptly as if he had stepped out from the wings of a stage. Already the sun was beginning to shine weakly through clouds, burning off the mist. Geraldine held up her warrant card, and the uniformed officer blocking her path stepped aside with a barely perceptible nod.

'Morning. He's in there. They only pulled him out of the water about half an hour ago, poor old sod. It's a bad business alright, leastways for him. The pathologist's with him now.'

Geraldine returned his greeting with a perfunctory 'Good morning constable,' and hurried on towards the tent, reassured to learn that the victim wasn't their missing female witness.

Her fingers numb with cold, she fumbled as she donned her contamination suit, white face mask and blue gloves. Finally she approached the opening to the tent. Pausing outside to pull on her overshoes, she ducked her head to enter and blinked in the bright artificial lighting that had been rigged up inside. The dead body was lying on the ground, half concealed by the pathologist who was kneeling beside it, gently probing discoloured flesh with delicate gloved fingers. The victim's drenched coat, shirt and vest had been neatly ripped open to reveal his mottled wrinkled skin. Gazing down at the dead man's flesh, Geraldine felt like a voyeur intruding on an intensely private scene. The body was childlike; pitiful.

The pathologist twisted round on his heels and she recognised Miles Fellows. He smiled wearily up at her before clambering to his feet to tower over her.

'Hi there, Geraldine.'

She nodded wordlessly, caught up in the suppressed excitement of her first viewing of a victim. She tried to focus on a factual analysis of the data in front of her, but was unable to distance herself from an instinctive response to the raw presence of death, as though her emotional reaction to George's corpse had relaxed the self-control she had previously shown in similar situations.

Grey and shrivelled, the body looked shrunken, almost impossibly small, like a wizened child.

'Did he drown?' she asked, wondering why her presence had been requested at the scene.

'I don't think so. I can't be sure until I've had a chance to examine his lungs but I'd say he was dead when he fell in the water.'

'Did he fall or could he have been pushed?' Geraldine enquired automatically, although she was still puzzled as to why she had been summoned.

Miles heaved a loud sigh.

'It's impossible to say how he ended up in the water. But I can tell you he's been in the water all night.'

'How many hours are we talking about, exactly?'

'I'd say he's been in the water for at least twelve hours.'

'Since yesterday evening then?'

'Sometime yesterday evening, yes.'

Geraldine took a step closer, her eyes fixed on the dead man.

'So if he didn't drown, how did he die?'

But she already knew the answer.

Miles pointed at a large purple area of bruising on the dead man's left temple surrounding a deep laceration.

'He was hit on the side of the head, here.'

'The skin's broken. Could he have knocked himself when he fell in the water?' Geraldine asked, as a matter of form.

She didn't need Miles to point out the nasty mash of bloodless flesh where the victim's genitals should have been.

'What about DNA?' she asked. 'Is there any sign of female DNA on this body?'

Miles shook his head.

'There's no evidence of any contact, as far as I can tell. The water's affected him of course, but apart from the injuries to his head and genitals, he looks reasonably intact.'

Looking down at the withered and bloated corpse, Geraldine wasn't sure she would have chosen those words to describe the body.

'I might find something more for you when I get a proper look at him, but he doesn't appear to have put up much of a struggle. I'd guess he was taken by surprise. The killer's been more careful this time.'

Geraldine stared down at the dead man. Even with swollen features and distended torso, the body was still recognisably that of an old man. He appeared to have been small and although it was difficult to tell, he gave an impression of frailty.

'Maybe this victim was just easier to deal with,' she said. 'He doesn't look like he would've put up much resistance.'

'Yes, the joints are severely arthritic and he wasn't exactly what you'd call robust.'

He pointed to the victim's spindly legs.

'He would have been easy to overpower.'

Having seen more cadavers than she could readily call to mind, Geraldine was taken aback to feel her eyes begin to water. She couldn't help wondering whether the dead old man had a wife and children, anyone to mourn the violent death of this diminutive human being, or if he had lived on his own. Like her. On balance she wasn't disturbed to discover that a victim could still touch her emotions after all her experience with death; nevertheless she turned her face away from the young pathologist. Some things were best kept private.

CHAPTER 42

'Will you tell him or shall I?'

Reg shook his head and gestured wearily towards her. His tall figure looked slightly bowed and there were grey creases under his eyes she had never noticed before.

'You can have that pleasure, Geraldine.'

'You never thought it was him anyway, did you?' Sam asked when the detective chief inspector had left the Major Incident Room.

The question sounded like an accusation.

'No, but—'

Geraldine didn't finish the sentence. They were all dismayed that a third murder had been committed while Guy was being held in the custody suite. Under normal circumstances they wouldn't have been able to keep Guy in custody past Thursday night without a formal charge. The detective chief inspector had been jumping through hoops to extend the period they could hold him for questioning, while a team of officers had been tied up investigating the wrong man. And all the time the killer had also been busy, pursuing his dreadful business

* * *

The heavy door swung open. Its shadow moved slowly across the grimy floor. Guy suppressed a shudder. His rage had given way to exhaustion with the effort of keeping himself together. It wouldn't do to show his alarm. Far better to tough it out and act as though he felt aggrieved, like any innocent man would do. It was an effort to keep his temper under control. Shouting only succeeded in making them even more smugly assured of his guilt. It was insane. Everyone he knew lost their temper sometimes. It didn't make them all murderers.

'What now?' he asked.

He made no move to stir from the bunk where he was sitting, shoulders hunched forward, hands dangling between his knees.

'Mr Barrett, you're free to go.'

Still he sat without moving.

'You're free to go, Mr Barrett,' the inspector repeated. 'You can go home now.'

She smiled at him.

'You mean – that's it? I can go?'

For an instant he didn't believe it. He thought it was a trick to catch him off guard. Then it crossed his mind that he ought to make a stink about wrongful arrest or something, but he couldn't help returning her smile as he stood up and stretched his legs.

The relief as he strode out of the police station in his own shoes, his wallet back in his pocket, was like nothing Guy had ever experienced before. Every day of his life he had been free, but he had never before appreciated the joy of simply walking along the street. He had checked his cash and cards before leaving the station. It was all there. He was free, the sun was shining, and he had close on fifty quid in his pocket. Although he hadn't been banged up for long, he felt as though he had been released back into the world after an absence of weeks, or even months. It reminded him of his first game of football after a long childhood illness. He whistled at an attractive girl who passed him on the street, short red skirt swinging with the rolling motion of her butt. He was free and life was full of possibilities. And he knew exactly where he was heading.

It took Guy a few attempts before he managed to fit his key in the lock and open the door. He staggered along the narrow hallway to the toilet, eventually flinging himself onto his bed to savour the familiar tangy odour of the sheets. He fell asleep almost immediately. It was eight o'clock when he opened his eyes, groggy with alcohol and sleep. At first he thought it was morning and he had been woken by his alarm. It took him a few seconds to realise it was the evening, and his phone had disturbed his sleep. With a groan he turned on his side and waited for it to stop. It was Amy calling, and he didn't intend to have anything more to do with her. After all her protestations of love her behaviour had been unforgivable. She had tried to manoeuvre her way out of trouble by using him as a scapegoat. He wouldn't put it past her to have deliberately set him up. She might have been planning to kill her old man all along and blame it on him. He had seen a film where that had happened. He couldn't remember the ending, but no doubt the dupe had taken the rap for the conniving woman. Amy was clever enough to do that, and he had been stupid enough to fall for it. At twenty-three, he should have known better.

The phone stopped and he breathed a sigh, stretching out in bed, enjoying the comfort. After a moment the phone rang again. And again. Finally he caved in and answered it.

'Guy? Guy? Oh thank God.'

Amy sounded hysterical. The neediness that Guy had once found endearing now infuriated him.

'Where are you? Are you alright?'

'No thanks to you.'

His voice sounded slurred with sleep or alcohol, or both.

'I need to be with you,' she gasped, her voice choked with sobs. 'Come over, please. I'm all on my own.'

She broke down.

'Leave me alone,' he yelled into the phone.

He was startled by the force of his own fury. He

hadn't realised quite how angry and disappointed he had been with her.

'No, no, you don't understand. I'm all on my own here. My poor Mitzi . . .'

For a second he was confused, listening to her babbling incoherently. She was crying so hard that he could barely make any sense of anything she said; something about her dog. He couldn't have cared less about her stupid dog, or her.

'She's gone, she's gone,' she kept repeating.

Clearly she was more upset about losing her bloody dog than about the death of her husband. He wondered how she would react if anything happened to him, once she tired of his attentions.

'Get off my case, you bitch. Don't call me again. Don't ever call me again.'

He hung up and chucked the phone on the bed. Generally useless at remembering what anyone told him, he couldn't forget what the inspector had said. Silently he mouthed the words to himself.

'Mrs Henshaw doesn't see things as you do. . . . Amy Henshaw made a statement accusing you of murdering her husband.'

A moment later the phone started its shrill summons again. Guy rolled out of bed clutching it.

'It's over between us. Get the message and stay the fuck out of my life. I don't know what the hell

I was doing with you in the first place. Leave me alone you sad old cow!'

Switching the phone off and throwing it across the room, he rolled over and went back to sleep.

CHAPTER 43

Like Sam, the sergeant Geraldine had worked with in Kent had been repulsed by corpses, but Ian had made a far better job of covering up his discomfort. Even so, he had frequently paled when confronted with a cadaver and had even on occasion rushed from the room when the victim's appearance was particularly gruesome. Geraldine smiled as she thought about her ex-colleague.

'I don't know what's so funny,' Sam grumbled.

Accustomed to her colleague's irritable mood when they were about to view a body, Geraldine no longer made any attempt to distract her young colleague by talking in the car on the way to the morgue.

Geraldine had never understood how she retained her own composure so easily, but she had always viewed dead bodies as no more than pieces of evidence in the jigsaw of a case. As her first detective inspector had impressed upon her, in a murder enquiry the dead were vital. Several officers had exchanged smiles at his inept turn of phrase.

'Is something amusing you, Geraldine?' he had demanded, turning on her like a predator.

'No, sir.'

An arrogant man, patronising towards his team, he had taken every opportunity to undermine the female officers in particular.

'I hope you're not going to pass out on us,' he had said sharply, the first time he and Geraldine visited the morgue together. 'We've got no room for weakness here.'

Concealing her indignation, she had entered the examination room determined not to react to the body. To display even a flicker of an eyelid might be interpreted as a sign of feminine weakness. But she had felt only curiosity on seeing the corpse.

They drove to the morgue in silence and entered the cold corridor where Miles was waiting for them. With lanky frame and large grinning teeth, his gloves and apron stained with blood, he looked like a character out of a horror movie as he turned and led them to where the victim lay spread-eagled on the table.

'Here he is,' he said cheerfully.

He caught sight of Sam's expression, and his smile faded.

'Are you alright?'

Sam nodded.

'She's fine,' Geraldine reassured him, glancing at Sam whose face had gone white.

'I'm fine,' Sam echoed weakly.
'Good, then let's crack on.'

Miles turned his attention to the body.
'I gather there was no identification on him?'
'We're working on that,' Geraldine replied.
'Hmm. Well, he was in his late seventies, I'd say, not very well nourished, and he had a variety of health issues going on. He was small, not much over five foot, and had advanced arthritis and was developing scoliosis of the spine giving his shoulders this hunched appearance. He suffered a coronary some years ago, but he was basically healthy.'
'Sounds like it,' Sam muttered.
'What I mean to say is, he didn't die of natural causes.'
'People fished out of the canal generally don't.'

Geraldine threw Sam a cautionary glance, vexed by her surliness. No one liked to see dead bodies, but there was no need to antagonise Miles. It wasn't his fault the old man was dead. It was important the pathologist remained committed to helping them. Any tiny piece of information he could provide might prove crucial in solving the case. Without his full co-operation they might only hear the minimum facts of the examination, and Geraldine wanted more than that. She wanted Miles to feel comfortable enough to share his gut reaction with them.

* * *

'As you can see, the method of killing was the same as that used in the Henshaw and Corless cases.'

Gazing down at the cadaver, its skin hideously wrinkled and discoloured, Geraldine could distinguish little similarity between the other two bodies and this one. They could have belonged to different species. The pathologist swept the victim's hair aside to reveal an ugly gash on the side of his head, alongside a large area of bruising.

'He was hit on the left side of his head, a severe blow which probably knocked him out, and almost certainly killed him.'

'So it might not have knocked him out but—' Sam had barely begun to speak when Geraldine interrupted her.

'Go on, Miles.'

Sam scowled and fell silent.

'He was hit here,' he indicated the victim's genitalia, 'in exactly the same way as your earlier victims.'

'So this was the same killer?'

'I'd say so, yes.'

'Is there any doubt about it?' Geraldine pressed him.

'No. I'd say not. Of course I can't be a hundred per cent sure but I'd say there's no doubt really that the same person committed all three murders, unless the killers were communicating with each other about their methods. It's an identical murder.'

'But very different victims.'

Geraldine gazed at the grotesque cadaver. It looked like a monstrous frog with its skinny legs and bloated torso.

Miles shrugged.

'That consideration doesn't really fall within my remit. All I can tell you is that the three bodies have been killed in the same manner. That the three murders were carried out by the same hand is a matter on which you can speculate, but it's not a matter of scientific interest. He hadn't eaten since around midday but had been drinking shortly before he died, beer from the look and smell of it. Not an excessive amount but he might have been intoxicated, depending on his tolerance. Like I said, he's a small man.'

'Did you find any female DNA on this victim?' Geraldine wanted to know.

'For goodness sake,' Sam said before the pathologist had a chance to reply. 'Look at him. He was hardly likely to be gallivanting around with women. He could barely stand up on those.'

She gestured at the dead man's frail legs. Miles inclined his head at Geraldine, pointedly ignoring Sam's outburst.

'I believe so.'

'How do you mean?'

'Wouldn't it have all been washed away in the water?' Sam asked.

* * *

He shook his head impatiently.

'Not necessarily. But this victim hadn't engaged in pre-mortem sexual intercourse.'

They all glanced down at the shrivelled body, none of them voicing their thoughts.

'So it's not the same as Patrick and George at all,' Sam said.

'The cause of death was the same. The disposal of the body was different in each case. As for the motive – well, as I say, that's not for me to determine.'

'So what about the DNA?' Geraldine prompted him.

'Yes, I was coming to that. We found a strand of hair entangled in the victim's watch strap.'

'A shoulder-length dark hair?' Sam said, her voice raised in excitement.

'No, it was a shoulder-length blonde hair.'

Geraldine and Sam looked at one another in surprise.

'Do you mean to say there are two women committing these murders?' Sam asked.

'That doesn't necessarily follow,' Geraldine pointed out, but she couldn't conceal her dismay at this new twist in the case.

It was all becoming disturbingly complicated.

CHAPTER 44

'Still no identification for the old man?' Reg asked. 'It's over four hours since he was found.'

'Four hours since he was found, but around sixteen hours since he was killed,' Sam replied. 'He was in the water all night but no one's reported him missing yet.'

'It's only one night,' the detective chief inspector pointed out. 'I don't suppose anyone's noticed yet.'

'But an old bloke like that,' Sam protested. 'Wasn't there anyone keeping an eye out for him? You'd think someone would have noticed when he didn't go home last night.'

'The divers are still out looking in case a wallet fell out when he went in the water, but they haven't found anything yet,' Geraldine told the detective chief inspector.

He gave her a worried frown.

'It's an expensive business searching underwater,' he said tetchily. 'And they could look for days without results if the contents of his pockets were carried further along with the current, or buried in sludge at the bottom. He was in the water overnight. Is it worth continuing with the search, I wonder? For all we know, this could have been a mugging that went wrong and all his possessions might have been taken before he went in the water. He wasn't wearing a watch, was he?'

Geraldine realised the detective chief inspector was posing a series of rhetorical questions. It was hardly worth pointing out that muggers didn't normally mutilate their victims' genitals.

'I'm going to call off the search,' Reg said, suddenly decisive, then hesitated. 'We'll give it another twenty-four hours and then call it a day.'

'Twenty-four hours is generally called a day,' Sam pointed out with a grin.

Reg glared at the sergeant as he left the room and Geraldine couldn't help laughing.

Later that morning a woman telephoned the station to report that her neighbour was missing. He was an elderly gentleman, she said, very small and quiet. Geraldine had nothing pressing on her desk so she went to question the concerned neighbour herself.

'It's probably nothing,' she told the duty sergeant as she left the station, 'but I might as well go and check it out, seeing as this is the only missing person whose description might possibly match the body that was fished out of the canal.'

* * *

Dudley Court was a depressing development of run-down concrete blocks off Dartmouth Park Road; a row of identical ugly constructions put up when high rise flats were seen as the answer to a spiralling housing shortage. One wilting tree grew in the corner of the estate in apologetic recognition that this dreary artificial zone was more than a hideous vision of the future, it was a fragment of a green planet. Having tracked down the right block in a maze of streets around Archway, Geraldine gave the foul-smelling lift a miss and chose instead to trudge up the stairs to look for Mrs Edie Foster on the third floor.

The interior of the block was as miserable as its façade, and she restrained a grimace at the greasy feel of the bell. A dog began yapping hysterically on the other side of the door while she waited. The door was opened by a rotund woman in her seventies who peered anxiously at Geraldine through thick lensed spectacles before issuing a shrill command to 'Get back in here,' as a bedraggled Yorkshire terrier rushed out to snuffle wetly at her ankles. The little terrier continued sniffing at Geraldine's feet, its short tail wagging with excitement. The woman lunged forward and made a grab for the dog which slipped around behind Geraldine's legs, growling softly. Geraldine held out her warrant card to introduce herself.

'Come on in, then,' the woman said, with a hurried glance along the corridor. 'Only we're not supposed to keep pets here. Everyone does of course, but it's best not to advertise the fact. It's against the rules – oh!'

She broke off, remembering who she was talking to.

'It's not like it's against the law,' she added, flustered, 'it's just the rules. But as long as he's quiet – anyway, Toby's not mine, he belongs to Maurice next door, my neighbour that's gone missing. I phoned you about it. That is why you're here, isn't it?'

As she followed Mrs Foster into a tiny living room, Geraldine reassured her that she wasn't calling about the dog, but in response to Mrs Foster's report about her neighbour.

'It's his dog,' the old woman repeated. 'And that's how I discovered he was missing. Poor Toby.'

She leant down to pat the little creature's head and the dog twisted round to lick her fingers.

'Toby never makes a sound, he's a good boy, aren't you, Toby? Yes, you are. But he's been making a terrible racket all day, howling and yelping, so I knew something was up. I left it as long as I could bear it and then I went in to have a look, he was making such a din. I just knew something had happened.'

'How did you get in?'

'Me and Maurice, we've got the keys to each other's flats. We're not close, nothing like that – he's a funny man, very private, very shy. But we keep each other's keys, just in case. It's so easy to lock yourself out, isn't it? We've done it a few times, both of us, so it's handy to be able to knock next door for the spare.'

Geraldine waited a moment while Mrs Foster patted the dog's head and fussed over him.

'What happened?'

'I don't know. That's why I phoned you people.'

The old woman's eyes opened wide as she described how she had gone in next door fully expecting to find her neighbour had passed away.

'To tell you the truth, I was that relieved he wasn't there, dead or dying. I was afraid I'd find him on the floor, you know, in a pool of blood or something, like you see on the telly. I mean, it could have been an intruder, couldn't it? But he wasn't there, only poor Toby going crazy all on his own. That's how I knew something was wrong because Maurice would never have left Toby like that without food or water. Not in a million years. He loves Toby, doesn't he? Yes he does.'

She bent forward to fondle the dog again.

Geraldine could have shown the old woman a photo of the body, but she decided not to tell the old woman the police suspected Maurice had been pulled out of the canal. Instead she asked for the key to the flat next door, hoping to find a photograph as a means of establishing whether the body found in the canal was indeed Maurice.

'Do you think I ought to let you in there?'

'I can call the station to send a couple of officers to break the door down if you prefer.'

'Oh dear no. Wait a minute then, while I fetch the key.'

It was a depressing job searching the musty flat next door: a free standing wooden wardrobe stuffed with cardigans and jumpers, grimy bathroom, kitchen smelling of dog food, living room covered in a fine film of dust. She wished she had brought Sam with her for company. Hidden in a drawer she found proof of the dead man's identity: his face gazing stoically up at her from a small framed photograph. She found no evidence of alcohol anywhere in the flat.

CHAPTER 45

When she called the police station on Friday morning Amy learned from the desk sergeant that Guy had been released the previous day. Although pleased, she was nevertheless upset that he hadn't been in touch with her as soon as he had left the police station. She went straight home to check the answer phone machine on her landline, though Guy always called her mobile. There were no messages. Puzzled, she keyed in his number on her mobile.

'This is Guy. I can't speak right now. Leave a message and I'll get back to you.'

The normality of his tone was reassuring, but she needed to know where he was. She punched the number in again and then again, although it was pointless; each time she heard the same message after the beep.

'Where are you?' she asked out loud.

With gnawing unease she ran out to her car and drove to Guy's flat. If he was there she should be with him, like old times, before all the problems that had beset them since Patrick's death. She drove fast, swearing at a red light, unbearably impatient now that she had decided to go to him. She knew that once he saw her, he would stop being angry with her.

The door creaked open. A wiry little man peered at her from beneath a straw coloured fringe.

'I'm looking for Guy,' she blurted out.

'You're looking for a guy?' the man repeated.

He looked her up and down before shaking his head. He looked wary.

'Sorry, love, not interested.'

Amy felt her face burn.

'No, you don't understand.'

She felt close to tears.

'I'm looking for someone whose name is Guy. He lives here.'

'Alright, love, keep your hair on. I was pulling your leg. I can see you're not on the game, at your age. Now, who was it you were after?'

Forcing herself to speak calmly, Amy repeated that she was looking for Guy.

'He's a friend of mine, a close friend.'

The man shook his head.

'Sorry, love, you're too late.'

'Too late? What do you mean? Where's Guy?'

She should have realised something terrible had happened when he hadn't been in touch or answered his phone.

* * *

'He's not here any more. He moved out,' the man explained.

He started to close the door.

'Moved out?'

'Yes. He'd been in some sort of trouble with the police from what I heard. Anyway, he scarpered without giving notice. Left a load of gear here as well. I only moved in here yesterday. It was all a bit sudden, but the room came up and I was desperate and here I am. So it worked out well in the end.'

He grinned at her.

'You missed him. Isn't that just typical?'

'Where did he go?'

'How would I know? I'd have thought you'd know that, seeing as you're close friends.'

He spoke the last two words with a sneer and Amy felt herself blush.

As the door shut, she stared at the familiar peeling paintwork on the front door, fighting back tears of frustration. A horrible sick feeling clutched at her guts, like a parasite sucking her energy. Panicking, she drove home and ran through the house to Patrick's study. She hesitated before opening the door to what had been her husband's private space. She hadn't been in there since his death, had hardly ever gone in there when he was alive. Only the police had been there, looking through his papers. Entering, she thought she caught a faint whiff of Patrick's aftershave and felt the breath catch at the back of her throat. She wanted to be out of there as quickly as possible.

To her relief she discovered the household files all neatly organised and she found what she wanted in a box file labelled Maintenance: a series of invoices from Winhold and Co, the firm which had constructed their conservatory three years earlier. Pleased that Patrick had kept the relevant documents, she jotted down the address and phone number of the firm which employed Guy. He might want to avoid her after all that had happened, but she knew he would change his attitude once he saw her again. He had to. He couldn't abandon her now.

To begin with, the receptionist at the building firm where Guy worked didn't understand Amy's request. Her pencilled eyebrows frowned elegantly.

'If you have a complaint against one of our employees, it's Mr Furrows you need to speak to. He's out on a job at the moment but he should be in later. If you'd like to leave your number, I'll see he gets the message—'

Amy interrupted impatiently to explain that she didn't want to lodge a complaint against Guy. She just needed to speak to him.

The receptionist looked edgy. Tapping the end of her biro on her cluttered desk, she gave a forced smile.

'I'm afraid we don't give out personal details of our employees to—'

She paused and stared at Amy, one eyebrow raised as though questioning her motives for wanting to know the whereabouts of the young builder.

'He's a friend . . .' Amy stammered, 'I just need to see him. Surely there's no reason why you can't tell me where he's working. I'm not asking for private information. He's – he's a family friend.'

The receptionist tapped her biro more rapidly on the table and here eyes flicked sideways to a white board on the wall. Amy followed her gaze.

'It's not really for me to deal with this – if you can wait until Mr Furrows comes in . . .'

Amy adopted an authoritative tone with the young woman.

'I'm afraid this can't wait.'

'I'm sorry, madam, but I really have to check with Mr Furrows. I can try and contact him?'

As the receptionist turned to her phone Amy glanced over at the white board, scanning down a list of names until she saw Barrett, the third name under a heading White House Hotel. Without another word she turned and hurried away.

Guy cringed when he saw Amy walk through the door. For an instant he considered blanking her, but he knew he could never carry it off. She might get hysterical, which would be even more embarrassing than if he just talked to her. He would get rid of her as quickly as he could and then wing it with his workmates; he would never live it down if they discovered the truth. He was rehearsing what he was going to say when Amy rushed at him, tears in her eyes. His fleeting sympathy was choked by anger that she had tracked him down to confront him in front of his mates.

She looked a sight, her eyes puffy, her hair a mess; even her lipstick looked ugly. She seemed to have aged in the few days since he had seen her. He couldn't believe he had once been so infatuated with her.

'Guy!'

She made no attempt to speak quietly so he seized her by the elbow and propelled her back through the open doorway into the hotel foyer where he led her into a shadowy corner, away from public scrunity.

'What the hell are you doing here?'

'I came to see you—'

Her voice wavered.

'Keep it down, will you? No one else needs to hear this.'

Through the open door, Guy thought he heard his mates laughing and felt his temper rise. She was lucky they were in public or he would have been tempted to teach her a lesson for showing him up like this.

* * *

At first Amy refused to believe he didn't want anything more to do with her.

'It'll die down,' she protested. 'All this fuss with the police. They can't keep hassling us forever. It'll be alright. You'll see. You're not even a suspect any more. We can go back to how we were . . .'

'No,' he assured her, speaking as firmly as he could in a low undertone. 'Things will never go back to how they were. It's over, Amy.'

'You can't mean that.'

He replied in a furious whisper.

'Leave me alone, will you? Don't you get it, I'm sick of you, sick of the whole damn business.'

'But you and me, we're—'

She reached out and put her hand on his arm. Guy stepped back but she clung on, her long nails clutching at his sleeve. He looked at the bright red varnish that had once seemed so glamorous, and felt sick.

'There is no you and me,' he hissed. 'What the hell are you thinking?'

He glanced over his shoulder to check no one was watching.

'You told the police *I* was responsible for what happened to your old man,' he reminded her. 'How the hell could there be anything between us after that? I can't trust you any more. I can't stand the sight of you, not after what you put me through. Just get lost will you, I don't want to see you again.'

* * *

Amy gave a low whimper, like a small dog. He pulled away from her, vexed that she was making such a fool of herself. All he wanted to do was forget the whole horrible affair.

'I don't want to see you again,' he repeated.

He turned and marched off without a backward glance.

CHAPTER 46

Maurice Bradshaw had never married. His only sibling had emigrated to Australia over thirty years earlier. A relative was traced living in South London, the grandson of a cousin who had moved to Scotland. The local force sent an officer round to notify him, and the young man reluctantly agreed to identify the body. Geraldine decided to go along and question him, hoping to discover a connection between Maurice and at least one of the other victims, other than the identical manner in which they had been killed. But she didn't feel very optimistic about the outcome. Maurice clearly couldn't afford to patronise a restaurant like Mireille, and there was no evidence of gambling in his meagre financial arrangements.

Maurice's distant relative, Edgar Hilton, turned out to be a young man in his twenties, sharply dressed in a pin-striped suit, brilliant white shirt and no tie. His shoes, which were highly polished, beat out a loud rhythm on the floor as he followed close on Geraldine's heels to where the old man's small body lay almost hidden. Only a tiny head with a peaked nose showed above the covering, his face ashen, as though carved in marble. The young man glanced down for a second before turning away with a perfunctory nod, his face twisted in a grimace.

'Yes, that's him alright. That's Uncle Maurice.'

A gold ring glittered on his little finger as he ran a hand through his cropped dark hair.

'Jesus, I hardly recognised him. He looks well weird. What the hell happened to him?'

'He was found in the canal.'

'He drowned?'

'Something like that.'

Leaving the viewing room, Geraldine steered the young man towards a row of chairs, asking if he would sit down for a moment to answer a few questions. Once they were seated she told him that although his uncle had been found in the canal, he hadn't actually drowned. She felt a flicker of anger when the young man didn't seem in the slightest bit curious.

'He's more of a distant cousin of some sort, not really an uncle,' he explained, as though that made a difference.

He looked interested for the first time when Geraldine explained that his relative had been murdered.

'Why? I mean, who on earth would want to kill

CHAPTER 47

›ugh she had been waiting for him to
:, Sam entered the office shortly after
went out.
he?'

glanced up from her screen, frowning.
Bradshaw. What do we know about
·epeated, a hint of impatience in her

turned to face the sergeant who had
the edge of Nick's chair and was
/ard, her hands palm down on her
.g intently at Geraldine. An enthusi-
ıt was more useful than any online
Geraldine had read all the reports
:ral times over. She could have recited
he witness statements by heart but
information so well was pointless if
ave the right information. She focused
on Sam.

ıo he is. The answer's in the question.
Maurice Bradshaw.'

him? He was completely harmless, and it's not like he had money or anything. According to my mother, he was as poor as a church mouse, just a poor old bloke living on his own. Oh well, takes all sorts I suppose. But bloody hell, he must have been some sick bastard to do away with poor old Uncle Maurice.'

When Geraldine was silent, he shrugged and stood up.

'That's it, then, is it? I can go now? Only I really do have to get back to work.'

Geraldine nodded and he thanked her glibly for letting him know about the death.

'Will you keep us posted? I mean, when you find out who did it. I think my mother would like to know it's all been sorted out. She was quite upset when she heard he was dead. Seems she was quite fond of the old bloke, even though we didn't see him any more. I mean, he's still family, and all that. I think she'd like to know that you got the bastard who mugged him.'

Geraldine assured him they would be in touch as soon as they had any news.

At the door Edgar half turned, his slender fingers on the handle.

'We can leave it to you to sort out the funeral and all that, can't we? I mean, my parents are in Scotland. I would see to it myself but I've got a lot on right now and I can't really commit myself without knowing what's involved. In any case,' he went on apologetically, 'I hardly knew my uncle, not really. I haven't seen him in years. He used to come over to us for Christmas when I was a kid but then my parents moved to Edinburgh so I started going up there for Christmas, and we lost touch with Uncle Maurice. You know how it is.'

Geraldine smiled sadly at him.

'Yes, I know how it is.'

Discussing the gist of the case with Nick, Geraldine couldn't hide her dismay at the fact that they seemed to be going backwards with the investigation since the discovery of a third victim. Geraldine had dealt with murderers who knew their victims, and with rarer instances of psychopaths who killed random strangers, but she hadn't often come across killers who combined the two. It didn't make sense. Nick leaned back in his chair, his lopsided grin suggesting that he was amused by her frustration.

'That's where you're going wrong,' he told her. 'You can't seriously expect any of this to make sense. Remember you're dealing with a psycho. He's insane. You're never going to figure out what a nut job is thinking.'

'We have to try,'

'That's the job of the profilers. It's nothing more than stating the obvious. Think about it. The profiler tells you to look for some poor misunderstood damaged bloke with an uncontrollable

desire to commit a c
to find the bastard a
out to be someone
uncontrollable desir
the rest of it, at whic
of the corner where
text books while we'v
and says "I told you

Nick shook his head,
as a waste of time,
She had been throug
colleagues. No one
her conviction that
killer was an essenti
down murderers. T
ator was sending th

'Don't worry,' Ni
a mistake sooner o

Geraldine nodded
right, and that th
murdered Henshav
Bradshaw before th
They were three de
had stumbled on s
alleys.

As th
leav
Nic

'So who

'What?'

Geraldine

'Maurice
him?' Sam
voice.

Geraldine
perched o
leaning for
knees, stari
astic sergea
information
anyway, sev
chunks of
knowing th
they didn't
her attentio

'We know w
His name's

'Yes, but who *is* he? I mean, we know how Henshaw and Corless are connected. Obviously someone wanted them both out of the way, as an act of revenge or to get their hands on the restaurant, or something. That much makes some sort of sense.'

'If you say so.'

Geraldine sighed. She wasn't sure any of it made any sense, even if it turned out to be true that the first two murders had been committed for the sake of a business, however successful it was. The killer must have known the two restaurant owners and she was confident they would uncover the motive in time, but Bradshaw was a conundrum. He seemed to have been such an innocuous little man, leading such an inoffensive life. Geraldine wondered if there was anything that could link him to the other two victims, and hence to the killer. Speculation was futile. She needed to find out more about the third victim.

She set Sam the lengthy task of trawling through the statements again to look for inconsistencies, anything that didn't ring true. Geraldine had already been through the whole lot, but a fresh pair of eyes might spot something she had missed. Geraldine drove to Archway and stood for a moment gazing at the dingy block of flats where Bradshaw had lived. She waited outside the depressing building but no one went in or out so, after a brief hesitation, she got back in her car and headed for the nearest station, thinking. According to the pathologist, Bradshaw had been drinking beer within an hour or two of his death, but there was none in the flat, and no empty beer bottles or cans in the crammed rubbish bin which hadn't been emptied since his death. Unless someone else had been round and taken the empty bottles or cans away at the time, which seemed unlikely, Bradshaw had not been drinking at home on the night he was murdered. Geraldine wondered where he had been and if he had been drinking alone.

Dudley Court was a few yards along from the junction with Dartmouth Park Road. Bradshaw couldn't have walked far with his arthritic limbs and bent spine so, seeing a bus along the main road, Geraldine followed its route on a hunch. After a while she executed a U-turn and retraced the bus route in the opposite direction. Two miles past the entrance to Bradshaw's side turning she saw a bus stop right outside a pub. She pulled over straight away and parked. It was growing late and the silence was oppressive as she crossed the pavement. As if from nowhere, a gang of youths appeared on a nearby street corner, and stood watching her as she approached the pub. Automatically, she quickened her pace.

The interior of the pub was shabby. Rings glistened on unwiped tables and dust gathered at the foot of the skirting boards as though someone had gone through the motions of sweeping the floor, careless of the outcome. In spite of the uninviting atmosphere, it was surprisingly busy for a weekday evening. Most of the tables were occupied and a few men lounged at the bar. Geraldine showed a photograph of Bradshaw's face to the landlord who shook his head.

'Can't say I recognise him but that's not to say he's never been in. We get all sorts and it gets mobbed, especially when the football's on.'

He sighed, as though customers were an unwelcome imposition.

'Please check again,' Geraldine said. 'I need to know if this man was in here yesterday evening.'

'Sorry, love, I can't help you there. Wednesday was my evening off.'

He turned away and called out.

'Who was behind the bar last night?'

'Angela.'

The landlord half turned and nodded at a short plump barmaid leaning on the bar, chatting with a customer. Angela scrutinised the picture carefully.

'Do you know, I'm not sure,' she said at last. 'Was he in here yesterday? That's a jolly good question.'

She paused. Geraldine waited.

'Yesterday, you say?'

'Yes, yesterday evening.'

'Yesterday evening?' Angela echoed.

Geraldine hid her impatience.

* * *

'That old codger's here all the time,' another barmaid announced, glancing over Angela's shoulder.

'I know that,' Angela conceded. 'But was he here last night? That's what they want to know.'

'Last night?'

The other barmaid looked up at Geraldine, suddenly suspicious.

'Who wants to know?'

'She does. She's police.'

'Flipping heck.'

'Was this gentleman in here last night?' Geraldine asked. 'We need to track his movements, find out who he was drinking with.'

'Oh, that's easy enough,' the second barmaid said. 'He always drinks alone, that one.'

'Was he in here last night?'

The plump barmaid shrugged and turned away, losing interest.

'Last night? He could have been.'

The barmaids' answers were inconclusive, but at least Geraldine had established where Bradshaw habitually drank. It was frustrating that no one could say for sure if they had seen him there the previous evening but it was a fair bet he had been in the bar on the night he was killed, drinking on his own if the barmaids' information was accurate. As she drove home, Geraldine thought about the old man, hunched and misshapen, eking out a solitary existence, travelling two stops on the bus from his lodging to a bar where they took his money without registering his presence, before he caught the bus back to his empty flat. At least his dog had noticed his absence.

CHAPTER 48

More statements had been taken from employees of companies that came into contact with Mireille: food suppliers, employment agencies, laundrettes, even refuse collectors, but no one was able to give any indication as to who might have wanted the two proprietors dead. The detective chief inspector briefly considered making enquiries into rival restaurants, but although criminal action to sabotage Mireille's menu was perhaps credible, a double murder seemed too far-fetched, even without the complication of Bradshaw who had nothing to do with the restaurant, as far as they knew.

The whole investigation was fraught with inconsistencies. Not only was the third victim's involvement an enigma, but different coloured hairs had been found at two of the crime scenes. It was of course possible the different coloured hairs found on Henshaw and Bradshaw came from the same woman, if she had dyed her hair in between the first and the third attack. If the DNA of the blonde hair him? He was completely harmless, and it's not like he had money or anything. According to my mother, he was as poor as a church mouse, just a poor old bloke living on his own. Oh well, takes all sorts I suppose. But bloody hell, he must have been some sick bastard to do away with poor old Uncle Maurice.'

When Geraldine was silent, he shrugged and stood up.

'That's it, then, is it? I can go now? Only I really do have to get back to work.'

Geraldine nodded and he thanked her glibly for letting him know about the death.

'Will you keep us posted? I mean, when you find out who did it. I think my mother would like to know it's all been sorted out. She was quite upset when she heard he was dead. Seems she was quite fond of the old bloke, even though we didn't see him any more. I mean, he's still family, and all that. I think she'd like to know that you got the bastard who mugged him.'

Geraldine assured him they would be in touch as soon as they had any news.

At the door Edgar half turned, his slender fingers on the handle.

'We can leave it to you to sort out the funeral and all that, can't we? I mean, my parents are in Scotland. I would see to it myself but I've got a lot on right now and I can't really commit myself without knowing what's involved. In any case,' he went on apologetically, 'I hardly knew my uncle, not really. I haven't seen him in years. He used to come over to us for Christmas when I was a kid but then my parents moved to Edinburgh so I started going up there for Christmas, and we lost touch with Uncle Maurice. You know how it is.'

Geraldine smiled sadly at him.

'Yes, I know how it is.'

Discussing the gist of the case with Nick, Geraldine couldn't hide her dismay at the fact that they seemed to be going backwards with the investigation since the discovery of a third victim. Geraldine had dealt with murderers who knew their victims, and with rarer instances of psychopaths who killed random strangers, but she hadn't often come across killers who combined the two. It didn't make sense. Nick leaned back in his chair, his lopsided grin suggesting that he was amused by her frustration.

'That's where you're going wrong,' he told her. 'You can't seriously expect any of this to make sense. Remember you're dealing with a psycho. He's insane. You're never going to figure out what a nut job is thinking.'

'We have to try,'

'That's the job of the profilers. It's nothing more than stating the obvious. Think about it. The profiler tells you to look for some poor misunderstood damaged bloke with an uncontrollable desire to commit a crime, we do the donkey work to find the bastard and surprise, surprise, he turns out to be someone with criminal tendencies, an uncontrollable desire to commit a crime, and all the rest of it, at which point the profiler creeps out of the corner where he's been hiding behind his text books while we've been out finding the bastard, and says "I told you so".'

Nick shook his head, dismissing her determination as a waste of time, but Geraldine was adamant. She had been through this same debate with other colleagues. No one had yet been able to shake her conviction that understanding the psyche of a killer was an essential tool in helping them to track down murderers. The trouble was that this predator was sending them mixed messages.

'Don't worry,' Nick reassured her. 'He'll make a mistake sooner or later.'

Geraldine nodded miserably. She hoped he was right, and that they would find whoever had murdered Henshaw, Corless and old Maurice Bradshaw before the killer found another victim. They were three deaths in, and the only clues they had stumbled on so far had led them up blind alleys.

CHAPTER 47

As though she had been waiting for him to leave, Sam entered the office shortly after Nick went out.

'So who is he?'

'What?'

Geraldine glanced up from her screen, frowning.

'Maurice Bradshaw. What do we know about him?' Sam repeated, a hint of impatience in her voice.

Geraldine turned to face the sergeant who had perched on the edge of Nick's chair and was leaning forward, her hands palm down on her knees, staring intently at Geraldine. An enthusiastic sergeant was more useful than any online information. Geraldine had read all the reports anyway, several times over. She could have recited chunks of the witness statements by heart but knowing the information so well was pointless if they didn't have the right information. She focused her attention on Sam.

'We know who he is. The answer's in the question. His name's Maurice Bradshaw.'

'Yes, but who *is* he? I mean, we know how Henshaw and Corless are connected. Obviously someone wanted them both out of the way, as an act of revenge or to get their hands on the restaurant, or something. That much makes some sort of sense.'

'If you say so.'

Geraldine sighed. She wasn't sure any of it made any sense, even if it turned out to be true that the first two murders had been committed for the sake of a business, however successful it was. The killer must have known the two restaurant owners and she was confident they would uncover the motive in time, but Bradshaw was a conundrum. He seemed to have been such an innocuous little man, leading such an inoffensive life. Geraldine wondered if there was anything that could link him to the other two victims, and hence to the killer. Speculation was futile. She needed to find out more about the third victim.

She set Sam the lengthy task of trawling through the statements again to look for inconsistencies, anything that didn't ring true. Geraldine had already been through the whole lot, but a fresh pair of eyes might spot something she had missed. Geraldine drove to Archway and stood for a moment gazing at the dingy block of flats where Bradshaw had lived. She waited outside the depressing building but no one went in or out so, after a brief hesitation, she got back in her car and headed for the nearest station, thinking. According to the pathologist, Bradshaw had been drinking beer within an hour or two of his death, but there was none in the flat, and no empty beer bottles or cans in the crammed rubbish bin which hadn't been emptied since his death. Unless someone else had been round and taken the empty bottles or cans away at the time, which seemed unlikely, Bradshaw had not been drinking at home on the night he was murdered. Geraldine wondered where he had been and if he had been drinking alone.

Dudley Court was a few yards along from the junction with Dartmouth Park Road. Bradshaw couldn't have walked far with his arthritic limbs and bent spine so, seeing a bus along the main road, Geraldine followed its route on a hunch. After a while she executed a U-turn and retraced the bus route in the opposite direction. Two miles past the entrance to Bradshaw's side turning she saw a bus stop right outside a pub. She pulled over straight away and parked. It was growing late and the silence was oppressive as she crossed the pavement. As if from nowhere, a gang of youths appeared on a nearby street corner, and stood watching her as she approached the pub. Automatically, she quickened her pace.

The interior of the pub was shabby. Rings glistened on unwiped tables and dust gathered at the foot of the skirting boards as though someone had gone through the motions of sweeping the floor, careless of the outcome. In spite of the uninviting atmosphere, it was surprisingly busy for a weekday evening. Most of the tables were occupied and a few men lounged at the bar. Geraldine showed a photograph of Bradshaw's face to the landlord who shook his head.

'Can't say I recognise him but that's not to say he's never been in. We get all sorts and it gets mobbed, especially when the football's on.'

He sighed, as though customers were an unwelcome imposition.

'Please check again,' Geraldine said. 'I need to know if this man was in here yesterday evening.'

'Sorry, love, I can't help you there. Wednesday was my evening off.'

He turned away and called out.

'Who was behind the bar last night?'

'Angela.'

The landlord half turned and nodded at a short plump barmaid leaning on the bar, chatting with a customer. Angela scrutinised the picture carefully.

'Do you know, I'm not sure,' she said at last. 'Was he in here yesterday? That's a jolly good question.'

She paused. Geraldine waited.

'Yesterday, you say?'

'Yes, yesterday evening.'

'Yesterday evening?' Angela echoed.

Geraldine hid her impatience.

* * *

'That old codger's here all the time,' another barmaid announced, glancing over Angela's shoulder.

'I know that,' Angela conceded. 'But was he here last night? That's what they want to know.'

'Last night?'

The other barmaid looked up at Geraldine, suddenly suspicious.

'Who wants to know?'

'She does. She's police.'

'Flipping heck.'

'Was this gentleman in here last night?' Geraldine asked. 'We need to track his movements, find out who he was drinking with.'

'Oh, that's easy enough,' the second barmaid said. 'He always drinks alone, that one.'

'Was he in here last night?'

The plump barmaid shrugged and turned away, losing interest.

'Last night? He could have been.'

The barmaids' answers were inconclusive, but at least Geraldine had established where Bradshaw habitually drank. It was frustrating that no one could say for sure if they had seen him there the previous evening but it was a fair bet he had been in the bar on the night he was killed, drinking on his own if the barmaids' information was accurate. As she drove home, Geraldine thought about the old man, hunched and misshapen, eking out a solitary existence, travelling two stops on the bus from his lodging to a bar where they took his money without registering his presence, before he caught the bus back to his empty flat. At least his dog had noticed his absence.

CHAPTER 48

More statements had been taken from employees of companies that came into contact with Mireille: food suppliers, employment agencies, laundrettes, even refuse collectors, but no one was able to give any indication as to who might have wanted the two proprietors dead. The detective chief inspector briefly considered making enquiries into rival restaurants, but although criminal action to sabotage Mireille's menu was perhaps credible, a double murder seemed too far-fetched, even without the complication of Bradshaw who had nothing to do with the restaurant, as far as they knew.

The whole investigation was fraught with inconsistencies. Not only was the third victim's involvement an enigma, but different coloured hairs had been found at two of the crime scenes. It was of course possible the different coloured hairs found on Henshaw and Bradshaw came from the same woman, if she had dyed her hair in between the first and the third attack. If the DNA of the blonde hair found on Bradshaw's body matched the sample of female DNA found at the scene of Henshaw's murder, the as yet unidentified woman would be placed at the scene of two out of the three murders. A close search might even discover the same DNA at the site where Corless's body had been deposited. That area was still being checked. In the meantime, they were all pinning their hopes on the blonde hair providing them with more information.

Reg veered towards suspecting Corless's young mistress. Desiree was a gold-digger who had embarked on the affair with the intention of getting her hands on his fortune. She had the opportunity, stood to gain a substantial share of his restaurant on his death, and had shoulder-length blonde hair. But the hair found in Henshaw's car was dark and, in any case, Reg agreed with Geraldine that it was a leap to suppose Desiree had killed both men in the vain hope of getting her hands on a share of the restaurant. It didn't add up.

Geraldine was convinced that Desiree had genuinely cared for Corless.

'What if George killed Patrick, for sole ownership of the restaurant, and was then killed in turn by Desiree?' Reg suggested. 'She might have put him up to it. Perhaps it was Desiree, not Amy, who manipulated her lover into committing a murder.'

He rubbed his hands together, warming to his theory.

'George might have told his mistress exactly how he'd killed his business partner, giving her the idea of doing the same to him. It's possible, isn't it?'

He sounded quite animated and Geraldine shook her head cautiously. Reg was, after all, the boss, and she had to be diplomatic, especially when she was sure he was wrong.

'But I don't think we can read too much into the blonde hair,' Reg went on, 'not until we get the results of the DNA test.'

'Amy was blonde,' Sam pointed out, and Reg groaned.

They all agreed the DNA results were crucial. They would be available soon, expedited for the murder team. The discussion was beginning to go round in circles. Until they had more information they could only speculate. Just as Geraldine was about to suggest returning to her desk to double-check Desiree's statement, the door opened and the psychological profiler, Jayne, entered the room, her long skirt sweeping the floor behind her. Geraldine had been disappointed with the profiler's contribution to their last case. Nevertheless, she listened closely as Jayne gave a brief overview of what they had been considering.

'What can you bring to the table, Jayne?' the detective chief inspector asked.

Jayne spoke very slowly.

'One thing we can be sure of is that this is a hate crime. The nature of the injuries tells us that. Whoever killed the two restaurant owners—'

'We've got three victims,' Geraldine corrected her, struggling to control her impatience.

'Whoever committed these murders was making the attacks very personal. Inflicting injuries after death is a different kind of assault to one where the perpetrator just wants to dispatch the victim, to get him or her out of the way as efficiently as possible, without leaving any clues behind. Some murders are really quite functional in that sense, a means to an end, where the victim is killed for his or her money, for example. In this instance the violation of the bodies is probably the killer's end in itself, or why would he hang around to mutilate them, increasing the risk of discovery? There's something going on here, some expression of loathing, a venting of a deep-seated anger.'

'You mean the killer didn't like his victims?' Sam asked.

She turned her head to wink at Geraldine, who ignored the signal. Geraldine had very little respect for the profiler, but she did her best to hide her disdain, and her irritation that Reg set so much store by what Jayne said. The profiler was only doing her job.

'I think the killer is driven by more than mere dislike,' Jayne replied evenly.

'We wouldn't have thought of that, would we?'
Sam appealed to Geraldine who hesitated, tempted to support her sergeant in disparaging the profiler. Instead, she deflected the conversation to a new topic.

'Do you think the killer's a male then?' she asked.
It was a straightforward question, but Jayne looked unexpectedly flustered. Her naturally pinkish complexion turned deeper red as though she suspected Geraldine might be intending to catch her out.
'That's a tricky one—' she hedged. 'Was there anything at the scene to suggest the killer could have been a woman?'
Reg explained about the DNA found on Patrick's body.
'Flecks of skin on his cheeks and under his fingernails, suggesting defence wounds or at least close contact of some kind, and evidence of sexual activity shortly before he died, although that wasn't conclusive because of his injuries.'
Jayne nodded.
'In the light of that, we had more or less decided we were probably looking for a woman. And there's more, but also inconclusive, confusing even,' he added with a sigh.

Geraldine explained about the hair found at two of the scenes.
'So it looks rather like two women might have

been involved, one dark-haired, one blonde, yet the injuries are virtually identical, and singular.'

Jayne shook her curly head. 'That doesn't rule out one killer. The hair evidence could easily be misleading. The woman – if it was a woman – might have dyed her hair.'

They proceeded to discuss the third victim, who didn't seem to have any connection to Henshaw and Corless.

'Let's assume for now that the first two men had some sort of connection to the killer,' Jayne said. 'Having killed twice might have released some impulse in the killer who then went on to attack again, perhaps even selecting the next victim at random.'

'Bradshaw was an easy target,' Sam agreed, persuaded by the sense the profiler was making.

'Perhaps the killer gave in to some long suppressed urge—' Geraldine said.

'And having started found himself, or herself, compelled to kill again,' Jayne finished the thought.

No one put into words the obvious conclusion that they were dealing with a serial killer. Once the desire to kill had been triggered, the murderer might be unable to stop.

CHAPTER 49

Given her reluctance to view cadavers, Sam was surprisingly keen to accompany Geraldine to the morgue again.

'It gets easier, doesn't it?' she asked as they donned their protective clothing.

Geraldine nodded as she dabbed underneath her nostrils with a small tube of Vic. The pungent smell helped to mask the stench. For her, bodies had always held a clinical fascination. She had never felt in the slightest bit queasy until she had seen Corless. That had been an aberration.

The pathologist had confirmed what they could see for themselves, that the third victim had been mutilated in the same way as the other two bodies. The gruesome details had not yet been revealed to the press and the singular nature of the fatal assaults left the police in no doubt that they were looking for a serial killer. Although they had several suspects for the murders of Henshaw and Corless, Bradshaw was another matter altogether. With no apparent link between the first two victims and the third, it appeared the killer was extending the area of his or her attacks, possibly settling old scores. A team of constables were busy checking into Bradshaw's history. So far they hadn't found anything even faintly interesting.

The long blonde hair found on Bradshaw's body had been sent off for analysis. Its owner had to be the killer or else a key witness. The results of the DNA testing hadn't yet arrived but the pathologist was able to tell them that evidence of bleach suggested the owner wasn't originally blonde. That meant the blonde woman might easily be the same woman whose dark hairs had been discovered in Henshaw's car. If that turned out to be the case, that same woman would be implicated in the murders, even if she wasn't actually responsible for them. They had to find her.

While they waited for the all-important results, Geraldine decided to look into the woman whose DNA appeared to have been found on Henshaw's body, the woman who had been in prison for twenty years. Arriving back at the station she joined Sam for a rushed coffee in the noisy canteen before settling down to work.

'Aren't you having lunch?' Sam asked, seizing on a jacket potato. 'I'm starving.'

Geraldine shook her head. She wasn't hungry. After a hurried coffee she returned to her office to look up Linda Harrison, the female prisoner who had been locked up for murder twenty years earlier – whose name had mysteriously turned up again in connection with the current investigation when her DNA had appeared on a murder victim.

In her mug shots, Linda looked rough. Her dark hair was matted, as though it hadn't been combed for weeks, her lips hung slightly open in a slack snarl, and her eyes bored through the screen, seeming to follow Geraldine when she shifted her position. But more striking than signs of neglect in her appearance was the coldness of her eyes. She looked like a woman who had given up on life. Geraldine stared back, trying to fathom the strange expression on the woman's face, almost triumphant.

Geraldine printed out the image and went back to the canteen. Sam had gone. Geraldine found her deep in conversation with a female constable in a corner of the incident room. The two fell silent when Geraldine joined them. She felt as though she was intruding on a private conversation.

'What's going on?'

'Nothing,' the constable muttered.

Sam was more forthcoming.

'We're talking about Nick Williams,' she replied in an undertone.

'Sam,' the constable hissed.

'It's OK,' Sam reassured her colleague. 'Geraldine won't say anything.'

'Then perhaps you'd better not tell me,' Geraldine retorted.

She didn't like secret gossiping in corners.

Dragging Sam away from her conversation, she showed her Linda Harrison's picture. Sam glanced at the grainy image and shook her head.

'No, I can't say I recognise her, but the trial was a bit before my time! All the same, there is something vaguely familiar about her. It's odd, but I could swear she reminds me of someone. No, it's gone. But I could have sworn I saw her picture recently.'

Geraldine returned to her desk, puzzled.

'Something up?' Nick asked, leaning back in his chair to indicate a readiness to converse.

Nick listened to her account of Linda Harrison being linked to the crime scene, despite being incarcerated.

'She couldn't have been there.'

'Yes, I know that, but how do you explain her DNA being found at the crime scene?'

'Parole?'

'None.'

'Did she have an identical twin? It has been known.'

'She had one sister who died thirty years ago.'

'How about a daughter then? Can't DNA be strikingly similar in some cases?'

'She didn't have any children.'

Nick gave a sympathetic grin.

'I see your problem.'

Geraldine wondered what Sam and the constable had been saying about him. He struck her as committed and professional.

'The funny thing is,' she went on, 'I don't know what it is, but there's something about her that Sam found familiar.'

'Did she recognise her?'

Geraldine shrugged.

'Kind of. But not really—'

Nick nodded.

'I've had that exact same sensation with offenders in high profile cases years back. And it must've been a very serious crime if she got life.'

Geraldine nodded.

'So twenty years ago this woman's face would have been all over the press, in the papers, on the news. Seeing her picture probably triggered Sam's memory of what she saw when the case came up all those years ago. The thing is, these cases can make a huge impression once the media get hold of them.'

Overlooking the fact that Sam would have been about five at the time Linda Harrison was convicted, Nick turned back to his desk with an air of finality, as though he had cleared up Geraldine's problem. She considered what he had said. Linda had no children. All the facts indicated that Nick's theory must be right. Sam's mind was playing tricks on her, throwing up an image from the past as though she had seen it only yesterday. With a sigh she filed the printout of Linda Harrison's face and went to find out what the constables' research into Bradshaw had thrown up. There must have been more to his existence than his shabby flat, his dog, and his occasional trips to the pub.

CHAPTER 50

Removing her long blonde wig, she shook her own hair free as she kicked off her outdoor shoes and placed them neatly, side by side, on the rack by the door. Wearing her indoor shoes, she went to the bedroom to put her wig away. Her head felt light without it, as though she was floating. She liked the strange empty feeling in her brain. Remembering the pills her doctor had given her, she smiled. Life was too difficult to face with a clear head. Better to be cushioned from it, unable to think about anything. She had already had her medication for the day but she swallowed just one more pill, knowing they were good for her. The stillness calmed her. Nothing disturbed the order of her rooms. Everything remained in position, precisely where she had placed it.

Her eyebrows twitched with annoyance as she noticed a picture had shifted so that it no longer hung exactly parallel to the wall. She reached forward and gave it a little nudge. Straightening up, she stepped away so she could scrutinise it with narrowed eyes until she was satisfied the picture was back where it belonged. She would have to be more careful in future. It must have shifted when she walked past, touching it with her arm without noticing. Unnerved that she had unwittingly displaced the picture, she turned her attention to the rest of the room. She had the same problem with the rug, which had moved a fraction out of place. It was almost brand new, because her dog had pissed on the last one. That was the final straw. She had bought the dog for protection, but the animal had become unbearably unpredictable, jumping up at her with dirty feet and barking. To begin with she had loved it, but in the end she had to get rid of it.

It took her twenty-eight minutes to take all her cutlery out of the drawer, wash and dry it, and replace it tidily in the drawer. Each knife, fork and spoon was stacked tidily in its own compartment, lined up with the rest of the set. It was an uncomplicated part of her daily routine, and necessary. Germs could find their way through the smallest cracks. People picked up all sorts of nasty diseases by eating with cutlery that wasn't clean. As a teenager she had refused to eat out. Even at home she wouldn't touch metal knives and forks, throwing the plastic ones away after one use. Once it occurred to her that she should wash plastic knives and forks before they came in contact with her food, there seemed no point in wasting money on plastic cutlery. So she had to be satisfied with washing all her cutlery regularly. At first she had carried out the task at least five times a day, just to be sure, but she had managed to reduce this to twice a day, along with brushing her teeth. It was important not to let these daily chores take over her life. There were other demands on her time that were equally important.

She finished washing her cutlery and consulted her list. Usually she knew what to do without checking, but her mind wasn't feeling very sharp this morning. It was her day for wiping the paintwork, which she did once a week. It helped keep her mind quiet if everything was clean. She went into the bedroom and sat down for a moment, overwhelmed with tiredness. While she sat, immobile, something stirred right on the periphery of her vision. It was barely a movement, more like a faint twitch of an eyelash but in that still room any activity was impossible to ignore. She folded her damp cloth neatly and hung it on the side of the plastic bucket before standing up and walking across to the window. A tiny creature was wriggling across the window sill. She leaned forward to look at it more closely. It was a round grey speck. As she watched, the mite uncurled and curled up again, to progress slowly across the sill, looking like a minute caterpillar or the larva of a tiny fly. To her surprise, she noticed a second insect, then a third. She fetched a chair and sat beside the window, watching, counting the tiny creatures as they appeared. Small enough to crawl through invisible cracks, they seemed to appear from nowhere, in growing numbers. She counted twelve of them while she sat there in silence, transfixed by the only living creatures visible in the place apart from her. She could scarcely believe what she was seeing.

There was something devastating about their minute crawl into the light. To them one wall must seem like an entire universe. If they only knew what else lay out there, beyond their wit to understand, they would never crawl out of the cracks in the woodwork to make their slow journey across the painted window sill. Had they travelled across it before, or were these pioneers, searching for a new life? Either way, it made no difference. She fetched her cloth and wiped them away. This was her domain. She wouldn't brook any intrusion, however small. Having given the sill and its surrounds a thorough scrub, until some of the paintwork flaked away, she rinsed the cloth, changed the water in the bucket, and prepared to start again. The paintwork still had to be washed down before she could relax. While she worked, she glanced over at the window sill from time to time, checking to see if any more little grubs had surfaced. None did.

When she had finished cleaning she went straight out to buy insect spray. The assistant in the supermarket wasn't helpful when she asked which spray could be guaranteed to eliminate her infestation.

'This should do the trick,' was all he would say. 'Without knowing what the insects are, it's impossible to offer any guarantee. But there shouldn't be a problem.'

She felt like screaming at him, because there already was a problem: there were bugs in her bedroom. Having read all the instructions, she settled on six different sprays, between them claiming to kill all flying and crawling bugs. The insecticides might not be healthy, but at least she knew what she was dealing with. She glanced down the list of contents: Permethrin, Tetramethrin, Cypermethrin, Imiprothrin. She had no idea what any of them were, but they sounded toxic. They all warned that they must be used in a well ventilated area. Of course they would say that, thinking they were being clever. Opening the window would entice more insects to fly in, so she would end up having to buy even more of their products. It was hard to believe most people were stupid enough to fall for that. She saw through it straight away.

She considered trying the insecticides one at a time to discover which worked best. The drawback with that plan was that the sixth one might be the most effective at eliminating her particular infestation, and it would take her nearly a week to reach it. There was no guarantee any of the sprays would work for the bugs she had found earlier in which case she would have to contact the pest control people who would tramp through her bedroom in their outdoor shoes, spreading dirt and germs. Rather than risk that, she decided to spray all six insecticides around the window sill and hope at least one of them worked. Clutching the cans, she went into the bedroom. There were no insects in sight. That made her nervous because she knew they were waiting, out of sight, until she was in bed. As soon as she lay down, they would come back. And when they did, they would hurt her. Unless she stopped them.

CHAPTER 51

Geraldine was only five minutes away from home. Tired and dispirited, all she wanted to do was get in, kick her shoes off, put her feet up and watch some rubbish on television. When she heard the shrilling of her phone she had a horrible presentiment that another body had been discovered. The thought made her feel slightly nauseous. She desperately hoped she was wrong as she drove on, doing her best to ignore the fact that her phone was ringing. Nothing could be so urgent it wouldn't wait for five minutes, but knowing someone was trying to contact her spoiled her anticipation of reaching home at the end of a frustrating day and relaxing with a glass of wine. Closing her front door she went into the living room, reluctantly fished her phone out of her bag and sat on the sofa. She resisted pouring herself a glass before she had found out who had called. Allowing herself to relax would be tempting fate.

It was a pleasant surprise to see the name on the display. Detective Inspector Ted Carter had acted as Geraldine's mentor in Kent when she had been training for promotion to inspector. He had been consistently helpful, an unusually attentive listener. She leaned back on the sofa and was just wondering if it was too late to return Ted's call when he phoned again.

'Geraldine!'

He sounded genuinely pleased to hear her voice and she couldn't help smiling.

'I thought you must be working. How have you been? I hear you're in London now! Is it all bright lights and excitement there?'

Geraldine felt a stab of guilt. Ted was one of the people she had intended to keep in touch with because she genuinely liked him, but time and circumstances had dictated otherwise. Although it worked both ways, he had more of an excuse not to have been in touch as he had family commitments in addition to work.

'So how are you keeping?'

Hearing his familiar voice reminded Geraldine how keen she had been, how hopeful about the future when she was first promoted, as though there was nothing she couldn't achieve. The reality had turned out to be very different.

The initial exchange of greetings over, he explained the reason for his call. He wanted to invite her to his retirement party.

'I daresay you're too busy to come along but—'

'No,' Geraldine interrupted him. 'I'll make the

time. It'll be great to see everyone again. Who else is going to be there?'

Ted mentioned some names. A few were unfamiliar but she recognised most of them from her time spent working on the Kent constabulary.

'And Kathryn said she'll come,' he finished, a hint of triumph in his voice. 'I know she'll be pleased to see you too.'

Geraldine smiled on hearing the name of her former detective chief inspector. When she had first worked for Kathryn Gordon, Geraldine had found the older woman intimidating. Only when the senior officer had fallen ill had the two women begun to form a personal friendship. Geraldine felt another stab of guilt when she remembered her promise to keep in touch with Kathryn when she had retired.

'So you're in the Met now,' Ted said. 'I always knew you'd do well.'

Hearing the smile in his voice, Geraldine tried to ignore the pressure of expectation his words engendered. It was gratifying to know that other people had faith in her ability, but she was afraid of letting everyone down. She almost launched into a diatribe about the disastrous case she was currently working on, getting nowhere as they investigated a growing body count. Nothing made sense. But there was no point concerning him with the details. He would only tell her to hang on, they'd get a result in the end. What else could he say? Only the same useless platitudes she would offer him if it was the other way round. Her problems were of no consequence to an older colleague on the point of retiring.

'I'll put the date in my diary straight away,' she said cheerily.

'We're meeting about eight but it's an informal gathering, no speeches and all that, so just come along when you can. You won't miss anything if you're not there on the dot.'

That was what everyone said, *no speeches, no presentations, no fuss*. She would insist on that herself when the time came and her wishes would be ignored, just as Ted's colleagues would take no notice of his request that nothing be said on the occasion of his retirement after a lifetime on the force.

'Sounds perfect.'

It would certainly be good to see Ted and Kathryn again. She expected to see her former sergeant, Ian, there as well although Ted hadn't mentioned his name. Geraldine could count the number of people she had felt close to in her life on the fingers of one hand. Ian Peterson was one of them. They had worked together on a number of cases and she still missed working with him. The call ended, Geraldine went into the kitchen to fix herself something to eat.

* * *

Talking to Ted had reminded her how readily she had once trusted her instincts about people. Somehow the more experienced she became, the less confident she felt. Sitting down to eat in front of the television, she found her attention wandering from one of her favourite comedy shows; intermittently she was aware of the audience roaring with laughter but she missed the jokes as she reviewed her gut feeling about the suspects in her current case.

She had never believed Guy had killed Henshaw, let alone Corless, and now they knew Guy was out of the frame. Amy and Amanda Corless seemed equally unlikely to have killed each other's husbands. Even if it had been credible to begin with, Sam's desperate suggestion that the two women might be jointly culpable, acting out a pact to despatch their husbands, was completely discredited by the discovery of old Bradshaw's body. Not only had Geraldine doubted that either of the women were in any way involved in the murders, she hadn't thought any of the suspects guilty yet. How much time and energy they would have saved if the investigation had simply followed her hunches. But so far her instincts had merely rejected all the suspects they had come up with. Even she couldn't home in on an unknown killer.

She felt in her bag for her diary. The retirement do was exactly one week away. She hoped it wasn't too optimistic to trust they would have made some progress with her current case before she met up with her old colleagues again. The way the investigation was going, they were more likely to discover another victim than the killer.

CHAPTER 52

Geraldine didn't completely disapprove of her young sergeant's fecund imagination, although Sam's latest theory was particularly far-fetched. Nevertheless, Geraldine had to agree it was feasible. She had seen too much not to admit that if something was possible it didn't really matter how improbable it might seem. When an investigation seemed to be going nowhere, any idea was welcome. Geraldine nodded at Sam to indicate she was listening as she continued to outline her latest theory, warming to her narrative as she spoke.

'So what I was thinking is, let's say Patrick was having it off with Desiree and George found out.'

Sam sat forward in her chair, her short blonde hair falling forward to form an irregular fringe above her eyes. Geraldine couldn't help smiling at the young sergeant's enthusiasm.

'You make it sound like a soap. This isn't *Eastenders*, Sam.'

Geraldine laughed but Sam didn't join in.

* * *

'No, but think about it for a moment,' the sergeant insisted earnestly, undeterred by Geraldine's amusement.

'Patrick and Desiree must have known each other, mustn't they? At the very least they must have met. They can't not have known each other.'

'OK, I get it, Patrick Henshaw knew Desiree. They knew each other. So what? Where is this going, Sam?'

Geraldine glanced over at her screen, rapidly losing interest in Sam's idea which seemed to be nothing but gossip.

'Well, what if George found out that Patrick was having an affair with Desiree and killed him? George would've had plenty of opportunity, plus there's the added inducement of getting his hands on the entire proceeds of the restaurant which would've come in very handy. He might have been considering getting rid of his partner for a while, only not in any serious way, and then the sexual jealousy pushed him into doing it. Well? What do you think? It makes sense, doesn't it? Sexual jealousy can be a powerful drive.'

Geraldine nodded, thinking about Corless's gambling debts. His creditors might well be the kind of people who wouldn't hesitate to resort to threats. There was a strong possibility he was being pressurised to settle up, and didn't have the money. Sole ownership of a lucrative business would have been an attractive prospect to someone in his financial straits.

'George might have gone to Patrick asking for help and been refused – or – well, there could be any number of other reasons why George might have resented Patrick. It's hardly unheard of for business partners to fall out. The affair with Desiree might have been the last straw, and it would explain the injuries we saw on Patrick's body as well. This was a personal attack motivated by cupidity and sexual jealousy.'

Sam paused expectantly. Geraldine still made no comment.

'Then, when Desiree found out George had bumped Patrick off, she killed George.'

Sam leaned back in her chair with an expectant grin, as though she was waiting for Geraldine to congratulate her for cracking the case.

'Because?'

'What?'

'Why would Desiree want to kill George?' Geraldine asked.

Sam scowled.

'I thought that was obvious. She killed him in revenge, because she found out he'd killed Patrick. Perhaps George told her. She might have been infatuated with Patrick—'

She broke off, frowning, as though suddenly sceptical of her own idea.

'After all,' she resumed in a more reticent tone of voice, 'Desiree was living with George. And she must have known how much she stood to gain from George's will. Even if she didn't know, she must've suspected it. Well, it's possible, isn't it?'

Geraldine considered. The theory could have hung together except for two considerations: not only was she convinced that Desiree had genuinely cared for Corless, but there was the puzzling question of the DNA found on Henshaw; the DNA of a woman in prison. The records had been carefully checked and it appeared Linda Harrison had never given birth, yet the most likely explanation for the DNA match was that it had been left on Henshaw's body by a daughter of Linda Harrison. And there was still the third victim.

Geraldine called the forensic team who dealt with the DNA profiles but they were only able to confirm what they had already told her.

'But it's reasonable that this DNA belonged to a daughter?' Geraldine persisted. 'Theoretically, I mean, if there *was* a daughter.'

'Yes, it's certainly a possibility,' the scientist agreed amiably, as though the conversation was purely conjectural, and there was no murder investigation to consider.

Geraldine paused, phone in hand.

'Don't forget we're checking against a DNA sample that was taken twenty years ago,' the scientist said.

'Yes, that's true, but we could easily get another sample if a current one would help clinch it.'

'Well, there have been a lot of changes in the way DNA is—' the scientist began before Geraldine interrupted him impatiently.

'Yes, thank you very much. What you've told me has been very helpful. Thank you.'

She didn't want another lecture about the progress with DNA, impressive though the recent advances were.

'What if she did have a child and the child was adopted?' Sam enquired with an anxious glance at Geraldine.

'The child – it could have been a daughter – would have a different name so wouldn't be immediately traceable.'

'Good thinking, but we've checked Linda's medical records and there's nothing to indicate she ever had a child. That's not an easy thing to keep quiet about.'

'But twenty years ago . . . It's possible, that's all I'm saying.'

Geraldine had to agree it was possible. Twenty years ago Linda could indeed have given birth in secret and offered the child up for adoption without leaving any official record of the birth. It was the simplest explanation of the DNA discovered on Patrick's body, and the truth was often simple.

'The only problem now is, without any record of a birth how are we ever going to find out if she had a child?'

Geraldine stood up.
'That's not a problem.'
'What do you mean?'
'Leave it to me. I'll keep you posted.'

Geraldine didn't tell Sam she intended to confront Linda to ask her outright if she had ever given birth to a daughter. Sam was usually the one to come up with fantastical notions, but Geraldine was harbouring an idea so fanciful she wasn't prepared to share it with anyone until she had discovered the truth.

CHAPTER 53

Geoff was in a bad mood as he carried the rubbish out at the back of the café early on Sunday morning. It was a foul job at the best of times, humping bags out to the stinking bins where the pungent odour of mildew and rotting food hung in the air like a fog. To make matters worse he was suffering from a thumping hangover and the sight of a homeless tramp propped up against the bins, blissfully asleep, did nothing to improve his temper. The sleeper's face was barely visible, concealed in shadows beneath the protruding hood of a dark anorak. No doubt he was adding to the stench of the place.

'Here, you, shove off out of it,' Geoff snarled, nudging the stranger with his foot.

The other man keeled over slowly until he was lying on his side in a puddle, legs stuck out in front of him at an odd angle. He was well out of it, oblivious to his clothes which were sodden after the heavy rain overnight.

'Wake up!' Geoff snapped. 'You're in my way.

Push off! Some of us are trying to earn a living here.'

He gave the tramp's leg another kick, harder this time. The sleeper still didn't stir. With a flash of rage Geoff booted him viciously but the man lay without moving, blocking the access to the bins. A few drops of rain began to fall. A horrible thought struck Geoff who set down the rubbish bag he was clutching and stooped down. Lifting the edge of the hood he glimpsed a face, grey and rigid. Geoff swore softly. That was all he needed, some bloody homeless yob dropping dead right outside his café. He considered dragging the inert body a few feet along to the far side of the bins, out of sight, where he could leave it for some other unlucky bugger to deal with. He had enough on his plate without having to faff around with strangers who drank themselves to death and then went and parked themselves right on his back doorstep.

Geoff wanted to open the café in less than half an hour and really didn't have time to start messing about with the police, and goodness knows what else besides. The geezer could have gone and croaked outside one of the big chains that could afford to close up for a day while the police investigated the area and removed the body. But he knew he couldn't ignore it. With a sigh he pulled out his phone and hesitated for a second, uncertain who he should speak to. In the end he dialled 999 to report that he had discovered a dead person lying in the gutter outside his café.

He seemed to be waiting for ages, fiddling with place settings on the tables, until a patrol car drew up in the street at the front of the café. He opened the door to admit two young uniformed police officers who followed him through the empty café and out of the back door to the bins where the three of them stood in a semi-circle gazing down at the body, still lying on its side. Glancing up, Geoff saw that the face of one of the policemen had gone slightly grey and he wondered if this was the first time the lad had seen a stiff.

Geoff looked back down at the hooded face, half submerged in an oily puddle.

'Can you move it now, please? Only I need to get to the bins.'

He indicated the black rubbish bag he had left standing by the kerb.

'I can't get my litter in the bin.'

His relief that the police had responded so promptly to his call soon vanished.

'What do you mean you can't move it out of the way?' he protested. 'What about my rubbish?'

The younger of the two police officers suddenly darted away behind the bins. Geoff and the other officer watched his bent back for a second, listening to sounds of vomiting, before the older policeman politely suggested Geoff take his rubbish back inside for the time being.

'And then we'll need to ask you a few questions, sir.'

Geoff gaped.

'I'm sorry, but I can't stand around jawing. I need to open up. It's already gone nine, and this is costing me money. I'm not bleeding Starbucks.'

'I'm sorry, sir, but we need to alert local CID and they'll decide whether to call out the Homicide Assessment Team.'

'What does that mean? Homicide team? Who's talking about homicide? It's just some old soak, isn't it? Just take it away will you? This is outrageous – take it away. I've got a café to run here.'

'I'm sorry, sir.'

The policeman turned aside and began talking rapidly on his phone.

The younger officer rejoined them, slightly red-faced, and blustering officiously as he turned to Geoff.

'We'll need to take a statement from you, sir. I appreciate this must have been a shock for you, finding a body like that, but—'

George shook his head and interrupted impatiently. He insisted that he was fine. All he wanted to do was open up his café.

'I'm losing customers. My regulars will all be going somewhere else. I might lose them altogether . . .'

'I'm sorry sir, but there's no question of your opening the café until we've established what happened here.'

'What happened? I can tell you what happened. Someone kicked the bucket, that's what happened. He took an overdose or his liver packed up, or something.'

'Have you seen the victim before, sir?'

Geoff was already heading for the door and the police officer scurried after him, notebook in hand.

'Sir, I need to ask you a few questions.'

Geoff turned on him.

'*I've* got a question for *you*.'

But the police were unable to give any indication as to when the body might be removed.

'Hang on a minute,' Geoff sighed. 'Don't worry, I'll answer your questions, but first I need to put up a closed sign.'

Grumbling to himself, he put a note on the door: 'Closed today, Open tomorrow as usual.'

CHAPTER 54

The post office was forwarding Geraldine's mail. There was one such envelope on the doormat that morning, with a printed redirection label. Since her conversation with Celia, Geraldine wasn't surprised to pull out an invitation to her father's birthday celebration. After a moment's hesitation, she slipped it into her bedside table, along with the single photograph of her mother. Although she was neither superstitious nor religious, she hoped and prayed the proximity of the two pieces of paper would bring her luck and her adoptive father would be able to tell her where to find her birth mother. Then she turned her attention to the serious business of the day.

As she drove out of London along side roads lined with green hedges, the weather turned chilly, threatening rain. Nearing her destination she passed through a pleasant residential district before the area changed again. She followed the main road, which was a bus route; its verges were overgrown, and beyond them only waste ground was visible. From the road she turned into a lane that led to the prison complex. The women's prison was directly opposite the entrance to the car park. The outer high metal gate was locked behind her and she was admitted through a second gate. She followed a chatty blonde prison officer through a neatly laid out garden, into a secure building where she checked in and was finally taken along a rabbit warren of corridors to the visitors' room.

Not for the first time, Geraldine wondered what it must be like to hear a key turn, knowing that door wouldn't open again for years, decades in some cases. Did the young prisoners she passed in the corridor wake up every morning thinking, 'Oh shit, I'm still here,' as they gazed around at the four walls of their cells? The penalty of a lengthy incarceration was harsher for women. A man could leave prison after twenty years and start a family. Yet the recidivism rate indicated how many prisoners preferred the security of prison care to the life they faced on the outside.

The blonde woman who had let Geraldine into the building handed her over to a cheerful square-jawed officer who led her outside. They walked briskly along a path bordered with small bushes that skirted the main prison block. Another jangling of keys, another door closed. Geraldine followed her guide into a large room where a prison officer stood unobtrusively by the door. She smiled and jerked her head in the direction of a solitary woman seated at a table, waiting.

'There she is. Good luck trying to get anything out of her. She's not much of a talker.'

Geraldine looked at the prisoner's grey bowed head and hesitated. Rehearsing the approaching meeting in her mind she had envisaged a terrible outcome. In a nightmare scenario Geraldine stared at the convicted murderess, like Dorian Grey gazing at an aged image of himself, knowing she was meeting her own mother for the first time.

'Yes, I had two daughters,' she imagined Linda Harrison saying. 'One of them was about your age. I called her Erin.'

'So where are they now?'

In the terrible fantasy, Linda shook her head.

'I've no idea. I did hear one of them had joined the police force, and the other one is a killer. Seems to run in the family.'

Geraldine's first sensation on sitting down was an overriding sense of relief. The woman facing her looked nothing like Geraldine imagined her own mother would look now. She had a photograph of her mother aged around sixteen. There was no way the prisoner was the same woman as the one in that faded image. In the precious photograph,

Geraldine's mother looked uncannily like Geraldine as a teenager, with large eyes so dark they appeared black, and a small crooked nose.

Geraldine didn't recognise the prisoner in the flesh from the photograph she had found online in an old newspaper. Taken when Linda was barely twenty, the image had been on the front pages of all the papers, so it was possible Sam might have seen Linda's face in the press during her trial. At that time Linda's hair hadn't been grey and badly in need of a wash, hanging down on either side of her pinched face in greasy straggly locks. Together with her extreme pallor, her unkempt appearance made her appear a lot older than forty. She pursed her thin lips and glared at Geraldine, her green eyes guarded.

'Linda.'

The prisoner continued to stare fixedly at Geraldine who smiled uneasily.

'I'd like to ask you a few questions.'

The other woman didn't respond.

'It would help you if you helped us,' Geraldine added untruthfully.

Silence.

Geraldine took a breath and plunged in with a direct question.

'Do you have a daughter?'

The green eyes flickered for an instant.

'Do you have a daughter?' Geraldine repeated.

Linda's face had resumed its blank expression. Geraldine leaned forward and repeated her question once more, studying the other woman closely while Linda sat in stony-faced silence.

'It would really help us if you answered my questions.'

Unexpectedly, Linda erupted in hoarse throaty laughter, simultaneously beating a tattoo on the table with the flat of one hand. Behind her the prison officer at the door stepped forward, tensed for action.

When the prisoner was quiet, Geraldine posed her question yet again.

'What's it to you?'

Linda's voice was gruff, as though she was unused to speaking.

'It would help our enquiry.'

'Help you?'

Linda spoke with scathing derision. Too late, Geraldine amended her statement.

'I don't mean it would help the police exactly. You'll be helping innocent people.'

'Sod off!'

'Linda, you don't understand. It's really important you tell me the truth.'

'I don't want to continue with this.'

Linda enunciated the words coldly.

'Please, Linda, if you could just answer a few straightforward questions—'

It was no good.

* * *

Frustrated, Geraldine watched the prisoner shuffle from the room without a backward glance, her past as secret as if she had died twenty years ago. In a way, she had.

CHAPTER 55

It was hard to credit how quickly the body count had risen without anyone coming forward with information. Henshaw, Corless, Bradshaw, and now a fourth victim had all been killed within a fortnight of each other. There were two gaps of four days between the first three murders, then only two days had elapsed before the fourth man was killed. A fifth body might be discovered at any time. It was all happening so fast, the killer must surely be making careless mistakes. By now someone must be harbouring suspicions about a family member, a neighbour or a colleague. Someone must have knowledge that could help point the investigation in the right direction, but apart from the usual cranks, the public had remained obdurately silent.

Observing a press briefing, Geraldine watched as Reg stated the facts of the case, his calm delivery making no impression on the reporters. He had done a good job to conceal his irritation with their lurid suggestions and hysterical comments.

'So you're hunting for a serial killer?'

'If you know who he is, why is he still on the loose?'

'Are the streets of London safe any more?'

'Can you assure us there won't be any more killings?'

Amy and Desiree joined Reg. Amy spoke stiffly about the loss of her wonderful husband.

'This was a senseless murder,' she concluded lamely.

Desiree wanted to speak, but she kept breaking down in tears, and in the end Reg had to take over.

'If anyone has any information, however unimportant it might seem, please contact us on this number.'

'Why was Maurice Bradshaw a victim?' Sam asked for the twentieth time, when the press briefing was over. 'Who would even notice him, let alone want to kill and mutilate him?'

Geraldine nodded without answering. She understood her colleague's disquiet. It was certainly hard to understand how anyone could have been provoked to attack an inoffensive nonentity like Bradshaw. But without motive the murder was reduced to a senseless act of violence not only somehow more vile but also more worrying, since it suggested the killer was selecting victims at random. In the absence of any pattern, it became almost impossible to trace or predict the killer's movements. And after four murders it was clear this killer would strike again and again, until he was stopped.

It was drizzling when Geraldine and Sam arrived at Camden station. They hurried along the crowded pavements of Camden High Street past shop windows filled with bizarre shoes, boots and belts, to Gino's Café. When she had lived in Kent, Geraldine had rarely travelled by public transport, but parking in London was so difficult, even with police parking privileges, that she was just as likely to use the tube.

'Is it always like this?' she had asked Sam the first time they had travelled on a packed train together.

'No. It's usually worse.'

From the outside Gino's wasn't inviting, with its grimy glass front, a yellowing menu displayed in the window, and the 's' from the tawdry red sign missing: *Gino'*. It was decent enough inside with wooden chairs and formica-topped tables displaying white china cruet pots; a cramped space packed with dark-uniformed officers and white-clad scene of crime officers jostling one another in the aisles between tables. As soon as they entered the room the stuffy atmosphere hit them, airless and buzzing with voices.

'It's this way.'

A young constable greeted them with a grin, as though he was throwing a party and showing them to the kitchen where the drinks were.

'It's all happening out in the alley.'

He looked as though he wanted to jump up and down with excitement. Geraldine wondered if this was his first experience of a homicide investigation. She gave him a level stare. He might be enjoying the bustle and thrill of a murder case on his patch, perhaps on his first day on the job, but this was a serious investigation. All the same, she couldn't help feeling a flicker of empathy for his zeal.

They manoeuvred their way to the back exit, past a man seated at a corner table watching the melee. From his wretched expression Geraldine assumed he was the café proprietor. There would have been something heartening about the purposeful atmosphere in the place were it not for the fact that another victim had been discovered, making a total of four bodies in barely two weeks. And for all their hard work and investigation they were no closer to finding out who was responsible. Geraldine had an unpleasant feeling that they were running around like a bunch of unfocused amateurs.

Outside the rear exit of the café the alleyway was narrow and dirty, spattered with shiny oily puddles, barely wide enough for one-way traffic to pass between the high kerbs on either side of the flat cobbled roadway. The rain had stopped but it was wet underfoot and everything gleamed: tall grey garbage cans, grey paving slabs and cobbles, brick buildings, one painted white, all looked grey in the weak sunlight. Only the forensic tent loomed white and spectral.

Geraldine hoped her visit would turn out to be a mistake, an error of judgement on the part of an eager junior officer. It was still possible the café proprietor had stumbled upon a vagrant who had succumbed to an overdose of toxic drugs, or downed a few drinks more than his damaged liver could survive. Maybe this would turn out to be a death from natural causes. But a quick glance at the victim was enough to persuade her that she was viewing the fourth victim of the killer one newspaper had glibly called The Hammer Horror.

CHAPTER 56

On Monday morning, Geraldine tracked down the firm of solicitors who had defended Linda Harrison twenty years earlier. It didn't take long to find them. When she telephoned, she learned that the solicitor who had dealt with the case had retired around ten years ago. The secretary at the law firm obligingly called back straight away with contact details for the retired lawyer, who was happy for Geraldine to call her. Unable to shake off the feeling that Linda held the key to the case, Geraldine preferred to speak to the woman in person. She didn't want to risk missing any nuance in the conversation. Half an hour after she had first contacted the firm, Geraldine was on her way to Richmond.

The weather was overcast. After a few miles, a steady drizzle began to fall although the autumn sun was shining behind her, lending the air a luminous quality. Geraldine wondered if she would see a rainbow and sure enough before long a faint arc appeared up ahead, spanning the sky. She smiled, hoping it was a good omen. In the meantime, the traffic was building up and she soon regretted her decision to drive. If she had taken the tube she could at least have read the paper on the way. As it was, she listened to the radio and took a minor detour to drive through Richmond Park. She didn't see any of the famous deer, but the open parkland made a welcome change from the busy streets.

Melissa Joyce lived in a smart terraced house near the river. Geraldine didn't generally park in restricted zones but on this occasion she had no choice. It was impossible to find a space that wasn't on a double yellow line or in a residents' bay. Melissa came to the front door straight away and led the way into a living room, small but tastefully furnished.

'How can I help you? I take it this is about someone I represented?'

Geraldine nodded.

'You must appreciate a few years have gone by since I left the firm. I can't promise to remember the details of every case I worked on, but I'll do what I can. So – what was the case?'

When Geraldine explained the reason for her visit, the other woman's anxious expression relaxed into a smile.

'Good lord, yes. I certainly remember the Linda Harrison case! I can see the defendant as clearly as if it happened yesterday. She wasn't the sort of woman you forget. Let me make some coffee and then we'll get down to it – and perhaps you can tell me why you're interested in the case after all this time. It must be twenty years since she was convicted and there was no controversy about it at the time. She made a full confession. It was cut and dried. All we could do was plead diminished responsibility, but the jury threw that out straight away. She refused to show any remorse for what she'd done, just insisted she would do it again if she had the chance—' Melissa broke off with a sigh. 'It was a domestic affair, very sad. Now I'll fetch the coffee and then I'll answer your questions as best I can after all this time.'

Over coffee Geraldine explained that she wasn't able to share the reason for her interest. The solicitor nodded her understanding and, without reference to any notes, launched into a detailed account of the case. Linda had been nineteen when she had killed her husband. They had been married for less than two years. She was a strange woman, according to Melissa, with no family to support her. Her parents were both dead and her only sister had died some years before the murder took place. To begin with Linda had blamed the murder on an intruder, but the police had found no evidence of a break in.

'What was odd was that she stuck to her guns, insisting the attack was the result of a burglary that went wrong. No amount of questioning could shake her account. And then she altered her story for no reason at all. It wasn't as though she broke down or anything, she just changed her mind. It was bizarre.'

She paused, frowning, still puzzled by the memory.

'What happened?' Geraldine prompted her.

'She claimed she'd murdered him herself. She flatly refused to explain why she had decided to confess, after such strenuous denials. We pleaded self-defence in court, of course, but the jury didn't go for it because she refused to express any remorse. "I did it so you can punish me for it," she said, in the most matter-of-fact voice. "If I found out that bastard was still alive, I'd do it again," was what she said, without a trace of emotion. And the only reason she ever gave was that she didn't like him. How could we build a case with that?'

Melissa paused to pour more coffee from a gleaming cafetiere.

'All we could do was plead diminished responsibility. It was obvious there was something not quite right with her. But the psychiatric report came back saying she showed no signs of mental disorder or disturbance of any kind. Linda Harrison had known exactly what she was doing when she took her husband's life, they decided. There was nothing we could do for her. To be honest, she didn't exactly help herself. It was as though she wanted everyone to put the worst possible construction on what she'd done, and even that fact didn't sway the jury into believing she was unbalanced. Or the judge for that matter. In his summing up he described her as a genuinely evil character. But is there such a thing? Still, if there is, she came closer than anyone else I've ever encountered. "A cold-blooded killer," that's how the papers described her.'

As they talked through the details of the case, Melissa let it slip that the only reason she could come up with to account for the defendant's change of heart was that she didn't want her niece to be questioned.

'Her niece?'

Geraldine sat forward, alert.

'What niece? I didn't know she had a niece.'

Melissa shrugged.

'There was a niece. Linda's sister had a daughter. The niece went to live with Linda when her mother died. We never found out who the father was. He disappeared before the child was born. I'm not sure Linda's sister even knew who he was. Linda didn't, at any rate. So when the sister died – I can't remember what it was, leukaemia or something – the child went to live with Linda. There were no grandparents by then. They'd died years before.'

'How old was she?'

'Linda's sister?'

'No, the niece.'

'I can't remember exactly. She was about twelve or thirteen when the murder took place, maybe fourteen. There were some questions raised about her being cared for by her nineteen-year-old aunt, but social services thought it was best for the child, to be with family.'

Geraldine felt the skin on the back of her neck prickling with excitement.

'You said Linda confessed to killing her husband to protect her niece from being questioned in court?'

'That was one theory we came up with, just between ourselves. We were trying to understand why she changed her mind.'

'What made her think her niece would be questioned?'

'The child was in the house when Linda killed her husband, so she could have been called as a witness. But then Linda confessed and it wasn't felt necessary to put the youngster through the ordeal.'

Geraldine could barely phrase her next question; she already knew the answer.

'How was he killed?'

Melissa shrugged.

'He was battered to death. It was a violent assault.'

'What do you mean, violent?'

'He was knocked out and then beaten to death—'

'Beaten where exactly?'

Melissa threw Geraldine a shrewd glance. After a brief hesitation, she answered.

'You could check the records – he was beaten in his genitals.'

'What was the niece's name?'

Melissa shook her head.

'I'm afraid I can't remember. We never saw her. Social services had taken her away by the time the case came to us.'

'So you're telling me Linda confessed to protect her niece from being questioned?'

'That's one possibility. It's what I believed at the time, because nothing else seemed to make sense. She realised that questioning the girl would only confirm her guilt, so there was no point putting the girl through it. Quicker and better all round for her to confess, and the outcome was the same anyway, even without the niece's corroboration.'

'There is another possibility,' Geraldine said quietly.

The solicitor shook her head, her expression suddenly tense. She stood up and when she answered, her voice was sharp.

'Linda Harrison confessed to murder. There was no doubt about the woman's guilt. No doubt at all. Now, I've taken up too much of your time already, and I've told you all I know, so I won't keep you any longer.'

Geraldine thanked her, pleased that she had taken the time to question Melissa face to face. The retired solicitor's uneasy expression had confirmed what Geraldine already suspected. She too had realised that there was another possibility.

CHAPTER 57

Geraldine struggled to contain her excitement on hearing that Linda Harrison had a niece. This had to be the answer to the conundrum of the DNA found in Patrick's car. The existence of a niece could even explain why Sam thought she had seen Harrison before. If their DNA was sufficiently similar for the niece's traces to be confused with Harrison's twenty-year-old sample, then it made sense that the two women would look alike. Suddenly everything was beginning to fall into place. All that remained was to trace the niece.

Arriving at her flat, she regretted returning home instead of going straight to her office. She couldn't settle to anything. She fiddled around in the kitchen making herself supper but although she was hungry she couldn't eat. She switched on the television but couldn't concentrate. In the end she went to bed very early but lay for hours unable to sleep, thinking about Linda and wondering where her niece was. By the time Sam arrived at work the next morning, Geraldine had been at her desk for a couple of hours, searching for the niece.

Sam perched on Nick's chair.

'What are you doing?'

'If he catches you sitting on his chair, there'll be hell to pay,'

Sam leaned forward, peering earnestly at Geraldine.

'So what you're saying is that if you don't agree to come to the canteen with me for breakfast, I could end up in serious trouble. Is that really what you want?'

Geraldine shook her head, laughing.

'I had breakfast hours ago. I've got work to do, Sam.'

'All the more reason for you to come to the canteen for a coffee. It'll clear your mind. Plus you'll have the added bonus of a super-intelligent and sympathetic listening ear to run your theory by.'

'Who says it's only a theory?'

Geraldine stood up. She would value Sam's views about Linda's niece.

Sam wasn't helpful. To begin with she was sceptical about the idea that Linda's niece might have murdered her uncle.

'Think about it, Geraldine, it doesn't really stack up. I can understand that you might suspect she killed her uncle, although why her aunt would have confessed to it, I can't imagine.'

'To protect her.'

'Well, maybe. But serving more than twenty years in prison for a crime she didn't commit, is that likely? And anyway, the case was closed. A jury found Linda Harrison guilty. End of. Even if there was a miscarriage of justice twenty years ago, and Linda was sent down instead of her niece, you're saying that, after a gap of twenty years, the niece suddenly decided to kill Henshaw, Corless, Bradshaw, and this new victim, four murders in the space of a fortnight? That doesn't make sense.'

'The method of killing was similar,' Geraldine insisted. 'Linda's husband was battered to death in exactly the same way as the four recent victims. Hit on the head and beaten in the genitals.'

Sam wasn't persuaded.

'So? The method of killing was similar. So what? That doesn't prove anything. The Harrison killing was all over the news twenty years ago, wasn't it? Going by what you've said, and what I've seen, it was front page stuff for weeks. Anyone could have been influenced by it.'

'But like you said, after twenty years, why would anyone start copycat murders?'

'Exactly. Why start up again after twenty years? That's what I was saying to you.'

'No, it's not. You're talking about copycat crimes. What I'm saying is that this might be the same killer repeating the same murder, reliving the original event for some reason. Perhaps something triggered it off.'

They argued round in circles for a while, neither of them prepared to concede. Geraldine hid her increasing irritation. At length she returned to her desk, her conviction shaken. Despite her exasperation, she knew the sergeant had done her a favour, warning her against giving her theory undue credence without proof. It was a desperate trap to fall into, in the absence of any useful leads, and all too easy to do. Without her theory that Linda's niece was culpable she had no leads, but that was no reason to believe the niece was guilty.

Despite Sam's scepticism about using DNA from twenty years ago, Geraldine focused her attention on looking for Linda's niece. She discovered a girl called Emily Tennant had gone to live with Linda Harrison and her husband a year after their marriage. Emily was only six years younger than Linda. As her sister had been ten years older than Linda, it was likely that Emily was her niece. Emily Tennant's birth certificate and school records weren't difficult to trace. The school had her registered as living at the Harrisons' address. Nearly two years later, when Emily was fourteen, Linda was arrested and the girl was taken into the care of social services.

After leaving school at sixteen, Emily vanished from the system. Her name didn't appear on any census records, she was too young to be on the electoral register, and she wasn't registered with a doctor or dentist. It was frustrating. Geraldine could find no record of any marriage or death, and no trace of her leaving the country or even applying for a passport. The only obvious explanations were that she was homeless or had changed her name, or perhaps both.

Geraldine's research had thrown up no indication of where the name Tennant came from. Linda Harrison's maiden name was Buckingham, and there was no record of her sister having married. Tennant could have been the name of Emily's father, but no father was named on her birth certificate. Perhaps her mother had adopted a new surname to hide the fact that she was unmarried. In any event, Geraldine could find no records from the life of Emily Tennant after she reached the age of sixteen. The only vaguely encouraging piece of information was that she had found no record of her death. Linda was the only person who could help her.

Returning to the prison, Geraldine was admitted by a different prison officer wearing the same cheerful expression as the woman who had accompanied her on her previous visit. Once again she was led along a walkway around the prison building, past small scrubby bushes and weedy flowers. The place was eerily silent. Her guide led her through several secure doors, along corridors, until they reached the cavernous visitors' room. It was empty. Minutes crawled by as though time had stopped. For some of the prisoners, incarcerated for decades, it effectively had.

At last another prisoner officer entered the room. She was alone.

'Linda doesn't want to see you.'

'I just want to ask her one question.'

'I'm sorry, Linda is refusing to see you.'

The prison officer led Geraldine back along dim corridors, her keys jangling as she locked and unlocked the heavy doors they passed through on their way back through the prison gardens. The outer gate closed behind her, and Geraldine walked slowly back to her car. Somewhere in the normal world to which she had returned, an unknown killer was hiding.

CHAPTER 58

'We have a match!' Reg crowed, grinning at Geraldine from behind his desk.

His broad shoulders were hunched forward over his keyboard as she entered his office but he straightened at once, his face bright with enthusiasm. She couldn't help returning his smile, he looked so pleased with himself.

'Is it Emily Tennant?'

Her voice echoed his excitement. The detective chief inspector's grin faded as he leaned back in his chair, frowning.

'What's that? Emily who?'

'Tennant. Emily Tennant.'

'Emily Tennant? Who's Emily Tennant? The name they gave me is Lolita Wild. She's the woman who was there when Bradshaw was murdered.'

It was Geraldine's turn to look baffled.

'Lolita Wild? Who the hell is she?'

Reg smiled, misconstruing her surprised expression.

'Lolita Wild. I know, highly unlikely, isn't it? But it's probably a false name, although you can never tell, especially these days—'

'Who the hell is Lolita Wild?'

'That's exactly what you're about to find out.'

The misunderstanding was swiftly clarified. The forensic team had identified the owner of the blonde hairs found on Bradshaw's body. The bad news was that her DNA did not match that of the brunette who had left her hair in Patrick's car, which meant that different women had been at the two crime scenes. It wasn't one woman who had dyed her hair, after all. They were looking for two women. The only other information they could gather from Lolita Wild's hair was that she was a habitual heroin user.

'But we already knew that from her record,' Reg added.

'Lolita Wild? That can't be her real name,' Sam laughed when Geraldine told her about the development. 'What sort of a name is that?'

'What's so funny about it?' Geraldine responded sourly.

She was vexed that her theory about Emily Tennant appeared to be foundering. She had been so convinced she was right.

'Do you ever get a strong feeling about something, for no reason?' she asked her colleague. 'I mean, you just know you're right, only you can't prove it—'

'You're the one who's always insisting on facts,' Sam reminded her.

Geraldine sighed.

'Come on, then, let's find this blonde Lolita. Whoever she is, she was there when Bradshaw was murdered.'

'Lolita Wild sounds like a stage name,' Sam said. 'At least there can't be too many women around with that name.'

'That should make your job a whole lot easier then.'

It took Sam less than half an hour to track down the woman calling herself Lolita Wild. Real name Lynn Jones, she had been working in Soho as a prostitute. Over two years earlier she had left the hostel in London where she had last been recorded as living temporarily. After that the paper trail had gone cold. Leaving Sam to continue her search online, Geraldine paid a visit to the hostel. Even though it was a long time since Lolita had left, it was the only lead they had to her current whereabouts.

The hostel was a dreary block for homeless women, situated in a rundown street near Marylebone Road. A plaque in the dusty lobby informed visitors that it was a charitable foundation established in Victorian times as a refuge for fallen women. It was now run by a particular church sect. A grey-haired woman was seated behind a small glass partition. She watched with sharp black eyes as Geraldine approached. The woman enquired who she was visiting and smiled ruefully when Geraldine introduced herself.

'We are a Christian house,' she said softly. 'Our aim is to help these poor women, but they struggle to follow the path.'

When Geraldine outlined the purpose of her visit the woman shook her head and explained that even if they could find a record of a resident going by the name of Lolita, they would be unable to provide any information about where she might have gone after leaving the hostel. It was difficult enough keeping a record of who was living there. They certainly didn't have time to keep track of where the women moved on to when they left, even it was possible to do so. Mostly the women slipped away, changed their names, and ended up on the streets. Sometimes they returned for a while, before disappearing again.

'I don't want to sound callous, Inspector. It's not that we don't care about all the women who stay here. We do everything we can for them. We put a roof over their heads. But they come and go all the time. It's that sort of a place. We like to think our doors are open to all comers, providing we have a bed for them, of course. Everyone is welcome here. We do what we can. But whatever we do for them, it's never enough to keep them here for long. It's usually drugs that lure them away. The devil's at work, even here.'

* * *

Geraldine glanced around the drab hallway, trying not to feel dejected. It was hard to remain positive standing in such a depressing place. She wasn't surprised people didn't want to stay there long, although the miserable truth was that this was probably the best many of these women could hope for. She turned back to the woman sitting behind her glass partition.

'It's really very important we trace this woman.'

'I'm sorry, Inspector, but there's nothing I can do. We don't record where the women go on to when they leave. It would be a pointless task. Most of them move on again fairly soon. They don't stay anywhere for longer than a few months at a time. It's never long before they're back on the streets, soliciting to support their habit. And once they've left us, well, we'd help them if we could but they're not our responsibility, after all. We're very limited in what we can do for them.'

Geraldine thanked the woman. She asked if there was anyone at the hostel who had been there two years earlier and might know what had happened to Lolita.

'Only Rowena. She's in and out all the time. But you won't get much sense out of her.'

Rowena was an emaciated woman with olive-coloured skin and almond-shaped eyes. She must once have been beautiful. Now her skin was blemished and blotchy, and she glanced suspiciously at her visitor with eyes that were bloodshot and inflamed. When Geraldine introduced herself, Rowena dropped her gaze and stared doggedly at the floor. Nevertheless, she admitted that she had known Lolita.

'We were friends,' she mumbled.

She had a faintly Far-Eastern accent, and Geraldine had to lean forward to make out what she was saying. But when Geraldine asked where Lolita was now, Rowena just shook her head without answering.

'Rowena, it's very important we find her,' Geraldine insisted. 'You have to help us. You are the only person we can find who knew her. Do you have any idea where she could be right now?'

She paused. Rowena stared at the floor.

'It will help Lolita if you tell us,' Geraldine lied. 'After she left here we can't find any trace of what happened to her. She just disappeared. Do you know if she had another name?'

Rowena nodded slowly.

'Lolita wasn't her name. It was her working name. Lolita.'

She smiled at some recollection.

'Could she be using another name now?'

Rowena shrugged.

'Did you hear her use the name Lynn Jones?'

The other woman just shook her head. It was unclear if she couldn't remember, or had never known.

* * *

'Lolita wasn't her real name,' Rowena said after a pause. 'She used it because it made her sound foreign. That's what she thought, anyway. She said it sounded exotic, like it wasn't really her. She was somewhere else. She wasn't the woman living here. She wanted to be someone else, you see.'

She looked around the shabby corridor.

'We all do.'

'Where did she come from? Rowena, it's really important. Please try to remember.'

Rowena nodded.

'She came from—' she paused, wrinkling her brow as she struggled to remember. 'I can't remember.'

She sighed.

'She was my friend.'

It didn't help in the search for the woman who had at least witnessed a murder, if she hadn't wielded the bludgeon herself.

CHAPTER 59

Leaving the hostel where the missing suspect had once stayed, Geraldine drove straight to the morgue. Confident in her sergeant's tenacity, she left Sam at the station researching Lynn Jones' whereabouts. They couldn't afford to let that line of enquiry wait. Jones was now their main suspect and the sooner they pulled her in for questioning the better. While she remained at large, there was a possibility there would be more deaths. Calling the station, Geraldine had smiled on hearing the relief in Sam's voice when she learned she was to give the morgue a miss for once.

Geraldine's previous sergeant, Ian, had been just the same. Over six foot tall and physically tough, he used to turn pale whenever they witnessed an autopsy. He had covered it up well, but Geraldine had worked too closely with him for him to conceal his feelings from her.

'It's the smell that gets me more than anything else,' he had confided to her when they were out for a drink together one evening. 'Only don't let on to the boss, will you?'

He shuddered.

'I can't stand the smell of the place. And the thought that it could be me one day, up there on the slab, or it could be—'

'Oh my God, don't even think about it,' Geraldine had interrupted, laughing.

Ian had joined in her laughter, his amusement obviously fake; he couldn't laugh about death. Geraldine wondered if the natural way in which she was able to divorce herself from any personal engagement with the cadavers she viewed in the course of her work meant she was unfeeling, inhumane even. But her detachment certainly helped her to function efficiently at her job.

Miles looked up from the body he was working on as Geraldine entered. The body found outside Gino's Café had been identified as John Birch, a thirty-two-year-old bus driver. Miles grunted in acknowledgement of her greeting, hazel eyes meeting her gaze solemnly.

'Looks like we've got another one for you,' he said, pointing a gory finger at the injuries the dead man had sustained.

Frustrated, Geraldine stared down at the battered body. The wounds appeared to match those of Henshaw, Corless and Bradshaw exactly. That made four virtually identical deaths in just over two weeks. The exact details hadn't been made public so the murders must all have been carried out by the same person, or group of people, and apparently with an identical weapon. Meanwhile the police could only speculate about the killer's identity. They had no real evidence.

'Must make you sick, seeing this again,' the pathologist said.

He sounded a trifle surly.

'That's four of them in a row. Isn't it time you found out who's killing all these poor buggers, and put a stop to it? Or at the very least can't you get him to use a bit more imagination if it's going to carry on like this, unless you want another death on your hands, because I might just die of boredom writing these pathology reports. Maybe you can put out an appeal on the TV, asking the killer to vary his methods.'

Geraldine sighed.

'We're doing our best, Miles, we're doing our best. It's a tricky one.'

'At the rate he's killing people, he can't be that difficult to find, surely?'

Geraldine looked down at the victim.

'I take it this was the same cause of death?'

Miles shook his head.

'Well, no, as it happens it's not quite the same, although the injuries are identical.'

Geraldine frowned.

'What was the cause of death this time then?'

'He died from a massive coronary while the

previous three victims all died from blood loss. It was a close run thing, but it was the heart attack that killed him.'

'So you're saying he died from a coronary that was brought on by the attack?'

The pathologist shrugged.

'It's impossible to say for certain what caused the coronary. Who can say? It could have been going to happen anyway, couldn't it?'

Geraldine considered.

'Had he suffered previous heart trouble?'

'No. He had a clean bill of health before this.'

With John Birch's injuries, there was no possibility his killer could get away with a charge of manslaughter. In any case the direct cause of death was irrelevant, if the murderer was implicated in the deaths of the other three victims. Once they had arrested the killer, a life sentence was inevitable. But first they had to find whoever was responsible.

'Still no leads then?' Miles asked, watching her expression closely.

Unsure whether his enquiry was sympathetic or censorious, Geraldine faced him squarely across the table. John Birch's cadaver lay between them, white and staring.

'Whatever makes you say that?' she asked. 'Of course we've got leads. That's what we're doing, all the time, following up leads. Why do you think Sam isn't here with me today? She's back at the station following up a suspect right now. We'll have this wrapped up soon.'

Miles nodded.

'Glad to hear it,' he replied, turning away, but Geraldine hadn't finished yet.

'I need to get back to the station, but before I go, is there anything else you can tell us, anything at all?'

Miles gave her a quizzical look. She repeated her question. Any small snippet of information the pathologist could supply might help. She wanted to beg him to give her some clue to work on, anything that might blow the case wide open. It was all right for him to stand there, smugly patronising. While he dealt with tangible evidence, Geraldine was struggling with obscure intimations.

'What kind of detail are you looking for?' he asked. 'Are we talking about DNA? There's nothing yet. Nothing that matches anything we found at the other scenes. And I'm afraid the killer didn't leave a calling card.'

She refused to be rattled by his goading. He was probably intending to be light-hearted, but she was too stressed to be amused. She wanted to know if there was anything different about this victim.

'Apart from the cause of death? Well, yes, there is one other thing.'

He looked down at the body.

* * *

'This chap was standing up when he received the initial blow. As you've seen, he was hit on the back of the head. The other three victims were all hit on the temple, assaulted from the front. In this case, the assailant approached him from behind.'

Geraldine asked to see the bruise on the back of Birch's head again. The body was carefully turned and they examined a large gash on the back of his head, surrounded by bruising. The dead man's hair had been shaved to disclose the damaged skin.

'What was it done with?'

Miles shook his head.

'It's impossible to say what the weapon was, and in any case a different weapon was used in the attack on Henshaw. But they were all forceful blows, hard enough to bruise and break the skin. It must have stunned him, maybe even knocked him out. He suffered a coronary almost immediately afterwards which would have caused him to fall to the ground—'

He indicated bruising on the dead man's knees.

'The other injuries were inflicted after his collapse, the first impact while he was still alive, the others post-mortem.'

Geraldine focused on the blow to the victim's head.

'So he was standing up when he was first hit?'

The pathologist nodded.

'You're sure of that? I need to know . . .'

'Yes, but—' he broke off and nodded, his eyes narrowing. 'You want to see what that can tell us about the killer.'

Geraldine leaned forward.

'Is it possible to estimate the killer's height from the angle of the impact? Can you tell that without knowing about the instrument that hit him?'

Miles nodded thoughtfully. The dead man had been hit on the back of his head, just above the nape of his neck, with a heavy implement.

'But what was used, exactly?'

'Still no sign of a murder weapon then?' he asked.

They studied the injury. The bottom edge of the weapon had made a deeper impression than the top edge, suggesting he had been hit from below. The dead man was five foot ten. The pathologist estimated the killer's height to be somewhere between five four and five six, although it wasn't conclusive.

'The weapon might have been swung, like a hammer, and made an impact on the upward trajectory,' he pointed out.

'Was he killed where he was found or moved after death?'

'He was killed there, in the alley.'

Geraldine was pursuing her own line of thought.

'Could he have been hit by a woman? I mean,

five foot four isn't that tall. How powerful would you say the blow was?'

'Powerful enough to knock him down – but yes, it could certainly have been dealt by a woman, if the victim was caught off guard. And he was hit from behind. If he'd had any idea what was coming, surely he would have turned round and tried to stop it.'

He looked up at Geraldine, frowning.

'You've got no idea who did this, have you? You don't even know if he was killed by a man or a woman.'

'We're following several leads right now,' she replied frostily. 'We'll get the killer. It's just a matter of time.'

CHAPTER 60

While Geraldine had been at the morgue, Sam had been painstakingly tracing Lynn Jones' history. As a teenager Lynn had left her family home in Acton after a falling out with her parents. They had reported her missing, but she had turned sixteen by the time she was traced. At sixteen she could not be compelled to return home, and she refused to go back voluntarily. After that the trail had gone cold for about a year until she had turned up in central London under her new name, Lolita. Somewhere in the interim she had become an addict and begun working for a pimp and dealer known to the drug squad. They had finally nailed him and he died of pancreatic cancer while serving a prison sentence. There was no record of how Lolita had managed without him. Presumably she had moved on to a new pimp.

After lunch, Sam and Geraldine drove to the address in Peckham where Lynn's mother still lived. The man who came to the door must have been in the hall because the door opened as soon as the bell chimed. He looked about fifty, with grey stubble on his cheeks and chin, and a balding head. Small eyes peered out at them, almost completely concealed in fleshy pouches.

'What do you want?'

His voice was shrill and he screwed up his face as though they had brought a bad smell with them. 'We don't buy no shit on the doorstep and we're not interested in no crap religion.'

He made to close the door but Geraldine stepped forward, explaining the reason for their visit.

The man's belligerence slipped in surprise.

'Lynn?' he repeated. 'Did you say you're looking for Lynn?'

A woman's voice screeched incoherently from inside the house and the man turned away to yell in reply.

'Someone's here asking about Lynn!'

A woman appeared in the hall, hovering just behind the fat man, who shifted his bulk aside to allow her to speak to Geraldine. With wrinkled skin and stooped shoulders, she looked old enough to be her companion's mother. She too seemed startled when she heard the purpose of their visit.

'You want to know about Lynn?' she repeated in surprise, her vacant eyes animated with fleeting interest. 'After all this time, why would you want to know about her now?'

'I know it's a long time since she left home—' Geraldine began.

'Home!' the fat man interrupted, rolling his piggy eyes. 'If she ever thought of this place as her home, I'll eat my hat.'

At her side, Geraldine heard Sam cough. It sounded as though she was trying not to laugh. Geraldine turned and glared at the sergeant who looked down, biting her bottom lip. Geraldine turned back to Lynn's mother.

'May we come in?'

Mrs Jones nodded dumbly and led them off the narrow hall into a small untidy living room at the front of the house, sloppily furnished with a couple of armchairs that didn't match, and a pair of grey plastic chairs. There was a stale smell, as though the windows were never opened. Mrs Jones perched on one armchair, the fat man sank into the other, and the two visitors sat down on plastic chairs. The place appeared neglected, as did Mrs Jones. Her hair was greasy, her clothes creased and threadbare, her lips cracked.

'We want to know about Lynn,' Geraldine said when they were all sitting down, 'anything you can tell us.'

The woman sat brooding silently.

'She won't tell you anything,' the fat man said. 'She never talks about Lynn.'

'Can *you* tell us about her then?'

'Me? No. She'd left home long before I came to live here.'

Geraldine turned back to Mrs Jones.

'We need to find Lynn urgently. It will help her if we can talk to her,' she lied.

'You can't help Lynn,' her mother said in a flat voice.

'I think you'll find we can—'

'No one can help Lynn. She's dead. She died eighteen months ago.'

'Are you sure?' Geraldine asked.

She regretted the question straight away. As though a mother would make a mistake about such a matter.

'That's that then,' Geraldine said tetchily as she climbed into the driving seat. 'Lynn Jones isn't our murderer because she's dead.'

'Funny we didn't find any record of her death.'

'That's because we were looking under the wrong name.'

Geraldine thought about her own fruitless efforts to trace Emily Tennant, and wondered if she too was looking under the wrong name. She sighed. They were scratching around for leads, and every time they thought they were onto something, they ended up going nowhere.

'Where are we off to now?' Sam asked, glancing at her watch.

Geraldine thought aloud.

'Why was hair from two different women found on the bodies? They can't both be killers, because one type of hair belonged to Lynn, and she's dead.

Did Lynn sell her hair to be made into a wig that was worn by the killer? If we can trace whoever bought Lynn's hair—'

Geraldine didn't finish the sentence. She knew it was an impossible task. To begin with, they had no idea when Lynn had sold her hair. Even if Rowena could help them to pin down a time, she was unlikely to know where the hair had gone. And if they found the wig-maker who had purchased it, the hair would most likely have been bought for cash, or sold on, or lost, and picked up by the murderer without any trace. Realistically, there was no chance they would find a record of the transaction, or that anyone would remember that one wig and its owner after so long; just another junkie desperate for money.

'I know, leave no stone unturned,' Sam muttered.

'Sooner or later something has to go in our favour,' Geraldine responded, but she no longer believed what she was saying.

Not for the first time, she wondered what it would be like to work in a job that lacked any kind of moral responsibility, a job where failure was acceptable. First the DNA found at the scene of Henshaw's murder had been a match with a woman in prison, and now the DNA found on Bradshaw's body turned out to be that of a dead woman. Nothing about this case seemed to make any sense. She was beginning to think they would never find the person who had killed four men – so far.

'Failure is not an option,' she muttered fiercely as they drew up outside the hostel and left the car on a double yellow line again.

Rowena greeted them indifferently, as though their visit was nothing unusual. Geraldine asked her straight away when Lynn had cut her long hair. Rowena frowned with the effort of remembering.

'She had long hair,' she offered at last.

'Yes, but then she had it cut off. We need to know when that was.'

Rowena stared blankly at a black smear on the floor and didn't answer.

'Rowena, when did Lynn get her hair cut?'

'We called her Lolita.'

'All right, but you know who I mean. When did Lolita get her hair cut off?'

Rowena looked troubled.

'Lolita had long hair,' she repeated.

'Did she ever have it cut in all the time you knew her?'

She shook her head.

If Rowena's testimony was reliable, Lynn must have sold her hair after leaving the hostel. On the streets and desperate to feed her habit, she would have been making what money she could by any means possible. She might have been finding it difficult to earn money from soliciting without the protection of her pimp, with her looks no doubt fading as a result of her habit. A wig seemed the only possible explanation for Lynn's hair turning up like that, but they had no way of finding out who had bought the wig and presumably worn it while killing Bradshaw.

'Well, that'll be a nice little job for you tomorrow,' Geraldine said to Sam as they drove away, 'checking the records of every wig-maker in striking distance of London.'

'I know it's got to be done, but you don't really think there'll be an official record in writing somewhere of blonde hair bought from Lynn Jones, or Lolita, do you?'

Geraldine ignored the question.

'Let's get some chips on the way back,' she said instead.

'That's the first sensible thing anyone's said to me since we started on this crazy case with people committing murders from behind bars, and beyond the grave,' Sam answered cheerfully. 'I know where there's a great chippy not far from here.'

'I was counting on it.'

CHAPTER 61

Geraldine knocked at a dirty white door and waited patiently. She could have delegated the visit to a local constable but preferred to carry out the task herself, her judgement coloured by an experience in her early years as a sergeant. She had despatched an inexperienced constable to break the news of a fatality to the parents of a youth who had been knifed in a pub brawl. Geraldine still wondered if she was responsible for his crass performance. Her instruction had seemed innocuous enough: 'Deliver the message and come back here straight away.'

Years later she still felt cold when she remembered questioning the young constable. With hindsight she suspected his rapid return to the station had alerted her to the fact that something was wrong. If she hadn't been there on his return she would never have discovered what had happened, and the outcome could have been dreadful. Finding the house empty, the young constable had put a note through the door informing the parents of their loss. Shocked, Geraldine had rushed to the house. Fortunately the family had not yet come home. She had waited in the car for five hours to intercept them and tell them in person that their son had been stabbed to death, before they saw the note that had been posted through their letter box.

The latest victim to be bludgeoned to death by 'The Hammer Horror' had lived in Wealdstone, not far from the bus garage. Geraldine caught the overground from Kings Cross and walked for about a mile along the High Street past small dilapidated shops. Turning off the noisy main road, she found the small terraced property where John Birch had lived with his wife. This time she only had to wait a few minutes before the door was opened by a tall lanky woman. Dark hair streaked with grey hung in a straight fringe, through which her eyes gleamed anxiously from a narrow face with a small pointed nose.

'Where—' she began in a screechy whine.

Seeing Geraldine, she pressed her thin lips together and stood poised, one hand on the door, while the other hand wandered absent-mindedly to her face. Long bony fingers cupped her chin.

'Mrs Birch?'

The woman nodded without speaking. Behind her fringe, Geraldine saw her eyes narrow with suspicion.

'May I come in?'

Mrs Birch's eyes widened in sudden apprehension when Geraldine held up her warrant card, and her grip on the door tightened visibly, bony knuckles whitening under the pressure. Without another word, she ducked her head and led Geraldine into a cluttered front room. Tattered magazines covered a coffee table, women's magazines and car periodicals jumbled together as though they had fallen on the floor and then been thrown together on the surface of the table without any care.

A fat ginger cat strolled into the room and scrutinised Geraldine before leaping onto Mrs Birch's lap with surprising agility as soon as she sat down. She scooped the animal up in her thin arms and dropped it on the floor. Offended, it raised its tail in the air and stalked out of the room.

'Where is he?'

'Mrs Birch, I'm afraid your husband's dead.'

The widow looked confused.

'What are you talking about? Who are you?'

Geraldine took out her warrant card again and held it up.

'I'm here to tell you that your husband is dead. I'm so sorry for your loss,' she said softly.

Neither of them spoke for a moment, then Mrs Birch dropped her head into her hands. Geraldine waited. The cat reappeared and rubbed itself against the bereaved woman's legs, purring loudly. She moved her leg, shifting the cat away from her. It settled down on the carpet, wrapping its tail around its body. After a moment it rose to its feet and leaned against her shins again, mewing plaintively.

'He knows,' Mrs Birch said dully.

'What?'

'Ginger. The cat. He knows what's happened. He can tell. That's why he's not purring.'

She began stroking the cat, while tears slipped down her gaunt cheeks.

'So he's dead?'

'I'm afraid so.'

'What happened?' She turned her tear streaked face to Geraldine. 'Was it his fault?'

'His fault?'

'The accident. It was the other driver's fault, wasn't it? John was a safe driver. He'd been driving the buses for ten years without an accident. He – he was a good driver—'

'This wasn't an accident, Mrs Birch.'

'But – the bus—'

Gently Geraldine explained that her husband hadn't died in a traffic accident.

'I don't understand.'

'Your husband was murdered.'

'How?'

'He was assaulted, hit on the head and knocked out.'

★ ★ ★

Mrs Birch shook her head.

'I don't understand. Why? Why would anyone kill John?'

Geraldine asked the bereaved woman if she could contact anyone. Mrs Birch shook her head.

'There is no one else. There was only ever the two of us, me and John.'

'Do you have any family you could call?'

Again she shook her head and her fringe quivered above her eyes.

'We never had children.'

She explained she was an only child, and her husband's only brother had gone abroad and died.

'Do you have a neighbour who could be with you?'

Mrs Birch shook her head again.

'Be with me?' she repeated, bemused. 'There's only Ginger.'

As if rejecting her dependence, the cat arched its back and trotted lightly out of the room.

Back in her own flat, Geraldine slumped down on her sofa and scowled at an ink stain she had made with a biro the night before. The sofa was dark, so it wasn't particularly noticeable, but she knew it was there. She made a mental note to ask her sister how to remove it, when they next spoke. It was the kind of domestic detail her sister would know about. With a bowl of pasta and a small glass of wine on a tray, she flipped through channels on the television but couldn't settle to anything.

The memory of John Birch's widow wouldn't leave her. It wasn't as though it was the first time she had delivered news of a tragedy to an unsuspecting family, but there was something about the woman's isolation that was unsettling. The detective chief inspector had considered it fortunate there were no children in the marriage, but children might have given the widow some support.

Usually efficient at detaching herself from homicide victims and those they left behind, for no obvious reason Mrs Birch perturbed her. Sitting disconsolately in front of the flickering television screen, she replayed the widow's words in her mind, like a voice over. 'There is no one else.' Geraldine tried not to see parallels with her own situation. She had her work. But in twenty years' time she would be retiring. What company would she have then? She thought of Sam as a friend. An intimacy had sprung up between them as they worked closely together. But either one of them might relocate at any time and even if they continued as a team for twenty years, their relationship would inevitably lose its immediacy once they no longer worked together.

Apart from her colleagues at work, there were very few people Geraldine felt close to. Even before she had learned about her adoption, she had never felt at ease with her adoptive family. Looking back on her early life, it was almost as though she had sensed that she didn't belong with them. Now she went through the motions with her sister, pretending nothing had changed. Hannah was a loyal friend, but she had her own family to fill her life. It struck Geraldine that her birth mother might be in a similar situation to Mrs Birch, living an isolated and lonely existence. Perhaps she too had only a cat for company. For the first time Geraldine wondered whether she owed it to her mother, as much as to herself, to find the stranger who had given birth to her.

CHAPTER 62

Charlie hesitated as he reached the estate. It was already dark and he never knew when or where they might be waiting for him. His main advantages were that he was a sprinter, and he wasn't worth the effort of chasing. There was nothing on him worth nicking. They already had his phone and he never had more than a couple of quid which they were happy to take off him, but only if it was no trouble. If he didn't get too close before they noticed him, he could usually escape. If not, they would rough him up a bit, jeering and twisting his arms, spitting and throwing the odd punch. But they were too thick, or too carefree, to conceal their presence. As soon as he was aware of them, loitering on a street corner or hanging about in one of the alleys between the blocks of flats, he would be off.

His mum didn't like it. She was always on at him, wanting to know who was in the gang that kept picking on him so she could complain to the school, or harangue the police about the violence on the streets. He assured her he had no idea who they were, so there was no point in reporting it. It was difficult enough keeping her out of it and she didn't even know the extent of his problem. She thought he had lost his phone, as well as his new school bag. That had probably been a mistake, because she flatly refused to replace his phone, calling him irresponsible and a waste of space, and a host of other things besides.

'You think I'm made of money?' she'd screeched at him. 'Do you know how much that phone cost?'

'But Mum, I need a phone.'

'Well life is full of disappointments, you little sod. Get your own phone.'

He nearly told her he'd been mugged, but the truth would only set her off again, doing his head in with her questions.

The problem with narrow alleys was that, once one of the gang pushed past him, he was trapped. They had caught him like that a couple of times. Since then he tended to go the long way round, walking along Hornsey Road until he could turn right and double back to Birnam Road where he lived. It was raining and he deliberated over whether to risk it. As he hesitated, a woman approached. He seized his chance and entered the estate right behind her. He had no idea if they were in there, skulking in the shadows, but he couldn't smell cigarette smoke or hear their voices. Even if they were there, waiting silently, they would probably leave him alone with the woman walking in front of him. Safety in numbers, he thought. He began to hum under his breath.

It was very quiet on the estate. Charlie's trainers padded softly and the woman moved silently ahead of him. Her pace quickened as she entered an alley between the blocks. It crossed his mind that she might be afraid of him. The idea made him smile and he walked faster to keep up with her. In the half light he saw the woman glance anxiously over her shoulder and he felt a slight thrill. There was no longer any doubt about it. She was frightened of him. That could only mean one thing. She was expecting him to mug her. He glanced around. There was no one else in sight. Grinning, he trotted closer, eyeing the bag slung across her shoulder. If his mother refused to replace his phone, he would sort it himself. He should have thought of this before, it was so obvious.

Catching up with her half way along the alley, he looked back over his shoulder. The place was deserted. With one short stride he reached her, grabbed hold of her bag and yanked it. It was unexpectedly heavy. The wide leather strap slipped off her shoulder and down her arm. But instead of letting go, the stupid cow clutched at the bag with both hands, jerking it out of his grasp. She didn't turn round. He couldn't see past her hunched shoulders but she seemed to be fumbling inside the bag. Close up he could see she was wearing a smart coat and her hair smelled of some poncy perfume that probably cost a bomb. With renewed vigour he grabbed at the strap of her bag. She must have a few quid in there, a decent phone and some feminine stuff he could wrap up and give his mother for Christmas.

He tugged harder at the strap with one hand, at the same time giving her a smart shove between her shoulder blades to make her lose her footing. It wouldn't be difficult to whip the strap from her shoulder as she struggled to keep her balance, and by the time she found her feet he would have vanished. It was that simple. He hung on. Instead of letting go, the woman spun round. He caught a glimpse of her eyes, staring maniacally as she raised her arm above her head. He was so startled that for a fraction of a second he didn't realise what she was doing. In the nick of time he dodged back and the hammer she was wielding hit him only a glancing blow on the side of his head. The pain was excruciating. If he hadn't darted back out of reach, she would have killed him.

For a second he was dazed. He was vaguely aware that his back was pressed against the wall. His legs were too weak to support him and he was sliding slowly down the wall to the ground. A movement alerted him to his assailant, still there in the alley. With difficulty he opened his eyes. Her arm was raised, her face a mask of loathing. He tried to stammer an apology, but his mouth wouldn't work. All at once she stopped, her arm above her head, turned and fled. As he slumped to the ground, he became aware of voices echoing along the alley.

A moment later two women hurried past. He thought they hadn't noticed him lying against the wall, but as they scurried by he heard them muttering. One of them said something about a tramp, and how it shouldn't be allowed. Her voice floated back to him, sour and disapproving.

'There must be places for them to go.'

He didn't care what they were saying. Those women had probably saved his life.

He heard hoarse moaning and realised the noise was coming from his own throat. He pressed his lips together and sat up. Feeling the side of his head gingerly, his fingers slid in wetness. He was bleeding. With a groan he staggered to his feet, blinking. Everything looked strangely fuzzy and he felt dizzy. Without warning he threw up. Sitting on the ground, stinking of sick and bleeding, he began to cry. Regularly mugged by other boys, he hadn't even managed to mug a lone woman.

Thankfully the house was empty when he finally staggered home. In the bathroom he studied his face in the cloudy mirror. A layer of skin had been scraped off the side of his face, the deep graze bordered down one side by a nasty bruise. He touched the surface of his damaged skin and winced. With trembling fingers he stroked his hair sideways across his temple to cover the bruise as well as he could, resolving to tell no one how a woman had bettered him in a fight. It was lucky his straggly hair was so overgrown. He would tell his mother he had fallen over, scraping the side of his head. At school he would have to spin a yarn about how he had fought off three muggers, all by himself. He could just imagine what his classmates would say if they found out he had been beaten up by a woman. He smiled grimly at his reflection and flinched when the movement made the side of his head smart.

CHAPTER 63

Geraldine sat down at her desk with a take-away and logged on. She hadn't gone to the canteen for lunch because she wanted to be alone to check through all the files stored on the internal data system. Details of everyone interviewed or questioned in connection with the victims had been entered and there were a lot of documents to look at. It promised to be a tedious job. What made it even more time-consuming was that she didn't yet know what she was looking for. All she could do was hope she might stumble upon some piece of information that would point her in the right direction. It was going to take her days to read through everything again, and would probably prove pointless in the end, but she had to do something. Every time she closed her eyes she saw Mrs Birch's scrawny figure sitting alone in her untidy front room.

Picking at her lunch, she left most of it to grow cold while she scanned through all the earlier suspects' statements, starting with Amy. As she read, she remembered the widow's expensive clothes and immaculate hair, and wondered what she was doing right now. Not grieving over her dead husband, that was for sure. She turned her attention to Guy. Since Amy and her lover had first been suspects, the case had become far more complex. There was no way they could be responsible for all four murders that had taken place.

It seemed like months since they had started the investigation and there were still many unanswered questions, like Stella's role in Henshaw's life, but beyond curiosity there was no reason to investigate those early suspects. Nothing they had said helped establish who had killed Henshaw, Corless, Bradshaw and now Birch. And if the police didn't find the killer soon, there might be other victims before long. It wasn't her fault the killer remained at large, but Geraldine couldn't help feeling accountable. She focused on her reading with renewed determination. She had access to all the information so far gathered. If there was any hint of a clue that had been overlooked, she had to find it. That she had done her best wouldn't exonerate her.

'Hey, you look miles away.'

Nick's desk was placed at right angles to hers; he must have walked right past her without her noticing. She gave him a cursory glance. His features softened into a smile, inviting conversation.

'I'm thinking,' she answered tersely, not wanting her train of thought to be further interrupted.

She turned away, signalling that she wanted to be left alone. To her annoyance, he stood up and came over to perch on the edge of her desk. Resisting an impulse to snap at him, she kept her eyes fixed on her screen.

'Must be interesting,' he ventured.

He smiled warmly as though he was perfectly comfortable twisting round to look at her. She didn't answer.

'Still working on the Hammer Horror?'

She looked up on hearing him use the term coined by some idiot reporter.

'The Hammer Horror?' she snorted. 'That's what the bloody tabloids are calling him.'

'Oh, I wouldn't pay attention to anything those hangers-on say. You just get on with the job.'

'That's what I'm trying to do right now.'

'Well, don't let me stop you.'

He waited for a few seconds but she didn't look up from her screen so he retreated to his own desk where he sat shuffling papers.

Geraldine scowled. Her attempt to pre-empt distraction had failed, because now she was bothered by the possibility that she had offended her colleague. She had nothing against Nick and besides, they had to share an office.

'I'm sorry to be unsociable, it's just that I'm bogged down in all this.'

'Can I help?'

'Hardly. I mean, you don't know the case from the inside, and it's really a matter of going over details again. If I had to start explaining, it would – well, it would waste time . . .'

He was back on her desk, smiling in his relaxed way that really wound her up in her present state of agitation. It was hard to believe he could be so dense as to ignore the obvious fact that she wanted to be left alone to get on with her work.

'I'm very experienced,' he said. 'I'm sure I can be of assistance, and I can easily spare half an hour to help reduce the load on an overworked colleague.'

Now Geraldine felt irritated with herself for resenting his tone. She knew he didn't intend to come across as patronising, but genuinely wanted to help. All the same, she began to understand how he could have riled Sam.

'Thanks, but I really need to get on.'

No longer caring if Nick took her abrupt dismissal the wrong way, she settled back to work.

She went over what Corless and his girlfriend had said. Closing the last document, she turned her attention to witnesses and studied Keith Apsley's statement. It was growing late and she was nowhere near finished.

'I'm off,' Nick announced. 'If you're sure I can't help you out?'

Geraldine looked up. Maybe she should go home

and forget about work for the evening, so she could return to it fresh in the morning. She was wasting her time, going over and over the same old documents.

'I think I should pack this in too,' she said, leaning back in her chair with a sigh.

Nick raised his eyebrows.

'I mean for today,' she added.

'I thought you were saying you'd had enough of the job altogether.'

'I do feel like that sometimes,' she admitted.

'Leave it for the evening and come for a drink then,' he suggested.

She was tempted but shook her head.

'I'll take a rain check on that,' she replied, turning back to her terminal. 'I really should crack on for a bit longer.'

He wished her luck and left, whistling cheerily.

For a moment she was tempted to run after him. Instead, she turned her attention back to the screen and pressed on resolutely, knowing she would carry on until exhaustion forced her to stop for the night. Although that was hardly an efficient way to proceed, ideas often occurred to her when she was mentally exhausted, immersed in a case that was going nowhere, as though she found inspiration in despair. They suspected the killer was a woman, but that didn't narrow the search down very much. She forced herself to keep her eyes open, fixed on the screen, but her concentration kept wavering.

She must have dozed off. Suddenly she opened her eyes, wide awake, and reopened Desiree's file with fingers that fumbled at the keyboard in her hurry. After rereading the document, she fished in her bag to retrieve her notebook and flicked through the pages to check her original record of the meeting.

'Desiree met GC while she was singing at restaurant – he offered a lift home.'

Setting the book down on the desk beside her half eaten takeaway she leaned back in her chair, frowning. Desiree was a singer. She met George Corless at the restaurant. He had given her a lift home. That was how they had met. The words revolved in her head, forming a possible new scenario which she examined from different angles. Whichever way she considered it the story made sense, apart from one glaring problem.

A singer called Ingrid had performed at Mireille on the evening of Henshaw's murder. The records kept by the restaurant were incomplete, but the same singer could have been there on the evening Corless was killed. The two men might both have offered her a lift home, as Corless had done at least once, with Desiree. If the cleaner was to be believed, Henshaw had 'an eye for the girls.' Geraldine looked up what Ginny had said. 'He was the one wanted those girl singers, and he'd have had them do more than sing, I daresay—' Ignoring the conundrum of Linda Harrison's DNA in the car, she speculated about a violent encounter in the car with a singer who had accepted a lift home, an encounter that ended with a brutal murder. Sam had spoken to Ingrid in Shepherds Bush. Was it possible that the singer was the killer? Sam had described her as slight and unprepossessing. At the time she hadn't aroused their interest. Now Geraldine wanted to know more.

Sam hadn't recorded Ingrid's surname, which was irritating, but Geraldine understood that pressing someone for information could backfire. According to Sam's notes, it had been hard to wheedle anything out of Ingrid. It didn't matter. In a few seconds, Geraldine would be able to find out all she needed to know. The manager at Mireille hadn't been able to help her but the information was available at the click of a 'live music' icon on the website of the café in Shepherds Bush. It couldn't have been easier to find. With trembling fingers she looked up the singer who was listed only as 'Ingrid' and found a link to her website. Geraldine held her breath. Another click of a button revealed that the website was 'under construction'. She was still no closer to finding the singer, but if Ingrid really was the killer, Geraldine couldn't afford to wait nearly a week to find her singing in Shepherds Bush.

CHAPTER 64

For once, Charlie didn't oversleep. His night had been restless, disturbed by a pounding headache. When he had managed to doze off, his dreams had been troubled by images of a mad woman charging at him wielding a variety of weapons: an old-style police truncheon, a long gleaming sword, a snake that hissed by his ear before snapping crocodile jaws at the side of his head, hacking off chunks of flesh until his head had all but disappeared down its gullet. The snake withdrew and Charlie saw his own face staring back at him. He wondered how he could still see when his own eyes were gazing at him from the serpent head. The snake lunged forward. He tried to run but couldn't see where he was going. In the darkness he tripped and woke with a jolt, muzzy and fretful from pain and lack of sleep.

By the time his mother banged on his bedroom door, bawling at him to get up, he was already awake and staring in dismay at his blood stained pillow. His head wound had bled onto his school jacket, the discolouration barely visible on the dark fabric. He could sling it over his arm when he left the house, after which he would conveniently 'lose' it, just to be on the safe side. He hardly ever wore it anyway. It was best not to take any chances where his mother was concerned. Once her suspicions were aroused he would never hear the end of it. He could hide his wound without too much trouble, concealing it beneath his hood. It wasn't ideal, but it was the best he could do. Once he had left for the day, he would stay out of the house as long as possible, and run straight upstairs when he got in. With any luck she would never notice he'd been injured.

His pillow was not so easily disposed of. He could hardly throw that away. He racked his brains, trying to come up with an excuse for a missing pillow, because even if he succeeded in leaving the house without his mother catching sight of the gash on his head, the pillow would give the game away. Although he had banned her from his room, she went in there all the time, nosing around, checking up on him, ever since she had found a packet of her fags beside his bed. She was bound to go in and see the bloody pillow and then all hell would break loose. He would be grounded, and his mother would insist on marching off to the school to complain, as though that would make any difference. She was always complaining, and it only made things worse for him. All the teachers hated him because of her fussing, and the other kids knew it. Anxiously, he pushed the pillow under his duvet.

With the stained pillow concealed for the time being, he felt more positive. She probably wouldn't notice. By the time she saw it, the gash on his head would have healed and he could make up some bull about having cut his finger or something equally innocuous. Anything to prevent her finding out that he had been set upon again. There was no way he was going to tell anyone the truth about being attacked by a woman. The more he thought about it, the less he liked the idea of anyone finding out. Apart from the fact that he would become a laughing stock at school, it raised all sorts of awkward questions.

Adults always closed ranks. They were bound to suspect the woman had been acting in self-defence, raising questions about what he had been up to, setting on her. The only alternative was to convince everyone he was the victim of an assault. And if he lied about his attacker being a woman, his mother would start banging on about going to the police who would check CCTV and find out he had been lying about being beaten up by a gang of lads on the estate. It was all so complicated, it made his aching head spin. Only one thing was clear. No one must ever find out what had happened. He skipped out of the house without stopping for breakfast.

'Gotta go, I'll be late for school.'

'When did you ever care about being on time? And take that bloody hoodie off. What's wrong with your jacket? I spent good money getting you a proper uniform for that school.'

Ignoring her raised voice as he ran through the door, he raced along the walkway and down the concrete staircase. He had no intention of going back to school until his head had healed. As long as he kept his hood up, he could move around without attracting attention. His head was still throbbing but he didn't feel too bad, and he had a tenner in his pocket that he had borrowed from his mother's purse. Stupid cow should have been more careful. She would blame it on him, of course, as per usual, but in the meantime he was on his way to the shopping centre with a free day ahead of him and ten quid in his pocket. Stuff her. Stuff them all. This was his time and he intended to make the most of it.

Talk about unlucky. He still had the note in his jeans pocket and could have paid for the bar of chocolate ten times over. They shouldn't leave goodies on display like that, if they didn't want people to help themselves. It was there for the taking. The sodding security guard caught him just outside the shop.

'Fuck off! You've got to be joking. It's only a fucking bar of chocolate! Here, have it.'

He squirmed but the security guard kept a tight grip on his arm. Inexorably dragged back into the shop, he continued his protest, keeping his head down because people had started to look at him.

'I can pay for it if you let go of my fucking arm. I've got ten quid on me. I'll pay for it. Take the money. Let me go.'

The office was a poky room with a desk and some rusty filing cabinets along one wall. Charlie thought the manager would have had a more impressive place to work. He looked the old geezer straight in the eye and decided to appeal to his good nature. He looked like a goody goody sort. After all, it was only a bar of chocolate.

'I'm very sorry, sir,' he stammered.

He tried to sound scared, which wasn't difficult, because he was shitting himself in case his mother found out. He could just imagine her reaction.

'I don't know what come over me, sir. I've never done nothing like it before, and—'

'Take off that hood,' the manager barked.

Charlie's heart sank. So much for expecting kindness and charity.

'It was a mistake, sir. I forgot I'd picked it up. Jesus, it's only a fucking bar of chocolate. Here, you can have it and I'll pay you the money – I've got ten quid—'

He chucked the Toblerone down on the manager's desk and rummaged in his pocket for the note.

'I don't even want it. It was for me sick granny. For fuck's sake, it's not fair to make such a bloody fuss over a fucking bar of chocolate. I've never been in no trouble before. It'll kill me mum.'

He stared at the old man, trying to look all young and innocent, but the manager wasn't taken in.

'You should have thought of that before you attempted to steal from my store. I've had more than enough of you youngsters carrying on as though the world owes you a living. It's all take with you lot, isn't it, all rights and no responsibilities. Do you have any idea how much money this store alone loses every month from this sort of petty pilfering?'

Charlie tried to think of a way out, but he was well and truly screwed, his escape route blocked by the security guard who was built like a tank. The manager refused to listen to reason and kept banging on about responsibility. It was so boring, Charlie might as well have been at school. There was no getting away from it. He was nicked.

CHAPTER 65

Geraldine fretted at her desk, checking her phone and her screen for updates, but there was no news. Every few minutes she slipped along the corridor to check with the intelligence officer who was liaising with the borough intelligence unit, working to trace the singer. Each time Geraldine went in her colleague shook her head.

'Not yet. I'm still waiting to hear, but it shouldn't take long.'

Trying to quell her impatience, Geraldine returned to her desk and fiddled about but she couldn't concentrate on anything else until she had followed up her hunch about the singer, Ingrid.

'Is everything alright?' Nick asked, swivelling his chair round to face her.

She found his fixed stare disconcerting.

'Fine, thank you.'

'Only you're like a cat on heat this morning.'

Instead of replying, she turned back to her screen. Nick was only trying to be sociable, but his approaches were increasingly grating on her nerves. She wasn't sure if Sam's antipathy for him was colouring her own feelings. Certainly she resented the fact that Sam rarely wandered into the office to talk over cases since Nick had returned to share Geraldine's office. When challenged, the sergeant acknowledged so readily that she was being petty, that Geraldine suspected there was more to the falling out than either Nick or Sam had told her. Perhaps he had been insulting about Sam's sexual orientation, without realising she was a lesbian. Whatever the cause of their bad feeling, Sam didn't feel comfortable in Nick's presence.

'We're getting somewhere,' her colleague told her at last, looking up with a smile. 'Ingrid used to sing with a band called Lazy Bones but she split from them nearly a year ago. Since then she's been working alone, singing with a variety of different groups and doing solo gigs in pubs and restaurants mainly. She seems to float about.'

'And the address?'

'We're still checking. We're working our way through all the venues where she's worked over the past year trying to get her full name, but it's a slow job. All the managers who organise music seem to be taking a day off today. And we can't raise any response from the agent listed on one of the venue's sites. The email address doesn't exist.'

The intelligence officer was called Jessica, which reminded Geraldine of Hannah's daughter, and her insistence on changing her name.

'We've drawn a blank so far for Emily Tennant,' she said, 'but we haven't tried Ingrid Tennant. Let's try that. Ingrid Tennant.'

'Did you say Ingrid Tennant?'

'Yes. Go on, try it. It's just an idea.'

'OK. If you say so.'

Reg looked puzzled when Geraldine told him she was looking for Emily Tennant, the woman she believed was the niece of a convicted murderer, Linda Harrison.

'Not sure where you're going with this, Geraldine. Just because her aunt's a convicted killer, that doesn't make her a suspect. I'm not sure what your point is.'

He sounded tired and leaned back in his chair with his eyes closed as she explained her suspicion that the DNA found on Patrick might have come from Linda's niece.

'Oh, I see. Very well, of course you must follow it up in that case,' he told her, opening his eyes and sitting upright. He glanced at his watch.

'Reg you have to admit—'

'Yes, yes, I said follow it up, Geraldine.'

Narked by his apathetic response she left the office, her enthusiasm dampened. She was on her way back to her desk when a sergeant stopped her. A constable had come across a boy he thought might have encountered the killer. It sounded like a long shot, but they had to follow it up. The most unlikely of possibilities sometimes turned out to be invaluable.

She went back to her office and was about to summon Sam when her phone rang. The intelligence unit had come up with an address for a singer called Ingrid Tennant.

'What are the chances it's her?' Geraldine asked.

'Oh, it's her alright. We checked it out with the pubs and restaurants where she sings. Most of them were pretty cagey – no doubt paying her cash from takings on the side – but a few of them came up with the same mobile number and it checks out. She's renting a flat from a Mr Delaney. I've just sent you all the details.'

Geraldine thanked her colleague and hung up, checking her screen as she did so. A second later the details came through.

'Bingo,' she muttered.

Sending her sergeant to speak to the constable who had interviewed the boy, Geraldine decided to proceed to Bounds Green and check out the singer's address. Without a DNA sample from Ingrid Tennant, the evidence was circumstantial. The girl had performed at Mireille on the evening when Henshaw was killed, and may have been there when Corless died too, but that was inconclusive, as she often sang there. Apart from that, there was nothing to link her to the other two murder victims.

'You've found out nothing at all about her earlier life?' Geraldine asked. 'There must be something, surely.'

The intelligence officer just smiled and shook her head.

'Not yet.'

'Isn't that a bit unusual? I mean, doesn't that suggest there's something dodgy about her?'

'Oh, we'll dig something up, sooner or later. Do you want us to ask around? Although you'll have to sort out the man power.'

Geraldine shook her head.

'No, don't worry, you've got her address. That's good enough. We can ask her to tell us what she's been up to.'

The address she had been given was only a short walk from the station but she would have to take the Northern line into Kings Cross and change to the Piccadilly line out to Bounds Green so she decided to drive to the dingy street of terraced properties where Ingrid lived. Climbing a few stone steps to the front door she rang the unnamed bell for 26a. There was no answer. She rang again then knocked loudly several times until she heard footsteps approach. The door swung open to reveal a short stout man in his fifties, wheezing from the exertion of running downstairs, his bald head emphasising his ruddy complexion and bulging eyes.

'What's all the racket?' he demanded.

* * *

Geraldine introduced herself and explained she was looking for the woman who lived at flat number 26a. As soon as she mentioned her business his stance altered. No longer posturing belligerently, he ducked his head in an obsequious gesture, his expression suddenly craven. He blinked up at her with eyes almost closed by creases of flesh that threatened to envelop them.

'It's about time you lot turned up,' he declared. 'One blinking constable, that's all I've ever seen, and he didn't do anything, just took down a few details, and that was the end of it. I never heard anything more. I've been calling you for months.'

'I'm sorry, calling about what?'

'The woman at 26a. The one who lives downstairs. It's about time someone started to take this seriously.'

Ingrid's neighbour laboured his point, but what it boiled down to was that her singing irritated him. His face turned a deeper shade of red as he worked himself up into a temper.

'All the bloody time,' he fumed, 'she's at it all the bloody time with her bloody racket. It's a cut and dried case of noise pollution, all out of tune she is and out of time. It wouldn't be so bad if she sang some proper songs, not all this modern rubbish.'

Geraldine didn't tell him the purpose of her visit.

'Out at all hours, she is,' he went on, warming

to his invective. 'And up to no good, I've no doubt. Caterwauling like that, it's not normal.'

'Do you know when she's likely to come back?'

He shrugged.

'In and out all the time, she is. There's no knowing with that one. But I can tell you she's usually home late afternoon. And then she goes out again for the evening. I'm telling you, there's something not right about the way that girl's allowed to carry on. I'm glad something's finally being done about it. I'm not saying she should be locked up or anything, but she can't carry on causing such a disturbance. It's not legal, is it?'

Geraldine pressed him to say more.

'Off the record, Mr—?'

'Parker. Jeff Parker. I don't care if it's on the record. It bloody well should be on the record by now. She's a complete basket case.'

'Basket case?'

'With all that singing.'

Geraldine's phone rang and she excused herself and walked back to her car as she took the call. It was Sam, enquiring how she was getting on, and asking if she wanted company. Geraldine quickly brought her up to speed. There wasn't much to say. In return Sam told her about a possible witness a constable had spoken to: a young boy who had been caught shoplifting. He had been assaulted prior to his arrest. Under questioning he had broken down and admitted he had been attacked by a woman.

'Is that it?'

'Yes.'

'So there's nothing concrete to link him to the case?'

'Only that he was bashed on the side of the head by a woman on the Andover Estate, about a mile or so from where Henshaw's body was found.'

'But she didn't kill him?'

'No. He's only a kid.'

Geraldine thought about it. The chances were the incident had nothing whatever to do with the murder investigation, but it was possible the boy had encountered the killer, and had a lucky escape.

'It could have been the same woman. Luckily the manager of the shop called up about the theft – it was only a bar of chocolate – and the constable who attended the scene was on the ball. It looks like the boy might have survived an attempted fatal assault. He wasn't exactly forthcoming – I think he was petrified his mother would find out he'd been nicked for pilfering. But if he can identify his attacker . . .'

'Find out exactly where it happened and alert Visual Images Identification and Detection Office,' Geraldine told her. 'We need to view all CCTV we can get hold of from the area at the time of the attack, check who else was around, and see if we can get a look at his attacker. At the very least we should be able to confirm the gender and general appearance.'

They agreed that Sam should speak to the boy and find out more about the attack. Meanwhile, Geraldine intended to sit tight and wait for Ingrid to come home. She couldn't afford to let her slip away. Geraldine hoped a DNA sample from the young singer would place her at the scene of the murders. If not, it was best to find out soon so they could stop wasting time on her.

'Are you sure you don't want to see the boy?' Sam asked. 'This could be the break we've been waiting for. He might have seen the killer.'

Even down the phone, Sam's excitement was clear. Geraldine smiled.

'No,' she replied, 'I'll leave it to you. I'm going to sit it out here for a while. Ingrid's neighbour said she's usually home late afternoon. Find out what you can and I'll see you back at the station in a couple of hours.'

CHAPTER 66

Sam never liked being stuck at her desk, staring at the four constables on her team. It wasn't that they didn't have enough to do, checking the VIDO reports, liaising with borough intelligence, beavering away hunting for information, and right now they were fully occupied searching for anything that could link the four victims. With Henshaw and Corless the case had presented a tidy picture. The two men had not only worked together and known one another's wives, they had no doubt been privy to the skeletons each had squirreled away in their closets. Bradshaw remained an enigma, and the addition of Birch to the death toll did nothing to clear the obscurity that seemed to grow around the case with every passing day. While she appreciated the necessity of spending hours ferreting out information, she was always happiest when she was out and about looking for answers in the real world, leaving the virtual maze for others to track online. Missing Geraldine, she set three of her constables to assist the VIDO team in viewing CCTV, and took Detective Constable Christian Whittaker with her to see what they could find out about Charlie Lewes, the young boy who had been attacked on the Andover Estate.

Charlie was a skinny lad, with floppy light brown hair and narrow brown eyes that glared from beneath lowered lids. Either his memory had been knocked out of him in the attack or else he was deliberately refusing to co-operate, because whatever question was put to him, he was unable to come up with an answer.

'How did you get that bruise, Charlie?'

'Can't remember.'

'Who hit you?'

'Don't know.'

'How can you not know who did that to you?'

'Can't remember.'

'Was it your mum?'

'Me mum? You having a laugh? She knows better than to lay a finger on me.'

Despite vociferous protests, the boy had been given a medical examination.

'It's for your own good,' Sam had explained.

'What would be good would be to let me go home. It was only a bleeding bar of chocolate.'

The medical officer was positive the blow had been indirect. If the implement had struck full on, there was no way the boy would have escaped serious damage. As it was, he had suffered a flesh wound that looked nastier than it actually was. Skin had been scraped away as the bludgeon slid along the side of his head, but internal damage appeared minimal. The boy was sent for an x-ray to make sure, but the doctor was confident the victim had suffered only superficial damage.

'Would it have been enough to knock him out?' Sam asked.

The doctor shrugged.

'He might have been stunned, in the sense that he'd received a terrible shock. As to whether he actually lost consciousness or not, that's something you'll have to ask him.'

Charlie's form teacher at school was a harassed-looking middle-aged woman, who groaned when she heard the police had come to see her about Charlie.

'What's he done now? I noticed he wasn't in school today. He's not in trouble is he?'

Without answering the question, Sam asked if Charlie had been in any fights in school recently. The teacher said she wasn't aware of any such incident.

'What about injuries?'

'What sort of injury are you talking about? He's a boy. They fall over, knock each other about playing football, that sort of thing. But we don't have any trouble here with fighting and—'

'I'm talking about a nasty-looking head injury, on the right side of his head, bruised and perhaps bleeding. You couldn't miss it.'

* * *

The teacher shook her head.

'A head injury, you say? That wouldn't go unrecorded.'

'When did you last see him?'

Flustered, she checked her register.

'Yes, here it is, 9S,' she muttered. 'He was here yesterday, but not today. I saw him at the end of the school day yesterday and he didn't have any head injuries then as far as I'm aware. Whatever it is you're investigating, it must have happened after he left school yesterday.'

She looked up with a smile as though relieved the injury hadn't happened in school.

'He's in my tutor group,' she added, sounding more confident.

'What about his mother? Could she be beating him at home? Enough to cause potentially serious injury?'

The teacher shook her head.

'I doubt it very much. She's the overprotective type, always coming into school complaining.'

'About what?'

'Some parents just complain a lot, it doesn't seem to matter what it's about. Most of them just want to blame the school for their children's bad upbringing. It happens a lot, especially when there's no father at home. The mothers are either violent or over-indulgent. Sometimes both.'

She laughed nervously.

* * *

A figure resembling Charlie was spotted on camera near his home at eight thirty that morning. Close examination of the film disclosed a stain on the side of his hood that could have been blood. It was difficult to tell on the grainy black and white film, but comparison with a blood stain on Charlie's jacket confirmed the identity of the figure, so he had been injured at some time between leaving school at four on Wednesday and leaving home around eight on Thursday morning. The entire Visual Images Identification and Detection Office was tasked with following Charlie after he left school the previous day. There was much interruption as he travelled unwittingly from camera to camera, until he was picked up turning into Todds Walk, not far South of his home.

'He entered the estate all right,' the VIDO officer said, 'but he didn't arrive at Birnam Road for nearly an hour. It's less than half a mile. It shouldn't have taken him more than ten minutes at the most.'

'Was anyone else around on the Hornsey Road who might have seen something? Could he have fallen over . . .?'

'The only other figure there at the same time was this – hang on—'

The officer rewound the tape back to the point where Charlie went into Todds Walk. A woman had turned off a few seconds earlier.

'He was hanging around for a few minutes before

he turned off,' the VIDO officer said, 'almost as though he was waiting for her.'

'Or for someone. According to his mother he'd been mugged twice on his way home from school. She insists it's all the fault of the school, but the Andover Estate is notorious for its gangs and she knows that. She told him not to cut through the estate but to go the long way round along the main road. Perhaps he just didn't want to go in there on his own.'

'I'll check back and find out who else was around,' the VIDO officer said.

'If there was anyone else there,' Sam muttered under her breath.

She turned back to her colleague.

'Before you do that, I want images of the woman, enhanced to give as clear an image of her figure and her face as possible, and send them to me as a priority.'

'But—'

'Now please!'

Picking up the urgency in Sam's voice, the VIDO officer set to work.

Sam called Geraldine but there was no answer. With growing unease she rapped at the detective chief inspector's door and brought him up to date with the CCTV evidence.

'So it's looking like this singer might be responsible,' she concluded. 'It looks like a woman, at any rate.'

'We don't know the woman who assaulted the boy in the tunnel has got anything to do with the murders,' Reg pointed out.

'But it's a possibility. Shall I go after her?' Sam asked.

'Who?'

Sam explained that Geraldine had gone to question Ingrid Tennant. She hadn't returned and wasn't answering her phone. Reg listened closely, frowning, and nodded when she finished speaking.

'Go on then,' he agreed. 'Take a couple of constables and go over there. And let's hope this singer can tell us something useful.'

CHAPTER 67

Geraldine waited outside Ingrid's flat for almost an hour. It hadn't taken long to scan through the sketchy information the intelligence unit had dug up on her. By contrast there was a lot of background detail on Linda Harrison. She read and reread it while she waited, familiarising herself with the prisoner's history. Comparing pictures of Ingrid and Linda, there did seem to be a resemblance, although the pictures she had of Ingrid weren't very clear and it was impossible to be sure.

Absorbed in her reading, she almost missed her target. It was drizzling and the woman walked so quickly up the path she had reached the front door before Geraldine spotted her black raincoat and grey scarf. She had only ever viewed a picture of the singer online and could see nothing of the woman's face as she unlocked the door and hurried inside. Geraldine barely caught a glimpse of the black coat, grey scarf and large bag slung across one shoulder before the figure vanished inside. Nevertheless she felt a thrill of anticipation. She was almost sure she had just seen Ingrid Tennant. Deciding not to stop to summon Sam, she climbed out of the car and scurried across the road. She didn't want to risk losing her suspect now. The rain was falling heavily in fine drops that swept sideways under her umbrella, and by the time Geraldine reached the front door, her ankles and shins were soaked. Clutching her jacket closer to her chest, she reached out to ring the bell. As she did so, Jeff Parker opened the door.

'Oh it's you,' he greeted her, surprised but pleased. 'Come to speak to her at number 26a about her bloody racket, have you? About time too. Number 26a, it's that door there.'

He pointed along a corridor brightly illuminated by lights placed at intervals along the walls.

'Wish I could stay around to hear you give her a dressing down but my sister's expecting me and I'll be in hot water if I'm late. I hope you give her what for. She's had it coming for a long time.'

With a quick grin, he bounced down the steps and trotted away, whistling.

There was no response when Geraldine rang the bell. Wondering if Ingrid was in the shower, or listening to music, she pulled out her phone to call Sam. As she did so, the door to the flat was suddenly opened by a blonde woman in steel rimmed glasses. The interior behind her was dark as she peered out, blinking into the brightly lit hall. There was a strong stench coming from the flat. It smelled like insecticide.

'What do you want?' the blonde woman asked in a low voice.

'I'm looking for Ingrid Tennant.'

'Ingrid? She's my flatmate.'

The woman took a step back, her head lowered. Her shoulders were bowed and a bedraggled fringe fell down to her eyes, brushing the top of her glasses.

As Geraldine introduced herself, something warned her to be discreet. She played her interest down, claiming she just wanted to have a brief word with Ingrid concerning an ongoing enquiry.

'What's it about?'

Ingrid's flatmate didn't sound very interested. She shuffled back so Geraldine couldn't see her features, half concealed by the door. Geraldine hastened to reassure her it was nothing important. When the other woman wanted to know if it was to do with the neighbour upstairs, Geraldine gave a non-committal grunt, adding that she was unable to disclose the reason for her visit.

'Do you know when Ingrid will be back?'

The blonde woman shook her head, hesitating. 'You can come in and wait if you like.'

She turned and led Geraldine into a small kitchen where she pulled a three-legged stool out from underneath a work surface.

'You can sit down there, while you're waiting.'

'Thank you.'

'Would you like a cup of tea? Or coffee?'

Geraldine sat on the stool and looked around the kitchen which was small but immaculate. The worktops were clear, four matching mugs stood in a neat line next to a polished kettle, and two identical saucepans stood on the hob, their handles exactly parallel. A row of metal kitchen implements hung on pegs by the sink, beside a row of sharp knives. Geraldine checked that none of the knives was missing, even though the victims had been battered, not stabbed; it was an automatic reaction. Everything was gleaming as though the kitchen had just been scrubbed.

With her back to Geraldine, the blonde woman switched on the kettle and took a carton of milk from the fridge.

'How long have you shared a flat with Ingrid?'

'What did you say you wanted to see her about?' the girl answered with a question.

Her voice was oddly flat. As she shut the fridge she turned to face Geraldine for an instant, before her eyes flitted away. Something about the situation didn't feel right, although Geraldine couldn't pinpoint what was wrong. She had experienced that sensation before, a feeling that she had seen or heard something significant, if she could only work out what it was.

'I didn't,' she replied, smiling pointlessly because the woman didn't look round.

It was odd how Ingrid's flatmate had invited her into the flat, although she was apparently too shy to even look at her.

'What's your name?'

The woman didn't answer. Instead she stretched out her arm to lift a large black handbag from the floor, still without turning round. Thankful that everything in the kitchen was polished and gleaming, Geraldine kept her eyes fixed on the woman's reflection in the metal toaster, watching closely as the distorted image reached into the bag. Something moved in the reflection, glinting silver. As the woman spun round and threw herself across the room, Geraldine leaped from the stool. Out of the corner of her eye she was aware of something flashing past the side of her head to crash down on the edge of the work top. She was trapped in a cramped kitchen with a homicidal maniac. Her mind raced as she registered what the woman was wielding. A hammer. It had struck the worktop with such force it made a dent in the surface, leaving scattered dark flecks. The blow would have crushed a human skull.

Ingrid brandished her weapon again as she turned to face Geraldine, her eyes glistening with frenzied triumph. Geraldine saw that the blonde hair had slipped to one side of her head, revealing dark hair beneath.

'You won't get me this time,' Ingrid hissed.

She lunged forward, swinging the hammer above her head.

CHAPTER 68

Sam hurried from the detective chief inspector's office, stabbing at her phone as she made her way along the quiet corridor back to her own office.

'This is Geraldine Steel. Please leave a message. For urgent calls please contact . . .'

Reg was a cold fish, as a rule, sitting at his desk working out strategies and calculating odds from the safety of his office. He rarely expressed emotion, but even he had seemed concerned about Geraldine.

Sam nipped into her office and collected a couple of constables who scurried after her, like children eager for an outing.

'Where to?' one of them asked as they left the building.

They were both smiling, pleased to be away from their desks, young and enthusiastic. At the sight of their grinning faces, Sam felt her tension dissipate. The sun was shining. Geraldine had gone to question a witness who might possibly turn out to be a suspect. There was no reason to suppose she might be in any more danger than any other officer out meeting the public. Besides, Ingrid was only a slip of a girl. Geraldine could take care of herself. Nevertheless, Sam ran to the car, urging her colleagues to hurry.

'We're going to Bounds Green,' she told her companions as they set off. 'Geraldine's gone to question a suspect, and we're going over there to check how things are going.'

'Has she called for back up?'

'No.'

The two constables exchanged a glance.

'She's not answering her phone,' Sam explained.

'Why not?'

'That's what we're going to find out.'

'You don't think anything's happened to her, do you?' one of the constables asked.

'More likely her phone's the problem, don't you think?' the other one pointed out.

Sam didn't answer.

On the way she tried Geraldine's phone again. There was still no answer.

'Can't we go any faster than this?' she complained.

The constable accelerated to catch up with a queue at the next red light.

'Where the hell do all these people come from? It would have been quicker to take the tube,' she grumbled, even though she was aware that would have involved travelling into central London and out again on a different line. 'We're hardly moving.

At this rate it's going to take us an hour to get there.'

A lot could happen in an hour.

Unable to contain her disquiet, she called Reg and told him they were stuck in traffic. She wasn't sure whether to feel reassured or unnerved to hear that he had already notified the nearest station to send a patrol car to Ingrid's flat. Evidently he too was worried that Geraldine wasn't answering her phone.

'I'm sure everything's fine,' he added, as though reading her mind, 'but it does no harm to be cautious.'

They crawled along until the constable who was driving darted into a side turning and they made their way through a maze of side streets, avoiding the congested main roads.

'Where the hell are we?' Sam wanted to know.

'At least we're moving,' he pointed out cheerfully and she scowled at him.

She tried Geraldine's phone again. There was no answer.

It was a comfort to know that a local patrol car had been alerted and help would arrive imminently. But that wasn't enough. If Geraldine was in trouble, Sam wanted to be there. They worked together, partners on the same team. Geraldine had only been in London for a few months but Sam thought of her as a friend, and she hoped the feeling was reciprocated. Besides which, Sam had questioned Ingrid just over a week ago. If Ingrid was the killer, and harmed Geraldine in any way, Sam would feel responsible.

'Get back to the main road and put the siren on for God's sake,' she snapped.

'Righto, sarge.'

Sam thought back to when she had first met Geraldine, and how distant her new colleague had seemed initially. It hadn't taken Sam long to penetrate her diffidence and discover that Geraldine was lonely, living on her own in London where she knew no one. On the face of it her life was perfect. Having inherited family money she was buying her own flat in a select part of Islington, and she had a reputation on the murder squad for getting quick results.

'You're lucky to be working with Geraldine Steel,' was the general response people gave when she had told colleagues about her new boss.

Few people appreciated how much Geraldine embodied the cliché of a successful career woman isolated in her private life. A failed relationship with a man who had unexpectedly left her for another woman after six years, followed by a succession of unsatisfactory affairs, had left her bitter and isolated. What made it worse was her discovery in her thirties that she had been adopted as a baby, leaving her feeling cut off from the people she had believed were her blood relatives. Although they had only been working together for just over a month, Geraldine had shared the secrets of her past with Sam, who appreciated her confidence. Out of such familiarity, friendships were forged. Geraldine trusted her. If anything were to happen to her, Sam would never forgive herself. She had met Ingrid. She should have spotted her as a suspect straight away. Now Geraldine might be in danger, and it was all her fault. She glared at the busy road ahead, frustrated with herself for not being there to help her friend, and angry with Geraldine for going out on her own.

Driving on blues and twos they made faster progress through the busy streets and finally arrived at their destination. A patrol car was parked outside number 26. Sam leaped from the car and saw two uniformed officers knocking on the front door of the building.

'When did you get here?' she yelled as she ran up the path.

'We've been here about five minutes, but no one's answering,' a burly constable replied.

'Oh shit. Let's hope we're not too late. Get that door open.'

'But—'

'Just get us inside.'

The constable glanced at his companion and then together the two of them kicked the door open with a resounding crash. They ran inside, Sam close on their heels.

'It's number 26a,' she shouted and one of the officers put his shoulder to the door of Ingrid's flat.

CHAPTER 69

Despite her terror, Geraldine couldn't suppress a wild feeling of relief. At last they had tracked down the woman who had been carrying out the killing spree. Geraldine raised her arms to protect herself as, with a loud grunt, Ingrid raised the hammer again. This time Geraldine was ready. She dodged, at the same time clenching her fists together and punching up against her assailant's arm as it descended, jabbing it sideways to deflect the blow. The hammer landed on the floor with a heavy thud. Ingrid was slight, but she was agile and surprisingly strong. If she had pressed on with her attack, she might have dealt Geraldine a serious injury. But she was distracted by her weapon. As Ingrid lunged to recover the hammer, Geraldine turned and fled.

She ran from the gleaming kitchen and raced along the narrow hallway to the front door, almost slipping on the polished floor. Ahead she could see the door was bolted, top and bottom. By the time she reached it, Ingrid would have caught up with her, hammer raised. Geraldine darted sideways into another room and shut the door, glancing around for a window. They were on the first floor, but she would be better off risking a few broken limbs than a caved in skull. She was in a pristine bedroom. On the bed a pillow lay precisely parallel to the top of the duvet cover which appeared freshly ironed. Looking around she noticed the paintwork on the window sill was faded and flaky, as though it had been scrubbed. Apart from that, the decor was flawless.

Before she had time to cross to the window, the door flew open. Flipping out her truncheon, Geraldine turned and braced herself for the next attack. There seemed little point in trying to reason with Ingrid. Geraldine's heart was pounding, yet her mind felt unnaturally clear as she faced her assailant. She looked completely demented, blonde wig askew, dark eyes burning.

'What are you doing in my bedroom?' she shrieked.

Ingrid was shaking so violently, Geraldine wondered if she would be able to hang onto the hammer she was grasping, let alone wield it.

Ingrid's scream sounded barely human as she charged forward, hammer raised. Even as she feared for her life, Geraldine registered the absurd sight of Ingrid's blonde wig, precariously attached to the side of her head by a few hair pins, swinging crazily. Geraldine had to time her defensive leap just right. Taking a deep breath, she grabbed at her assailant, twisting her arm up behind her back until Ingrid was forced to surrender to the pressure of extreme physical pain. The timbre of her screams altered as her hammer dropped to the floor once more.

Panting, Geraldine snapped handcuffs on the woman, and shoved her onto the bed. Geraldine stepped back and leaned against the wall, her legs shaking from the shock of the attack.

'Ingrid Tennant?'

All the fight seemed to have gone out of her assailant who lowered her head submissively. She didn't answer.

'Back-up is on the way, so you might as well stay calm now and co-operate. I know who you are. There's no point in keeping up the pretence. You're Ingrid Tennant, and Linda Harrison's your aunt.'

It was easy to resume control with her assailant handcuffed. Ingrid nodded and sat passively while Geraldine tugged away her dishevelled blonde wig and spectacles. Shoulder length dark hair tumbled down in a straggly pony tail. Without her wig and glasses Ingrid resembled Linda Harrison more closely, despite her heavy make-up. Ingrid stared straight ahead, with the same sullen expression her aunt had worn. Geraldine was startled by the similarity.

* * *

The silence was broken by a sudden loud crash as the door to the flat was smashed open. Geraldine heard voices calling out her name.

'In here!'

She kept her eyes fixed on Ingrid who didn't appear to have noticed the fracas out in the hall. Two uniformed officers came trampling into the room, followed a moment later by Sam with a pair of constables at her heels.

'Take off your filthy shoes, all of you!' Ingrid yelled suddenly. 'Take off your shoes. Take off your shoes,' she shrieked. 'Get out of my bedroom. This is my bedroom.'

She began to cry.

'You could have rung the bell,' Geraldine said quietly. 'There was no need to break the door down.'

'We thought – I thought—' Sam stammered. 'There was no answer—'

'Get out of here, all of you, and Sam, call SOCOs to come and take the place apart, starting with those.'

Geraldine pointed at the wig and hammer lying on the floor.

'There should be enough blood samples on there to confirm what Ingrid has to tell us. And there's no need to look so stressed,' she added firmly. 'I had everything under control.'

She remembered the dented worktop and shuddered.

CHAPTER 70

Ingrid refused to speak on the journey to the police station where she emptied her pockets without a word, handed over her watch and shoes, listened to the custody sergeant's questions and submitted to being searched. She gave her finger prints and DNA and even submitted to a medical examination, all without breaking her silence.

'Maybe a few hours in the hotel will loosen her tongue,' the custody sergeant said cheerfully.

He led her into a cell to wait for the duty solicitor. As she had doggedly refused to answer one way or the other when asked if she wanted a solicitor present at her interview, Geraldine called one anyway to avoid unnecessary delay once the interview started.

At last they were ready. The duty brief had arrived, the tapes were spinning, those present had been introduced and the regulations had been read to the suspect who had been formally arrested on a murder charge. Ingrid refused to answer questions about the deaths of Patrick Henshaw, George Corless, Maurice Bradshaw and John Birch.

'I don't know what you mean, I don't know who you're talking about, I wasn't there, it wasn't me,' was all she said.

Geraldine tried a different approach.

'You can sit there and claim ignorance of these murders until you're blue in the face, but you can't deny your attempted assault on me earlier this evening, in your kitchen.'

She paused for effect.

'Attempted murder of a police officer. That's not in question. You'll go down for that, for a long time.'

She paused, ignoring Sam's gasp. Out of the corner of her eye she could see the sergeant staring at her, wide-eyed. The solicitor's eyes flickered from Geraldine to Sam and back again, a quizzical expression on his sharp features. But nothing seemed to register with Ingrid who sat, staring dully at the table.

'You never wanted to kill me, did you?' Geraldine resumed. 'It wasn't me you were after. I'm not the one you want. Why don't you tell us what's going on, Ingrid? What exactly happened in your flat today, and why did you attack me? Ingrid?'

There was a silence. The tapes whirred gently. Somewhere outside a phone rang. The solicitor cleared his throat. Geraldine leaned forward and spoke gently.

'You didn't mean to kill me, did you? So why did you attack me? You know you could have killed me. Why did you do it?'

Ingrid didn't answer.

'Tell me about your uncle,' Geraldine gently. 'Tell me all about it.'

'He had to be stopped!' Ingrid suddenly cried out, raising bloodshot eyes and staring wildly round the room, as though looking for someone. 'I had to do it.'

She half rose to her feet and the solicitor leaned towards her and muttered under his breath.

'What did he do, Emily? Tell me about your uncle.'

Ingrid stared at the solicitor for a second, trembling, and he drew back as though unnerved by her expression. She turned back to Geraldine.

'It was all his fault,' she muttered.

'You went to live with your uncle after your mother died, didn't you? Linda's husband, William.'

'Yes.'

It was barely a whisper now, she spoke so softly. Her eyes never left Geraldine's face.

'Tell me about Uncle William. Did he hurt you?'

Ingrid nodded again. Tears streamed silently down her pale cheeks.

'What happened with your uncle, Ingrid? What did he do?'

Ingrid was sobbing too violently now to speak. Dropping her face in her hands, she cried without restraint.

'What happened with your uncle?' Geraldine

resumed after a few moments, when Ingrid's crying fit had died away.

'I had to stop him, I had to stop him.'

Her voice was muffled, her hands still over her face.

'Stop what?'

'He came into my room every night and I didn't want to – I didn't want to – it hurt so—'

Geraldine sat back in her chair.

'So you stopped him.'

Ingrid looked up.

'I tried to get away but he followed me downstairs. I wanted to leave by the back door, run away from there and never return. But he found me, hiding in the shed. He grabbed me by the arm. I was screaming. He pushed me down on the floor. There was a hammer. I reached for it and I hit him and hit him – I just wanted it to stop—'

Her eyes were streaming again. Wiping them on the backs of her hands she looked slowly round the room. Her eyes rested on the solicitor, thin and balding, moved past Sam, and came to rest on Geraldine.

'I stopped him all right,' she said, and her thin lips curved into a smile.

'How did you stop him? What did you do? Tell me what you did, Ingrid.'

'I hit him on the head.'

'And what happened then? Did he fall? Or what?'

'I heard his skull crunch and then he fell backwards. He was moaning and making a disgusting wheezing noise. His hands kept groping in the air, pulling at me. He wouldn't stop, so I hit him, again and again, until he was dead.'

'Where did you hit him?'

'I hit him where it hurt.' She grinned. 'Right in the balls.'

'What about the others, Patrick Henshaw, George Corless, Maurice Bradshaw and John Birch, why did you kill them? What had they done to you?'

Ingrid gazed earnestly at Geraldine, staring straight at her, dry-eyed for the first time. She spoke clearly now.

'I had no choice. I had to stop them.'

'Stop them?'

'They shouldn't have done it.' Her voice rose hysterically again. 'They shouldn't have touched me. They shouldn't have done it, they shouldn't have done it. I had to stop them.'

She leaned forward suddenly, her thin arms encircling her chest, her head down, as she rocked on her chair, moaning.

'You stopped him, and then you let your aunt take the blame. You let her go to prison for twenty years for something she hadn't done,' Geraldine said. 'Your aunt, who had taken you in, given you a home when your mother died.'

Ingrid dropped her arms and sat bolt upright.

'She deserved it.'

'Why?'

Geraldine leaned forward.

'Why, Ingrid? I want to understand. What had your aunt done to deserve going to prison for twenty years?'

'She knew what he was doing. I was only twelve when it started. She knew it was going on and she did nothing to help me.'

Her expression was bitter now, her eyes hard.

'She should have protected me, but she didn't even try to stop him.'

'How could you be sure your aunt knew what was going on?'

'Because she used to watch. She watched everything, right to the end.'

CHAPTER 71

Geraldine was relieved that Reg didn't query her going alone to question a suspect. Of course he didn't yet know that Ingrid had assaulted her. But now that Ingrid had confessed to five murders, there was no need to dwell on the circumstances of her arrest. Geraldine had brought it up during the taped interview, but there was no reason to draw any further attention to it before the trial. She had asked Sam to exercise discretion, and it would hardly be in Ingrid's interest for her brief to make a feature of it. The prosecution would doubtless raise it in court, having listened to the interview, but by then the arrest would be history. The details of Geraldine's part in it would hopefully be buried in general triumph.

In the meantime, Geraldine had other matters on her mind. She felt a familiar tremor hearing prison doors close behind her as she followed a prison officer to the visitors' room. A long time seemed to pass before Linda shuffled in and sat down without looking at Geraldine. Her dark hair was greasier than Geraldine remembered it, and her extreme pallor looked sickly.

'You've heard the news?'

Linda gave no response.

'About Ingrid.'

Almost imperceptibly, Linda's face coloured.

'I don't know anyone called Ingrid.'

'You know very well who I mean. I'm talking about your niece. She's changed her name to Ingrid, but you used to call her by her first name, Emily.'

Linda raised her head. Her green eyes glittered wretchedly.

'Leave Emily alone. She doesn't need you pestering her after all this time.'

'Linda, your niece has been arrested because we know what happened to your husband. We know it wasn't you who killed him. Emily's confessed. You're going to be released.'

'Released?' she repeated, gazing around the room with an expression of bemusement. She turned back to Geraldine, suddenly angry.

'I don't know what the fuck you're talking about. Leave me alone.'

She stood up but Geraldine told her to wait.

'You can help Emily,' she added.

With a grunt, Linda sat down again.

'Why did you take the rap for your niece when she killed your husband? You weren't responsible for his death. Why lie about it?'

Linda didn't answer.

'For twenty years you let his killer go free. You've spent a lifetime incarcerated for a crime you didn't commit. Why did you do it, Linda?'

Linda's face relaxed into a smile. She leaned forward on her chair and spoke very rapidly, in a low voice. As she explained, her eyes stared ferociously at Geraldine, with a fervour that was almost manic.

'I wouldn't expect you to understand. But you're right. It wasn't me, it was Emily who killed him, and he deserved it, the sick bastard. I should have done it myself, not left it to the child. Because he deserved to die. And I deserved to be punished.'

'You think what you did was right?'

Linda shrugged, unrepentant.

'You sacrificed twenty years of your life to protect your niece, knowing she had murdered your husband. You knew it was her, didn't you, because you were there, in the shed. You watched her batter him to death and you didn't do anything to stop her. But what I don't understand is why you abandoned her like that.'

Linda's eyes opened wide in surprise.

'Abandoned her? What are you talking about?'

She raised her voice. The prison officer started forward. Geraldine shook her head and raised a hand to indicate she didn't want to be interrupted. Linda dropped her voice.

'You don't understand. How could you? I promised my sister I'd take care of Emily, promised when she was dying. And then – then . . .'

She drew a deep shuddering breath. Geraldine glanced over at the warder whose eyes were fixed on Linda.

'It was all right to begin with, when she first came to live with us. I wasn't sure how William would take to it, having her there all the time, but he was very nice with her, very attentive. But then it started. They were very close and one night I heard her whimpering. I went into her bedroom and I saw them. He was on top of her and I could see her face over his shoulder . . .'

She broke off, lost in the horror of the recollection.

'I can still see the terror on her face. She was only thirteen. But I didn't do anything. I just stood there, watching.'

She lifted her face to Geraldine in sudden appeal.

'I didn't know what to do. I was only nineteen, not much more than a child myself. You don't know what it was like. It was such a shock. I'd had my suspicions before then, but yes, I didn't want to believe it. You don't want to believe it of your own husband. And what was I meant to do? I was too scared to confront him—'

'Scared?'

'I was so much younger than him and he was

so sure of himself. I can't explain it, but he wasn't the kind of man you could argue with. He never listened to me anyway. But he must have realised I knew, because he changed. He stopped being furtive. I'd go into the lounge and he'd be there, with his arm around her, and he wouldn't move away from her when I sat down. Nothing was the same after that.'

She dropped her face into her hands as though to shut out the memory.

'So you closed your eyes to what was going on. Wilful blindness.'

It was a statement, not a question. Linda lifted her head and nodded, with an expression almost serene.

'When it happened, when she killed him, I finally saw my way to doing the right thing by her—'

'The right thing?'

'I'd promised my sister I would protect Emily, look after her. When I was given this chance to make it up to her, I took her place in prison, so she could go free. None of it was her fault. She was only a child. She didn't deserve to be punished.'

'But you did, because you had kept silent about your husband's abuse—'

'Yes. I don't regret what I did, not for a second, not even now you've caught up with her. Because she knows my sentence gave her twenty years of freedom, twenty years of life she would have missed out on. Twenty years of freedom while she was still young—'

Coldly Geraldine interrupted to explain that if Ingrid had received professional help when she was fourteen, she might in time have been able to live a normal life, with a new identity. There were extenuating circumstances to her murdering her uncle. In sacrificing twenty years of freedom to assuage her own guilt, Linda had sentenced her niece to a lifetime of torment and hatred.

'She's insane, Linda; completely insane. Maybe she has been ever since she killed your husband. God knows what has been going through her mind for the last twenty years. You dealt with your own guilt, but left her to deal with hers alone. If she wasn't damaged enough already, you abandoned her to turn into a psychopath, beyond hope of recovery.'

Linda gave Geraldine a baleful glare.

'What do you mean, a psychopath? You're forgetting that Emily was the victim in all this, not William. He got what was coming to him. She never deserved to be abused. She never asked for it. That's exactly why I didn't want her to be put on trial, because of that kind of attitude. You don't understand anything. She killed her uncle, so you immediately assume she must be evil, when she was just a frightened child.'

* * *

Geraldine shook her head.

'That's not what I'm saying. Whoever was responsible for what happened to your husband, Emily needed help. In the course of a month your niece has battered four men to death, and who knows how many more she's assaulted over the years. She was abused and seriously disturbed as a young teenager. I don't know if her urge to kill people is part of her nature or was brought on by her early experience. I'm not qualified to hazard an opinion on that. But she's a psychopath now, if she wasn't born one. There's a chance that, if she had received professional help after killing your husband, she might have grown up to lead a semblance of a normal life. She might have recovered from her experience. People do. But by refusing to acknowledge her guilt, you stole that chance from her.'

With a cry of rage, Linda scrambled onto the table and tried to fling herself at Geraldine who dodged out of the way, just as the prison officer reached them.

'You'd think she'd be pleased she's going to be let out,' the officer called over her shoulder as she led Linda away. 'We only told her this morning.'

'That depends,' Geraldine called after her. 'There are worse sentences than prison.'

CHAPTER 72

Geraldine had only taken a few days off work when she had moved to London. Her holiday entitlement had been accumulating for a while. Nevertheless, she experienced a twinge of guilt when she locked her front door and set off for the airport. It was a long time since she had left work behind her for more than a few hours. A hire car was waiting for her at the end of her short flight. She set off to the small town where her father had settled, about fifty miles from Shannon airport. She drove along a well maintained motorway, bypassing the city of Limerick, and turned North towards her destination. Reaching her father's small town, she gazed appreciatively at the picturesque scene that spread out in front of her.

The town had grown up on two banks of a river beside a large lake. The square tower of a church appeared above the trees behind her. In front of her a row of boats bobbed gently up and down in a marina on the lake. Before going to her hotel, she parked the car and explored the streets on foot. It didn't take long to do a circuit of the main roads on her side of the river. Traffic lights on either side of a narrow bridge allowed cars to cross singly, in one direction at a time. Even with little traffic on the roads, there were a few cars waiting to cross. She dreaded to think what the queues must be like at busy times. But gazing around, she wondered if the place was ever busy, it appeared so sleepy and quiet. A few people sauntered in and out of the shops, occasionally stopping to greet one another on the pavement. No one seemed to be in a hurry.

There were several pubs offering accommodation in the town, but only one hotel. Studying the choices online, she had plumped for the most expensive option. Catching sight of the hotel from the bridge, she was pleased with her choice. With landscaped gardens leading down to a marina, and windows facing out over the lake, the setting couldn't be more beautiful. Her pleasure was complete when she checked in and was shown to a spacious room with large windows overlooking the lake. No wonder her father had chosen to spend the rest of his life here.

Although he had been married to Molly for longer than he had been with Geraldine's mother, she had never met her father's second wife. Soon after they met, Molly had taken him back to the town where she had lived as a child, and they never left. Celia and Geraldine had ignored his letters, begging them to visit him. Without mentioning his name, it was clear their mother would regard any contact with him as a betrayal. Even now, Geraldine had been reluctant to tell Celia when she decided to visit Ireland. In the end, she had merely told her sister she was going away for a few days. She hoped Celia wouldn't realise her trip coincided with their father's birthday celebration.

'Where are you going?'

'I haven't decided yet. I'm due some time off—'

'You can say that again!'

'And if I don't take it soon there'll be another investigation and then I'll never get away.'

'It sounds like a good idea. You could do with a break from all those dead bodies! Tell you what, do you fancy going somewhere together? Just for a few days. One of my friends knows this fabulous retreat . . .'

It sounded wonderful, but Geraldine had her own plans.

'Not this time.'

'Don't tell me you're going with someone else?' Celia wanted to know. 'You dark horse. There's a man involved, isn't there?'

Geraldine sighed. In a way, Celia was right. But she didn't suspect the man was their father.

'No, I'm not going with anyone else. I really need some time to myself right now. It's a great idea to do something together, just not right now. Let's do something together soon.'

The woman at the door had grey hair and sad blue eyes. She smiled nervously when she saw Geraldine on the doorstep, and greeted her by name as though they weren't strangers.

'You must be Molly,' Geraldine responded.

She tried to inject as much warmth into her voice as she could. She hadn't travelled all this way to be hostile to the woman her father had fallen in love with over twenty years ago.

'I brought you these.'

'Thank you, they're beautiful.'

The flowers between them resolved any awkwardness about whether they should shake hands or attempt an embrace.

Geraldine's overriding feeling on seeing her father was sadness; he looked so old. She could have passed him in the street without recognising him. It was odd to think that he hadn't been much older than she was now when he had left her mother for Molly nearly a quarter of a century ago. She looked for the father she remembered in the old man rising stiffly from his chair to greet her. Everything about his features had been clearly defined. Now it was as though he had been drawn in soft charcoal and someone had come along and smudged the edges of his portrait; his chin lost in sagging jowls, eyes peering from wrinkled folds of skin, the mop of fair hair she recalled all but vanished, leaving a shiny pate bordered by a few wisps of white. But when he smiled and held his hands out shyly, the years slipped away.

'How are you, Dad?'

He nodded and they embraced wordlessly. When she pulled away he covered his face, but not before she had seen tears in his eyes. All at once she was struggling to keep her own emotions under control.

'I'll put the kettle on,' Molly said. 'The others will be here soon.'

Geraldine was glad she had arrived early, to meet her father without his neighbours and friends there to gawp.

The rest of the afternoon passed in a blur of introductions. Molly seemed to be related to half of Ireland. Her three sons and seven grandchildren all turned up. Geraldine hoped her father wasn't grieved that not one of the guests at his birthday party was his blood relation. Even Geraldine was a stranger who had shared his home for ten years. She wondered if her parents' inability to have more children after Celia's birth had contributed to the breakdown of their marriage. But that was all in the past. Her adoptive mother was dead, and he had a new life.

Seeing him surrounded by Molly's family, it felt inappropriate to raise the issue of her search for her birth mother. She would ask him another time. In any case, it was unlikely her father would be able to help her. After all her anticipation, she decided against mentioning it, even though searching for her birth mother had been the main factor influencing her decision to travel to Ireland. Her father didn't ask about his own daughter until Geraldine was leaving, speaking quickly, as though the words pained him.

'Celia's fine.'

'And the child?'

'Chloe? She's fine too.'

She didn't know what else to say.

'Still just the one?'

Geraldine nodded.

'And you?'

'No-one, Dad. Just my work.'

He smiled sadly at her, not knowing what to say. He had forfeited the right to pass judgement on her adult life before it had begun.

Geraldine was relieved when it was time for her to leave. She suspected her father felt the same way. It would have been nice to have spent more time with him, and get to know him better. As it was, their parting was oddly formal.

'It's been great seeing you again.'

'Yes, we must keep in touch.'

Geraldine agreed, and this time she really meant what she said. She turned to wave as she drove away, but her father had already closed his door.

CHAPTER 73

It was glorious to oversleep and spoil herself with a late breakfast. At her favourite café along Upper Street she lingered over freshly squeezed orange juice, brown toast, and fluffy scrambled egg and bacon, with a cafetiere. England was enjoying an unexpected spell of beautiful autumn sunshine. After breakfast she strolled along the busy main road and back down the quiet side street to her flat. Picking up her car she drove into work to start on the paperwork which had to be completed before the case could finally be closed. However cut and dried the result, everything had to be in order for the prosecution, to ensure the case was watertight. Even after a confession, facts could be twisted. With a decent lawyer even those who were blatantly guilty could evade conviction on a technicality.

It was hard to focus on her report. So many people had been involved in the case: widows and witnesses, victims and families, suspects and passersby, those who had been touched for an instant, and those whose lives had been transformed forever. Just twenty-four hours earlier, Geraldine could have recited chunks from key statements in the investigation. She had known names and relationships, and could have stated where suspects had been at the time of any one of the four murders, without recourse to her notes. This morning, she had to double-check the name of Patrick's former mistress. The investigation over, she was already losing her grasp of names and dates, actions and injuries, that had occupied her thoughts over the past few weeks to the exclusion of everything else. Now she was exhausted, and her head felt empty.

She didn't stay late at work, wanting to reach Kent in time for the start of her former mentor's leaving party. Out of all her ex-colleagues, she had only been in close contact with her previous sergeant, Ian Peterson, and wasn't sure how it would feel to return to her old work place and meet her former colleagues on the Kent constabulary. As it turned out, they all seemed pleased to see her and teased her about deserting them for the bright lights of the capital. Ted Carter seemed delighted that she had made the effort to turn up.

'I really appreciate your coming,' he said, beaming at her over the rim of his glass. 'I know how busy you must be in London.'

'As it happens, we've just wrapped up a case,' she told him, 'but I wouldn't have missed this anyway.'

She waved her hand around to indicate the

gathering. 'Timing is everything,' he told her and she smiled.

They both knew she wouldn't have made it if she had been tied up on a case.

'It's good to see you, Geraldine.'

'Very good,' a familiar voice chimed in.

Geraldine turned to see her former sergeant, Ian, towering over her.

'You saved me a stamp,' he grinned, reaching into his pocket.

He pulled out an envelope, only slightly crumpled.

'What's this?'

'An invitation.'

'Another do?'

'Ian's not leaving, more's the pity,' someone called out.

'No life of freedom for him,' Ted laughed.

'He can kiss that goodbye,' another voice added.

Geraldine smiled, understanding that she had been handed an invitation to Ian's wedding.

'You're really doing it then?'

'Finally. The wedding's in December. I hope you can make it.'

'Work permitting.'

'Such commitment,' he said, shaking his head at her as though her dedication was something shameful.

'That's why she's a DI on the Met,' Ted told him.

'And there I was putting it all down to your brilliant mentoring,' Ian replied.

Ian put the invitation in her hand. She was pleased to see him looking so happy. Last time they had spoken he had been stressed over his wedding plans. Ignoring an unexpected stab of dismay, she smiled at him.

'I hope it's all going smoothly now?'

He shrugged.

'I'm leaving everything to Bev.'

'I'm sure that's the best thing to do.'

'Yes, except that now she's complaining I'm not involved. Seems I can't win.'

'It'll be fine once you're married,' she reassured him.

She was surprised to see how her words cheered him up. What did she know about marriage?

Although she was pleased for him, as she slipped the envelope in her bag she felt strangely abandoned. They had worked so closely together in the past, it was almost like losing a friend. Of course she knew his marriage wouldn't make any difference to the way he behaved towards colleagues, and in any case she hardly saw him any more since her move to London. She shrugged the feeling off as several other officers joined them. They all quizzed her about the capital, as though they couldn't possibly imagine what it would be like to live there.

* * *

Geraldine mumbled something about having been too busy to explore London life, which was no exaggeration.

'What with the move, and then I've been involved in a couple of tricky cases—'

'Nothing you can't handle, I'm sure,' someone said.

Geraldine paused, remembering Ingrid's frenzied attack, Linda's despair, and the horrific injuries sustained by Patrick Henshaw, George Corless, Maurice Bradshaw and John Birch.

'I bet they aren't as friendly on the Met as we are,' a constable chipped in.

Geraldine recollected Sam's spat with Nick after his outrageous comment about a rape victim. *"She probably asked for it."* No one spoke like that about Ingrid's victims, although there was no way of knowing what appalling behaviour on their part had provoked her attacks.

'They're friendly in a different way,' she said, shrugging off her troubling memories.

It was strange to return to the camaraderie of her former work colleagues. Looking back on her time in Kent, she realised they had been a close-knit team. Although they hadn't all been on first name terms, as was the norm in London, they had all known one another. Looked at from outside, the familiar form of address adopted by her colleagues in London seemed superficial. She experienced a fleeting regret at having moved away from Kent.

'So you're OK in London?'

Ian was at her side. He always seemed to sense when she was feeling despondent.

'It's different—'

She hesitated, tempted to confide her reservations. But now was not the time. She hoped Ian's future wife appreciated his sensitivity and consideration, and realised how lucky she was to be marrying him.

It was late when Geraldine arrived home at the end of a tiring day, with one last task to carry out before she went to bed. Sitting at her desk she sent an email to her father, telling him how much she had enjoyed seeing him again, and giving him her new address. Then she went to bed, without setting her alarm for the morning.